The Golden Hour

ALSO BY BEATRIZ WILLIAMS

The Summer Wives

Cocoa Beach

The Wicked City

A Certain Age

Along the Infinite Sea

Tiny Little Thing

The Secret Life of Violet Grant

A Hundred Summers

Overseas

The Golden Hour

A Novel

BEATRIZ WILLIAMS

WILLIAM MORROW
An Imprint of HarperCollins*Publishers*

July 13, 2019 B+T

HarperCollins books may be purchased for educational, business, or
sales promotional use. For information, please email the Special Markets
Department at SPsales@harpercollins.com.

FIRST EDITION

Designed by Bonni Leon-Berman

Library of Congress Cataloging-in-Publication Data has been applied for.

ISBN 978-0-06-283475-1

19 20 21 22 23   LSC   10 9 8 7 6 5 4 3 2 1

To women and men everywhere who live with depression.
You are loved. You are needed. The night will pass.

In August 1940, the Duke of Windsor is appointed governor of the Bahamas by his brother, George VI, on the recommendation of Winston Churchill.

While the former king feels the appointment is beneath his station, he accepts, in the expectation that loyal service in this colonial outpost will lead to more prestigious assignments in the future.

But despite an exemplary public record of governorship for the duration of the Second World War, and the energetic support of the Duchess of Windsor as the governor's wife, the duke is never again asked to serve his country in an official capacity.

The Golden Hour

PART I

LULU

I N THE FOYER of the Basil Hotel in Cadogan Gardens, atop the tea-colored wallpaper, a sign advises guests that blackout hours will be observed *strictly*. Another sign reminds us that enemy ears are listening. The wallpaper's crowded with tiny orange flowers that seem to have started out life as pink, and they put me in mind of a story I once read about a woman who stares at the wallpaper in her room until she goes batty. Although that wallpaper was yellow, as I recall, so I may have some time to go.

I consult my watch. Three twenty-two.

Outside the windows, the air's darkening fast. Some combination of coal smoke and December fog and the early hour at which the sun goes down at this latitude, as if the wallpaper and the signboards and the piles of rubble across the street aren't enough to make you melancholy. I check the watch again—three twenty-three, impossible—and my gaze happens to catch that of the desk clerk. He's examining me over the top of a rickety pair of reading glasses, because he hasn't liked the look of me from the beginning. Why should he? A woman shows up at your London hotel in the middle of December, the middle of wartime, tanned skin, American accent, unmistakable scent of the foreign about her. She pays for her room in advance and carries only a small suitcase. Now she's awaiting some no-good rendezvous, right in the middle of your dank, shabby, respectable foyer, and you ought to telephone the authorities, just to be on the safe side. In fact, you probably *have* telephoned the authorities.

The clerk's gaze flicks to the window, and then to the clock above the mantel behind me. He steps away from the reception desk and goes to pull down the blackout shades, to close the heavy chintz curtains. His limbs are frail and stiff; his suit was tailored in maybe the previous century. When he moves, his white hair flies away from his skull, and I catch a whiff of cologne that reminds me of a barbershop. I consider whether I should rise and help him. I consider whether he'd kill me for it.

Well. Not *kill* me exactly, not the literal act of murder. It seems the killing of people has got inside my head somehow. War will do that. War will turn killing into a commonplace act, a thing men do to each other every day, every instant, for no particular reason except not to be killed yourself, so that you start to expect it everywhere, murder hangs darkly over you and around you like an atmosphere. The valley of the shadow of death, that's war. Killing for no particular reason. At least in regular life, when somebody kills somebody else, he generally has a damned good reason, at least so far as the killer's concerned. It's personal, it's singular. As I observe the feathery movement of the clerk's hair in the draft, I wonder how much reason a fellow like that needed to kill someone. We all have our breaking points, you know.

A bell jingles. The front door opens. A blast of chill air whooshes inside, along with a pale woman in a worn coat and a brown fedora, almost like a man's. She brushes the damp from her sleeves and looks around, spies the clerk, who's just crossing the foyer on his way back to the desk.

"I beg your pardon, my good man," she begins, in a brisk, quiet English voice, and the light from the lamp catches her hair, caught up in a blond knot just beneath the brim of her hat. She's not wearing cosmetics, except maybe a touch of lipstick, and you might say she doesn't need any. There's something Nordic about her, something that doesn't need ornament. Height and blondness, all those things my own Italian mother couldn't give me, though she gave me plenty else. There's also something familiar about her. I've seen that mouth before, haven't I? Those straight, thick eyebrows soaring above a pair of blue eyes.

But no. Surely not. Surely I'm only imagining this, surely I'm only seeing a resemblance because I want to see one. After all, it's impossible, isn't it? Margaret Thorpe won't receive my letter until this evening, when she arrives home from whatever government building she inhabits during working hours. So this woman can't be *her*, cannot possibly be my husband's sister, however much the sight of those eyebrows sets my heart stuttering. Anyway, her head's now turned toward the clerk, and from this angle she looks nothing like Thorpe, not at all. Unless—

The bell jingles again, dragging my attention back to the entryway. Another draft follows, and a man shambles past the door in a damp over-coat of navy blue, a hat glittering with mist. His face is pockmarked, the only notable thing about him. He casts a slow, bland expression around the room, and it seems to me that he takes in every detail, every flock on the wallpaper and spot on the upholstery, until he arrives, quite by accident, on me.

The woman's still addressing the clerk. No notice of us at all. I climb to my feet. "Mr. B——?"

He steps forward and holds out his hand. "You must be Mrs. Thorpe," he says warmly, and he takes my fingers between his two palms, as if we are father and daughter, meeting for tea after a short absence.

INSTEAD OF REMAINING INSIDE THE Basil Hotel foyer (in which the enemy ears might or might not be listening, but the desk clerk certainly is) we head out into the gloom. I tend to step briskly as a matter of habit, but Mr. B— (I'm afraid I can't reveal his real name) shuffles along at an awkward gait, and it's a chore to keep my limbs in check. I tuck my hands inside my pockets and drum my fingers against my thighs. I feel as if he should speak first. He's the professional, after all.

"Well, Mrs. Thorpe," he says at last. "I must congratulate you on your resolve. To have made your way to London in wartime, to have approached my office with such an extraordinary request—why, it's the most astonishing thing I've seen in some time."

"I hope you don't mind."

"Mind? Of course not. If there's one thing we admire in this country, it's dash. Dash and pluck, Mrs. Thorpe, which you appear to possess in abundance. How long had you two been married?"

"Since July."

"This past July?"

"Yes. The seventh."

"Ah. Just before he was captured, then. How dreadful."

"It was months before I had any word at all. At first, I thought he'd been called out on another of his—whatever you call them—"

"Operations?"

"Yes, operations. But when he didn't return . . ."

We pause to cross the street. I've allowed him to choose the route; I mean he's the one who lives here, after all, the one who understands not just the map of London but the habits of the place. A couple of bicycles approach, one after the other, and while we wait for them to pass, Mr. B— speaks again.

"Mind you, it was quite against the rules."

"What? What's against the rules?"

Mr. B— stares not at my face, but along a line that passes right above my head, down the street to the approaching bicycles. "Marrying," he says blandly.

The bicycles pass. We cross the street to enter a foggy square of red brick and white trim. Several of the houses are missing, simply not there, like teeth pulled from a jaw. Mr. B— leads me to the gardens in the middle, where we choose a wooden bench and sit about a foot apart, so that our arms and legs aren't in any danger of touching, God forbid. The button at the wrist of my left-hand glove has come undone. I attempt to refasten it, but my fingers are too stiff.

"Of course, I quite understand your distress, Mrs. Thorpe," he says, in the voice you might use to console a child. "It's for that reason that we tend to discourage men such as Thorpe from forming any sort of personal attachment. To say nothing of marriage."

"We're all human, Mr. B—."

"Still, it's unwise. And then to allow you any hint of his purpose there in the Bahamas—"

"Oh, believe me, he never said a word about that. I was the one who put two and two together. I was on the inside, you see. A friend of the Windsors."

"Were you really? Remarkable. Although I suppose . . ." He reaches into the pocket of his coat, brushing my arm with his elbow as he manipulates his fingers inside. He draws out a familiar white envelope. I recognize it because I carried this envelope myself, in a pocket next to my skin, for the entirety of the thirty-nine hours it took to cross the Atlantic, from Nassau to London, in a series of giant, rattling airplanes, before I stamped the upper right corner and posted it from a red metal postbox yesterday evening. And it's funny, isn't it, how a letter you mailed with your own two hands no longer belongs to you, once it begins that fateful drop through the slot. I glimpse my own handwriting, the stamp I placed there myself, and it's like being reunited with an estranged child who has grown into adulthood.

"You suppose?"

Mr. B— taps the edge of the envelope against his knee. "I suppose it depends on what one means by *friendship*."

"In wartime, friendship can mean anything, can't it?"

"True enough. This note of yours. Quite astonished me this morning, when my secretary delivered it to my desk."

"But you must have known Thorpe was captured."

"Naturally. I take the most anxious interest in my agents, Mrs. Thorpe, and your—ah, your husband—he was one of—*well*. Well. That is to say, Mr. Thorpe in particular. We took the news very hard. Very hard indeed. Colditz, my God. Poor chap. Awful show."

He takes out a cigarette case, opens the lid, and tilts it toward me. I select one, and he selects another. As he lights the match, he covers the flame with his cupped hand. We sit back against the bench and smoke quietly. The wind on my cheek is cold, and the air tastes of soot, and the sky's blackening by the instant. At first I don't quite understand what's missing, until I realize it's the absence of light. Not a pinprick escapes the windows around us, not a ray of comfort. It's as if we're the only two people alive in London.

"There used to be a railing," says Mr. B—.

"What's that?"

"Around the square gardens. A railing, to keep residents in and everybody else out, you see. They took it away and melted it down for iron."

"I suppose it's more democratic this way."

"I suppose so. Here we are, after all, the two of us. Sitting on this bench, quite without permission."

"And that's what we're fighting for, isn't it? Democracy."

He straightens his back against the bench. "Well, then. Leonora Thorpe. Plucky young American from across the ocean. What are we to do with you?"

"I don't understand."

"Why are you here? You'll forgive me, but London isn't the most peaceful of cities, at the moment. I imagine, wherever you come from—"

"Nassau."

"Yes, Nassau. But you weren't born there, were you?"

"No. I was raised in New York. I arrived in the Bahamas a couple of years ago, to cover the governor and his wife for a magazine."

"A *magazine*?"

"*Metropolitan* magazine. Nothing serious, just society news. The American appetite for the Duke and Duchess of Windsor is just insatiable."

Mr. B— sucks on his cigarette. "I must confess, it puzzles me. You Americans went to such trouble to rid yourselves of our quaint little monarchy."

"Oh, we like to gossip about them, all right. Just not to let them rule over us and all that."

"I imagine you were well paid?"

"Well enough."

"A plum assignment, Mrs. Thorpe, spending the war in a tropical paradise. Plenty of food, plenty of money. Why didn't you stay there?"

"*Why?* Isn't it obvious?"

"But what's to be gained by coming to London? Look around you. It's the middle of the afternoon, and it's already dark. Decent food in short supply. The weather—as you see—is simply dreadful, to say nothing of air raids and the threat of invasion. You ought to have stayed in the tropics, nice and safe, to wait for news."

I crush out my cigarette on the arm of the bench.

"But that's the thing, Mr. B—. I don't mean to sit around and wait. That's why I've come to London."

I say this carelessly—*come to London*—as if it were as easy as that. As easy as boarding an ocean liner and waddling from meal to meal, deck chair to deck chair, until you step off a week later, and *poof!* you're in England. And maybe it *was* that easy, in another time. These days, it's not so simple. That ocean teems with objects that hope to kill you. And if you want to reach London in a hurry, well, the challenge grows by geometric leaps and bounds, because there's only one way to cross the Atlantic in a hurry, and it doesn't come cheap, believe me.

And then you contrive to meet this challenge. Clever you. You pay the necessary price, because you must, there's no other choice. You find yourself strapped inside the comfortless fuselage of a B-24 Liberator as it prepares to separate you from the nice safe sun-soaked ground of the Bahamas and bear you, by leaps and bounds, to darkest England, a place you know only by hearsay. The engines gather power, the noise fills your ears like all the world's bumblebees pollinating a single rose. The metal around you bickers and clatters, the world tilts, the air freezes, and there you are, eyes shut, stomach flipping, ears roaring, mouth watering, chest rattling, lungs panting, nerves screaming, heart aching, wishing you had goddamn well fallen in love with someone else. Someone you could live without.

But you can't. So now you're here in London. London at last, on a garden bench in the middle of a darkened city, next to the only man in the world who can help you. Except the fellow's shaking his head, the fellow's got no faith in you at all.

"Come to London," he says. "How on earth did you manage it?"

"I managed it because I had to. I'd do anything to free my husband."

"Free your husband? Is that the idea?"

"I damned well won't run around Nassau going to parties while my husband rots away in the middle of Nazi Germany."

Mr. B— extends his arm and flicks ash onto the gravel. His shoes are beautifully polished, his trousers creased. Standards must be kept. "Mrs. Thorpe," he says, "I don't know quite how to express this."

"How about straight out? That's how we Americans prefer it."

"Then I'm afraid you've wasted your time. Once one of our men falls into enemy hands, why, he's on his own. Thorpe knew this. We can't possibly risk more agents on hairy schemes that—you'll forgive me—

offer almost no chance of success. We're stretched enough as it is. We're scarcely hanging on."

"But I'm not asking you to risk anyone else. I'd go myself."

"I'm afraid it's impossible. Thorpe's been trained. He knows it's his duty to escape, not ours to spring him out, and I've no doubt he's doing his utmost."

"That's not enough for me."

"I'm sorry, Mrs. Thorpe," Mr. B— says. "I don't mean to be unkind. Naturally you're suffering. It's the most beastly news. One hopes for the best, of course. But one soldiers on. That's all there is, just to soldier on."

"That's all terrific, if you're a soldier. If you're allowed to do something useful instead of twiddling your thumbs."

"There are many ways in which women are able to serve the war effort, Mrs. Thorpe. And I can offer you my steadfast assurance that we're doing our best, in my department and in Britain as a whole, all the services, every man Jack, to defeat Germany and bring your husband safely home."

Across the street, a pair of women hurry down the sidewalk, buttoned up in wool coats and economical hats. The clatter of shoes echoes from the bricks, and it occurs to me how silent a city can be, when gas is rationed and private automobiles are banned. You can hear an omnibus rattle and grind from a couple of streets away, and you realize how alone you are, how desolate war is.

The women turn the corner. A man begins a slow, arthritic progress from the opposite direction, bent beneath the weight of his coat and hat. He's smoking a cigarette. I figure the fellow's probably deaf, but I speak softly anyway. Soft and firm.

"I understand your position, of course. I guess it's about what I expected. I understand, I really do. But now I need you to understand *me*, Mr. B—."

He turns his face toward me and lifts his eyebrows. At last, his voice goes a little cold, the way a man speaks to another man, his equal. "Oh? Understand what, Mrs. Thorpe? Let us be perfectly clear with each other."

"All right, Mr. B——. Listen carefully. In the course of my service in Nassau, in my capacity as a journalist, as an intimate associate of the governor and his wife, I became privy to certain information. Do you catch my drift?"

There is this silence. I think, *Well, he knows this already, doesn't he?* I wrote as much in my note. At the time, I thought I conveyed my meaning in circumspect sentences, that my note was a clever, sophisticated little epistle, but now it seems to me that my note was probably a masterpiece of amateurism, that Mr. B—— probably laughed when he read it. Probably he's suppressing his laughter right now. His silence is the silence of a man controlling his amusement.

He examines the end of his cigarette. "What kind of information?"

"You know. The kind of information that might prove embarrassing—embarrassing to say the least—were it to be made known to the general public."

He drops his cigarette to the gravel and crushes it with his shoe. "Embarrassing to whom?"

"To the British government. To the king and queen."

Mr. B—— reaches into his jacket pocket and removes another cigarette from the case. He lights it with the same care as before, the same series of noises, the scratch and the flare, the covering of the flame. "Mrs. Thorpe," he says softly, "I'm afraid I have a little confession to make."

"Oh?"

"I may have stretched the truth just a bit, when I told you I was astonished by the contents of your letter."

We still sit side by side, except we've turned a few degrees inward to address each other. Mr. B——'s elbow rests on the top slat of the bench. Because he's looking at my face now, almost tenderly, I make a tremendous effort to keep my expression as still as possible. My fingers, however, have developed some kind of tremor. Imagine that.

"How so?" I ask.

"I received a memorandum a day or two ago. From a certain member of the Cabinet, in response to a cable sent him from Government House in Nassau. So we had some warning, you see, of your imminent arrival. We had some notion of what to expect."

"I see."

"Still, your note was—well, it was marvelous. I don't wish to take anything away from that. My own men couldn't have done better."

"I'm flattered."

He leans forward, so I can smell his cigarette breath, the faint echo of whatever it was he ate for lunch. "Mrs. Thorpe, I simply can't allow that information to go any further. Do you understand?"

"Of course I understand. That's why I'm offering to—"

He drops the cigarette in the gravel and crushes it with his heel. "No, my dear. I don't think you really *do* understand."

And I'm ashamed to say it's only now I realize what an idiot I've been. Not until this instant does it occur to me to ask why, if Mr. B— received my note in the morning—my note hinting delicately of treason at the highest level, treason within the royal family itself—he waited until the fall of night to meet me, to draw me outside, to walk with me into a darkened square before a thousand windows closed for the blackout.

Why, indeed.

I rise from the bench. "Very well. If you're not going to cooperate, I have no choice—"

With remarkable swiftness, he rises too, draws a small pistol from his pocket, and lodges the end of it in the middle of my coat, just above the knotted belt.

"Mrs. Thorpe. I'm afraid I must insist you give me whatever evidence you've obtained in this matter."

"I don't have it. Not right here."

"Where, then?"

"In my hotel room."

He considers. The pistol remains at my stomach, moving slightly at each beat of my heart. Though my gaze remains on his, I gather the details at the edge of my vision: the trees, bare of leaves; the shrubs, the plantings, all of them shadows against the night, against the murky buildings surrounding us. I observe the distant noise of another omnibus, a faint, drunken cheer from a pub nearby. Possibly, if I screamed, someone might hear me. But I would be dead by the time this noise reached a pair of human ears.

"It's well hidden," I continue. "I could save you a lot of trouble."

Mr. B— nudges the pistol against my stomach. "Very well. Move slowly, please."

As I begin my turn, I jerk my knee upward, bang smack into the center of his groin. A shot cracks out. I grab the pistol, burning my hand, and slam it into his head, right behind his left ear. He slumps to the ground, and let me tell you, I take off *running*, hoping to God I don't have a bullet in me somewhere, hoping to God I knocked him out as well as down.

As I dart across the street, there's a shout. I don't stop to discover where it came from, or whom. The sidewalk's empty, the street's dark. The sky's begun to drizzle. I pass a red postbox, the house with the grand piano in the window I noticed this morning, except you can't see that piano right now, I can't see anything, the whole world is dark and wet, each stoop concealing its own shadows. I cross another street, another, not stopping to check for traffic—there isn't any, not with wartime restrictions on brave, threadbare London—until the familiar white signboard resolves out of the mist, BASIL HOTEL in quaint letters.

I pull back, undecided, but my momentum carries me forward into another human chest, female chest.

Oomph! she says, and snatches me by the arms. I lift my hands to push away. I spy a coat, a neck, a fringe of blond hair gathered into a bun.

The woman in the foyer.

"Miss Thorpe?" I gasp.

Her eyes are paler than her brother's, but I recognize the shape, and the straight, thick eyebrows, though his are a darker gold. The same milky skin, the same freckles. She has pointed cheekbones, a wide, red mouth, a slim jaw. I'm able to drink in all these details because the world seems to have gone still, the clock seems to have stopped, and even the molecules of air, the motes of dust, have stuck in place. Only my blood moves, against the scorched skin of my right hand.

"You must be Leonora," she says.

"Yes."

She snatches my elbow and pulls me down the sidewalk. "Come along, quick. My flat's just around the corner."

And it occurs to me, as I career along in her wake, that this is just how her brother appeared in my life. Out of the blue in some foreign land, like a genie from a lamp, just when you needed a wish granted.

LULU

O N THE MAGAZINE cover, the woman sits on a rattan sofa and the man sits on the floor at her feet, gazing not at the camera but upward, adoringly, at her. She smiles back in approval. She has a book in her lap, open to the frontispiece or maybe the table of contents—she doesn't look as if she actually means to *read* it—and in her hair, a ribbon topped with a bow. (A *bow*, I tell you.) A pair of plump Union Jack sofa pillows flanks either side of her. A real domestic scene, a happy couple in a tasteful home. THE WINDSOR TEAM, reads the caption, in small, discreet letters at the bottom. At the top, much larger, white type inside a block of solid red: L I F E.

I'd been staring at this image, on and off, for most of the journey from New York, having paid a dime for the magazine itself at the newsstand in the Eastern Air Lines terminal building at LaGuardia Field. (It was the latest issue, now there's coincidence for you.) I'd held it on my lap as what you might call a talisman, throughout each leg of the journey, each takeoff and landing, Richmond followed by Savannah followed by some swamp called Orlando followed by Miami at last, smacking down to earth at half past five in the afternoon, taxi to a shabby hotel, taxi back to the airfield this morning, and I still didn't feel as if I'd quite gotten to the bottom of that photograph. Oh, sometimes I flipped the magazine open and read the article inside—the usual basket of eggs, served sunny-side up—but mostly I studied the picture on the cover. So carefully arranged, each detail in place. Those Union Jack pillows, for example. (*We just couldn't be any more patriotic, could we? Oh, my, no. We are as thoroughly British as afternoon tea.*) That hair ribbon, the bow. (*We are as charmingly, harmlessly feminine as the housewife next door.*) The enormous jeweled brooch pinned to her striped jacket, just above the right breast— and what *was* it, anyway? The design, I mean. I squinted and peered and adjusted the angle of light, but I couldn't make any sense of the shape. No matter. It was more brooch than I could afford, that was all, more jewels than I could ever bear on my own right breast. (*We are not the housewife next door after all, are we? We are richer, better, royal. Even if we aren't quite royal. Not according to the Royals. Still, more royal than you, Mrs. American Housewife.*)

The airplane lurched. I peered through the window at the never-ending horizon, turquoise sea topped by a turquoise sky, and my stomach—never at home aboard moving objects—lurched too. According to my wristwatch, we were due at Nassau in twenty minutes, and the twenty-one seats of this modern all-metal Pan American airliner were crammed full of American tourists in Sunday best and businessmen in pressed suits, none of whose stomachs seemed troubled by the voyage. Just my dumb luck, my dumb stomach. Or was it my ears? Apparently motion sickness had something to do with your inner ear, the pressure of fluid inside versus the pressure of air without, and when the perception of movement on your insides didn't agree with the perception of movement from your eyeballs, well, that's where your stomach got into difficulty. I supposed that explanation made sense. All the world's troubles seemed to come from friction of one kind or another. One thing rubbing up against another, and neither one backing down.

So I crossed my arms atop the magazine and gazed out into the distance—that was supposed to help—and chewed on the stick of Wrigley's thoughtfully provided by the stewardess. By now, the vibration of the engines had taken up habitation inside my skull. *This? This is nothing, sister,* said the fellow sitting next to me on the Richmond–Savannah hop yesterday, local businessman type. *You shoulda heard the racket on the old Ford tri-motor. Boy, that was some kind of noise, all right. Why, the girls sometimes had to use a megaphone, it was so loud. Now, this hunka junk, they put some insulation in her skin. You know what insulation is? Makes a whole lot of difference, believe you me.* Here he rapped against the fuselage with his knuckles. *Course, there ain't no amount of insulation in the world can drown out the sound of a couple of Pratt and Whitney Twin Wasp engines full throttle, no ma'am. That's eight hundred horsepower apiece. Yep, she's a classy bird, all right, the DC-three. You ever flown the sleeper model? Coast to coast in fifteen hours. That's something, ain't it?* And so on. By the time we reached Savannah, I would gladly have taken the old Ford tri-motor and a pair of earplugs.

On the other hand, it could have been worse. When the talkative fellow from Richmond disembarked in Savannah, he was replaced by another fellow entirely, a meaty, sweating, silent specimen in a fine suit, reeking of booze and cigarettes, possessed of a sticky gaze. You know the type. By the time we were airborne, he had arranged himself luxuriously on the seat, insinuated his thigh against mine, and laid his hand several times on my knee, and as I slapped away his paw yet again, I would have given any amount of money to have Mr. Flapping Gums in his checked suit safely back by my side. And then. *Then.* The damned fellow turned up *again* this morning in an even more disreputable condition to board the daily Pan American flight to Nassau, fine suit now rumpled and stained, eyes now bloodshot and roving all over the place.

Thank God he hadn't seemed to notice me. He sat in the second row, and by the stricken expression of the stewardess, hurrying back down the aisle this second with the Thermos of precious coffee, he hadn't mended his ways during the night. I caught her eye and communicated sympathy into her, woman to woman, as best I could. She returned a small nod and continued down the aisle. The chewing gum was turning stale and hard. The wrapper had gone missing somewhere. I tore off a corner of page fourteen of *Life* magazine, folded the scrap, and slipped the wad discreetly inside.

In the seat next to mine, a gentleman looked up from his newspaper. He was tall and lean, almost thin, a loose skeleton of a fellow, and he'd made his way aboard with a small leather suitcase, climbing the stairs nimbly, the last in line. I hadn't paid him much attention, except to note the interesting color of his hair, a gold fringe beneath the brim of his hat. He wore spectacles, and in contrast to my earlier companions, he'd hardly acknowledged me at all, except to duck his head and murmur a polite *Good morning* and an apology for intruding on my privacy. Though his legs were long, like a spider's, he had folded them carefully to avoid touching mine, and when he'd opened his newspaper, he folded the sides back so they didn't extend past the armrest between us. He'd refused the chewing gum, I remembered, though the tropical air bumped the airplane all over the sky. Other than that, he read his newspaper so quietly, turned and folded the pages with such a minimum of fuss, I confess I'd nearly forgotten he was there.

As the stewardess swept by, he bent the top of said newspaper in order to observe the fellow up front, unblinking, the way a bird-watcher might observe the course of nature from the security of his blind. I felt a stir of interest, I don't know why. Maybe it was the quiet of him. Under cover of looking back for the stewardess, I contrived to glimpse his profile, which was younger than I thought, lightly freckled. All this, as I said, I captured in the course of a glance, but I have a good memory for faces.

After a minute or so, the gentleman folded his newspaper, murmured an apology, and rose from his seat. He set his newspaper on the seat and walked not to the front of the airplane, which he'd observed with such attention, but down the aisle to the rear, where the stewardess had gone. The airplane bumped along, the propellers droned. I looked back at the magazine on my lap—THE WINDSOR TEAM, what did that mean, what exactly were they trying to convey, those two—and then out the window again. A series of pale golden islands passed beneath the wing, rendering the sea an even more alluring shade of turquoise, causing me almost to forget the slush in my stomach and the fuzz in my head, until the gentleman landed heavily back in the seat beside me.

Except it wasn't the same gentleman. I knew that instantly. He was too massive, and he reeked of booze. A thigh came alongside mine, a paw settled on my knee.

"Kindly remove your hand," I said, not kindly at all.

He leaned toward my ear and muttered something I won't repeat.

I reached for the hand, but he was quicker and grabbed my fingers. I curled my other hand, my right hand, into a fist. I still don't know what I meant to do with that fist, whether I really would have hit him with it. Probably I would have. The air inside our metal tube was hot, even at ten thousand feet, because of the white June sun and the warm June atmosphere and the windows that trapped it all inside, and the man's hand was wet. I felt that bile in my throat, that heave, that grayness of vision that means you're about to vomit, and I remember thinking I must avoid vomiting on the magazine at all costs, I couldn't possibly upchuck my morning coffee on the pristine Windsor Team.

At that instant, the first gentleman returned. He laid a hand on the boozer's shoulder and said, in a clear, soft English voice, "I believe you've made a mistake, sir."

Without releasing my hand, the fellow turned and stretched his neck to take in the sight of the Englishman. "And I say it's none of your business, *sir.*"

His voice, while slurred, wasn't what you'd call rough. Vowels and consonants all in proper order, a conscious ironic emphasis on the word *sir*. He spoke like an educated man, thoroughly sauced but well brought up. You never could tell, could you?

"I'm terribly sorry. I'm afraid it *is* my business," said the Englishman. "For one thing, you're sitting on my newspaper."

Again, he spoke softly. I don't think the other passengers even knew what was going on, had even the slightest inkling—if they noticed at all—that these two weren't exchanging a few friendly words about the weather or the Brooklyn Dodgers or Hitler's moustache or something. The Englishman didn't look my way at all. The boozer seemed to have forgotten me as well. His grip loosened. I yanked away my fingers and dug into my pocketbook for a handkerchief. The boozer reached slowly under his rump and drew out the crushed newspaper. The *Miami Herald*, read the masthead, sort of.

"There you are," he said. "Now beat it."

Those last words seemed out of place, coming from a voice like that, like he'd heard the phrase at the movies and had been waiting for the chance to sound like a real gangster. His empty hand rested on his knee and twitched, twitched. The fingers were clean, the square nails trimmed, the skin pink, except for an ugly, cracked, weeping sore on one of his knuckles.

The Englishman pushed back his glasses and leaned a fraction closer.

"I beg your pardon. I don't believe I've made myself clear. I'd be very grateful if you'd return to your own seat, sir, and allow me to resume the use of mine."

"You heard me," said the boozer. "Scram."

He spoke more loudly now, close to shouting, and his voice rang above the noise of the engine. People glanced our way, over their newspapers and magazines, and glanced back just as quickly. Nobody wanted trouble, not with a drunk. You couldn't tell what a drunk might do, and here we flew, two miles above the ocean in a metal tube. I myself had begun to perspire. The sweat trickled from my armpits into the sleeves of my best blouse of pale blue crepe, my linen jacket. The boozer was getting angrier, despite the soothing, conciliatory nature of the Englishman's voice, or maybe because of it. The force of his anger felt like a match in the act of striking, *smelled* like a striking match, the tang of saltpeter in your nose and the back of your throat. My fingers curled into the seams of my pocketbook.

"I'm afraid not," said the Englishman.

The boozer looked like he was going to reply. He gathered himself, straightened his back, turned his head. His cheeks were mottled. The Englishman didn't move, didn't flinch. The boozer opened his mouth and caught his breath twice, a pair of small gasps. Then he closed his eyes and slumped forward, asleep. The Englishman removed his hand from the boozer's shoulder and bent to sling the slack arm over his own shoulders.

"I'll just escort this gentleman to his seat, shall I?" he said to me. "I'm awfully sorry for the trouble."

No one spoke. No one moved. The stewardess stood in the aisle, braced on somebody's headrest, hand cupped over mouth, while the Englishman hoisted the unconscious man to his feet and bore him— dragged him, really—toward the empty seat in the second row. The airplane found a downdraft and dropped, recovered, rattled about, dropped again. The Englishman lurched and caught himself on the back of the single seat to the left, third row. He apologized to the seat's owner and staggered on. The stewardess then dashed forward and helped him lower the boozer into his seat like a sack of wet barley. Together they buckled him in, while the elderly woman to his right looked on distastefully. (I craned my neck to watch the show, believe me.)

Nobody knew what to say. Nobody knew quite what we had just witnessed. The engines screamed on, the airplane rattled like a can of nails. Across the aisle, a man in a suit of pale tropical wool turned back to his magazine. In the row ahead of me, the woman leaned to her husband and whispered something. I checked my watch. Only four minutes had passed, imagine that.

BY THE TIME THE ENGLISHMAN returned to his seat, the roar of the engines had deepened into a growl, and the airplane had begun to stagger downward into Nassau. A cloud wisped by the window and was gone. I feigned interest in the magazine, while my attention poured through the corner of my left eye in the direction of my neighbor, who picked his hat from the floor—it had fallen, apparently, during the scuffle or whatever it was—and placed it back in the bin. It turned out, his hair wasn't thoroughly gold; there was a trace of red in the color, what they call a strawberry blond. I turned a page. He swung into place and reached for the newspaper, which I had retrieved and slid into the cloth pocket on the seat before him. It seemed like the least I could do, and besides, I can't abide a messy floor.

"Thank you," he said. "I do hope you weren't troubled."

"Not at all."

He didn't reply. I had a hundred questions to ask—foremost, was the boozer still alive—but I just turned the pages of the magazine in rapid succession until I ran out of paper altogether and closed the book on my lap, front cover facing up, THE WINDSOR TEAM locked in eternal amity with their Union Jack sofa pillows. The loudspeaker crackled and buzzed, something about landing shortly and the weather in Nassau being ninety-two degrees Fahrenheit, God save us.

I cleared my throat and asked the Englishman what brought him to Nassau, business or pleasure.

"I live here, in fact," he said. "For the time being."

"Oh! So you were visiting Florida?"

"Yes. My brother lives in a town called Cocoa, up the coast a bit.

Lovely place by the ocean." He nodded to the magazine. "Doing your research, are you?"

"Not exactly," I said. "It was just a coincidence."

"Ah."

The airplane shook. I looked out the window and saw land, shrubby and verdant, and a long, pale beach meeting the surf, and a car flashing brilliantly along a road made of gray thread. "What a pair of romantics," I heard myself say.

"Romantics? Do you really think so?"

I turned my head back and saw a serious profile, a pair of eyes squinted in thought behind the wire-rimmed spectacles. He hadn't touched the newspaper. His lanky arms were folded across his chest, his right leg crossed over his left, immaculate, civilized. He didn't look as if he'd lifted a pair of boots, let alone two hundred pounds of slack human weight.

"Don't you? But it's the love story of the century, hadn't you heard?" I said. "The king who gave up his throne for the woman he loves."

"A thoroughly modern thing to do. Not romantic at all."

"How so?"

The airplane shuddered and thumped, bounced hard and settled. I looked out the window again and saw we had landed. The landscape outside teemed with color and vegetation and shimmering heat. I saw a cluster of palms, a low, rectangular building.

By the time we rolled to a stop, I had forgotten the question left dangling between us. The sound of his voice surprised me, but then everything about him had surprised me.

"A romantic would have sacrificed love for duty," said the Englishman, "not the other way around."

The airplane gave a final lurch and went still. He rose from his seat, removed his suitcase and his hat from the bin, removed my suitcase and gave it to me, and put his hat on his head. I said thank you. He told me to think nothing of it and wished me a good day, a pleasant stay in Nassau, and walked off the airplane. The sunshine flashed from the lenses of his spectacles.

As I passed the fellow from Savannah, he was still slumped in his seat, held in place by the safety belt, and I couldn't honestly tell if he was dead or alive. The stewardess kept casting these anxious glances at his chest. I told her thank you for a memorable flight.

"Wasn't it though," she said. "Have a pleasant stay in Nassau."

IN THE TERMINAL BUILDING, AS I waited my turn at the passport desk, I looked around for the blond man, but I didn't see him. He might have gone anywhere. He might have come from anywhere. A fellow like that, he was like a djinn, like an enchanted creature from a fairy tale. Except this wasn't a fairy tale, this was reality. He was made of common clay. He came from a woman and man, who fell in love, or had not. Who had married, or had not. Had spent a lifetime of nights together, or just one.

As I trudged out the terminal building to the street outside, I remember thinking a vast history lay behind this man, which I would never know.

ELFRIEDE

JULY 1900
(Switzerland)

THE ENGLISHMAN ARRIVES at the clinic about an hour after lunchtime, while Elfriede sits in the main courtyard with Herr Doktor Hermann, discussing something she dreamed the night before. When she looks back on this moment, from a distance of years and—eventually— decades, she will remember nothing about the dream or the discussion, but she will hear the exact noise of the cartwheels and the iron hoofbeats on the paving stones of the drive as if the interior of her head were a phonograph disc, and these sounds imprinted it forever. She'll remember the voices rising from the other side of the courtyard wall, and the smell of the pink, half-wild roses climbing that wall, and the way the sun burst free from the shade to warm the back of her neck and soak the courtyard in light.

Except that the sun doesn't really come out at that moment. Memory, it turns out, is unreliable. All on its own, your memory gathers up helpful details that match your recollection of an event, whether or not those details actually existed at the time. But does it matter? For Elfriede, the sun comes out when the Englishman arrives. That's how she remembers it. Sunshine, and the smell of roses.

ANYWAY, ONE OF THEM IS talking, Elfriede or Dr. Hermann, it doesn't matter which one, and they both fall silent at the clatter of hoofbeats and cartwheels. "A new arrival?" Elfriede asks, after a moment.

"Yes, a lung patient," answers the doctor. "Pneumonia."

"How awful."

"He'll be kept in the infirmary wing, of course. There is no danger of transmission."

"I meant, how awful for *him*."

Dr. Hermann nods and makes a note in his little book. He makes notes continually during these sessions—conversations, he calls them, as if purely social—and Elfriede feels sometimes like a laboratory experiment, an unknown specimen of plant or animal, something abnormal. "How do you feel about this?" he asks, still writing, and for a moment Elfriede isn't sure what he means, the note taking or the new patient. When she hesitates, he prompts her.

"I don't mind at all," she says. "I hope he recovers quickly. Why should I mind?"

"Indeed. Why should you mind?"

"I don't know. But you seem to think I should."

"What makes you say that?"

Another thing about Dr. Hermann, he never answers a question except with another question. He wants Elfriede to do all the talking, Elfriede to reveal herself. It's the very latest treatment for nervous disorders such as hers, and really, as compared to some of the others, it's not bad. Dr. Hermann is a large, soft-edged, round-shouldered man who folds his long limbs into normal-size chairs without the smallest irritation that they weren't designed to accommodate him. There's something malleable about him. Even his brown hair has a pliant quality. In later years, Elfriede will realize she never noticed the color of his eyes, nor can she recall his face. Just the soft, even shape of his voice, asking her questions.

She makes her answer as clear as possible, so he can't find another question in it. "When I said *How awful*, you told me there was no danger of infection. So you must have thought I was afraid of that."

Dr. Hermann adjusts his spectacles on the bridge of his nose. "Have you ever felt afraid of sickness, Elfriede?"

"No." She stands up. "I'm going to take a walk now."

ADMISSION TO THE CLINIC IS voluntary, and Elfriede is free to come and go as she likes, no restriction on movement, no requirement to stay. She could leave at any time, in fact.

Practically speaking, of course, that's nearly impossible. The clinic sits on the top of a mountain, surrounded by wilderness and reached by a single, steep road in poor repair. Until the middle of the last century, it was a monastery of the Franciscan order, and the last of the monks sold the grounds and the ancient buildings to Dr. Hermann for next to nothing, on the condition that the crumbling walls remain a sanctuary for healing and peace. Patients seek out its geographic isolation and clean, healthful air for a variety of reasons—lung trouble, nervous disorders, broken hearts, discreet pregnancies, discreet abortions—but the general point is to separate oneself from civilization. You can't leave without mountaineering skills or help from the outside, and Elfriede has neither. Also, she has no money—none she can produce from a pocket, anyway. So, when she rises from her bench and leaves the courtyard, walks along the covered passage to the old chapel, passes the chapel, and exits the building altogether to emerge on the fragrant, sunlit hillside, she doesn't imagine she could hail the driver of the Englishman's carriage and convince him to carry her back along the twenty miles of steep, rutted roadway, or that she could simply walk them on her own. Where would she go, anyway? Who would want her?

She just goes outside to be alone. That's all she wants. To be left alone.

AS YOU MIGHT IMAGINE, THE quarters in this former Franciscan monastery are austere, to say the least. Elfriede's bedroom is literally a monk's cell, or rather two of them knocked together, and contains a single bed with a horsehair mattress, a stool, a plain wardrobe in which she hangs her three dresses, a dresser, and a desk and chair. There are no bookshelves. Elfriede's free to borrow from the library, one volume at a time, but she wasn't allowed to bring any books from home, nor is she allowed to receive any while she's here. She's encouraged to write, however. Each week, a fresh supply of notebooks arrives on her desk. Herr Doktor Hermann wants her to record her thoughts, her memories, and especially her dreams, and to bring these notebooks to their daily conversations so he can review the contents. When her notebooks aren't sufficiently full, he doesn't express any obvious displeasure to Elfriede. Of course, that would be unprofessional! Still she feels his displeasure like a disturbance in the air, turning his flared nostrils all pink, so she writes her devoirs daily, sometimes for hours, in order to satisfy his hunger for her subconscious mind. She also keeps another notebook under the horsehair mattress. This is the notebook that contains her real thoughts.

In the evenings, or during the day when the weather's inclement, Elfriede has another way of finding solitude. She makes her way to the music room, which nobody ever enters except her, and plays on the piano from sheet music obtained from the library. Sometimes she'll go on for hours, in chronological order of course, Bach to Haydn to Mozart to Beethoven to Schubert to Chopin, one must be methodical about such things. Then it's midnight, and as the notes fade a silence fills the chamber like a thousand ears listening, an audience of spirits, and Elfriede can almost—but not quite—feel that her husband and son are among them.

TWO WEEKS LATER, ELFRIEDE ENCOUNTERS the Englishman for the first time. An orderly pushes him in a wheeled chair along one of the

paved paths in the infirmary garden, and she observes them both from
the hillside above. She's just returned from a long, solitary hike, and the
mountain air fills her lungs and her limbs, and the sunlight burns her
face in a primitive way. She sits among the wildflowers and wraps her
arms around her legs. Below her, about the size and importance of squirrels, the orderly and the Englishman come to a stop at the top of the
rectangular path, inside a patch of sun. The orderly adjusts the blanket
on the Englishman's lap and they exchange a few words, although the
breeze carries their voices away from Elfriede's ears. After a last pat to
the blanket, the orderly consults a pocket watch and heads back to the
infirmary building, leaving the Englishman in the sunshine.

For some time, he sits without moving. The chair's positioned at such
an angle that she can't see his face properly, and anyway Elfriede's a bit
nearsighted, so he might be asleep or he might just be too weak to move.
Still, he must be past the crisis, or they wouldn't have left him outside like
this, would they?

Judging from the proportion of man to chair, he seems to be on the
tall side, if slender. Of course, Elfriede's husband is a giant, two meters
tall and almost as broad, so most men look slender in comparison. Also,
this fellow's been sick, and he's wearing those loose blue infirmary pajamas. His hair's been shaved, and the remaining stubble is ginger, which
catches a little sun and glints. Elfriede creeps closer. The brief, vibrant
season of alpine wildflowers has arrived, and the meadow's packed with
their reds and oranges and violets, their sticky sage scent, clinging to Elfriede's dress as she slides through the grass. She just wants to see his
face, that's all. Wants to know what an Englishman looks like. In her
entire sheltered life, living in the country, small villages, Berlin once to
shop for her trousseau, Frankfurt and Zurich glimpsed through the window of a train, she's never met one.

Closer and closer she creeps, and still his face evades her. They're
pointed the same direction, toward the sun, and Elfriede sees only his

profile, his closed left eye. He must be asleep, recovering from his illness. His color's good, pale but not ghostly, no sign of fever, a few freckles sprinkled across the bridge of his nose. His left hand, lying upon the gray wool blanket, is long-fingered and elegant; the right hand remains out of view.

Elfriede stretches out her leg to slide a few centimeters closer, and without opening his eyes, the Englishman speaks, clear and just loud enough. "You might as well come on over here and introduce yourself."

"Oh! I didn't—"

"Yes, you did." Now he opens his eyes and turns his head to face her, squinting a little and smiling a broad, electric smile that will come, in the fullness of time, to dominate her imagination, her consciousness and her unconsciousness, her blood and bones and hair and breath. "My God," he says, in a more subdued voice, almost inaudible over the distance between them, "you're beautiful, aren't you?"

"Yes."

"What are you doing here? You don't look sick." He glances cheerfully at her midsection. "Not up the duff, are you?"

He says those words—*up the duff*—in English, and Elfriede doesn't understand them, so she just shakes her head. "A nervous disorder," she calls back.

"You don't look nervous." He smiles at her confusion. "Never mind. I was only joking. I'm the family jester, I can't help it. My name's Thorpe. Wilfred Thorpe. I'd offer my hand, but I'm supposed to be keeping my germs to myself, at the present time."

"Herr Thorpe. I'm Frau von Kleist."

"Frau, is it? You look awfully young to be married."

She hesitates. "I'm twenty-two."

"As old as that?"

"And I have a little boy as well," Elfriede adds, for no reason at all.

"Do you? Well, I won't ask any awkward questions." He turns his head back to the sun and closes his eyes. "Fine day, isn't it? Won't you come sit by me? I'll promise not to cough on you."

"I don't know if it's allowed."

"Bugger that." (In English again.) "I'll take the blame, I promise. I'll say I had a coughing fit, and you came to my aid in your selfless way."

She laughs rustily and rises to her feet. In the course of her creeping, she's come to within ten or twelve meters of the low stone wall that marks the perimeter of the garden, and it seems so silly and artificial to be holding a conversation in this manner, calling back and forth across the gulf, that Elfriede goes willingly to the brick wall and perches atop it, a meter or so from Herr Thorpe's left shoulder, crossing her legs at the ankle.

"That's better," he says. "Easier on my lungs, anyway. You smell like wildflowers."

"I've been sitting on them. You speak German very well."

"So do you."

She laughs again—*so* out of practice at laughing, but she can't seem to help herself. "But it's my native tongue, and you—you're an English-man, aren't you?"

"Indeed I am. I learned my German in school, from a fearsome and very fluent master. Used to beat me with a cane whenever I slipped accidentally into the informal address."

"That's terrible."

"It's supposed to build character." He opens his eyes and squints into the sun. He looks nothing like her husband, not just because he's smaller and his head is shaved and his bones stick out from his skin, not just because he's in a wheelchair while her husband is as huge and hale and hearty as a woodsman. Herr Thorpe is terribly plain, wide-faced and thick-lipped, freckled and ginger-haired, and the electricity of his smile can't disguise his current state of febrile emaciation. She holds her breath in disbelief at the sharpness of his protruding bones, at the length of his pale eyelashes. He's positively lanky inside his blue pajamas, and then there's this enormous pumpkin head stuck on top of him.

"I'm glad you're feeling better," she says. "Pneumonia can be so dangerous."

"Oh, I'm all right."

"You wouldn't have come here if you weren't quite sick."

"I couldn't have come here at all if I'd been really sick. It's a damned long journey from Vienna, you know. No, I came through the crisis all right, but the doctors were worried about my lungs, so they sent me here for recuperation. And my parents agreed because—well."

"Because why?"

"A personal matter."

"Some girl?" Elfriede asks boldly.

"Yes," he says. "Some girl, I'm afraid. But it all seems rather long ago now. What about you?"

"A personal matter."

"Let me guess. Coerced to marry some doddering old bastard against your will, and you've gone mad to escape him?"

"Nothing like that," she says.

"Crossed in love?"

"No."

"Some terrible grief, perhaps?"

"Nothing too terrible."

The man drums his fingers on the armrest of his chair. "Have you been here long?"

"Long enough."

"Ah. Then perhaps you can satisfy my curiosity on a small matter. You see, late in the evenings, when I'm meant to be sleeping, I sometimes hear the most extraordinary music floating into my chamber. Piano. Goes on for hours. I can't decide whether it's coming from outside the window or down the corridor. At first I thought I was dreaming. Do you hear it at all?"

"I—well, I . . ." She stops herself on the brink of a lie. "I'm afraid it's me."

"You? Ah. Ah."

"I'm terribly sorry. I didn't realize anyone could hear me. I'll stop—"

"No! No. Don't stop on my account."

"If I'm keeping you awake—"

"I don't mind at all, I assure you. It's enchanting. Last night, the Chopin . . . I had the strangest feeling . . ."

"What?"

"Nothing. Enchanted, that's all. Absolutely enchanted. And it was *you*, all along? All the more enchanting, then."

From another man, this compliment might have sounded unctuous. But Mr. Thorpe speaks the word *enchanting* with such easy intimacy, Elfriede laughs instead, and laughter feels so good in her chest, in her head. She looks down at her feet, crossed at the ankles, and only then does she realize she's blushing. She asks hastily, "What were you doing in Vienna?"

"What does anybody do in Vienna? Art, culture, philosophy. Opera and cafés and whatever amusement comes one's way. I suppose I was attempting what they used to call a grand tour, except I kept getting stuck in places." He pauses. "Delaying the inevitable."

"What's so inevitable?"

"Returning home. My father's found a place for me in chambers."

"What does this mean, 'chambers'?"

"Law. I'm meant to become a lawyer."

"How—how—"

"Grown up," he says. "Grown up and rather dull. Pretty soon I shall get married, grow a beard, and start a brood of rascals of my own, and the whole cycle will start over again." He looks as if he might say something else, but starts to cough instead. The sound is wet and wretched, cracking off the walls of the garden and the stone infirmary building across the grass.

"Are you all right?" Elfriede asks anxiously. "Shall I call the orderly?"

He waves the idea away. The fit dies down, and he leans his head back against the chair. "It's not as bad as it sounds. It's gotten much better, believe it or not."

"You must have been at death's door, then."

"Yes, I rather think I was. It's a real indignity, to catch pneumonia in the summertime. My mother says it was all the dissipation."

"Dissipation? Really? You don't seem like the dissipated sort."

"Well, my mother's idea of dissipation is a glass of sherry in the evening. Her side of the family is all Scotch Presbyterians. Strict," he adds, apparently realizing Elfriede isn't well acquainted with the tenets of Scotch Presbyterianism. "Damned strict."

"So you were escaping."

"Something like that. I finished university a year ago and thought— well, one's only got this single chance to sin, before that inevitable time of life when one's sins puncture the happiness of somebody else."

"It's not inevitable," Elfriede says. "You don't have to do it."

"Do what? Go home and take up the law and become a respectable chap?"

"No. You should go back to Vienna instead. Go back to Vienna and the cafés and that girl of yours—"

"Frau von Kleist," he says solemnly, "you're making me weary with all your talk of rebellion. I'm a sick man, remember?"

"Of course."

"I require a long period of rest and recuperation, not a program of debauchery."

"How long—" She clears her throat and continues. "How long are you supposed to stay here?"

"As long as it takes. A month or two, perhaps. Just in time for autumn. And you, Frau von Kleist? How long do you expect to stay?"

She shrugs. "As long as it takes."

"A month or two, perhaps? I'm afraid I don't know much about nervous disorders."

"More time than that, I think."

There is a queer, heavy silence, the kind for which the clinic is famous. The deep peace of the mountains settles over Elfriede, a sense of motionless isolation that sometimes unnerves her, or increases her melancholy, because it seems as if she's the only human being in the world, and she wants passionately to belong to somebody, anybody, almost anybody. Elfriede smells the wildflowers, the faint odor of something cooking in the refectory kitchen—it's nearly lunchtime—and something else as well, a peculiar, indecipherable scent she will come to recognize as that of Herr Thorpe himself, a scent that will forever remind her of mountains, even in the middle of a teeming, dirty city.

Herr Thorpe murmurs, "There's the orderly."

Elfriede glances to the infirmary door, and the white-uniformed man presently emerging from it. A shimmer of panic crosses her chest, the way you feel when the nurse arrives to draw your blood from your veins. She climbs to her feet atop the wall.

"I must be going, Herr Thorpe—"

"Wilfred."

"Wilfred." She hesitates. "My name is Elfriede."

He presents her with that wide grin, one eye squinted. "Why, it's practically the same as mine! What are the chances, do you think?"

"Very slim, I think."

Wilfred puts his hand to his heart. "Shattered. Will I see you again?"

She leaps back to the meadow side, which is about a half meter higher than the garden, rising upward along a soft, rounded hill. "I don't see why we should. We occupy entirely different wings of the clinic."

"And yet you're here."

"A mistake!" she says, over her shoulder, as she starts to climb the hill.

Wilfred's voice carries after her. "There are no mistakes, Elfriede the Fair! Only fate!"

Elfriede climbs quickly, and the word *fate* is so thin and distant, it's almost out of earshot. Nevertheless, she hears it. In fact, it echoes inside her head, over and over, in time to the heavy smack of her heart as she approaches the summit of the hill. She tells herself it's only the effort of the climb, the thin air, the anticipation of the view from the top.

LULU

JULY 1941
(The Bahamas)

E VERY TOWN HAS its watering hole, where everybody gathers to share a few drinks and some human news, and in Nassau that particular place was the bar of the Prince George Hotel. You couldn't miss it. If, newly disgorged from some steamship onto the hot, smoky docks of Nassau Harbor, you staggered with your suitcase across Bay Street to shelter from the sun, you found yourself bang under the awning of the Prince George. And since the Prince George, as a matter of tradition, offered the arriving tourist his first glass of rum punch gratis, why, you can see how the bar developed a loyal following. I should know, believe me, even though I'd arrived by air instead of by sea. That punch went down so well, I made straight for the reception desk and booked a room. Three weeks later, I had almost forgotten I'd lived anywhere else. Every evening at six sharp, I made my way downstairs and took up a stool three seats down from the left, and the bartender—we'll call him Jack— whipped up a cocktail while I lit a cigarette from a case full of Parliaments, a brand relatively rare in New York City but nigh ubiquitous in this British Crown colony. So began my twentieth night in Nassau. Now pay attention.

Jack was the kind of bartender who sized you up first and decided for himself what kind of drink you needed. On this particular evening, with the place just loosely occupied and the afternoon sun still filling the windows, he took a bit of time and asked, "Be a double for you, Mrs. Randolph? Look like you been dropping bombs all over Germany today."

"Nothing as exciting as that." I rested my left hand on the thick, sleek varnish and stared at the gold band on my fourth finger. "Just a day with the ladies at the Red Cross."

Jack made a low, slow whistle. "Since when?"

"Since this morning, when the nice fellow in charge of the magazine was so dear as to send me one of his telegrams to go with my breakfast."

"The good kind of telegram?"

"See for yourself." I set the cigarette in the ashtray, pulled the yellow envelope from my pocketbook, and removed the wisp of paper, which I spread out flat on the counter before me. How I hated the color yellow.

HAPPY ANNIVERSARY STOP TODAY NOW THREE
WEEKS SINCE YOUR DEPARTURE NASSAU STOP
TOTAL EXPENSES TO MAGAZINE $803.22 STOP TOTAL
EXCLUSIVE WINDSOR SCOOPS ZERO STOP RETURN
TO NEW YORK IMMEDIATELY REPEAT IMMEDIATELY
STOP NOT ONE MORE PENNY EXPENSES WILL BE PAID
BY THIS MAGAZINE=
=S. B. LIGHTFOOT

Jack peered over and whistled. Above our heads, a ceiling fan purred and purred, lifting the ends of my hair. Jack shook his head and returned to his bottles.

"So you see," I continued, replacing telegram in envelope and envelope in pocketbook, "my time in Nassau may be winding to an end."

"Don't you like it here, Mrs. Randolph?"

"Very much. But I can't stick around if the magazine's cutting off my expenses."

"You could write them a story, like this fellow suggests."

I inclined my head to the pocketbook. "This fellow? You mean Lightfoot? That's a nice way of putting it. *Orders*, is more like it."

"So? Write the fellow a story."

"It ain't that easy, sonny," I said. "There's only one thing to write about in this town, this blazing, backward, godforsaken burg, and it turns out you can't just waltz right into Government House and ask to see the Duke and Duchess of Windsor, *s'il vous plaît*, and make it snappy."

"I guess not, at that."

"No, sir. You've got to weave your way into society, it seems. For starters, you have to join the local Red Cross, of which said duchess is president, and make nice with the ladies."

"That bad, was it?"

"It was awful."

Jack set the drink in front of me. A martini, it turned out. "Compliments of an admirer."

"A *what*?" I sputtered into the glass.

"An admirer, like I said. And that's all I'm saying." Jack zipped his lips.

I set down the glass and lifted the cigarette. Jack observed me with interest, thick eyebrows cocked. When I'd taken the first long drag, and another sip from the martini, I crossed my legs and began a survey of the room around me. As you might expect, there was plenty of room to survey, plenty of height and arch, plenty of solid rectangular pillars done in handsome raised wood paneling, plenty of large, masculine chairs and ashtrays on little tables. Not so many customers. Everybody still out enjoying the sunshine, no doubt, and aside from the elderly gent near the window, buried in his newspaper, and the two fellows in linen suits having an earnest discussion in an alcove, the joint was empty. I turned back to Jack.

"Not the old man with the newspaper, I hope?"

"He's mighty rich, Mrs. Randolph. Beggars can't be choosers."

"Are you calling me a beggar, Jack?"

Jack's face assumed an aspect of innocence. Above his head, the glasses glittered in their rows, highballs and lowballs, champagne coupes and brandy snifters, not a speck of dust, not a hair's width out of order. "Just an old saying, Mrs. Randolph," he said. "Something my mama used to tell me, that's all."

"I have my faults, I'm the first to admit. But I've never begged for a dime in my life, and I don't intend to start now." I tilted my head toward the window. "Certainly not with some old moneybags trying his luck in a hotel lounge."

"You have your standards, is that what you're getting at?"

"I have my standards."

"Oh, then I should take back this little glass here?"

I slapped away his hand. "Don't you dare. The poor fellow's perfectly free to buy me all the drinks he wants. So long as he understands he's not getting his money's worth."

"Aw, he's not so bad. Just look at the poor sucker. Got most of his hair. Nice clean suit. Shoes all shiny. Can't see his teeth, but I bet he's got a few left."

"I'll take your word for that."

"You're a real tough dame, you know that? A lot of pretty girls might take pity on a nice guy like that, money to burn. A one-way ticket to Easy Street."

"I'm not a lot of girls, am I? Besides," I said, reaching for the ashtray, "I happen to know firsthand where that kind of arrangement ends up, and it's not Easy Street, believe me."

The ashtray, if you're asking, was a heavy old thing made of silver and embossed in the middle with what seemed to be a tavern scene. A border wound around the edges in a series of scrolls, dipping now and then to make space for a resting cigarette. I knocked a crumb of ash inside and measured the weight of Jack's curiosity on the top of my head. Not that I blamed him. You said a provocative thing like that, you expected someone to wonder what you meant by it, to clear his throat and ask you for a detail or two.

Jack's black waistcoat shifted in the background, his crisp white sleeves. He put away the bottle of gin on the shelf behind him and said, over his shoulder, "Just as well, I guess, he ain't the fellow who bought your martini."

"But you said—"

"*You* said." Jack turned back to me and grinned. "I was just following along, you see?"

"I can't tell you how delighted I am to have amused you."

"Now, don't be sore with me, Mrs. Randolph. I'm sworn to secrecy, that's all."

"You're teasing me, aren't you? I'll bet this admirer of yours doesn't even exist. You just poured me a free drink for your own entertainment."

"Oh, he exists, all right. Paid me up front and everything. Nice tip."

"Is he here right now?"

"In this room?" Jack's gaze slid to the door, traveled along the walls, the panel and polish, the glittering windows, and returned to me. "'Fraid I can't say. Kind of a shy fella, your beau. But don't you fret. I got the feeling he'll make himself known to you, when he's good and ready."

Before me, the martini formed a tranquil circle in its glass, a cool pool. Not a single flaw disturbed its surface. I pondered the chemical properties of liquids, the infinitesimal bonds of electricity that secured them together in such perfect order, the beautiful molecules held flat in my glass by gravity. The great mystery eluded me, as ever.

"How long have you tended bar, Jack?" I asked.

"How long have I tended bar? Or tended this bar here?"

"Tended bar at all, I guess."

"Well, now." He shut one eye and judged the ceiling. "Landed here in Nassau in twenty-one when I was just a wee lad, helping my dad with the old schooner—Lord, what a sweet ship she was—"

"Rum-running, you mean."

"Just engaging in a little maritime commerce, Mrs. Randolph, serving the needs of you poor suckers dying of thirst back home. Used to load and unload them crates of liquor all the livelong day. Oh, but we lived like kings in Nassau back then. Those were good years." He shook his head and wiped some invisible smudge of something-or-other from the counter. "Then they brought back the liquor trade stateside."

"Hallelujah."

"For you folks back home, maybe. Come to find out, my dad spent all the money from those years, every damn penny, Mrs. Randolph. Left me here in Nassau, broke as a stick. Lucky I knew a fellow who tended bar in those days. Took me under his wing, taught me the trade. Now here I am." Jack spread his arms. "Got my domain. Nothing happens here without my say-so, Mrs. Randolph, and don't you forget that. You got a problem with any fellow here, you come to me."

He was a large man, Jack, maybe more wide than tall, but still. I found myself wanting to wrap my arms around that comfortable girth and kiss his rib cage. At the thought of this act, the image it evoked in my imagination, I directed a tiny smile at the remnants of my drink and asked, "Why do you like me so much, Jack?"

"Because you're an honest dame, Mrs. Randolph. Honest and kind-hearted."

"This fellow of yours. Is he good enough for me?"

"Nobody's good enough for you, Mrs. Randolph, not in my book." He leaned forward an inch or two. "Between you and me, there's been a lot of fellows asking. Pretty lady, drinking alone, kind of sad and don't-touch-me. But this fellow is the first fellow I said could buy you a drink."

"A fine endorsement."

"Now it's up to you, Mrs. Randolph. You're a real good judge, I'll bet. You just watch yourself around here, that's all."

"I thought you said he met your approval."

"Oh, I wasn't talking about *him*." Jack pulled back and set the glass back on its shelf. "Talking about everything else, everything and everyone else on this island, but especially that duchess and her husband, them two sleek blue jays in a nest, looking out for nobody but themselves. You watch yourself."

"Watch myself? What for? When I can't seem to buy myself even a peep inside that nest. I spent all morning at their damned headquarters, the Red Cross, stuffing packages and sitting through the dullest committee meeting in the world, going out of my mind, just to wrangle myself an invitation to the party at Government House on Saturday, and then the duchess finally turns up, and do you know what she says?"

Jack makes a slice along his throat. "Off with your head?"

"Worse. *Enchanted to meet you, Mrs. Randolph.*"

"That's all? Sounds all right to me."

"You don't know how it is with these people. She locks eyes with you, see, like you're the only person in the room, the only person in the *world*, pixie dust glitters in the air around you, and she takes your hand and says, *Enchanted to meet you*, and you think to yourself, *She likes me! She's enchanted, she said it herself! We're going to be the best of friends!* Then she drops your hand and turns to the next woman and locks eyes with *her*, and you feel like a sucker. No, you *are* a sucker. Sucked in by the oldest trick in the book." There was a stir to my right, somebody approaching the bar. I glanced out the side of my eye and recognized, or thought I recognized, a certain man sliding into position a few stools down, tall, polished, Spanish or French or something, air of importance. Jack, on the other hand, made not the slightest sign of having noticed him. I leaned my elbow on the counter and said, "Maybe I ought to just read the stars and give up."

"Give up?" said Jack. "Now what kind of talk is that?"

"The smart kind, brother. The realist kind."

He glanced at last to the newcomer. "Excuse me one minute, Mrs. Randolph."

The drink was finished. I stubbed out the cigarette. Jack had taken the newcomer's order and turned to the row of bottles behind him. I stood up, a little more unsteady than I ought to have been after a single martini, and fished a shilling from my pocketbook.

"I beg your pardon," said the gentleman to my right. "I couldn't help overhearing."

"Of course you couldn't."

"You are not leaving, surely?"

"I'm afraid I am."

"But you haven't eaten yet."

"Maybe I'm having dinner elsewhere."

"Now, Mrs. Randolph," the man said slowly, "we both know that isn't true."

Up until this point, I'd been speaking into air. I wasn't in the habit of addressing bold men, it was a stubbornness of mine. But you can't ignore a fellow who calls you by name, can you? I turned my head. As I said, I had taken notice of him before. He was one of the regulars at the Prince George, and besides, you couldn't help but notice him. He was tall and lustrous and strapping, dressed in a pressed suit and white shirt and green necktie, and even though his nose was large and his jaw a little soft, you had to admit he was handsome, especially when he looked at you dead on from that pair of wicked, intelligent eyes. Also, he had an elastic way of moving, like an athlete.

"I beg your pardon," I said. "I don't believe we've been introduced."

He held out a large hand. "Alfred de Marigny."

"I've heard that name before, I believe."

"I'm afraid I have something of a reputation." There was a note of apology in his voice.

"I'll say. If you believe all the stories."

"*Do* you believe the stories?"

"Naturally. I'll bet they're a hundred times more interesting than the truth. Thanks for the drink, by the by."

He lifted his eyebrows and signaled to Jack. "You're welcome."

"I didn't say I wanted another."

"Didn't you? But please, Mrs. Randolph, sit down. We cannot have you standing like that. We cannot have you *leaving* like this."

"Why not?" I asked. But I sat down.

He sat too, facing me, elbow propped on the bar. "What is this you are saying, about giving up? Give up on what?"

I reached into my pocketbook for the cigarette case. You know, something for my hands to do, something to occupy my attention while the most notorious playboy in Nassau settled himself on a nearby stool and fixed his attention on me. I tried to assemble a few facts in my memory. He was recently divorced from some wealthy Manhattanite who had left her previous husband for him. He was a yachtsman, a good one. A foreigner with a title of some kind, which nobody knew how he acquired, or whether it really belonged to him. In short, he was a—what was the word I had overheard? A mountebank. Fine ten-dollar word, *mountebank*. I plucked a cigarette and said, "Did I say that?"

"You did. I'm certain of it. Allow me." He removed a matchbook from his pocket and lit me up in a series of deft movements: selecting the match, striking flame, holding it just to the end of the cigarette, so that the blue core touched the paper in a tiny explosion.

"Thank you." I opened the case again and offered him the contents. He chose one and thanked me in turn. As we completed these little rituals, Jack returned with a pair of drinks: another martini for me, a whiskey for de Marigny.

When we had both tasted the waters, he said, "I hope I have not offended. I only wish to know if I might be of some assistance."

"Out of the kindness of your heart?"

He pressed his hand against his chest. "I am a gentleman, Mrs. Randolph. I ask nothing in return."

"Sure you don't. Not that I hold it against you, mind you. It's what makes the world go round."

"What makes the world go round?"

"Favors." I reached for the ashtray. "To answer your question, I'm a journalist. I've been sent here by an American magazine to give our readers an inside view of Nassau society in these interesting times."

"By Nassau society, do you perhaps mean the duke and his wife?"

"Well. That *is* what's interesting about it, after all."

"I see." He turned his face a few inches to the left, as if to regard the tables and chairs, which had begun to populate, mostly men in pale, pressed linen suits, like de Marigny, only shorter and pudgier, your commonplace middle-aged merchant, *Bahamicus mercantilis vulgarii*. A couple of conspicuous American tourists. "I'm afraid there isn't much I can do for you in this regard, Mrs. Randolph. I am not a favorite of His Royal Highness."

"Goodness me. Why ever not? I thought it was part of His Highness's duty to make himself agreeable to his allies."

"Allies?"

"I couldn't help noticing your accent, Monsieur de Marigny."

"Mrs. Randolph, I am a British subject by birth. I was born in Mauritius, which is a British colony, somewhat to the right of Africa."

"I see," I said. "How awfully exotic. Then it's *Mister* de Marigny?"

He made a small smile. "My friends call me Freddie."

"Well then, Freddie. How did a nice chap like you end up on the wrong side of the Duke of Windsor?"

"Do you ask me as a journalist, Mrs. Randolph, or as a friend?"

"Both. I'm a desperate woman, you know. Any little old tidbit might save my career."

"Then I don't mind telling you that the duke is a terrible bigot, a vain, weak, effeminate man, entirely ruled by his wife and his own greed."

He still wore the smile, but his voice was serious, and not at all hushed as you might expect, saying a thing like that in a place like this. I tapped my cigarette on the edge of the ashtray, taking care to keep my fingers steady despite the buzz along my nerves. "Golly. Say what you really think, Freddie."

"I beg your pardon. Mine is an outspoken nature."

"Oh, I don't mind a bit, believe me. Is he a traitor?"

"No," de Marigny said, "but he is the fool of the Nazis. I knew him a little before the war, you know, when I lived in London. It's no secret he admired Hitler very much in those days. His wife, I think, is of the same mind. You will remember, I think, their visit to Germany, shortly after they married?"

"I remember, all right. That was some show. Parades and factory tours and what have you. Wearing their best clothes and their best smiles."

"He is an idiot." De Marigny sucked on his cigarette. His gaze, which had been trained amicably on me, lost a little focus, lost a little amity, and slipped to some point past my left ear. "I had a friend in those days, a good chap, handsome fellow, clever, a Jew. He traveled back to Berlin to persuade his family to leave. This was in 1936, I believe, after they passed these terrible laws. That was the last I ever saw of him."

"Do you believe what some of the newspapers are saying? About the camps and so on? Or is it all just propaganda, like spearing the Belgian babies?"

He tossed down a considerable measure of whiskey and stared at the cubes of ice left behind. The air was warm, the way the air is always warm in Nassau, and you could almost hear the melting of the ice under the draft of the ceiling fan. His hand, holding the glass, was quite long, and the fingers looked as if they could crush rocks. I waited for him to speak. Most people will, if you give them enough time. Nobody likes a silence.

"I have a story for you," he said at last. "I think it illustrates rather nicely the character of the man."

"That's what I'm here for, after all."

"Some few years ago, when I first came to the Bahamas, I found a pleasant little ridge on the island of Eleuthera on which to build a house of my own. I had made some money, you see, in the London commodities markets, and I wanted what every fellow does. A castle of his own."

"Naturally."

He waved away a little smoke. "It's a pretty island, Eleuthera. Long and narrow and undulating, like a ribbon"—he made a gesture with his hand, illustrating this ribbon—"so you are never far from these beaches of beautiful coral sand. It lies to the east, about two days' sail from here. Eleuthera. This means 'freedom' in Greek, did you know that?"

"I did not. They don't teach much Greek at girls' schools, I'm afraid."

"No? I suppose not. In any case, I bought two hundred acres on a ridge, sloping right down to the beach, and assured myself of a source of plentiful fresh water on the property. Then I built a nice bungalow."

"So what happened? The duke decided he wanted it for himself?"

A large party burst into the room, six or seven of them, voices booming off the ceiling, reeking of sunshine and perspiration. De Marigny glanced across the furniture and observed them for a second or two, no more. Then he returned to me and said, smiling again, "Not quite. You see, in the village below this ridge, the Negroes have no fresh water of their own. The women boil seawater and collect rain in buckets, or else they walk for miles and then pay a penny a dipper. So I thought, since I was building this house in any case, I should also build a system to pipe water down to the village from my well, to these villagers who had nothing but dry rocks and barren soil. And I designed this system, and had the permit approved by the Executive Council, and all that was needed was the signature of the governor himself."

"Oh, dear," I said.

While he was speaking, Jack came silently in our direction and replaced the empty whiskey glass with a fresh one. De Marigny nodded his thanks and sipped. Though the sides of the glass were still dry, he held it gingerly. "Then this woman arrives," he said. "A woman named Rosita Forbes, a writer. An Englishwoman, the sporty sort, do you know what I mean?"

"I have an idea. Thinks she's Gertrude Bell and Good Queen Bess all rolled into one."

He laughed. "Yes, like that. So she buys her own land, not far away from mine, and builds herself a big, splendid house, and what do you think? She has no well, no source of her own. The silly woman did not think to ask these practical questions before she purchased her little empire." He shrugged his shoulders. "I suggested she build gutters and a water tank. We have plenty of tropical downpours in these islands, after all. But no. She has other ideas. And then I wait and wait for the governor's signature, and there is no signature, so I sail back to Nassau and make an appointment at Government House and explain the situation, how the villagers are waiting for their fresh water, and do you know what he says, this fellow who ruled as king of England and her dominions for almost a year? Emperor of India, et cetera?"

"I can't imagine."

"He says he wants the water in those pipes—*my* water, mind you, from *my* property—diverted to Mrs. Forbes instead. He says the natives are used to collecting their water in buckets, they have never had running water, it won't make a difference to them, while Mrs. Forbes, this munificent woman, she and her estate will provide work and money to the population, which is a gift of far greater value to them."

My fingers rotated the end of the cigarette in the ashtray, round and round. De Marigny had a contradictory mouth, a thin top lip over a full, sensuous bottom lip, from which the smile had disappeared. He drank again, not deeply, and when he put the glass down he stared at me. The voices hammered around us. By some imperceptible means, our two stools had drawn closer together, almost in intimacy.

"And what did you say to that?" I asked.

"I refused, of course. Then I said some rather uncomplimentary things, which I shall not repeat, and which he pretended not to notice. He left the room. His—what's the word—his aide-de-camp was horrified. I felt a little sorry for him, in the end."

"The aide-de-camp?"

"No, the duke. He spends the first three and a half decades of his life being told he is like a god on earth. And he believes it! And now it's a very different story. An attractive woman walks into his office and pays him the great compliment of begging for a boon, so he grants it—like a king, like an emperor—never imagining he cannot do this thing she asks. But what's this? His subject won't obey him. His subject crosses his thick colonial boots and tells the little emperor he's nothing more than the governor of a pimple on the arse of the British Empire."

"You *said* that?"

"Something like that, anyway." He ground out his own cigarette. "Listen to me. When I was living in London, before the war, I met him twice. Once at Ascot. The second time at a hunting party in Scotland. He arrives in his own airplane, you see, flies in late to join us on his own bloody airplane, the *Gypsy Moth*—what an ass—and proceeds to tell us over dinner what a fine chap this Hitler fellow is, has all the right ideas, Germany and England should be the best of friends, stand firm together against international Jewry—*pah*. Half of us were disgusted. The other half could not applaud him enough."

"Interesting," I said.

"Yes, interesting. That *is* what you wanted, after all, Mrs. Randolph. Anyway, you see what I mean. If you wish to become intimate friends with the royal couple, to learn all their secrets so you may write about them in your magazine, you had better not mention my name."

"Understood."

He looked at his wristwatch. "Forgive me. I have a dinner engagement. I am already late."

"We can't have that." I held out my hand. "It's been a pleasure."

Instead of grasping my palm, de Marigny pressed the fingers briefly to his lips. As he released me, he raised his eyebrows. "But perhaps you can join us? We are just a few dull sailors from the yacht club."

"I wouldn't dream of intruding."

He smiled. "Yes, you would."

"Maybe I would. But not this time. You've given me a little too much food for thought already."

De Marigny reached into his pocket to retrieve a fold of bills. He plucked at them almost without looking and laid a five-pound note on the counter, next to his empty whiskey glass, which amounted—if I knew my shillings—to a four hundred percent tip for Jack.

"Of course, you can do with this information what you wish," de Marigny said, rising from his stool, "but if I were you, I would not print these things I have told you, not yet, or you will never write another word in Nassau."

"Then what *would* you recommend?"

"Why, it's very simple." He picked up his hat from the counter and settled it on his head. His eyes had regained their luster, his smile its charm, and I believe every head in the room swiveled to take him in, on cue. He didn't seem to notice. "If you want to know all the best ladies in Nassau society, Mrs. Randolph," he said, "you must join the Red Cross, of course. The headquarters is just around the corner, on George Street."

I ORDERED A PORK CHOP for dinner and ate it at the bar, washed down by a glass of red wine. Afterward, I stepped outside and paused to light a cigarette. The sun was setting over the ridge, and the sky had that unearthly wash of color that stops your breath. Above my head, a pair of seagulls shrieked at each other. I stared north, toward the harbor and the slivery green paradise of Hog Island on the other side.

Having spent the last two years of my life in what you might call a prison, in a series of cheap boardinghouses in cheap American towns, I couldn't quite accustom myself to this landscape of heat and color and clarity, this excess of blue that was the Bahamas. When I'd stepped outside the metal skin of the airplane to the earth of Oakes Field, three weeks ago, I thought I'd traveled into another universe. I thought I'd stepped into another Earth entirely, a paradise lit by an eternal sun, a release from everything old, everything dreary. Then I touched land and discovered that freedom was not so straightforward, that you could move to a different universe but you couldn't escape the prison of your own skin.

Still, I hadn't entirely lost that sense of unreality, especially when I found the line of that horizon and searched in vain for any cloud. The British Colonial Hotel sprawled ahead on West Bay Street, white and crisp like a castle made of wedding cake. A breeze came off the ocean, smelling of brine. The sand, oh. How I'd miss the fluid, delicate sand, slithering between my toes. I dragged on my cigarette and stared again at Hog Island, now gilded by the rising moon. The lighthouse twinkled from the western tip. Some Swedish fellow owned the island, an inventor, built the vacuum cleaner and the electric icebox, God bless him. Came here to the Bahamas because of the taxes—the absence of taxes, I should say, and why not? A fellow who invents the vacuum cleaner, he's done his share for humanity. Let him wallow in profits and buy a goddamn island in paradise and call it Shangri-La. Let him buy the largest private yacht in the world and swan around the seven seas. Wenner-Gren, that was his name. Axel Wenner-Gren. There was a Mrs. Wenner-Gren too. No doubt Mrs. Wenner-Gren was invited to all the duchess's parties. And she hadn't even had to invent a solid-state electric icebox! Just to marry the man who had. I tossed my cigarette into the sand and turned to walk back to the Prince George Hotel.

As I reached the base of George Street, I hesitated. Instead of continuing to the hotel, I turned left, walked up the street, past the Red Cross headquarters to stand at the bottom of the steps that led to Government House. Darkness had drained away the pinkness of it, the confectionary quality. A constellation of lights shone through the various windows. I could just make out the guards at the main entrance, standing at brutal attention, and the perfume of the night blossoms, wafting from the gardens behind their wall.

BACK IN MY ROOM AT the Prince George, I changed into my pajamas, brushed my teeth, drank a glass of water, and took some aspirin. Fetched my suitcase from the wardrobe and opened it. There was a knock on the door, not entirely unexpected. I had asked for a final bill from the front desk, as I intended to check out tomorrow morning.

But it was not the bill at all. It was an envelope, addressed in an elegant, calligraphic hand to Mrs. Leonora Randolph. Inside lay an invitation from the Duke and Duchess of Windsor to a cocktail party this Saturday at seven P.M. in the gardens of Government House, to benefit the Central Bahamas Chapter of the International Red Cross Society.

ELFRIEDE

AUGUST 1900
(Switzerland)

Two weeks after the encounter in the infirmary garden, Herr Doktor Hermann offers Elfriede an unusual question in the middle of their afternoon discussion.

"Would you say, Elfriede," he intones, making a bridge with his hands, "would you say that you love your husband?"

ELFRIEDE'S HUSBAND. DOES SHE LOVE him? They were married four years ago. She'd celebrated her eighteenth birthday only a month before the wedding, in a small party attended by her parents and siblings and prospective sisters-in-law (her husband is an orphan) and Gerhard himself—of course—aged thirty-three, the giant Baron von Kleist who was doing her such a preposterous honor as to marry her. Of course, her beauty was to blame for that. Why else should a baron of such ancient lineage, of considerable fortune and figure, stoop to marry the daughter of a mere burgher? They had met skating on the village pond, a democratic location. Elfriede was an especially graceful skater, and Gerhard was not, and whether by accident or intent he had crashed into her, just gently enough that she wasn't hurt, but so decisively that he had no choice but to apologize profusely for the accident and buy her a cider. "Why, he's in love with you," her mother whispered eagerly the next day, after the baron paid an afternoon call to assure himself of Elfriede's recovery, and Elfriede—well, Elfriede was too overwhelmed, too flattered, too mesmerized to understand whether she returned that love or not. Gerhard von Kleist was not exactly handsome, but he was tall and magnificently built, he was well-dressed and well-read, he had a disarmingly earnest way about him, and above all he was Gerhard von Kleist! He was a nobleman, the hereditary master of Schloss Kleist; he was a great man, he was an officer in the army, he hunted often with the Kaiser himself. By April they were engaged; by June the banns were called, and on the first of July they were married in the beautiful church in the village, disapproving sisters-in-law to one side and ecstatic parents to the other, amid much good-natured congregational whispering about the baron's haste to make the flaxen-haired Elfriede his lawful bride.

Before they left for the church, in the carriage bedecked with flowers, Elfriede's mother pressed a lace handkerchief into her hand, as tradition required. Elfriede was to mop up her bridal tears with this linen square, and afterward to fold it and tuck it away in her drawer on her wedding night. There it's supposed to lie, until one day, when Elfriede dies, the Cloth of Tears will shroud her cold, dead features. Tradition. As it turned out, Elfriede didn't cry at all during the ceremony that united her to Gerhard, nor in the carriage to Schloss Kleist while Gerhard held her hand snugly beneath her massive wedding dress, nor during the wedding banquet in the schloss's baroque great hall, two hundred years old, bearing an exquisite resemblance to the wedding cake itself. (Her mother exclaimed over the dryness of the Cloth of Tears, when she extracted it unused from Elfriede's bodice as she prepared her daughter for bed.) And she did not cry when Gerhard himself entered the nuptial chamber, smelling pungently of soap, dressed in pajamas and a silk dressing gown. Elfriede had drunk several glasses of champagne, and her new husband appeared to her in a haze as he approached the monumental bed on which his bride sat. He knelt—such a big, powerful man, thirty-three years old, kneeling before her!—and covered her hands with kisses. Elfriede stared down at his wheaten head, worshiping her, and felt a sincere, loving warmth move her heart. A *sincere* connection to Gerhard, who had shared this day with her, who had stood by her side, the two of them united against all those curious guests and well-wishers. "I will be gentle, my dearest girl," he promised, removing her nightgown with trembling fingers, kissing her mouth and her breasts and everything else, and Elfriede, dazed and tender, lay back on the embroidered bedspread while he climbed on top of her, and still she didn't cry. He untied the belt of his dressing gown and shrugged it off, but he didn't remove his pajamas. Perhaps he didn't want to frighten her. In any case, he reached inside his pajama trousers and drew out his organ, primed for business, and Elfriede, being somewhat drunk for the first time in her life, couldn't help glancing at this thing that had consumed her curiosity since adolescence, this object designed by nature to plant seeds inside her womb. At the reality of her husband's erection, however, the tears sprang at last to her eyes. "Oh no!" she said, but it was too late. Gerhard's face had already clouded over with rapture, he was already fitting this startling, stiff machine—nothing like the harmless anatomy of the classical statues, God have mercy, of the Renaissance paintings—between her legs. As he shoved his way in, saying her name and invoking his love for her while he split her apart, she gripped the pillows and wept, but the Cloth of Tears was already tucked away in her bureau, unreachable and useless.

HERR DOKTOR HERMANN'S QUESTION IS strange not because of its intimacy—certainly they have touched on intimate subjects before—but because of its specificity. *How do you feel about your husband?* he should have asked instead. By inserting the word *love* inside the query, he's compromised the honesty of her answer.

Elfriede stares at the bridge made by his long, latticed fingers, and his face just above, which seems a little flushed, though today's weather is far from warm. "Why do you ask?" she says.

"Because it is important for me to know, as your doctor. As your doctor, I must know these vital details, Elfriede, so we may progress in your treatment."

Dr. Hermann's fingernails are small and shallow, almost as if the tips of the digits had been chopped off at some uniform length, or else cut short at his creation. Elfriede thinks of her son's tiny fingernails, like fragments of seashells, and how she used to gaze on them in awe and also fear, unable to understand how such delicate ornamentation could have come from her. From Gerhard and his bear paws.

"Of course I love my husband," she says.

Dr. Hermann considers. "You say 'of course,' Elfriede. Why do you say 'of course'? Is it necessary for a wife to love her husband?"

"A wife would be a beast if she didn't love a man such as my husband. She would be unworthy of life."

Herr Doktor's hands spring apart. He turns to his notebook, lifts the pen lying in the crease, and writes something down. When he looks up again, his cheeks are even more flushed than before, and the tip of his nose.

"Are you a beast, Elfriede?" he asks. "Are you unworthy of life?"

Elfriede rises from her chair. Because the weather's blustery, they're indoors, inside Dr. Hermann's private office, equipped with comfortable armchairs and a sofa. On the wall opposite Elfriede hangs a painting of the Ringstrasse in Vienna, where the large, baroque houses remind her of Schloss Kleist.

"Excuse me," she says. "I'm going to get a little air."

ACTUALLY, THERE'S NO SUCH THING as a *little* air in a place like this, a monastery arranged on the slope of a mountain so as to be far from mankind and nearer to God. You walked outside and encountered huge mouthfuls of it, you had to gulp to keep pace, to save yourself from drowning, and sometimes there was so much air you turned your back on the wind and made your way along with your shoulders hunched against this onslaught.

Today's such a day, a day that doesn't know it's supposed to be August instead of October. You can actually see the wind as it hurtles between the peaks, dragging along thick shreds of clouds, and you feel it as an ocean current. Cold and forceful it strikes you, sharp and wet at the same time, turning your cheeks and your fingers numb, any skin you dare to lay bare. Elfriede, wearing a thick, belted cardigan but no coat, no jacket of any kind, relishes the hardship. She trudges along the path that leads downward toward the trees, a trail she knows well, every rock, every kink of landscape. The heads of the wildflowers huddle low to shield themselves, like Elfriede herself. The surrounding peaks are invisible inside this mass of howling clouds. No, forget the surrounding peaks, even her own mountain is lost to sight, the slope disappears before her, and she walks on faith alone, curling her fingers inside her sleeves to keep them warm.

Then the first trees flash between the streams of mist. Grow larger, more certain, more plentiful. Elfriede quickens her stride. She reaches the stubby pines at the vanguard, and a hundred or so yards later she's enveloped by them, like stepping into a cathedral. The wind dies to a breeze. She finds a fallen log and sits in relief. Leans her head back against a thin, hardy trunk. She loves the smell of wood and rot and moss. She closes her eyes and dreams of her baby, whose features are blurred, but whose heart she feels clamoring inside her chest, whether she wants it there or not.

Though the trees muffle the howling of the gale, the forest is not silent. The branches rustle, the wind whines between the pine needles. Certain of her own solitude, Elfriede doesn't hear the sound of footsteps as they approach, only the voice that greets her, an instant after she senses the vibration of another human being.

"Frau von Kleist?" a man inquires, in a slight, courteous English accent.

TWO WEEKS HAVE PASSED SINCE Elfriede encountered the English-man in the infirmary garden. To be precise, sixteen days and a few hours, but who's counting? Her eyes fly open, she startles upward from the log. She beholds him, a pumpkin-headed skeleton belted into a thick Norfolk jacket, wool trousers, leather gaiters. A hunting cap covers his wide skull, his stubbly ginger hair. There should be a pipe sticking from his mouth, a shotgun nestled in the crook of his elbow to complete the picture, but mercifully no.

"You shouldn't be out in such weather," she exclaims.

"Probably not. Yet here I am. You might say the mountains called me. Do you mind awfully if I sit down? Still a bit short-winded, I'm afraid."

"No, of course not."

He doesn't move, just stands there smiling inquisitively, and Elfriede realizes that he won't sit until she does. A gentleman. So she drops back onto her log. Mr. Thorpe finds a boulder. Beneath the collar of his jacket, he wears a scarf of bulky wool. Elfriede drops her gaze to the ground before her, which is cushioned in old brown pine needles.

"You shouldn't be out," she says again.

"Do you know, that's exactly what the orderly told me."

"You should have listened to the orderly."

"Oh, I'm used to this sort of weather. I spent my summers in Scotland, with my mother and her sisters. Frightful, most of the time. Of course, when it was fine, there was no lovelier place in the world. Do you mind if I smoke?"

"*Smoke?*"

He was already drawing a silver case from his jacket pocket. "You're about to tell me I shouldn't be smoking, either."

"But it's true. You've had pneumonia."

"You're quite right, of course. I do all sorts of things I shouldn't do." He lifts a match, preparing to strike, then lowers it. "I say, you don't *mind*, do you? If you object to the smell, I mean."

"N-no." Elfriede thinks she should probably have said yes, because tobacco smoke is possibly the last substance on earth that should fill the passages of Mr. Thorpe's ravaged lungs at the moment, short of poisoned gas. But his pleasure, his anticipation is so obvious, she doesn't have the heart to deny him. A pattern that will shape all the days they spend together.

"Ah, but you *do* mind, don't you? How kind you are. If only I were good enough to return the favor." He strikes the match and lights the cigarette, and when he's taken a long draft, eyes shut in pleasure, and exhaled slowly, taking care to release the smoke in the opposite direction from Elfriede, he opens his eyes again and says, "I can't begin to express my gratitude. First fag in nine weeks. Tell me how to make it up to you."

"You can stop. You can take care of yourself, so you don't relapse."

Mr. Thorpe squints at a point a meter or so to her left. He has the kind of face that suits squinting. Crinkles his expression in a genial way. "I've been giving that some thought, actually."

"I hope so."

"I mean, my recovery has been altogether too rapid, if you know what I mean. Blessed as I am with my mother's formidable constitution. Just the other day, they were talking about discharging me."

"Isn't that a good thing?"

"Well." He turns back to her, turns the full force of himself upon her blushing cheeks. "That's the question, isn't it?"

"I don't think there can be any question. Of course you must get better."

"But *leave*? Aye, there's the rub."

"Don't you want to leave? To return to Vienna and your amusing life there?"

He sits there smoking, and his refusal to answer is answer enough. Just like her husband, who fell in love with her at a stroke—fell in love, at any rate, with her flaxen hair and celestial eyes, her round and childlike face, her expression of dreamy otherworldliness. Imagined she represented some kind of ideal, and was horrified to discover the reality.

"I'm not what you think," she says.

"How do you know what I think?"

"Besides, I'm married. I'm married and I have a baby, a son, three years old."

"I'm afraid I don't follow you. Haven't you already told me these facts? Believe me, I know them well. Except the age of your son, bless him. Three years old! He must be a sturdy little man by now."

"I wouldn't know," she says. "They won't let me see him. I have been living here for two—two years—"

"Oh, my dear girl."

Mr. Thorpe crushes out his half-finished cigarette on the boulder. Elfriede hides her face and doesn't see him rise to his feet and cross the carpet of pine needles between them. When he stops at the log and sits beside her, she feels the warmth of his body underneath the wool.

"Don't they send photographs?" he says. "Your people?"

"Herr Doktor forbids it. He says it will bring about a nervous relapse."

"Herr Doktor?"

"Herr Doktor Hermann. My analyst. He's well versed in the latest— the latest methods for disorders—like mine." Elfriede struggles to keep her composure, to speak rationally through the web of fingers covering her face.

"You'll forgive me, but Herr Doktor's methods strike me as a trifle barbaric."

Elfriede's so astonished, she lifts her face away from her hands and meets Mr. Thorpe's plain, large gaze directly. His freckles. His eyes, a startling blue. "But he's a doctor!" she gasps.

"What does that mean? He's got a paper of some kind, a degree in some scientific subject, which will probably prove entirely obsolete in a decade or so. Any fool would call that barbaric, to keep a mother away from her child. Not even a photograph!"

"You don't know. You don't know."

"Know about what? Your breakdown, as you call it?"

"I'm unnatural," she says. "An unnatural mother."

"Well, what the devil does that mean? You seem natural enough to me."

"I'm not, believe me."

By way of reply, Mr. Thorpe fixes her with an expression so compassionate, she has to look away. But looking away is not enough. The compassion remains in the air, on her skin, seeping into her flesh, inescapable. She stares at his shoulder and her heart crashes. Fear, or attraction? Are they perhaps the same thing?

"I went mad after he was born," she says. "An extreme form of nervous melancholy. It's a particular malady and one of Herr Doktor Hermann's special fields of interest."

"This Hermann fellow—have I met him?"

"I don't think so. He's in the psychiatric section."

"The loony bin, you mean?"

Elfriede refuses to laugh. Instead she examines the collar of his jacket. The woolen scarf tucked inside, protecting his neck and chest from the damp, cold air. She whispers, "You should be disgusted. You should be appalled."

"I'm just waiting to hear the rest of the story."

"There is no rest of the story."

"Rubbish. Of course there is. Lots of new mothers have a spell of the blue devils after their babies are born. My cousin spent a rough few weeks, as I remember. By God, I don't blame them. I should imagine the whole affair's rather a shock to the system, and then you've got this child to take care of, this mysterious little being keeping you up all hours and so on."

"Not like this. I couldn't—I couldn't get out of bed. I couldn't—it was like a shroud settled on me. I thought I was going mad. I should have been joyful, I should have been grateful. I had a rich, loving husband. I had a beautiful baby. Everything for me was perfect. But I felt miserable and terrified. I felt shadowed by doom. I can't even describe how black it all was. I looked at his face, his little squashed face, and he was a stranger. I thought, *I don't love you, I don't even know you, who are you?*"

"Poor Elfriede . . . my poor girl . . . and nobody understood . . ."

Now Elfriede raises her head to Mr. Thorpe's kindly, bony face. She defies his kindness. She defies this compassion of his. She defies his freckles and his pale, gingery eyebrows.

"I tried to kill myself." (She flings the words at his long eyelashes.) "I thought I *should* kill myself, because I was no use to my baby at all. I was a terrible mother. I was poisoning him with my own bitter milk. I thought I should kill myself before I killed my own baby."

Mr. Thorpe doesn't reply. Not in words, anyway. He lifts his arms and puts them around her. Her defiance crumbles. She leans into his ribs, into his shrunken chest, and shudders out a barrage of tears into the left-hand pocket of the Norfolk jacket, the one covering his heart. A shooting jacket, designed to withstand far more serious attacks than this one, thank goodness. His thumbs move against her back. He doesn't speak. She smells wet wool, and the particular scent she caught two weeks earlier, in the infirmary garden, soap and the salt of human skin. Mr. Thorpe's skin. Eventually she turns her face to the side and speaks again.

"I spent a month in hospital, and then they sent me home. Everybody pretended nothing had happened, that I had caught a bad cold or something. Except they wouldn't leave me alone with the baby. My milk had dried up. Everybody was so polite and cold." She pauses, considers, forges on brazenly. "And my husband—Gerhard—I wouldn't—I was afraid of having any more babies—"

"Dear me. Poor Gerhard. So they sent you here to recover your senses."

"Yes."

"When are you supposed to go back home?"

"When I'm cured," she says. "When Herr Doktor Hermann decides I'm well enough."

"Ah, this Hermann again. You know, I'm loath to point fingers at another man, but it seems to me that he's had two years to cure you. Two years, and you're clearly in your proper senses, no danger to anybody. Only a lingering sense of guilt, which a loving family ought to be able to conquer."

"Maybe it's better if I don't go back. Maybe my son—my little Johann—I'm a stranger to him—"

"Is that what this Hermann chap's been telling you?"

"No. He doesn't tell me things. He only asks questions, for the most part."

Mr. Thorpe makes a noise that Elfriede will one day recognize as coming from the Scotch side of him. She remains in his arms, laid comfortably against his chest, shielded from his sharp, skinny bones by the woolen jacket. She doesn't want to move. Has no ability, even, to stir from this place of refuge. His jacket, her Cloth of Tears.

"Anyway, he doesn't love me anymore," she says.

"Who doesn't? Your son?"

"My husband."

"Did he say that? Did he say he doesn't love you?"

"No, but I saw it in his face, after I came back from the hospital. I was alien to him. He thought he'd married an angel, and as it turned out . . ."

"Speaking from the male perspective," Mr. Thorpe says slowly, "of which I naturally consider myself something of an expert. Perhaps it was something else?"

"No. No. A woman can tell. A woman can tell when a man doesn't love her."

"Well—and I'm only speculating, mind you—a man whose wife— how do I put this? A man whose beautiful wife no longer allows him the singular privilege for which he married her—"

Elfriede starts to draw away. But Mr. Thorpe makes a little squeeze of his arms, not to keep her there, not so firm as that, but to let her know she's welcome to stay, if she likes. So she pauses, no longer pressed against his chest, but close.

"It's possible, you see, that he thought you didn't love *him*. And a chap who believes he's lost the love of a woman—forgive me—a woman such as you—well, I daresay it might ruin him." Mr. Thorpe pauses. "That's only conjecture, mind you. I haven't met the lucky Herr von Kleist."

"No, you haven't."

Another slight squeeze. Elfriede capitulates. The lure of comfort is too much for her. Warm human contact. Warm human arms, warm human chest. Things for which she's starved. A famine of touch.

"Thank you for your music," Wilfred says. "I was afraid you'd stop."

"I wasn't sure whether I should. I didn't want to keep you awake."

"Keep me awake? Kept me alive, I think."

"Oh!"

"So why did you? Keep playing, I mean."

"Because I . . . well, I . . ." She shouldn't say the words, but she must. She might conceal her true thoughts from the doctor, but she can't conceal them from Wilfred. Oh, his actual heart, thudding under her ear! She whispers, "Because I thought you might be listening."

"Damn it all," he says softly.

"What is it?"

"Nothing. Just hellish fate, that's all."

Elfriede says, "Tell me about this girl of yours."

"Girl? Girl? I'm afraid I don't know any other girls."

"You told me there was a girl."

There is a sigh from inside that ravaged chest, far more sigh than Elfriede might have imagined possible. It ends in a cough. Not a bad one. Not the cough of two weeks ago.

"Right. Her. Well, you know, she's quite the opposite of you. Older and rather cosmopolitan. Divorcée of a well-known composer, I won't say whom. Just the sort of woman to render a callow youth—an ugly, awkward fellow such as myself—dizzy with ecstasy."

"And did she?"

"Yes."

"Pardon me," says Elfriede, smiling a little, "but you don't sound ecstatic."

"That's because . . ."

"Because?"

"Because I shall have to go back to her shortly, I suppose. And the prospect is not what it once was. Don't ask why."

"Why?"

That noise again. "Let's just sit here a moment longer, shall we? I daresay we're not doing anybody any harm, just sitting here."

"No."

"I'm a man of honor."

"Yes."

"Unlike, I suspect, that blackguard Hermann."

"Let's not talk," she says.

"An ugly, awkward chap like me. Emaciated with fever. Head like a pumpkin—why are you laughing?"

"That's exactly what I thought, when I first saw you. Your head like a pumpkin."

"Ah, well. At least a fellow knows where he stands."

Elfriede stares at the trees opposite. The dark woods beyond. The wind whining quietly between the pine needles. "I love your pumpkin head."

"But you hardly know my head."

"You hardly know mine. Does it matter?"

Wilfred moves a little, turning his back to the tree as she had, settling them both more comfortably.

"No," he says.

LULU

JULY 1941

(The Bahamas)

ON SATURDAY EVENING, I walked to Government House in my best summer dress of blueberry organza and a pair of tall peep-toe shoes that would have fared much better in a taxi, if I could have spared the dough. It wasn't the distance; it was the stairs. Government House, as I said, sat at the top of George Street, aboard its very own hill, in order to ensure (or so it seemed to me, at the time) that the ordinary pedestrian arrived flushed and breathless for his appointment with the governor.

Still. As I passed Columbus on his pedestal and climbed the steps toward the familiar neoclassical facade of pink stucco—heavens, what a perfect representation of the Bahamian ideal—I had to admit to a certain human curiosity. Like everybody else, I knew Government House from the outside, as a passerby, an acquaintance. I hadn't the least idea what lay inside. Now its portico expanded before me, all pink and white, Roman columns and tropical shutters, windows aglow, music and voices, a thing of welcome, alive. I paused at the top of the steps to pat my hair, to adjust my necklace of imitation pearls, to gather my composure while the noise of an engine clamored in my ears, and an enormous automobile roared beneath the pediment and slammed to a halt exactly at the front door.

As I watched, too rapt to move, a stumpy man in a plain, poorly cut suit popped from the back seat and patted his pockets.

Now, in the many years since I inhabited the Bahamas, I've come to understand that memory is a capricious friend, and never more unreliable than when we trust it absolutely. But I'll swear on any Bible you like that I identified Sir Harry Oakes right there on the portico of Government House that evening with photographic precision. I remember the sense of awe I felt as I said to myself, *Why, that's Harry Oakes.* Maybe it was the car, or the confident electricity that inevitably surrounds the richest man in the British Empire. He had struck gold in Canada or someplace, after years and years of prospecting, one of the biggest strikes ever made, and now he lived here in the Bahamas, because of taxes. I guess he figured he had already paid his dues, like that Swedish fellow.

The car roared off. I slowed my steps to hang back, conscious that I had no companion, no escort, no friend of any kind. I was alone, as usual, and when you're alone you must time your entrance carefully, you must carry yourself a certain way, you must manage every detail so nobody suspects your weakness. A fellow in a uniform stood just outside the door, exchanging words with Oakes, who continued to pat his pockets in that absentminded way, while I crossed the drive at a measured pace, presenting my hips just so. As I reached the portico, I heard an oath. It was delivered, needless to say, in a plain, rough, American kind of voice, and I froze, a few yards away. I'd heard he was a flinty fellow, Sir Harry Oakes, that he had a hot temper and small patience—no wonder he'd married late in life, when he was already rich—and here's what I'd learned about men of temperament: stay the hell away, if you can help it.

But Oakes spun around and spotted me. In the course of patting his pockets, he'd discovered the same card I carried in my hand. He brandished it now. "In the gardens!" he bellowed. "The goddamn west entrance!"

"The west entrance?"

"Follow me."

He stumped off—there's no other way to describe it, as if he wore an invisible pair of iron boots—and I scrambled after him, because when the richest man in the British Empire tells you to follow him, you take your chances and follow, temperament be damned.

"Leonora Randolph," I ventured, when I reached his shoulder.

He stopped and spun again. He couldn't seem to turn like an ordinary man, but then he wasn't ordinary, was he? He stuck out his hand. "Oakes," he said, because of course there needed no further introduction.

I took the hand and shook it briskly. "I figured."

Well, he laughed at that. We resumed walking, at a more amicable pace, and Oakes said, "Where do you come from, Miss Randolph?"

"*Mrs.* Randolph. I'm from New York City, mostly. I came down to Nassau a few weeks ago for a change of pace."

"Change of pace, eh? I guess you've got your money's worth."

"I'll say."

"Your husband come with you?"

"My husband's dead, Sir Harry."

"I see."—*stomp, stomp*—"Awfully sorry."

"Don't be. He was a louse."

"A louse, eh? The lazy kind, or the drinking kind?"

"Take your pick."

"Did he beat you?"

"Oh, I wouldn't say *beat*."

Oakes grunted. "Good riddance to the bastard, then. Why Nassau?"

"Why *not* Nassau?"

"The heat, for one thing. It's goddamn July. My wife and kids left for Bar Harbor two months ago."

"I don't mind the heat at all, Sir Harry. Heaven knows it's better than the cold."

We had turned the corner of the mansion by now, and proceeded down a path that led, presumably, to the gardens at the rear. The music and chatter grew louder through the quicksand of warmth, the scent of blossom, the splay of palm fronds. Oakes raised his voice to bark, "Cold? *Cold?* A New York City winter's nothing to the goddamn Yukon, believe me!"

"Well, I'll take the tropics over either of them, any day. Even in July."

"And I say you're nuts. Nobody's here! Just the locals and the riffraff. Like me!" He rapped his thigh with his invitation card and laughed.

"And Their Royal Highnesses."

"*They* wouldn't be here either, if they could help it. Here we are."

We had reached an iron gate, where a sturdy, immaculate fellow wore his white uniform and white gloves bravely. He greeted Oakes by name. Oakes snatched my invitation card right from my fingers and thrust both of them, his and mine, toward this gatekeeper. "There you go, Marshall. This is Mrs. Randolph, just off the boat from New York."

"The airliner, actually," I said.

"The airliner. That new Pan American service from Miami, I'll bet."

"That's the one."

"Not afraid of flying, either. Good girl. Mrs. Randolph, this gentleman is George Marshall, butler at Government House. He's the fellow who runs just about everything. Isn't that right, Marshall?"

Marshall glanced down at my invitation card, glanced back up at me. I felt a cool inspection pass across my skin and my dress of blueberry organza, not unpleasant. "Good evening, Mrs. Randolph," he said. "Welcome to Government House."

"Good evening, Mr. Marshall. Delighted, I'm sure."

"How's the rum punch in there?" said Oakes.

"I mixed it myself an hour ago, sir."

"Good, good. The duke?"

"Their Royal Highnesses are still receiving by the goldfish pond, I believe."

Oakes took my elbow. "Come along, Mrs. Randolph. Might as well go in with reinforcements, I always say."

Together we walked through the gate, toward the crackle of human noise. By the sound of things, the party was already in full swing. Against the twilight, the flares of perhaps a dozen or more lanterns flickered opulently, illuminating the garden in patches of gold, illuminating spiky palmettos and white jasmine and pink bougainvillea, illuminating people and more people, drinking and smoking and laughing. I turned my head to Oakes. "I thought you said nobody was here, except locals and riffraff."

"Those *are* the locals, Mrs. Randolph. Conchie Joes, we call 'em. Merchants on Bay Street and their plump little wives. You'll get to know their faces, believe me. The pond's this way."

I allowed him to lead me down the path, toward a cluster of lanterns that had attracted—like mosquitoes, I thought—several people dressed in bright colors, next to a rock-lined pool. Oakes was grumbling to himself. I asked him if something was wrong.

"Receiving lines," he said. "Can't stand 'em."

"I'm sure they wouldn't notice if you just slipped past."

"*Their Royal Highnesses*," he muttered. "Nothing royal about *her*. You know that, don't you?"

I turned my head toward the man before me, the richest man in the British Empire. A dazzling fact, if you paused to consider it, but of course you couldn't pause in the middle of a cocktail party and consider the pounds, shillings, and pence that belonged to the fellow walking at your elbow. You just gazed in pity at his thinning hair, his frown in profile, and said gently, "I do. I also know it's wiser just to go along with things."

He didn't reply. I liked his face, his kind eyes and his even, sturdy, jowly features. Possibly I only imagined the ruggedness that clung to his skin, the hint of rock and earth, because I knew this about him. Or perhaps, when you spend half your life prospecting in the wilderness, no amount of Bahamas sunshine can burn away the scent of frontier.

As we drew closer, the cluster of people moved away, revealing a pair of familiar, ravishing figures, exactly the same height, one dark-haired and one fair. A half-dozen lanterns hung from the nearby palms. The light created a nimbus around them. What a show, I thought. What a goddamned brilliant show they put on. You almost wanted to applaud.

Oakes turned to me and said, "You know, you oughta meet my daughter Nancy. You'd like her."

"Would I?"

"She could use someone like you, a few years older. Take her under your wing."

I smiled. "Hasn't she got a perfectly good mother?"

"Sure, she does. But girls that age." He shook his head, and that was all, because we had reached the goldfish pond and the duchess and the duke, laughing warmly with a short, perspiring man who had materialized from nowhere. The duchess's head turned in my direction. She wore a dress of pale blue silk and an expression of brief, unguarded discontent, and a shock ran down my limbs because I thought perhaps someone had made a terrible mistake—God knew what, maybe that invitation hadn't been meant for me after all. But the duchess's frown smoothed away as I reached her. Oh, the duchess. It's a funny thing, when you encounter a face like that, a face you've seen frozen in a hundred two-dimensional photographs, and here it is before you, looking *at* you, alive. Those pungent blue eyes, that coronet of dark hair. That skin stretched over her cheeks and jaw, now endowed with breadth and depth and texture. Around her neck, a staggering circle of diamonds and rubies set off the blue of her eyes and her dress. How patriotic of her. She took my hand between two of hers and shook it firmly.

"My dear Mrs. Randolph! *And* Sir Harry. I see you've met our new recruit."

"Recruit?" he demanded.

"The Red Cross. Mrs. Randolph's volunteered her services."

"The Red Cross? What the devil for? You don't strike me as a Red Cross kind of gal."

"Just doing my bit," I said.

"But you're American. You've got no part in this damned war."

"Now, Sir Harry," said the duchess, "the Red Cross has nothing to do with taking sides. We are a *humanitarian* organization."

Well, Oakes rolled his eyes at this—as well he might—and stumped a few paces to the right, where he greeted the duke with about as much ceremony as he'd greeted the duke's wife. Stuck his hand out and grunted something. The duchess and I exchanged weary little smiles, almost intimate. A fellow like that can bind two females instantly. A pair of diamond and ruby earrings clung to her earlobes, matching the necklace. I thought she glanced down to assess the imitation pearls around my collar, but maybe that was my imagination.

"I'm so terribly sorry to be late," I said. "I didn't realize about the entrance."

"Not at all. I haven't anyone left to greet, thank goodness, so we can get to know each other a bit." She slipped her arm around mine. She smelled of face powder and perfume, and her arm was like her hand, bony and purposeful. "Don't you look *charming* in that dress."

I might have stuttered, so great was my amazement. "Why—well—this old thing?"

"Of course, you've got the kind of figure that suits any dress, you lucky duck. Now, stick with me. There's somebody I want you to meet."

"Meet *me*? I can't imagine whom."

She laughed. "David! David!"

Her husband stood a few feet away, dressed in a pale suit, speaking to the other man and to Oakes, who had turned toward them both. The duke's head snapped in her direction. For an instant, his eyes bugged in a terrified way. The lanterns poured gold on the duke's waving hair, his shocked, twitching, haggard face. Next to him, Oakes and the other fellow more or less disappeared—not physically, of course, but rendered invisible by the halo of glamour. "Yes, dear?" the duke asked, pitched anxiously toward his wife, not registering my presence in the slightest degree.

"David, it's Mrs. Randolph at last."

"Mrs. Randolph?"

"Yes, Mrs. Randolph. You remember, don't you?" She grasped my elbow. "Mrs. *Randolph*, David. The girl I've been speaking about."

"Oh! Oh, yes. Of course." He held out his hand to me, and although he'd turned in my direction and fixed his gaze politely on my face, I thought his eyes were unfocused, that he wasn't really looking at me. Not *past* me, mind you, the way some people do, searching out someone of greater interest, but the opposite direction. Inward, toward himself. "Duke of Windsor," he said, pronouncing the word *duke* like an American, *dook*.

I made a slight curtsy. "Your Royal Highness. Leonora Randolph. I'm honored to—"

"Charmed, of course." He dropped my hand—he had a grip that wasn't so much limp as motionless, without life—and turned to the duchess. "Have you seen Thorpe about?"

"Not since he arrived."

"Oh, damn." The duke cast his nervous eyes about the palms and the shadows. "Neither have I."

"Is something the matter?" she asked, but the duke was already bolting off. I suppose I stared after him, at least until his bright figure disappeared into the tangle of darker ones. I remember a feeling of disbelief—had I, or had I not, just met the former king of England, and did it matter if he hadn't actually perceived my existence?—and then the tug of the duchess's hand on my elbow.

"Mrs. Randolph, do you know Mr. Christie?" she said.

"I'm afraid not." I held out my hand to the other man, who was plain and balding, thick-necked, green-eyed. His temples gleamed with per-spiration. He was shorter even than Oakes, and next to Sir Harry's bull shoulders, looked as slight as a lamb. "Leonora Randolph," I said.

The man took my hand and smiled. "Harold Christie. Pleasure."

His palm was damp. I extracted my fingers and said the pleasure was all mine. "I've already heard so many *interesting* things about you, Mr. Christie."

"Ah." He cast a glance to the duchess—nervous or modest, I couldn't tell. "I hope—I hope—*good* things."

"Aren't you practically a one-man Bahamas development office? So they tell me."

"Oh, it's quite true," said the duchess. "Mr. Christie's done *so much* to improve the colony."

Back and forth glanced Mr. Christie. "That's too kind. I love the Ba-hamas, that's all. Only doing what I can for them."

"How awfully good of you," I said.

"Turns a nice penny, too, from time to time," said Oakes. "Isn't that right, Christie? Turned a few of those pennies on my account."

"From which *your* account profited considerably, I believe."

"Don't stop you borrowing a fortune from me, either. Eh, Christie? That Lyford Cay scheme of yours?"

"You'll be begging me for a plot of your own there, when it's finished."

Oakes turned to me. "Wasteland. Wasteland all the way on the other end of the island, miles from town. If I could pull my money out of that one, I would. I must've been drunk when you asked me, Christie."

Christie smiled. "Now, old fellow, I'm sure the ladies don't wish to listen to our business talk."

"On the contrary—"

"Tell me, what brings you here to our little paradise, Mrs. Randolph? Our oasis from this mad world? I certainly hope you mean to make a *lengthy* visit."

"Careful," said Oakes. "He'll ply you with booze and get you investing in his damned schemes."

As coincidence would have it, a waiter approached us right that second, bearing a tray on which a few champagne coupes glistened in the light of the lanterns. I reached out and snatched one by the stem. "How opulent. I haven't seen champagne since I left New York. Poor old France and all."

"We contrived to pack along a few bottles, when we left Paris in *such* a hurry," said the duchess, plucking a stem, smiling softly, so I couldn't help imagining a crew of stevedores unloading crate after crate at Prince George's wharf, while a flush-faced supervisor begged them to take care.

I raised my glass. "We're ever so grateful you found the time."

Naturally, the champagne was sublime. I knew precious little about wine, but I knew that the Windsors ate and drank and wore only the best, and I imagined, if they smuggled champagne out of France as the Germans closed in, the champagne would be the finest vintage fizz that credit could buy.

"To victory," said Mr. Christie. "May it arrive swiftly."

I remember thinking, as I clicked my glass against that of Harold Christie, that he didn't seem like much of a warrior.

BY THE TIME THE DUKE reappeared, I'd almost forgotten he existed to begin with. You know how it is during a party, how the minutes turn liquid and run into each other, how the words and faces form a separate universe in which you rotate endlessly on your axis, North Pole and South Pole tilted just so. Afterward, you never can remember the exact chronology, who said what, where and when it all occurred. And how.

Up he popped, anyway, just as the duchess was introducing me to two of her guests, a straw-haired mother and her teenage daughter. He jumped midsentence in front of the duchess's attention, the way a tennis player lunges for a ball, slicing neatly between us. A thick piece of hair had fallen from the shield atop his head. He pushed it back and said, "Darling, I can't seem to find him!"

"Who?"

"*Thorpe*, darling. *Thorpe*."

"Yes? Where is he?"

"That's the trouble. I've looked all over."

"Then I suppose we'll just have to start things off without him," said the duchess. "David, darling, will you please get everyone's attention?"

David—I beg your pardon, *the Duke of Windsor*—cast about for something or other, his long-abandoned cocktail glass perhaps, because he wound up snatching my champagne coupe and striking it forcefully with the manicured nail of his index finger. When that produced no discernible sound, he shoved it back to me and clapped his hands. "Good evening!" he called. "Good evening, all!"

At the sound of his voice, the din of voices went absolutely silent. The strangest thing, that instant silence, as if everybody had been waiting for this signal, even the birds, as if nothing else in the world held the slightest interest. Several dozen faces turned toward us, none of them quite sober. The duke smiled, and what a dazzling smile it was. Red-lipped and toothsome. He'd practiced it all his life.

"Good evening, my dear friends. We're so—ah, my wife and I, we're delighted to have so many of you gathered here tonight in our humble abode"—here he paused expertly for a ripple of chuckles—"in service of, really, an absolutely tremendous cause. I am just absolutely speechless with pride at all the great work my wife has done as president of the Red Cross chapter here in the Bahamas, which we couldn't possibly accomplish without your generous support. But my wife, I believe, has more to tell you about all that. Darling? Her Royal Highness, the Duchess of Windsor."

Nobody chuckled, nobody gave the least sign of knowing that the

Duchess of Windsor was *not*, in fact, royal: by express decree of those
who *were*. Certainly not Wallis herself. She painted on a thin, beautiful
smile and stepped to her husband's side. For the first time, I noticed that
she wore a jeweled brooch pinned to her breast, the same brooch as in
the photograph in *Life* magazine, and what do you know? It was a flamingo. She waved her ring-crusted hand. "Hello, everybody!"

Everybody murmured *Hello!*

"As David said. Thank you all for gathering here with us tonight. In a
few minutes I'll be coming round, cap outstretched, along with—I hope,
anyway—someone who seems to have gone . . . oh, *there* he is!" Her face
transformed, so that I realized she hadn't really been smiling before, and
now she was. She looked over my right shoulder, where a cluster of palms
bordered the rock garden. "Mr. Thorpe! Where *have* you been hiding?
Mr. Benedict Thorpe, ladies and gentlemen, a dear friend of mine and
David's, a scientist of international repute and a *true* patriot of our British
Empire."

She began to clap, and the crowd, shifting and straining to catch a
glimpse of this true British patriot, burst into applause. Though I kept my
gaze trained on the duchess—what a *show* she was, after all—I clapped
along. I mean, it would have been rude otherwise, wouldn't it? A scientist of international repute. I confess, I wasn't that interested in science,
at the time, but I could appreciate the affinity in others. Science was the
future, after all. Everybody said so.

"Mr. Thorpe—hello, everybody!—Mr. Thorpe's agreed to help me
collect donations for the Red Cross tonight, a cause close to both our
hearts, isn't that right, Thorpe? In fact, it's Mr. Thorpe's own hat we're
going to pass around, so don't be niggardly!" She paused for laughter.
She still hadn't taken her eyes from that patch of garden from which this
Thorpe had emerged. I felt a stir of curiosity—or maybe even premonition, who knows—and turned my head at last to catch a glimpse. A

palmetto spread its fronds between us, blocking my view. Before me, the duchess waved her hand. "Step up, Thorpus. Don't be shy!"

The crowd stirred, making way. I turned and stepped back with everyone else. A pair of shoulders swept past. In the slight draft of his passing, I smelled not the tang of cigarettes or cocktails or perspiration— those were endemic—but a soap of some kind, or else cologne, hair oil, whatever it was, and I believe I made a gasp of recognition. There was applause, delighted voices. The fellow stepped to the duchess's side and swept off his hat—he wore a towering silk topper for the occasion—to reveal that hair, short, glistening, ruddy-blond, and I covered my mouth with my hand. His spectacles were just slightly crooked.

He beamed across the crowd, left to right, and to my great relief his gaze passed right over me, though I stood in front, next to the duke. My cheeks ached, and I realized I was smiling back, even though he wasn't looking in my direction. *Thorpe*, I thought. He had a name. *Thorpe*.

"Right ho, chaps," he said. "Ladies. Let's make this quick and pain-less, shall we? Empty your pockets, so I don't have to go round the room again with my pistol."

BEFORE THE COLLECTION PARTY PASSED by, I slipped between guests and up the path toward the governor's residence. I don't believe I started out with any conscious intent. *A breath of air*, that's what I murmured as I sidled my way through the crowd, and this was true enough. Certainly I wanted air, and once free of the smokiness and perspiration of the party, I found air in abundance. I also saw a pair of French doors standing open to the evening air, allowing a glimpse of a hallway, and not a footman in sight.

Now, it wasn't as if I meant any harm. I had just sipped champagne with the duchess, I even felt a stir of liking for her, a warmth I hadn't expected. When somebody pays you compliments, pays you the favor of her attention and interest, you can't help but think she must be a person of great taste and discernment. I meant no disrespect toward either of them, duke or duchess; or their privacy. There was only curiosity, and the desire to escape, and a certain surge of audacity that visits me from time to time, and also the possibility—duchesses could be fickle, after all—that I might never again have the opportunity to enter this building and see its rooms for myself. Which, in retrospect, is just the sort of logic that lands a girl in trouble, in love affairs as in houses that don't belong to her.

Thus the inevitable. Instead of soothing my lungs and returning to the party or else to my own little room at the Prince George, snug and sound, I continued down that hall, the entire width of Government House, until I arrived at the door on the opposite side. I made no hesitation whatsoever. Hesitation's fatal, my father always told me, when he could be bothered to speak to me at all; deliberate all you like upon a course of action, but once you've made your decision, don't for God's sake waver. I laid my hand on the doorknob and opened it to find some sort of library. The duke's own study, perhaps. There was a desk and a fireplace, hissing the last remains of a good solid fire. The furniture was up-to-date, the upholstery fresh. I felt the duchess's taste hanging in the air, coating every surface, every detail, every Union Jack pillow, every club chair. Even in her absence, she possessed a magnificent presence.

Now we're getting somewhere, I thought.

I made a progress along the walls, examining each picture as one might examine the contents of an art gallery or a museum. I daresay I imagined I might discover some clue to the essential mystery of them—the Windsors, I mean—this exquisitely dressed pair of sybaritic bigots who had the power to fascinate millions, even those who weren't the slightest bit interested in fashion or luxury or jewelry or parties. This painting: Had the duchess chosen it for its form and its meaning or because the colors married so perfectly with the upholstery on her new sofa? I dragged my hand along the back of the sofa and made my way to the desk, orderly, untroubled by paperwork, adorned by photographs of Wallis. I had this idea—I remember it clearly—that if I opened any of the drawers in this desk, I would find them empty. I actually saw myself opening those drawers, as in a dream; I saw their emptiness. This fine, polished, beautifully proportioned desk, made of empty drawers. I curled my fingers around a brass handle. I don't believe I meant to pull it. Even if I had, the voice would have stopped me.

"My dear Mrs. Randolph. Are you looking for something?"

I spun to the door—not the one leading to the main hallway, but the door on the opposite side of the room, toward the back of the house, where the duchess stood in her beautiful blue gown with the jeweled flamingo on her breast. She was smiling.

"I—I seem to have taken a wrong turn," I said.

She moved forward. "It's a lovely room, isn't it? I had it redecorated. I had the whole place redecorated. It was a dump when we arrived."

"So I heard."

"Shabby and leaky and everything. Uninhabitable, really."

"You've done wonders. It looks just terrific."

The duchess paused at the corner of the desk, the opposite diagonal, and rested her fingers on the edge. "It's not what he's used to, of course. I did my best, but he ought to live in a palace, he ought to be doing something bigger. *That's* what he's used to. What he was raised for. Instead . . ."

I didn't know what to say. I had the feeling this was a test of some kind, and my answer would determine the course of my future association with the Windsors, or whether we had any association at all. Would determine the course of my existence altogether. The initial shock had passed, thank God. My face had begun to cool. I flexed my fingers, I drew in a long, steady breath and exhaled it slowly.

"You're both doing such a terrific job," I said. "Your talents are wasted in a place like this."

"How kind."

"Really, though. The Red Cross. It's such a smashing success. All those women, working so hard. Only you could raise all that money, organize everything so perfectly—"

The duchess laughed and turned her head. "Would you care for a drink, Mrs. Randolph? David keeps a few bottles handy in here. He's forbidden to start drinking before seven, but once the clock strikes, why . . ."

"No, thank you."

But she was already moving away, already opening the door to a cabinet of gleaming wood, the kind of cabinet you thought must hold important papers and that kind of thing, but actually contained about a dozen various bottles of liquor, several glasses, a siphon, a bucket.

"There's no ice, I'm afraid," she said, "but you don't mind that, do you?"

"No."

"Brandy? I like a glass of brandy in the evenings."

"I really shouldn't."

"Why not?" She turned to me. "You certainly look as if you could use a drink."

"I like to keep my wits about me."

"I see." She closed the cabinet door. She stood about fifteen or twenty feet away, about as elegant as a woman could possibly look, but then she had the kind of figure that sets off clothes to their best advantage. Long and angular, lean to the point of nonexistence; not exactly attractive by itself, but irresistible as a foil to what covered those bones, that flesh. Like all Southern ladies, she moved gracefully, shaping the air as she went. Her thin, tight, scarlet smile contained electricity. "Now, don't be afraid," she said.

"I'm not."

"Yes, you are. Most people are. But I don't bite."

"If you did, I'd bite back."

The duchess laughed. "You brave thing. That's exactly what I was hoping you'd say."

"I can't tell you how relieved I am to hear it."

She gestured to the window seat. "Can we sit a moment? I have a question for you, Mrs. Randolph. A proposition."

I hesitated only long enough to catch my breath. "Of course."

We sat. The window faced north, toward the twinkling of lights that rimmed the shore and the sudden blackness of the ocean. The stars were invisible. I smelled the duchess's perfume, her cigarettes. Around us lay that beautiful, masculine room of wood and photographs and, beyond that, the faint music from the party in the garden. I folded my hands in my lap and said again how lovely the place looked.

"Naturally the papers had nothing but bad things to say," she told me. "How extravagant I was. How out of touch with the common man. Never mind that the house—*Government* House, don't forget, the very seat and symbol of government, of the British *Empire*—was riddled with mildew and falling apart. Anyway, we paid for a great deal of the redecoration out of our own pockets. A great deal."

"I hadn't heard that."

"Of course you hadn't. They're all against me. I'm sure you read about our little tour this fall, how many pieces of luggage went along with us."

"I can't remember the number," I said modestly.

"A hundred and forty-six, they said, which wasn't remotely true, it was no more than seventy-three, and anyway it wasn't just ours. It belonged to our entourage as well. Our private secretary, Miss Drewes, and Major Phillips—that's David's aide-de-camp—and so on. But each and every story they print has to conform to this—this *idea* they have about me. I'm sure I don't need to tell you what *that* is. And it's all very frustrating. One can't answer back. One can try, of course, but that only makes one sound petulant."

"The duchess doth protest too much."

"Exactly. I see you understand the business, Mrs. Randolph."

"What business?"

"Journalism." Her smile took on a feline quality. "You're a journalist yourself, aren't you?"

I sort of choked. "Journalist?"

"Yes. *Metropolitan* magazine, isn't that right?"

"Yes. That is, no. That is, the magazine sent me out here to gather a little background information—"

"Now, Mrs. Randolph—"

"—I've never written a word for them. Not a word." I paused. "How did you know about that?"

"Oh, I hear things. It's my business to hear things. Not for myself, you understand, but for David's sake. All these stories in the press, these terrible things they print, it upsets him so much. I try to protect him, of course, but it's impossible. He *will* read them all."

I started to rise, and then remembered you weren't supposed to stand except with permission, and then remembered I was American, after all, not subject to such rules. I rose. I nearly said *Mrs. Simpson* and caught myself just in time. "Ma'am," I said instead, "I can't imagine why you're telling me all this."

"Oh, I understand, believe me," she said. "You've got a job to do. A girl's got to make her way in the world. I also suspect there was no *Mr.* Randolph. Am I correct?"

There was a noise through the window, a spray of brilliant laughter. The duchess gave no sign of hearing it, not a flinch.

"Oh, the husband's real enough," I said. "At least, he *was* real. But even a dead husband gives a girl on her own a bit more respectability."

"Of course. A girl like you, for example, a girl with no one to stand up for her. I understand completely. You haven't got a fortune. Just an allowance of some kind, I presume?" She tilted her head, narrowed her eyes intelligently. "Or not even that?"

"I'm afraid that's none of—"

"Mrs. Randolph." She rose to meet me. "What if you were to *become* a journalist?"

"Become a *journalist?*"

"A column of your very own, weekly or monthly, whatever suits. Syndicated in all the papers, or exclusive to *Metropolitan*, as you like."

"What kind of column?"

"Why, reporting from Nassau, from the middle of society, all our busy little doings here. Intriguing tidbits. The kind of details that only an intimate friend of the Windsors might know. Surely that would be of interest to readers in America?"

The exact shade of her eyes was so particular, so remarkable, a plush, vivid lavender, they had a name for it: Wallis blue. Her wedding dress, I'm told, matched that shade exactly. And I don't blame her. Those eyes, they held you in thrall, especially when she wanted them to. When she channeled the full force of her charm through them and into you. On that July day, the duchess was as much a mystery to me as to everyone else who wasn't married to her, and maybe even—maybe especially—to the fellow who was. I perhaps thought her morals a little wanting, her ethics a little thin, her mind a little shallow, her clothing a little fabulous and perhaps the most interesting thing about her. As for me, I was a pedigree twenty-five-year-old feline, blessed with a sleek, dark pelt and composure in spades, polished to a sheen by decent schooling and a little over a year of college, followed by a swift, brutal tutorial in the outside world to harden the skin beneath. I thought I was plenty of match for a woman like that, the Duchess of Windsor, the former Mrs. Ernest Simpson, the former Mrs. Earl Winfield Spencer, yes, *that* woman, striking, thin-lipped, blue-eyed, lantern-jawed, who nearly toppled the British Crown by the force of her ambition.

But here's the thing. You cannot possibly know somebody you've never met. You can observe her in a thousand photographs, a hundred newsreels, and not understand a thing about her. That person on the magazine cover is a character in a play, a character in a book, a character of her own creation and your imagination, and this immaculate namesake bears no more than a passing resemblance to the original. Remember that, please. You don't know her. You know only the fascinating fiction she's presented to you. *Surely that would be of interest to readers in America*, she had said.

"I bet it would," I answered.

Until that instant, I hadn't noticed the tension in her face. That tautness, I thought it was her natural state. Now everything loosened, her eyes and cheekbones and mouth, that fragile skin, like the softening of frosting on a cake. She looked almost human. I thought this couldn't be happening, I couldn't be standing here. She couldn't be offering me this prize. There must be some trick. But her eyes were so blue.

"Then we understand each other?" she said.

"I believe so."

"Good."

She held out her hand to me, and I clasped it. The coldness shocked me, but what did I expect? I always seemed to simmer a degree or two warmer than other women. I opened my mouth to ask her particulars, how all these lovely plans might be set into motion, but she spoke first.

"Let's return to our guests, shall we? There are so many people I'd like you to meet."

ELFRIEDE

SEPTEMBER 1900
(Switzerland)

I F SOMETHING WERE to happen to my husband," Elfriede says, "which God forbid, I wouldn't marry again."

"No. No. I don't see why you should. I never did understand why women agree to marriage, unless perhaps as a kind of business arrangement."

His answer so surprises her, she sits up and turns to stare at him. They're lying side by side in a meadow not far from the clinic, but shielded from view by the shoulder of the mountain and, for good measure, by a stand of shrubby trees. Though the sun's out and the temperature warm, the wildflowers have begun to die out by now. Color and scent have faded. Thank goodness for sunshine, then. Turning Wilfred's hair—growing out nicely—a bright, autumnal copper. He lies with his arms raised, elbows bent, hands cradling the back of his head, and he stares back at her in enchantment.

"You've got grass in your hair," he says.

Elfriede reaches for the back of her head. "Why do you say that? About marriage?"

"I just think it's a rum deal all around, don't you? Particularly for the women. Most wives—not all, by any means, but *most*—most wives strike me as chattel. They've got this dull, mute, complacent expression that says they've forgotten how to think for themselves. They simply go about their appointed daily tasks, keeping busy, and—oh, I don't know, maybe they're happy. But it's the dumb happiness of surrender. I'd rather be miserable than happy like that."

A long stalk of meadow grass hangs from the corner of his mouth. The day after their encounter in the woods, Wilfred had a relapse—a minor one, as it turned out, but he was in bed for another week and confined to the infirmary garden for the week after that, and Elfriede begged him not to smoke any more. He protested that it was the damp weather and not the cigarette (half-smoked) that had caused the relapse, but he threw away the rest of the cigarettes anyway. Instead he chews on the meadow grass. Like a bull, she tells him. More like a steer, he corrects her, mournfully.

Now he plucks the grass from the corner of his mouth and says, "Also, I've always suspected their husbands don't do much to please them in bed, these women."

Elfriede makes an O with her mouth and turns away to face the peaks of the neighboring mountains. "I don't think that's necessarily true," she says.

"You speak from experience?"

"You shouldn't ask such questions."

Wilfred makes a noise—not his Scotch noise, another one. He has a wardrobe of noises for every occasion. Each nuance of thought. Over the course of the past few weeks, Elfriede has learned and cataloged them all. This one's meant to convey amusement, tempered with just a lash of longing.

"Anything but that," Elfriede says. "You can ask me anything but that."

IN FACT, GERHARD WAS ALMOST touchingly eager to please her, after the disastrous deflowering. He had dreamed of nothing but consummation with Elfriede during those months of their betrothal, and when at last he lifted his damp, triumphant head from the pillow next to hers, he'd evidently expected to see his own expression of spent rapture mirrored in that of his bride. The tears astonished him. Well, they horrified him! Filled him with profound remorse.

The thing about Gerhard, he was so stiff and formal in public and to strangers and even to his own family, his two sisters, one married and one maiden. Inside the privacy of marriage, however, he was a pussycat. Not, not a pussycat. More like a spaniel, deeply emotional, almost abject, wholly bound to the late Romantic ideal of a singular, mystical, all-powerful love between husband and wife. Also as a Romantic, he worshiped nature. He loved to go walking with Elfriede, away from the schloss and its gardens, maybe rowing on the lake. He didn't say much during these expeditions, but tears often welled in his eyes as he gazed at her, especially once she became pregnant and her belly began to swell beneath her dress. He hated to leave her side, even to work in his study for a few hours, as duty demanded. Yet when he traveled to Berlin or to Vienna—to pay his respects to his Kaiser, to see to his business interests, to buy art for his collections—and Elfriede asked to go with him, he always refused.

No, he said. His angel Elfriede must not be polluted by the dirt of the city. He liked to think of her here, in the country, breathing the pure air that was so healthful for their growing child. Besides, he would say, kissing her tenderly, she wouldn't like Berlin, it was chock-full of merchants and artists and Jews. The worst, decadent aspects of Vienna transported into a kind of German Chicago, whatever that was.

Back to bed. Yes, the wedding night was a tearful disaster, but Gerhard was remorseful. The next evening he took greater care, and—a man of discipline—didn't allow himself the pleasure of penetration until he had coaxed Elfriede's first orgasm from between her legs, sometime past midnight. Following this victory, he became determined that they should experience climax at a simultaneous instant, in order to achieve the sublime, transcendental union of which he dreamed. In fact, so determined that Elfriede, touched but not inexhaustible, learned it was sometimes easier to simply pretend that she was about to reach the desired peak, so that Gerhard could join her there, or rather imagine he'd joined her.

Then she could go to sleep, stunned by the weight of his body.

STILL, SHE CAN'T DISCUSS THESE things with Wilfred. Something sacred should remain of that time, she thinks. Anyway, once she's recovered from her breakdown, once Herr Doktor Hermann determines she's completed her course of treatment, she must return to her husband and family. And can she face Gerhard again if she's disclosed these intimate secrets to another man? Another man than Herr Doktor Hermann, of course, who is a professional. (Although she hasn't described her conjugal experiences to Herr Doktor Hermann, either, despite how often he insists that her successful treatment depends on such revelations. That's the bind, in fact—she can't return to her husband *until* she's completed her treatment, and she can't return to her husband *if* she's completed her treatment.)

"FAIR PLAY, I SUPPOSE," SAYS Wilfred. "We'll leave that aside. But what *would* you do, if not marriage?"

"I don't know. I can't think about it. It would be like wishing he were dead."

"All right. We can speak in the abstract, if you like. If not marriage, then what?"

Elfriede draws her knees up to her chin. "I might travel."

"Travel where?"

"Everywhere. I want to see the ocean, first. I used to dream of traveling on a liner across the sea, and ending up in some exotic place, like America."

Wilfred laughs. "America's not as exotic as you think. Maybe the western part."

"Have you been there?"

"I went to Boston with my father, one summer. It was hot and dirty and businesslike, and the people were surprisingly prim. They draw from Puritan stock, I believe. Then we went to Cape Cod for a couple of weeks, which was rather nicer. It sticks out right into the ocean, you see, curling like a scorpion's tail, and we swam in the surf every morning at sunrise."

"Heaven," says Elfriede.

Wilfred struggles upward to sit beside her. "Not quite."

"Why not?"

"*This* is more like heaven, if you ask me."

A breeze comes upon them, stirring Elfriede's clothes. Stirring his. The sky is clear above the greens and grays of the mountaintops, except for a single, small cloud that sticks to the highest peak. The air smells of warmth, of sunbaked grass, and occasionally of Wilfred when his scent steals close enough.

"I don't understand . . ." she begins softly.

"Understand what?"

"Why *you* should move me like this, when *he* loved me so much. So terribly."

"It's strange, isn't it? This."

She leans her head on his shoulder. "What are we to do?"

"Nothing." He touches her hair. Then he says it again, in English. *Nothing.*

Nothing, she repeats.

"No-thing. Th-th-th. Put your tongue beneath your upper teeth."

"No-thing," Elfriede says again, paying particular attention to this English *th*, her Waterloo these past few weeks. In order to pass the anxious time while Wilfred lay in bed with his relapse—a friendly orderly passed the notes between them—she began to teach herself English with the books from the sanatorium's extensive library. She hoped to astound him when he recovered. *Good morning*, she said to him, when they met at last on the wall of the infirmary garden, the exact spot where they had spoken their first words to each other. (This by design, of course, in a note passed that morning from the orderly's pocket.) *I hope you are vell*. She remembers how he turned—she'd come up to him from the meadow behind—and how the sight of his face, pale but radiant, made her dizzy. How his smile, growing slowly across his face to expose his teeth, illuminated the universe. *Well*, he said. *W-w-w. Well*.

W-w-well, she repeated.

I am well, thank you. Are you well, my love?

I am wery vell.

Now it's a joke between them, how *wery vell* they both are during these slow, beautiful hours together. How *wery vell* the sun shines upon them, how *wery vell* the air smells, the ground feels, the skin glows. How *wery vell* she's progressing in her English lessons.

Nothing, Elfriede says again. *Nothing. Nothing. Nothing. We are doing nothing. How is ʒat?*

"I'm being discharged," Wilfred says in German.

BUT ISN'T THIS WHY THEY'VE fallen in love, so suddenly and so utterly? Because of course Wilfred must go home when he's better, because of course Elfriede and Wilfred must part. It's so easy and so safe to fall in love when the universe is against you. Now, they haven't quite said those words to each other—*I love you, we've fallen in love*—but Elfriede has no doubt they echo inside Wilfred's head, in the same way they echo in hers.

I am wery vell, she said aloud, on the wall of the infirmary garden. Translation: I love you.

Come, let's go for a walk, Wilfred replied, taking her hand. Translation: I can't bear to exist without you.

And they walked, and they existed with each other, and in the touch of Wilfred's hand Elfriede imagined the rest of him. When they sat to rest, Elfriede stared at their clasped palms in the grass, Wilfred's large, white bones curled around hers, and a premonition of grief came upon her. But what will I do when you've gone? she whispered.

I have an idea, Wilfred said. *Let's not speak of that day until it comes.*

NOW IT'S COME.

"*What?*" Elfriede says.

"After all, I've regained my health."

"But they don't ever *make* you leave, the doctors. You can stay as long as you like."

"Only if you've got the dosh, my dear."

"But I could—we could—I have plenty of money—"

"You mean your husband has plenty of money."

Elfriede bows her head to this truth. Across the meadow, about thirty yards away, the grass stirs. A rodent of some kind, or a rabbit. Making preparation for winter, though the sun is still warm, no hint of evil yet cools the air.

"We have until Thursday," Wilfred says. "Four more days."

"And then what?"

"Nothing. I go about my life, pretending my heart's not beating away somewhere else, beating inside your chest—"

"Oh, don't. Don't."

He doesn't. So they sit, as they always do, as they've done for the past few weeks, since Wilfred was first allowed out of the infirmary garden with strict instructions not to exert himself, not to expose his lungs to any hint of inclement weather. Lucky for them, the weather has been fine, an unprecedented succession of warm, dry, perfect days. Or maybe it's not luck, after all. Maybe some more conscious force has arranged their affairs in this manner. Either way, the result's the same. They sit side by side in the meadow grass, watching the sun make its eternal arc across the heavens. Sometimes he touches her, as he does now. His fingertips on the backs of her knuckles.

"I once met this fellow in the south of France, this painter. Do you know what he called this time of day? The hour before sunset?"

"No."

"The golden hour." Wilfred waves his hand at the sun, which now burns just above the jagged peaks that form their horizon. "He said that's when everything looks the most beautiful, just before the sun sets. This luminous air turning everything to gold. He said it made him want to paint the whole world. And then it's gone, just like that. The sun disappears. The night arrives."

"The golden hour." Elfriede stares at Wilfred's hair, which has indeed transformed into a gold so pure as to make the alchemists weep, like the sun itself. She wants to touch it, to bury her face in it, to lick the gold from each strand before it's gone. Before Wilfred's gone, and the night arrives.

"What about you, Elfriede?" he asks. "That's the important thing. What will you do?"

"I don't know. Except I can't stay here any longer if you're gone."

"Can't you?"

"No, it's impossible. It will hurt too much."

"Not so much as it hurts me to leave."

"No, more. Because you'll have Vienna, you'll have new sights and scenes, nothing to remind you of me. Whereas here, these buildings, this mountain, this meadow—everything is you now. And it will be empty."

"Is that so intolerable?"

"You know it is."

"Hmm." The fingertips make another waltz on her knuckles. A Blue Danube of longing. "I thought you needed approval from this doctor to leave. Are you certain you want to cross him?"

"He can't stop me. I'll find a way out, like you."

Find a way out. Once she says the words, once she releases them into the air, they become possible. The horror of the outside world loses all consequence compared to the horror of existing inside the sanatorium without Wilfred. Against that, she has no other fear: not the mountain roads or the trains or the stares of strangers, not the husband she has disappointed, not the baby who doesn't know her, not Herr Doktor Hermann and all his degrees and authority. She can leave. She is the wife of a baron, after all. She can arrange for a carriage, she can simply walk out the door if she wants. Who will dare to stop her?

Elfriede straightens her back. Her eyes are dry now, her blood's warm. "Yes. I can't stay here without you. I'll leave."

"Good," says Wilfred. "That's settled. But where will you go, my heart?"

She curls her fingers inside her palm, so that her entire hand disappears in the grass beneath Wilfred's hand. Sometimes, sitting in this patch of meadow under the sun, smelling the warm, dead flowers, she forgets that anything else exists except the two of them, disappearing into the grass and each other.

Where will she go? She belongs to only one other place. Only one other heart beats inside her chest, whether she wants it there or not.

"Back to my son, maybe," she says. "Maybe I'll go back to my son and miss your freckles. All twenty-six of them."

BUT NO SUCH AGONIZING DECISION needs to be made, after all. When Elfriede returns to the sanatorium—by a different path from Wilfred's, of course—Herr Doktor Hermann waits for her in her room. He takes her hands.

"There is terrible news, Elfriede," he tells her. "I'm afraid your husband is very sick. The family has summoned you home to his side."

LULU

B Y THE TIME the evening wound to its end, I'd lost track of all the names, all the faces. They passed in a blur while the duchess guided me around the garden, under the lanterns, introducing me like a prize filly, and I pranced and pawed and whinnied on cue, made almost dizzy by this extraordinary ascent of fortune. In the months to come, I didn't remember the exact moment in which I first met Mrs. Gudewill and her daughters, or Fred Sigrist, or the other men and women who were to figure so prominently in this Bahamian chapter of my life. I didn't remember the precise drip of information that fed its way through my ears and into my brain, to be picked through and examined later. I do remember that I stood once more in the duke's study, speaking to Axel Wenner-Gren—yes, *him*, the Swedish industrialist, owner of Hog Island, the sort of fellow attracted to tax havens like the Bahamas like ants to picnics—when Thorpe reappeared. By now, most of the guests had left, and only a few of us remained to drink bourbon whiskey from the Windsor cabinet and listen to the duke's collection of popular American songs on the phonograph. Mr. Wenner-Gren wanted to know more about my husband.

"How long were you married?" he asked.

"Only a year."

"Then you were newlyweds. What a terrible thing, this war."

"What's the war got to do with it?"

"Oh, I beg your pardon. I assumed he was killed in battle."

I tried to speak and realized the muscles of my throat were paralyzed, that my pulse struck like a hammer in my neck. The familiar panic. You never knew when it might seize you, when it might sock your gut at any sudden noise, any bang of a window, any innocent question. When it struck, you had to remember to breathe in through your nose and out through your mouth, to disguise your terror as something else, like grief. When the panic receded, when the muscles softened enough to enable you to speak at all, you spoke haltingly, as if mastering your anguish, so that no one would suspect you were lying.

"No," I said. "He was killed in an accident. A terrible accident."

Now, though he was all of sixty years old, this Wenner-Gren was still an attractive man, a man of silver hair and elegant movements and perceptive blue eyes of the X-ray variety, if you know what I mean. He smoked his cigarette and stared at me, not at all moved by my widowhood, while I resisted the urge to cross my arms over my chest and ask him if the rumors were true, that he was really a Nazi, that he was friends with Goering and that his real mission here in Nassau was to persuade the duke to cast his fortunes with a triumphant Germany. After all, wasn't that exactly the kind of worldwide exclusive the *Metropolitan* had sent me to the Bahamas to discover? Wasn't Axel Wenner-Gren exactly the kind of man with whom I'd been desperate to sidle myself into profitable intimacy?

He leaned his face toward mine. "This must be terribly lonely for you."

"Oh, I keep myself busy. Not as busy as you do, of course, with your yacht and your lovely estate."

"Ah. What do you know about my estate?"

"Isn't it right there on Hog Island? I can just about see it from my bedroom window."

"Can you, now?"

"And your yacht, of course. There's no mistaking her." I paused to sip my drink. "Where are you headed next? I hear you're much enamored of Mexico these days. You've started a bank there, haven't you? The Banco Continental."

His eyebrows rose. He turned his face politely away to blow out a stream of smoke, and while he did so, breaking gaze for just that instant, his eyes flicked downward to appraise the sharp, deep neckline of my dress. "You seem to hear a great many things, Mrs. Randolph."

"Oh, one keeps one's ears open. And Nassau is terrible for gossip. It's the favorite pastime. Everybody seems to be knee-deep in each other's dirty business."

"So my wife tells me. And what else have you heard about me?"

"Oh, this and that." I shrugged. "I can't remember most of it. But tell me more about Mexico. I've always wanted to go."

He took a long, slow drag from his cigarette, examined the diminished end, and said softly, "Perhaps you might join us on our next voyage. We intend to make an archaeological expedition to South America, and then travel up to Mexico in time for Christmas."

"How kind of you. When do you cast off?"

Wenner-Gren opened his mouth, but it wasn't his voice that answered me.

"Any day now, isn't that right? I'd go myself, if I wasn't already occupied."

The words came from somewhere near my right shoulder, causing us both to startle and turn to the doorway, where Mr. Thorpe stood in his white dinner jacket, long and wide-shouldered and lean as a wooden cross. His head was bare and the spectacles perched at the very end of his nose. He pushed them up and smiled.

"My dear Thorpe," said Wenner-Gren. "I thought you had disappeared, as usual."

"Merely counting my profits in the back office."

"Don't tell me you've finished raiding all the pockets already," I said.

"Every shilling accounted for." Thorpe held out his elbow. "Might I have a private word with you, Mrs. Randolph?"

I suppose I gaped. He hadn't shown the slightest sign of recognition earlier, and though I'd caught glimpse after glimpse of him during the course of the party, we had never come face to face, as if some contract had been drawn up between us, some agreement not to acknowledge each other. I thought he had probably forgotten me, forgotten the episode on the airplane, or at least my face in the middle of it. And now he held out his elbow to me.

"Thorpe, old chap," said Wenner-Gren, in the funny way that men of all nations will ape certain expressions of the English upper classes. "I didn't know you were a friend of Mrs. Randolph's."

"We met on an airplane," said Thorpe, pronouncing the word in three syllables, *air-o-plane*, "and formed an instant connection. Didn't we, Mrs. Randolph?"

His face was grave, his fair skin pink beneath the freckles. I considered his eyes, which were blue and slightly hooded behind his spectacles, giving you an impression of great depth. I glanced back at Wenner-Gren's face and discovered a cool, pale stare like a reptile's.

I set down my half-finished bourbon on the edge of the Duke of Windsor's desk. "That's a wonderful question, Mr. Thorpe. I guess we might as well find out."

WE DIDN'T SAY A WORD until we reached the center of the main hallway, right between the staircase and the front entrance, where the panic hit my stomach once more. I snatched my hand from Thorpe's elbow.

"Thanks very much for rescuing me in there. I won't trouble you further."

"Now, wait just a moment, Mrs.—"

But I was already pushing open the door, already hurrying across the portico. He caught up with me a few steps later and touched my elbow. I stopped and whirled to face him.

"Did I say I wanted company, Mr. Thorpe?"

"Look here. You can't just fly off alone like that."

"You can't possibly think I'd go off with you."

"Why not?"

"Why *not?* I don't even know you. For all I know, you're a homicidal maniac. Or worse."

"Worse? What could be worse than that?"

I lifted my chin and fixed him with a certain stare of mine. He gave my displeasure his full attention, while some bird trilled out a mighty evening song from the portico above. It takes a certain amount of strength, you know, to gaze without blinking into the eyes of a man you hardly know, a man as tall and dazzling as Thorpe, and to this day I don't quite understand how I held firm, or why. From the windows of Government House floated the mist of some jiggly, dancing tune I didn't recognize, the shadow of somebody's braying laugh. The dark air lay against Thorpe's skin. His eyes were narrowed and gray, the way the night drains color from everything. At last he sighed, glanced heavenward, and made a half turn toward the Government House entrance. "Taylor!" he called out.

For the first time, I noticed the footman there, or rather the doorman, straight-shouldered and tidy in his white uniform against the pink facade, lit by the windows behind him. "Yes, sir?" he said, staring straight ahead.

"You've seen me leave the premises in the company of Mrs. Randolph, correct?"

"Indeed, sir."

"If something untoward occurs, you're prepared to swear to that effect in a court of law?"

"Without hesitation, sir."

Thorpe turned back to me. "You see? Nothing to fear. Intentions entirely honorable."

I resumed walking toward the stairs. The air had cooled no more than a few degrees with the coming of night, but at least the brutal sun had sunk away. The atmosphere was hazy, the stars blurred in the sky above the nearby ocean. I didn't need to look over my shoulder; I knew Thorpe had joined me. "That doesn't prove a thing," I said. "For all I know, you're in collusion."

"You're a damned suspicious woman, Mrs. Randolph."

"Women need to be suspicious, Thorpe, suspicious of everyone and everything. A woman on her own, especially. It's a matter of survival."

"Not all men are beasts, you know."

"Enough of them are. Even one's enough. Once you encounter your first wolf, why, you start to notice them everywhere."

"I see," he said. "Are we speaking of Mr. Randolph, perhaps?"

We were tripping down the endless flight of stairs, had already passed the statue of Columbus. Below us, the street was dark and quiet. I stopped midstep and waited for Thorpe to halt, to turn, two stairs below, so that his face sat at last on the same level as mine.

"There was a girl back at college," I said. "Went off with a boy after a party, just like a little lamb. It didn't end well."

"I see."

"No, you don't. You don't have the smallest idea. You've never been anybody's prey."

"Not true."

I lifted my eyebrows and stared at his large, earnest face, his eyes behind the spectacles. I thought he was going to say more, tell me some story, even if it wasn't real. But the lips didn't move. Just those two words, *Not true*, a pair of words that covered a vast territory.

"All right," I said. "But I'll bet you were evenly matched, weren't you? A big cat like you. You could fight back."

"Fair point. But I might say the same of you."

"Me?"

"You might not be so big, of course. But you seem to me like the sort of woman who fights back."

The streetlamps cast a soft yellow heat on his face. He stood with one foot braced on the step above; his hand rested on his thigh. I was conscious of my daring neckline, my exposed skin, my scarcity of sleeves, my breath trapped in my lungs, my thundering heart. The goose bumps prickling my arms, which could not possibly have sprung from the tropical air.

"That man on the airplane," I said. "What did you do to him?"

"Nothing at all."

"No, that was something, all right. Something I wouldn't mind learning how to do, should another wolf come bounding into my life, for example."

Thorpe rubbed his fist on his knee and looked to the side, at an upward angle, as if considering the sky above the ocean. His nose was robust, almost Roman, and yet there was something vulnerable about his profile or else the way he presented it to me. "By *college*," he said, "do you mean you were at university?"

"Yes."

"And this girl. She was a friend of yours?"

I stared at his cheekbone. "We were inseparable."

"I see." He turned back to me. "I found myself at the bar at the Prince George a week or two ago. Happened to catch a glimpse of a girl sitting all by herself. She was drinking a Scotch whiskey, I believe, no ice, reading a book, and her hair kept falling over her forehead, and she kept pushing it back. Eventually she looked up and glanced my way—I imagine she must have sensed me watching—and I recognized her at once. The girl from the airplane."

I held out my hand. "Leonora Randolph. But you can call me Lulu."

"Lulu. I'm Benedict."

"Benedict?"

"I was named after my father. His middle name."

"I can't call you Benedict."

He shrugged. "Then call me whatever you want."

HE WALKED ME DOWN GEORGE Street to the hotel. We didn't touch, nor did we speak until we turned the corner of Bay Street and stopped. Thorpe stuck his hands in his pockets and looked toward the harbor. "Still the Prince George?" he said.

"Still the Prince George."

"Sounds rather temporary."

"I might be looking for something a little more permanent."

He turned his head. "Really?"

"Seems I'm about to enter paid employment. If all goes well."

"Congratulations. Splendid news."

"You don't seem surprised."

"I might have made a few inquiries regarding your intentions here," he said.

I snapped my fingers. "Jack! That old so-and-so. I might've known."

"I'm afraid I can't reveal my sources."

"There's no need. I can practically smell him on you. Say . . ."

Thorpe lifted an eyebrow and stared at me patiently. Behind him, the street was empty, except for the British Colonial rising brilliantly against the sky. The air smelled stickily of night blossom, of the nearby ocean, of the lingering afternoon ether of automobile exhaust. There's a particular odor to a Nassau evening, a perfume I've never encountered since. I wrapped my hands around my pocketbook and said, "I'll bet that was you, wasn't it? That drink the other night."

"I haven't the least idea what you're talking about."

"Jack said you were a shy kind of fellow."

"Jack was quite right. I'm practically a recluse."

"I wouldn't say shy. The way you swooped in, back there in the library. Plucked me out of Wenner-Gren's talons. The way you handled that fellow on the airplane."

Thorpe squinted upward again, judging the stars. His hands remained in his pockets, causing his wide shoulders to hunch slightly. "Well, what else was I to do? Allow the blackguard to continue occupying my seat?"

"Why not? Less trouble that way."

His gaze dropped back to my face, and I swear to God, he peered right through my skin and bone to the matter beneath. Those placid eyes. I couldn't move. I stood there like a fool, soaking it all up, the shining spectacles, the eyes and the pale skin, the hazy moon, the bare head glinting. "Tell me something, Mrs. Randolph," he said quietly. "What brings you to Nassau? And don't tell me some rubbish about your dead husband. We both know that's not the case."

I opened my mouth and made—to my eternal shame—nothing more than a strangled gasp.

"As I thought. You're a terrible liar, Mrs. Randolph. Not cut out for this business at all."

"And what business is that?"

"You tell me," he said.

I tucked my pocketbook under my arm. "I'm a journalist. Here to scoop the scoop of the century, if I can find it."

"Some kind of scandal, you mean? Parting the curtain of the Windsor boudoir for a breathless *Metropolitan* audience?"

"Now see here. How did you know the name of the magazine?"

"As I said, I made a few inquiries."

I threw up my hands. "Jack."

"Jack knows my intentions are entirely honorable."

"*Honorable.* There's a pact, you know, an unspoken pact of discretion between girl and bartender—"

"Don't blame Jack. I was persistent, and what's more, I pay well."

"No doubt. It's just I'm starting to think you're not the only one making our Jack sing like a canary, that's all."

"Oh?"

"The duchess knows everything about me." I waved my hand in the direction of Government House, which still glowed above us from the top of George Street. "Although I don't suppose it's done me any harm. She practically invited me inside the sanctum, just now. The chance I've been waiting for."

"Did she, now?"

"She did. She's concerned about the Windsor public image, poor dear. Wants to make sure it's shown in the most flattering light possible, by a pet journalist trained to eat right from her hand."

"And that pet journalist . . . ?"

"Yours truly. The idea's to feed me all the best tidbits, in order to keep body and soul together. Exactly what the magazine had in mind, in fact. If I play my cards, I'll have my own column, a nice salary, expenses all paid in an almost-tropical paradise. Everything a girl could want, and just exactly when I was down to my last dime. It's almost too good to be true, don't you think?"

"And that's it?"

"That's everything."

"That's the truth?"

"That's the truth."

"I see," he said again. He reached up to the basket of flowers that hung from the streetlamp and plucked a small pink flower I didn't recognize. "Some might feel themselves obliged to offer you a word of warning, where the duke and duchess are concerned. *Caveat emptor*, or something like that."

"Except I'm not buying anything, am I? I'm selling it."

He just looked at me, mere black and white in the darkness, the feeble crescent moon. I reached out and took the flower from his fingers.

Around us, Nassau had fallen asleep. The air was warm and still. If you listened hard, you might detect a faint hum of gaiety trailing from the windows of the British Colonial, an automobile rumbling down an unseen road. A dog barked from some great distance, no louder than the beating of our hearts.

"Where's home for you, Thorpe?" I asked softly.

"Home? Now there's a question. I was chiefly raised in the Scottish Highlands by my fearsome grandmother—"

"I mean here," I said. "Here in Nassau."

"Ah. I see what you mean. At present, I live in Shangri-La, Mrs. Randolph."

"Shangri-La? Do you mean Hog Island? Wenner-Gren's place?"

"A cottage on the property, yes."

"You're his guest? Why didn't you say anything? Back there in the study."

"Why should I?"

"Because it—because he—" I tucked my nose in the flower. Curiously, it had no scent. "How do you know him?"

"He was kind enough to offer his cottage as a base for my research, when I first arrived."

"Your research?"

"I'm a botanist, Mrs. Randolph."

"A botanist. Of course. A botanist of international repute, according to our hostess."

"A kind exaggeration."

"It's just—that fellow on the airplane—I pegged you for something else. Something a little more martial."

He pointed to the spectacles. "I'm afraid my eyesight got in the way of all that. In any case, my research requires a bit of space, you know."

"How will you get back?"

"Why, the same way I came over. By boat."

"At night?"

"Why not? It's not far."

He said this without irony, a little amazed at my amazement, as if sailing across the harbor were about the same thing as bicycling down the street. I don't know, maybe it was, around here. *Not far*, he said, and for an instant I thought I glimpsed this, him, a boat, moonlight, paradise, and for the space of that instant, that minute carved away from myself, I was somebody who stepped in a sailboat and fell in love.

And the instant passed, and I was myself, Lulu, standing on firm, dry land, ribs held together by a thick layer of scar tissue, impregnable.

"Well," I said, "be careful, that's all."

"I shall. Good night, Mrs. Randolph."

"Good night, Mr. Thorpe."

I turned to head down Bay Street to the Prince George, a few buildings down. The Royal Bank of Canada stood before me, a brick giant, all shut up for the night. As I forced my legs into stride, I heard him call out, "What did you read at university?"

"Read?"

"Study, I mean. What course of study?"

"French literature," I said. "And a minor course in music."

"Music? How interesting. My mother studied music."

I made a noise of exasperation and stepped under the awning of the hotel. From the street came the sound of whistling, a bar or two, and then Thorpe's voice, just as I crossed the threshold into the hall.

"It's how they met, I'm told. My parents. My father heard her playing the piano and fell in love."

NATURALLY I MARCHED STRAIGHT TOWARD the bar, with the fixed intention of giving Jack a piece of my temper. I was roiled, you see, overturned by the conversation on the corner of Bay Street, while the stars gazed fuzzily on Thorpe's bright head and the seagulls screamed. The salt air had done something to my head. I thought I was going to burst. Relief or disappointment or something, straining against the scar tissue, creaking my poor ribs.

"Jack, you son of a gun," I began.

Jack turned swiftly. "Now, *there* you are, Mrs. Randolph. Fellow came for you. Gave up about a half hour ago."

"What fellow?"

Jack reached into the pocket of his waistcoat and pulled out a piece of paper. "See for yourself."

I took the note and opened it.

My dear Mrs. Randolph,

Should you decide to prolong your stay in Nassau after all, may I humbly bring to your notice a convenient cottage on Cable Beach, available to let on reasonable terms, local landlord.

Yours sincerely,
A. de Marigny

PART II

LULU

DECEMBER 1943
(London)

MISS THORPE'S FLAT. AROUND the corner from the Basil Hotel it isn't, quite, although that might have something to do with the funny route taken there by Miss Thorpe, turning corners and doubling back, until we arrive at a house surrounded on both sides by empty lots, scattered with rubble.

"The Blitz," she says simply, jumping up the steps. She's got her key out already and shoves it into the lock. Thank God, it opens readily. She steps back and motions me through.

"Third floor," she calls softly.

I start up the steps while the sound of the bolt clangs behind me. Then her footsteps, tripping along as if the climb is nothing at all. We reach the landing and a single door, which she unlocks and opens, ushering me past into a hallway that smells of damp wool, just exactly as if I'm the ordinary kind of guest who drops by for tea and crumpets in the afternoon, pinky finger primed for business.

"If you'll hang your coat and hat on the hook, there," she says. "The radiator should dry them out. I do hope you haven't left anything important at the hotel."

"I haven't. Although that fellow back there thinks I have, which should keep him busy for a bit. Assuming I haven't killed him."

"You haven't," she says dryly. "That man's indestructible. I'll put the kettle on, shall I? You do drink tea?"

"When I must."

She disappears through a narrow doorway into what I presume is some sort of kitchen. I hang my hat first, then the coat. Before I turn away, I pat the left breast, and the stiffness of the paper beneath, tucked inside the inner pocket, is like a miracle. "Sit," calls Miss Thorpe, over her shoulder, and I sit, I simply collapse on one of the four chairs around the table, and it's only then that I realize my arms and legs are shaking, my breath is so shallow in my lungs that I can't seem to get any air. I lay my head on the wood. The room's dim, because of the blackout and because you're not allowed to use excess electricity around here, every ounce of energy must go to the war effort. *The radiator should dry them out*, Miss Thorpe said confidently, but if the radiator's doing its duty at the moment, I'll be damned. The atmosphere inside the flat is hardly any warmer or dryer than the atmosphere outside.

At the sound of Miss Thorpe's footsteps on the floorboards, I summon myself and lift my head from the table. Like her brother, she's tall and slender, and now that she's removed her hat, you can see the trace of ginger that links her to Thorpe, and to the pair of unknown parents who produced them. She has a sharp, neat profile and beautiful skin: so smooth and pale in this strange dark London room, it makes you think of the moon. She sets out the cups and asks me about milk and so on. She warns me there isn't much sugar, that the milk is the powdered kind. I make reply. The tea appears before me, and I can't remember what I told her, sugar or not. I raise the cup and sip, and she raises her cup and sips, and our eyes meet over the rims, Miss Thorpe and Mrs. Thorpe.

She sets down the cup. "Leonora—"

"Lulu."

"Lulu," she repeats, as if she's tasting something overly sweet.

"Only my mother calls me Leonora."

"I see. Lulu, then. I'm Margaret. Margaret Thorpe, but you know that."

"You received my letter, then."

"Yes. I came home early and found it in the post." She glances at my left hand. "Rather a shock. He never said a word about you. And now you're here, and he's—he's—"

"In prison."

She swears softly and reaches for her pocketbook. "Do you mind if I smoke?"

"Do you mind if I join you?"

She lights me a cigarette and then one for herself. The tea, the cigarette calm my nerves. Or maybe it's Margaret, who radiates that peculiar English calm, like there's nothing that can't be solved over tea. A cat leaps unexpectedly onto her lap, black with white points. She strokes him absently.

"What's his name?" I ask.

"What? Oh, this little criminal? Tuxedo. Not very clever, I know. Benedict brought him home one day, during the Blitz."

"Thorpe lived here?"

"We shared the flat. He was good company when the bombs were coming down. He kept me from panicking."

"Funny, you don't seem like the panicking type to me."

"When one returns home from a night spent on a Tube platform to discover both neighboring houses turned to rubble," she says crisply, tapping ash into the tray, stroking the cat, "it does try one's nerves."

"Was yours ever hit?"

"No. Not a scratch. I suppose even bombs have a sense of irony."

"Not really," I say. "That's just human illusion. We imagine there's an order to things, because it's too awful to consider the randomness of fate."

"I've never subscribed to the idea of fate."

I set down the cigarette and swallow tea. "Still, it must have been swell, having your brother around at a time like that. A fellow you could trust."

"Swell." She tests the word. "I suppose so. And then he was gone. Off to Nassau. I was so happy. I thought, well, at least one of us is out of danger."

"Did you ever find another roommate?"

The cat jumps from her lap to the floor and commences making love to the leg of the table. She reaches down to rub his chin.

"No. In case he came home in the middle of the night, you see."

"Oh, of course."

She lifts an eyebrow and stares at the mantel. A pair of small, framed photographs anchor the left side, too far away to see properly. "But I don't believe he'd mind if you shelter here for a bit."

A pool of silence spreads between us, but it's not the awkward silence that two ordinary women might experience, having just met, trying to think of something to say, trying to discover some common ground. It's the common ground that holds us silent, the common ground that lies between us. She finishes her cigarette first and stubs it out in the ashtray in slow, precise thrusts. Only then does her gaze return to my face, where it spends a second or two. I have the feeling she's trying to see me through her brother's eyes, she's trying to imagine me as her brother imagines me. The current in the light bulb fails, starts, fails, and returns—some interruption of the supply of electricity—and the flickering casts a strange pattern of shadows across her face, which she doesn't seem to notice.

The cat, having wound his way among the legs of the table and chairs, reaches with his nose to sniff my skirt. I lean down and hold out my fingertips, and the delicate texture of his tongue meets my skin.

"You know, you haven't asked me what happened," I say.

"What happened in Nassau, you mean? No."

"Why not?"

"I don't believe I'm supposed to know, am I? It's confidential."

"But you *want* to know."

"Only if you mean to tell me."

Tuxedo pulls back on his haunches, gathers himself, and leaps onto my lap.

"That's interesting," says Margaret. "He doesn't like strangers, ordinarily."

"Do you have strangers often?"

She starts to light another cigarette. "Not often. But sometimes."

Tuxedo kneads my thighs. A low purr starts up in his throat. He's got long, fluffy fur, a tail like a feather duster. I lay my hand on the top of his head and stroke all the way down his back. "There was a murder," I say. "A fellow named Harry Oakes was murdered last July, in his bed, in the middle of the night."

MURDER. IT'S ONE OF THOSE words, isn't it, that sounds as dreadful as the deed itself. Certainly it shocks me to say it out loud like that, though I have lived and breathed this thing for months now, though the terrible end of Sir Harry Oakes haunts me now as it did the first day I learned of it. And you would think that a statement like that—*There was a murder*—might pierce the composure of anybody, even Miss Thorpe. But maybe I forget that the rest of the world knows all about poor Oakes. Even in the middle of war, people will pay attention to the killing (there's another dreadful word) of a man so wealthy and famous as Sir Harry, in a location so exotic as the Bahamas, in a manner so gruesome as—well, as it was. So perhaps I shouldn't be surprised that Miss Thorpe's expression remains cool and ageless, that she doesn't so much as lift her eyebrows.

"The Oakes murder? What's that got to do with Benedict?"

"You've heard about it?"

"Heard about it? It was all over the newspapers. Such as they are, with paper rationed." She twitches the cigarette with her thumb. A strand of hair has come loose from the knot at her neck. She pushes it back over her ear. "Didn't they arrest somebody? Some French chap, I believe. There was a trial. A sensational trial."

"Not French," I say. "Mauritian."

"Oh, of course."

"Yes. The evidence was fabricated. It was all a giant cover-up. Not to cover up *who* committed the murder, mind you. Everybody in Nassau knows who killed Harry Oakes. Who *had* him killed, anyway."

"Then what were they trying to cover up?"

"*Why*," I tell her. "*Why* he was murdered."

"Oh, naturally. The *why* is always more complicated than the *who* or the *how*. More interesting and especially more dangerous."

"In this case, especially."

"And did Benedict know why?"

"Yes."

Tuxedo, having softened up my legs to his satisfaction, now settles in the center of my lap and purrs like a motorcycle. I stroke the fur behind his ears, beneath his chin. He seems to be smiling, though his eyes are shut. Margaret smokes her cigarette and stares at the photographs on the mantel, the images of which I can't make out.

"I should have known, I suppose," she says. "He told me he was just going to look after the duke, a sort of liaison officer. I should have known it was something more."

"Oh, I think you knew. Didn't you?"

Margaret rises from the chair and settles the collar of her dressing gown more snugly around her slender neck. Tuxedo lifts his head and blinks at her as she moves to the fireplace and brushes the frame of one of the photographs with her thumb. If I squint my eyes, I can just perceive a pair of monochrome figures set against the outdoors, drenched in sunshine. I ask if those are her parents.

"No. It's Benedict. Benedict and me. In Germany one summer, before the war." She drags on the cigarette. "Our mother was German."

"Yes, I know."

She lifts the photograph and strokes the picture's edge, as if she's rubbing something away. "We loved it there so much, like it was home. Isn't that strange? But we always visited in summer, when the sun was shining, unlike Scotland. Benedict loved to go hunting for new plants. That was his obsession, even then."

"Botany," I say.

"Yes. He was always outdoors. There was this lake at the edge of the garden. I taught him to swim there. He was six."

"Isn't that a little old to start swimming?"

"My grandmother wouldn't let him near the water."

"Really? Why not?"

She flicks ash into the fireplace and replaces the photograph on the mantel. The metal makes a decisive noise as it strikes the marble. She turns to me and folds her arms. "Grandmothers have their reasons. You haven't eaten, have you?"

"Not since lunch."

"Then I suppose we'd better make dinner."

DINNER IS BROWN BREAD, MARGARINE, pea soup with tiny pieces of ham, washed down with weak tea. I ask her about Thorpe as a boy, about summers in Germany, about this grandmother of theirs, but she doesn't want to answer me. Instead she asks me about my own childhood, about America, about my parents, and she listens earnestly to my replies. "How queer," she says, over and over, as if America is something exotic, as if my father and mother are a species of animal you find in a zoo.

We wash the dishes. She shows me to the lavatory and finds me a toothbrush. She shows me to my room—Thorpe's room—and only at the last second, as we exchange awkward good nights at the door, do I summon the resolve to press her again about her past.

"Do you miss it? Germany, I mean. Could you ever go back?"

"Go to Germany? Are you mad?"

I shrug one shoulder, like a question. Margaret bends down and lifts Tuxedo from the floor, where he's been winding around my legs, making suggestive noises. She strokes the fur between his ears. When she speaks, she addresses herself to the cat, not to me.

"I'm afraid there are certain places to which you can never return."

ELFRIEDE

OCTOBER 1900
(Germany)

O N THE CANOPIED bed where Gerhard von Kleist consummated his marriage by the light of two dozen beeswax candles—Schloss Kleist was not then electrified—he now lies in darkness, attended by a doctor brought in from hated Berlin, a Jew, the foremost expert in infectious disease, who once raised the Kaiser's own son almost from the dead.

Gerhard has typhoid. It's not hopeless, everyone insists, as they go about the corridors in dark clothes, mute voices, furrowed brows. Not hopeless at all. He's such a strong, big fellow. How could a puny germ conquer Baron von Kleist?

Elfriede knows how. It's five o'clock in the morning and she sits by the bed, reading aloud from *Faust*—naturally, Gerhard worships Goethe—but she doesn't hear her own words. Inside her head, she's begging God to let her husband live, not to punish Gerhard because Elfriede has fallen in love with another man and committed adultery in her heart. That last conversation with Wilfred, she hears every word echoing against her skull: *If something were to happen to my husband.* And: *It would be like wishing he were dead.* Almost as if she *knew*, as if she obtained some subconscious knowledge of what was happening in Westphalia while she sat on her mountaintop with her lover, speaking of Gerhard in the past tense. *He loved me so much.*

Everyone's asleep except Elfriede and, possibly, Gerhard, who exists in a febrile state of half slumber. When she first took her seat and began reading, he became calm, as if the sound of her voice gave him rest. But now he's twitching again. Tosses his head from side to side. Mumbles words. Twice Elfriede's bathed him with a sponge and a basin of lavender water, yesterday morning and yesterday evening, and still he carries that awful smell of sickness, that putrescent sourness. Now she breaks off her reading and touches his dry, warm, pale cheek. How devoted he was. A perfect husband. Never raised a finger against her, let alone his voice. She could have had no complaints, it was all her doing. Even when she told him she couldn't face the idea of having another baby—enduring that awful blackness again, that certainty of something deeply wrong at her core—he never objected. He moved his sleeping accommodation into the anteroom, now occupied by Dr. Rosenblatt. Only his eyes reproached her. Poor Gerhard. Now he suffers all over again, because of her. And her face is like an angel's.

Elfriede lifts the linen cloth that lies across the bowl of lavender water, sitting atop the nightstand. She wets its, wrings it, lays it along the beam of Gerhard's forehead. A paraffin lamp glows at the window. Just enough to see by. Under the coolness of the cloth, Gerhard goes still. A word sighs out between his lips, and after a moment Elfriede recognizes the syllables: her name.

She sets aside the book and walks to the window. Not the one with the lamp, the dark one, though her mind craves something light, something coppery and joyful. Craves Wilfred. His absurd figure. Big, plain, bony, ginger head atop long, spindly, freckled limbs. Laugh like sunshine. She's drawn to the thought of him like birds are drawn to the sky. But no. No sky for her. No sunshine. The hateful gazes of her sisters-in-law, blaming her for this catastrophe, for all catastrophes: that's what she deserves.

Elfriede lifts the curtain and stares through the glass. The peculiar darkness before dawn, the coldest time of day. Naturally the master's bedroom occupies a favored position at the back of Schloss Kleist, over-looking the formal gardens and the lake beyond, on which Gerhard used to take her rowing. A deep, pure lake, stocked with fish. On the opposite shore begins the woods, thickening eventually into acres of untouched forest, where Gerhard sometimes went hunting for boar. Altogether the estate is from another age, a feudal age. You might be gazing five hundred years into the past, gazing out this window. Except, at this hour, you can't see anything at all.

And yet. And yet.

There it is again. A tiny flash of white. On the ground below, the terrace, reflecting the light from the paraffin lamp in the other window.

A strange fear grips Elfriede's heart. Now her eyes adjust. The flash becomes an object, bobbing against the shadows. Elfriede turns and runs out of the room and down the corridor, down the back staircase, out the French door to the terrace. (Noting that the door was ajar.)

BY THE TIME ELFRIEDE RETURNED to Schloss Kleist from the hospital outside Berlin, the stitches in her wrists had been removed, the scars were fresh and pink, and she was—according to the doctors—healing nicely. Her baby had turned six months old and changed beyond recognition. He was enormous and round-cheeked, a roly-poly darling who sat up and ate pap and tried mightily to crawl. On his formerly bald head, a fine down of hair now grew, so pale it was almost white. They would not leave her alone with him, of course. The nurse remained in the room, within arm's reach. She was maybe thirty years old, blond and sturdy, and had been advertised for the instant Elfriede was whisked away to the hospital. *Wanted, nurse for infant, three months of age. Mother of recently deceased infant preferred. Female of good character only. References required. Wages 5 marks weekly.* The aunts desired a bereaved mother because they thought she would devote herself wholly to Johann, and this proved to be the case. Her gaze, pained and possessive, never strayed from Johann's white head. She regarded Elfriede with a suspicion bordering on hatred. Elfriede, cradling Johann to her chest, playing helplessly at peekaboo, felt like an intruder. When the baby cried for food, Charlotte snatched him back and assumed an air of command as she unbuttoned her bodice and produced a large, blue-veined breast for him to suckle. Which he did, eagerly. Closing his eyes in bliss. His tiny, beautiful fists clutching at Charlotte's skin. Elfriede watched those fingers knead and felt them ripping her flesh from her own chest, sucking her blood from her own heart. She had nothing to give him.

I have lost him, Elfriede thought. And then:

He was never mine.

BUT SHE CARRIED THE IMAGE of that round, fragrant white head to Switzerland with her. She carried it on the armchair in Herr Doktor Hermann's office, carried it on the bench in the courtyard, carried it along the narrow goat paths that crisscrossed the mountain, carried it in bed and at the table and buried in the meadow grass with Wilfred.

She carries it now as she darts across the cold terrace stone and calls his name.

Johann.

Johann.

Little white-haired boy, where are you?

She isn't allowed to see him. The germs, you know. Johann and Nurse sleep upstairs in the nursery wing and take their meals in the nursery kitchen, from food carried there directly from town. Herr Doktor Rosenblatt is specific in these points. Had, in fact, wanted Johann and Nurse to remove from Schloss Kleist altogether, except there's nowhere to send them except Elfriede's family, and *that's* out of the question, apparently. So Elfriede hasn't seen Johann once during the three days since her return to Westphalia. She's looked from the bedroom window, from the hallway, hoping to steal some glimpse of him, but her luck has turned, it seems. Or else luck has nothing to do with it. Maybe Nurse confines Johann strictly outside the potential arc of Elfriede's gaze, on her own initiative or someone else's. The aunts. Elfriede's sisters-in-law, Ulrika, who's married to the owner of a neighboring estate, and Helga, who still lives under her brother's roof, a maiden.

Still, her son's heart beats in her chest. She carries his image inside her skin. She calls his name now, stepping off the terrace to the darkened paths of the formal gardens, the parterres, the silent fountain, the alleys of linden and so on, searching each shadow for a flash of white, reflecting the half-moon. Listening for any rustle of fine gravel, any crackle of fallen leaves, any panting young breath. Anything she can hear above the thunder of her own terrified heart, that is. Surely he could not have gone so far as the lake.

Though she hasn't yet noticed the chill, this October morning is brittle with it. Spreading from the northeast, from the Baltic, from the Russian plains where the weather has already turned to autumn. Elfriede's hands and cheeks, if she cares to touch them, will prove icy. But she doesn't care. She has room in her head for only one thought. Only one sensation. Not fear, or terror or even panic—none of those words quite describes her state of mind, when she considers the possibility of Johann losing his way and wandering into the dark woods, or trundling down the dock to fall into the lake, even merely tripping on a stone and cutting his fat knee. The idea of his blood, she cannot fathom it. She cannot bear it.

Johann.

Johann.

Where are you?

In the cold air she doesn't notice, her words carry far and clear. After each call, she cants her head and sharpens her ears and listens, listens. But there's no answer, no small voice in the void. That half-moon sits behind a cloud now. It doesn't reveal much, just silvers the leaves and the stones, lightens the shadows from black to charcoal, so you see an obstacle in the instant before you run into it. Elfriede reaches the stone steps that end in the lake. In summer, a flat-bottomed boat would be tied to the mooring at the bottom of these steps, where the water's shallow. In summer, you could also stroll along the lake's edge where the water is deeper, where the bank's made of civilized cut stone, and you could sit on this stone and dangle your legs into the lake to cool them. Or maybe fish, if you brought your pole. Picnic. Gerhard enjoyed swimming. He'd dive in and stroke all the way across to the opposite bank and back again, to maintain a healthy physical fitness. But summer's gone, autumn has arrived, the sun's busy warming some southern part of the globe. The half-moon drizzles a little light on the lake's surface, and that's all there is to tell you a lake exists there at all. If you weren't expecting water, you might not even notice. Might simply walk off the edge, into the cold, black nothing.

Elfriede steps off the last stair and strides out into the shallows. She cups her hands around her mouth.

Johann.

Johann, please!

It's your mother, Johann.

It's Mama.

Where

are

you?

An echo floats back to her. Elfriede's own words, turned against her. Now she discovers the cold and starts to shiver. She thinks, maybe he went back to the house already, *maybe he wasn't outside to begin with.*

Maybe I imagined him in the moonlight, in the lamplight from the window. Maybe it was a ghost, a little boy who died a hundred years ago, a wee unfortunate von Kleist who caught typhoid or something.

Elfriede tells herself to be sensible. There would be ripples, surely, there would be some natural commotion. A sturdy little boy could not just fall into a lake without a fuss.

You have imagined all this.

You haven't slept, you're exhausted, your mind is playing tricks.

You're made of nerves right now.

You're a fool.

What the hell does it matter, you don't even know him. He doesn't know you. He probably thinks Nurse is his mother. Probably calls her mama. Probably—

A tiny sob.

Elfriede whips around and listens. Made of nerves. No, not *nerves*: one giant nerve, quivering, straining for sensation.

The wavelets trickle behind her. She's afraid to move, afraid to breathe, afraid of missing some vibration in the atmosphere. Her heart is too loud, her damned heart, getting in the way of everything. Why doesn't it just stop. Elfriede shuts her eyes. In the space between heartbeats, she strains, she reaches.

Sob.

To the right, to the right. Elfriede remembers in a flash, the summerhouse.

IT'S POSSIBLE THAT JOHANN WAS conceived in the summerhouse. There are other candidates, of course, but that's the interesting one. A hot, dreamlike afternoon at the end of August. Elfriede, by now accustomed to her husband, watches him hoist himself ashore after making his daily swim across the lake. Briefly, he looks like a god. The sun shines on his hair, his thick muscles run with water. (Of course he swims naked, he's a Romantic.) He catches her gaze. Drops his towel, clasps her, carries her into the summerhouse, and makes love to her twice in the suffocating heat. *Twice*. The perspiring Elfriede, fastened to some cushions by a hundred and twenty kilos of heroic bone and muscle, gazes through the blurred, sultry windowpanes toward the sky. A dream world, long ago.

A month or so later, she realized her courses were late. So throughout the rest of her pregnancy, whenever she and Gerhard walked past the summerhouse, arm in arm, he smiled and said, *Look, that's where we made our son, my dearest love, my Liebling, don't you remember?* Elfriede merely ducked her head and neither agreed nor disagreed. After all, she and Gerhard had frequent intercourse throughout the end of August, and only once—well, twice—on the chaise longue in the summerhouse. Also, what if the baby was a girl?

On the other hand, Gerhard was right about the baby being a boy. So maybe he was right about its place of conception, as well. Anyway, it's a good story.

THIS IS NOT AUGUST. IT'S October, and Gerhard lies dying in his bed upstairs, and nothing is a dream anymore, it is all reality. This son she scarcely knows, this child conceived in sunshine, now weeps in the nearby darkness, and Elfriede's arms and face and feet are numb with cold. She makes for the summerhouse. She can't hear the sounds of weeping anymore, but maybe she never did. Maybe the sounds originated in her own mind, because her mind needed to hear them. Maybe she doesn't expect to find anything in the summerhouse except some old cushions, some old dreams.

Still, when she finds the entrance with her hands, when she sweeps inside and sees a white head bobbing, hears a small voice crying, she feels no surprise.

She kneels on the stone floor and asks him what's wrong.

"My private," he says.

Elfriede experiences a moment of bemusement. "Your private?"

"My soldier. I left him here and he's gone!"

"Oh, dear. Oh, dear. This is terrible. Has he run off, do you think? Deserted his post?"

"No, no. He's a brave soldier. He wouldn't do that."

"Then we shall just keep looking, won't we?"

"I looked everywhere."

"Then we look everywhere twice. Come on."

On their hands and knees, Elfriede and Johann dredge every inch of stone, every seam of floor and wall, until Elfriede's fingers discover a small metal object wedged between the cushions on the chaise longue. Still too dark to see it properly, but Johann, clutching the figure, joyfully declares his missing private found.

"Now let's return to your room, before Nurse finds out you've stolen away," Elfriede says.

Already Johann's rubbing his eyes. "I sleepy," he tells her, losing his grammar to fatigue.

So Elfriede places her hands around his warm ribs and lifts him to her hip. "I'll carry you."

They emerge from the summerhouse to discover a fine pink light on the horizon, a smokiness in the air. Dawn steals over them. Elfriede turns her face so she breathes nothing but the scent of her son's hair. Ahead, the schloss rises from the earth in shades of gray. A lamp illuminates the master's bedroom, and Elfriede experiences a shudder of fear for the abandoned Gerhard, though not regret. If her husband's died of fever during this past hour, she will never regret leaving him to die alone. Not when she's saved a son, their son.

Because servants wake before dawn, the lights also burn on the third floor. Which is the nursery? Elfriede isn't sure. She carries Johann up the steps to the terrace—he's now asleep, his body slack against hers—and makes for the French door, still ajar, just as a woman flies outside in a blur of white nightgown.

"Oh! Oh! What have you done?" she cries.

Elfriede answers coolly. "I might ask the same of you, Nurse. How did my son come to be wandering alone outside at night?"

Nurse comes up straight and indignant. "He's been very naughty. Now give him to me before you kill him, if you haven't already."

The woman holds out her arms. In the feeble light, Elfriede can't see her face, but she knows the shape of that head, the shade of those blond braids. Johann stirs and lifts his head. "Nurse!" he cries, stretching his hands toward hers. "I found my private!"

"Have you, now," Nurse says. She thrusts again with her outstretched arms. "Frau von Kleist. You must give him to me at once."

"I don't—"

"You must. Haven't you hurt him enough already?"

Fury seizes Elfriede. *The insolence!* she thinks. I ought to dismiss her on the spot, I ought to slap her, how dare she.

And yet. Isn't she perfectly correct? Isn't that why Elfriede's fury is so fierce? Nurse is right. Elfriede's crawling with germs. Possibly she has already transmitted the fatal bacterium to her child. And it's true, God knows, she's hurt Johann enough already. What boy can recover from a mother's abandonment? His arms reach to Nurse and he whimpers with longing.

Elfriede presses her lips to Johann's hair. "I'll see you again soon, my love," she says, and she hands him carefully into Nurse's arms. As she does, a puff of air strikes her nose, the scent of schnapps.

INSIDE THE HOUSE AGAIN. ELFRIEDE wastes no time leaping up the stairs—not for nothing has she walked the mountains of Switzerland for the past two years, three thousand meters of altitude—and down the corridor to Gerhard's bedroom. The lights are now ablaze. Her sister-in-law appears like a phantom in a dressing gown.

"Come at once," she snaps, and turns back into the room.

Elfriede, terrified but unrepentant, follows Ulrika into the master's bedroom. But Gerhard is not dead. The opposite. He's awake, the fever ebbs. He spies her in the doorway and lifts his head, calling her name like a man risen from the dead.

LULU

DECEMBER 1941
(The Bahamas)

WE ALL HAVE a dream, don't we? And I don't mean some dream for the future, some grand desire of the heart. I mean that dream that comes to you in the dark of night. I mean that dream that visits and revisits, unbidden, crawling out from your subconscious while you sleep, the one that knows exactly how to make you scream. Mine goes like this.

I'm in some cheap room in some clapboard house in some hot, dusty prairie town in the middle of America someplace, I don't know exactly where, and I need to catch the next train out. The only train out. The trouble is, I can't seem to leave the room. My fingers won't button my blouse. My clothes won't stay in my suitcase. My hairbrush, my toothbrush, my lipstick—they go missing, time and again, so I have to go looking, and I can't find them. The room gets smaller and hotter. The clock ticks faster. The train approaches. And while I'm making these agonizing preparations that must be done, cannot be done, I've got to move silently, create not the smallest noise, because a stranger's passed out drunk on the metal bed against the wall, and he's going to wake up any second, any second, any second, goddamn, somebody get me out of here, somebody drag me out of this room, this scene, this dream I *know* is a dream, goddamn, it's just a *dream* but I can't get out, can't wake, stuck here forever like a black fly in a jar, he's going to wake, any second, any second.

Thump, thump.

Mother Mary, no. Don't wake him up.

Thump, thump.

BE QUIET, FOR GOD'S SAKE, STOP THAT THUMPING, YOU'LL WAKE HIM UP!

Thump, thump. Dragging me outside myself, outside this sticky, dusty, terrible scene in my head. *Thump, thump.*

A voice. *Miss Lulu? Miss Lulu? You sleeping still?*

Eyes fly open. Small, white room. No prairie, no train, no stranger passed out drunk in a bed. Unless that stranger was me.

FROM THE REAR PATIO OF my little bungalow on Cable Beach, I sat and watched the Hog Island lighthouse rising from the turquoise sea, so white and tranquil that you simply couldn't believe the entire world was now at war.

I remember the patio was paved in this quaint mixture of crushed seashells and concrete. There's a name for it, I believe, but I've since forgotten. Never mind. I liked the way it felt on my bare feet, the way there was nothing like it back home, the way it connected me to the beach beyond. I liked the way I could sit in a round-backed garden chair of cunningly wrought metal, lean my elbows on the small wrought metal table, smoke my morning cigarette, drink my morning coffee, like the only customer in a Parisian café that didn't exist, while I stared out to sea and pondered things.

This particular morning, I'd been pondering whether I ought to have mentioned the trifling matter of the Japanese attack in my monthly column—the "Lady of Nassau," inside back cover, perhaps you've read it—in between the account of the Silver Slipper Ball and the speculative frenzy over the invitations to Nancy Oakes's coming-out party at the British Colonial Hotel.

It wasn't as if we'd ignored the whole shocking incident, the barbarous attack on American soil. My goodness, Miami lay only a hundred and eighty miles to the east, whereas London was over four thousand miles away. In general orientation, Bahamians were more American than most of New York City. But there was this turquoise sea, you understand, these palm trees and sea grapes, this heat and this somnolence. When they broadcast the news about Pearl Harbor on the radio, everybody at the Red Cross and the sailing club just exchanged a blank stare with his fellow man. Shook his head and said how awful it was. Two weeks later, nothing had materially changed, except that the Americans had mostly fled and the hotels stood half-empty and sort of forlorn. At a loss what to do, really, since Nassau has nothing if it hasn't got American tourists to tend to, then as now. Nassau was where you came to escape the war, and now the war had landed smack among us, like a Japanese bomb of unknown explosive power, yet to detonate. Did you acknowledge this thing? Or did you tiptoe around it, pretending it didn't exist? This was supposed to be paradise, for God's sake.

The door creaked behind me. Veryl appeared, coffeepot in hand. "Telegram come for you, Miss Lulu," she said.

"New York?"

"New York." She refilled my cup in a long, steady stream. When she was done, she reached inside the pocket of her apron and pulled out a yellow envelope, which she placed on the table next to the saucer. "You decide what you gwine wear for the party tonight?"

"Not yet."

"I be leaving at noon for the afternoon shift, remember. Can't press no dress if I got no dress to press."

"I'm thinking of the blue velvet."

Veryl made a sound like *Mmm, mmm,* which might equally have meant approval or displeasure. I never could tell, but I did know that Veryl's taste in clothing—unlike mine—was infallible. Her mother had been a dressmaker, she once said. Of her father, she said nothing, but I had the idea—I can't recall why, maybe one of Jack's tidbits—that he was a white man, a Bay Street merchant, which was not an uncommon state of affairs in the Bahamas in those days. Certainly it would explain Veryl's canniness in the ways of the world.

"You don't like it?" I said.

"Nobody wear velvet in Nassau, honey. That dress look like something somebody Boston grandmother wear."

I plucked the cigarette from the ashtray. "Then what do you suggest?"

"That red silk. It got that V, Miss Lulu, that show off you bosoms."

"Veryl! It's a debutante ball, for heaven's sake. Anyway, there's nobody there to appreciate my bosoms."

Again, the *Mmm, mmm*, but in an entirely different tone of voice. She lifted the corner of her apron and wiped an invisible smudge from the surface of the coffeepot.

"Well?" I demanded.

"I hear that French fellow back in Nassau."

I poured in the cream, the sugar. "He's not French, Veryl. He's from Mauritius."

"He talk French. He French."

"Regardless. *I* heard he was off the island until the New Year. Hunting ducks or something."

"No, ma'am. He in Nassau. He fly here on that Pan American yesterday."

"Then I guess he had a change of plans. But I don't see what it's got to do with me. Or my décolletage."

"Miss Lulu," said Veryl, the way you speak to a child, "you ain't getting no younger."

I lifted the cup and wrapped my fingers around the bowl. Veryl waited, arms folded. Behind her, the surf fell placidly on the sand of Cable Beach, making comfortable noises as it landed. A woman of great and several talents, that Veryl. She was a chambermaid at the Prince George and we'd gotten to know each other on a daily basis during my period of incarceration. When Alfred de Marigny drove me out to Cable Beach in a giant Lincoln Continental to visit his properties there—no more than a week, I believe, after I received a check for two hundred dollars from *Metropolitan* magazine for the first "Lady of Nassau" column—and offered me this sweet little bungalow at a rent that was practically peppercorn, Veryl asked if I might be needing a housekeeper. I said, *Perhaps.* Not because I thought I needed a housekeeper—God knows I'd gotten along without them before—but because I thought it was generally a good thing to have someone trustworthy by your side in a strange, complicated country like this one, someone who knew the shape of the landscape. Someone to tend your mysterious tropical flowers, someone to brew your coffee just right and iron out the creases in just about everything, then to throw in the advice gratis. *Perhaps,* I said. Veryl said, *Fine, boss-lady, I be working morning at you place and afternoon at the Prince George, Monday to Saturday, thirty shillings a week.* I said, *Deal.* So I was bound to accept her advice, wasn't I? Even on such intimate matters as my romantic affairs, or lack thereof. That was implicit in the terms of Veryl's employment. I set the coffee cup back in the saucer and fluffed my hair.

"These are modern times, Veryl. I've got my own career to look after."

"Career not making you warm at night. Career not giving you no babies."

"I don't want babies, and the nights are warm enough already. Anyway, Freddie's a dear, but I'm simply not interested in him that way."

Veryl leaned forward. "I hear that Oakes girl got she own eye on that French fellow."

"*Nancy?* And *Freddie?*" I laughed. "Veryl, Nancy Oakes is seventeen years old. She's still in school. She's at the lycée in New York City, for God's sake. And he's not French."

"You meet this girl?"

"Just briefly."

"She pretty, ain't she?"

"Pretty enough, if you like that kind of pretty. But she's a child."

"She no child, Miss Lulu. She know what she want. She be wanting a big, strapping boss-man who take no sass from she father. And that Miss Nancy, she get what she want, just watch." Veryl swept up the coffeepot and turned for the door. "You wear you *red* dress, Miss Lulu. Veryl said so."

NOW, LET ME MAKE SOMETHING clear about the nature of my business arrangement with S. Barnard Lightfoot. I think it's important. Several months ago, when I sat before Lightfoot's desk in my best dress—such as it was—begging for a job, he had given me a piece of advice. Listen up, now.

It was the second Monday of June, and eleven stories below us, a few thousand sweating shoppers pullulated along the sidewalks of Madison Avenue. Inside Lightfoot's office, all was calm. A masculine sanctuary of dimpled leather chairs and trays of amber liquor, of wood the exact color and shine of maple syrup, an entire damned spectrum of brown. Except his suit, which was charcoal gray and pinstriped. Lightfoot lit a cigar, gave off a fulsome puff or two, and told me the *Metropolitan*'s Havana correspondent had been covering events in the Bahamas just fine, what could I possibly have to offer? I leaned forward and said there had to be something fishy going on, for God's sake, couldn't you just smell it. Everybody knew the Windsors had a soft spot for Hitler; everybody knew Wallis hated her in-laws like poison, and the venom was mutual; everybody knew that whatever differences in temperament existed between the royal couple, whatever mismatch in intellect or upbringing or what have you, they held this in common: they'd both sell their souls for a chest of gold doubloons. Besides all *that*. A Southern lady inhabiting the governor's mansion of a British colony that was eighty-five percent Negro—wasn't that rich, wasn't there bound to be trouble?

And what did the dear old fellow say to that? He laughed, that's what. Laughed around the corner of his cigar at me. Leaned back in his plush chair and explained that *Metropolitan* readers weren't interested in any of that, weren't interested in politics or war or the Negro problem. For these things, they might consult the *New York Times* over a pot of morning coffee. No. From the *Metropolitan*, consumed in the *après-midi* over a gin and tonic or a nice dry sherry, they wanted gossip, they wanted scandal— elegantly presented, of course, tied together with a bow of silken wit— not dreary things like death and poverty and the tragedy of color. (Here he took his cigar out of his mouth and paused to contemplate the sleek white ceiling, the curl of blue smoke drifting toward same.) Now. On the other hand. If I could charm my way into the beating heart of the matter, if I could discover a few tender tidbits, say, an intimate royal secret or two, and render them into the kind of sophisticated prose that sent delight shivering down the *Metropolitan* reader's superior spine . . . well then. For such a column, presented monthly, the *Metropolitan* might be willing to pay as much as two hundred dollars, plus expenses.

Having consumed nothing in the past twelve hours except a cup of coffee and a stale roll of brown bread, I thought perhaps I hadn't heard him correctly. I began at a squeak, cleared throat, proceeded in husky drawl: *Two hundred dollars?*

Lightfoot tapped the end of his cigar in an ashtray and said, *Plus expenses.*

I clenched my hands together in my threadbare lap and said, *Done*.

Lightfoot then stretched his pinstriped arm to the intercom box on his desk and pressed the button for his secretary. Miss Brown would arrange everything, he said, airplane ticket and expense account, perhaps a small advance—here he passed a disdainful glance over my costume—for a tropical wardrobe. I rose from the chair and said thanks. He rose too and actually troubled himself to travel around the desk and plant a damp, cigar-infused kiss on my cheek, interestingly close to the corner of my mouth. For an instant, I caught the smell of his hair oil. He pulled back, and his two hands captured one of mine, and his brow settled down atop his blue eyes. Lightfoot was then sixty-two years old, and possessed but five more in his allotted share before a mighty stroke was due to topple him (inside the bathtub or his mistress's bed, depending on whom you asked, and my money's on the mistress) but on that June day in 1941, he could still stare you right down to the carpet, by God, make you feel the full weight of his parting words:

But no politics, Lulu. Politicians, naturally, but no politics.

NOW, A HALF YEAR LATER, his advice had lost none of its weight. I finished my coffee, stubbed out my cigarette, stared at the yellow envelope tucked beneath the saucer. The sun climbed higher in the sky. Even in December, when the soupy heat of midsummer had long since eased, the Nassau sunshine bathed you in a peculiar soporific warmth I have never experienced elsewhere. Just you and that sunshine, drenching your bones, while you stare at a yellow Western Union envelope that must be opened, sooner or later. The latest Lightfoot salvo.

I tugged the envelope free and opened it.

As I said, after consideration, I'd crossed out any mention of Japanese infamy from my December "Lady of Nassau" column, even though the duke and duchess had talked of nothing else at a Government House dinner party on December the eighth. (I still have the invitation card somewhere.) I mean, the Nazi invasion of Poland was one thing. But a dastardly sneak attack by wicked Orientals on an English-speaking people! I remember the duke just about spat with rage. *The damned yellow disease is spreading right across the Pacific*, he said. *By God, I'd like to bomb those bloody Nipponese hoards myself.* The fury in his voice was enough to boil the vintage claret in our glasses. The next morning, I sat before my typewriter and painted the scene just as you see above, just exactly as I remembered it. Because why? Because it was so singular, you know. No act of Nazi barbarity had ever inspired that kind of outrage from the Duke of Windsor, at least in my experience. You got the distinct impression that the Jews had had it coming, rather, what with their cunning attempts to control the world's financial markets. So why this opprobrium for the Japanese? I just thought it was interesting, that's all. An interesting conversation around a dinner table, perfectly suitable for the Lady of Nassau to report to her readers. I stared at the brutal words, the elegant paragraph, pencil between my teeth.

Then I unscrolled the paper from the cylinder, crumpled it, and started again.

And now? One week later, S. Barnard Lightfoot, having received said column—Japanese infamy carefully redacted—had fired off one of his telegrams. He had an opinion, it seemed. Lightfoot never went to the trouble and expense of cabling someone unless he had a particular opinion to express.

I extracted the slip of paper from the envelope and held it in the air, between me and the turquoise sea.

FINE EFFORT STOP DAMN WELL BETTER WRITE
ACCOUNT OAKES BALL NEXT COLUMN OR ELSE=
=*S. B. LIGHTFOOT*

GIVEN THE CIRCUMSTANCES, I SUPPOSE I should have noticed the approach of the fellow around the corner of the house, but I didn't. I checked my watch and stuffed the telegram back in its envelope. I was due at the Red Cross headquarters at ten o'clock to count the takings from the Christmas bazaar, and my bungalow lay three miles from town along West Bay Street, which meant I had only a quarter hour to swim before duty called. I rose from my chair to untie the belt at the waist of my kimono, and then, and *only* then, did I see the man planted on the paving stones before me, wearing the curious felt fedora—who in God's name wore a felt fedora in the Bahamas, even in December?—and the expression of fearsome determination.

"Who the devil are you?" I exclaimed.

He was short, portly, middle-aged, dignified. He wore a suit of light-weight navy wool, almost like a uniform except it wasn't. He straightened his shoulders at me. "I beg your pardon. I was looking for Mrs. Randolph."

"I'm Mrs. Randolph. And you're intruding."

"Ah. Yes. I apologize. There was no answer at the front door."

"That usually means you should return at a more convenient hour."

"I'm afraid it's urgent."

"Urgent, is it?"

"Quite."

I stood there in my silk kimono, sizing his shoulders and his sharp, panicky expression, which reminded me more of a rabbit than the fox giving chase. Or maybe that was because of his ears, which burst from the sides of his head at dramatic angles. And his eyes, a wide-open silver behind a pair of thick round spectacles. The air surrounding him smelled of cigars. Where the devil was Veryl?

"May I ask your name?" I said.

The man's gaze shifted briefly to the door behind me. "Smith," he said. He reached inside his jacket pocket, and I confess I dropped the ties of my kimono and readied myself for a scene from one of those detective films. But his hand, when it emerged, contained only a small manila envelope, of the kind they used in offices.

"For me?" I said.

He nodded and urged the envelope forward, though he didn't approach any closer. It was for me to take that step toward him, around the edge of the round table, to extend my hand and extract the envelope from his thick fingers. The flap was sealed shut. No direction on the back, no mark of any kind.

"Couldn't you have just put it through the mail slot?" I said.

He shook his head. "I'm afraid not. You see, I was instructed to place that envelope in your hands *personally*."

"In *my* hands? Why?"

"You're Mrs. Randolph, aren't you? Mrs. Leonora Randolph?"

"So they call me, yes."

"Well, somebody wants to make sure you get that." He nodded to the envelope. "It's sensitive information, see?"

"Oh! Oh, I see. Sensitive information. How thrilling. Let me think. Shall I disguise the names in my next column, or do you want the sinners shamed before the world?"

Smith's eyebrows went up. He was already on the point of leaving, had already pivoted his shoulders in the direction of the frangipani in a gesture of extreme haste. "Column?" he said.

"That's what it's for, isn't it? 'Lady of Nassau'?"

Throughout this little interview, Mr. Smith's hat—as I said, a neat gray fedora of the kind you saw everywhere in New York City, but less commonly here in the tropics—had remained firmly on his head. If you'd asked me his hair color, in some police interview, maybe, or perhaps over cocktails at the Prince George, I wouldn't have been able to tell you. Brown, probably. Anyway, he tugged the brim now, all impatience, ready to bolt. "I haven't the foggiest idea what you're talking about, ma'am," he said. "I'm here to deliver an envelope, that's all."

"From whom?" I asked.

But he wasn't listening. He'd strode across the paving stones and around the right-hand frangipani shrub, out of sight, presumably toward the road at the front of the house, and though I started forward to chase him down, I checked myself the next instant. After all, what was the point? The envelope, *that* was the point. I raised it to my nose and sniffed. I don't know what I was looking for. Somebody's perfume, maybe, some lingering hint of the sender's identity. There was nothing, the smell of paper, a blank canvas.

I sat back in my chair, drew a hairpin from the knot at the back of my head, inserted it carefully at the envelope's seam and sliced.

A rare cloud passed before the sun as I reached inside the envelope and pulled the contents free. Or maybe it's just a trick of memory, maybe I only imagined that my patio darkened a degree or two as I sat there in my garden chair and stared at the instructions written in block letters on the back of the sealed packet before me.

FOR DELIVERY D/D WINDSOR ONLY, it said.

And beneath that, underlined, <u>CONFIDENTIAL</u>.

I rose, changed into my Red Cross uniform, noted Veryl busy in the kitchen, and slipped silently out the door. Well, I was due at headquarters at ten o'clock, wasn't I? You couldn't let a little thing like a clandestine envelope keep you from your patriotic duty.

DID I MENTION IT WAS Christmas Eve? I don't remember. Well, you can't blame me. For one thing, there was this business of the intruder on my patio. For another, it didn't seem like Christmas, what with the sunshine and the palm trees and all that, the straw hats and the bare arms.

Still, the approach of Christmas did not stay the Red Cross ladies from their appointed rounds, oh no. The headquarters had been festooned with wreaths and garlands and all those things—not genuine pine, mind you, because you couldn't import such things in wartime, just the tinsel kind—to say nothing of Christmas cards and bows and apple-cheeked pictures of Father Christmas, of ringing bells and incessant carols and a general Christmas keening in the air, if you know what I mean, such that you could just about smell the sugar cookies and the balsam that didn't exist. But parcels must still be packed, and bandages rolled, and socks knit, and besides all *that*, Miss Nancy Oakes herself was about to make her society debut, and if you weren't inside the walls of the British Colonial Hotel this evening, celebrating the coming of age of the richest girl in the British Empire, give or take a few shillings—why, you weren't anywhere.

For four whole hours, wrapping up the remaining presents for the poor children of Nassau—of which there were plenty, believe me—the ladies could talk of nothing else. What they would be wearing, what Miss Oakes would be wearing, did you hear the Count de Marigny had agreed to be her escort? It was true! She'd walked right up to him at the Prince George bar two weeks ago and asked him herself, a man almost twice her age, already divorced, a notorious playboy and sex maniac. Everybody knew the sordid circumstances of his marriage, how he'd seduced the wife of his friend, how she fell madly in love with him and went to Reno for a quickie divorce, how she couldn't keep up with de Marigny's boundless sexual appetites and left him a few years later. The ladies agreed that Sir Harry and Lady Oakes should really put a stop to it. But Miss Oakes was so very headstrong.

At two o'clock, the last toy truck was sealed up. Mrs. Gudewill was going to deliver them to Government House in her Buick. I tucked my hair back into my Red Cross cap and volunteered to help.

IN THE MIDDLE OF THE afternoon, struck on all sides by the glare of the Bahamian sun, Government House was a different creature, not nearly so formal. Smudged pink and a bit tired, like a confection left outside. The sun burned the tips of the palm trees and the windscreen of Mrs. Gudewill's automobile as it trundled up the drive to the west entrance. She kept up a friendly chatter as we went. She simply had to confess, she didn't think much of the duchess before all this, did I?

I said I hadn't really thought much on the matter. Royalty was never an interest of mine.

"Oh. Well, as I said, I always thought—and you mustn't ever repeat this, Mrs. Randolph—between the two of us, I always thought she was a bit of an *adventuress*." Mrs. Gudewill giggled nervously. Like the Oakeses, she was Canadian, a wealthy widow. She had two daughters, and the younger, a beautiful redhead named Marie, was rumored to be engaged, or pretty nearly engaged, to marry none other than the Baron George af Trolle, personal secretary to Axel Wenner-Gren. A terrific catch for Marie, don't you think? Exactly the reason you bring your gorgeous redheaded daughter to a place like Nassau. Anyway, Marie was thick as thieves with Nancy Oakes, also a redhead, so you see Mrs. Gudewill had authority to speak on pretty much anything, and I was happy to let her do it. Part of my job, to let people rattle on indiscreetly.

"Really? An adventuress?"

"Well, that was before I *knew* her, you know. Now I've seen all the good she does around here, how hard she works. And you can't deny the love they have for each other."

"No, indeed," I said. "It just touches the heart."

The windows were open, and as I rested my elbow on the doorframe, I thought I tasted the humid, golden, salty scent of summer. In New York, the air would taste of garbage and car exhaust, would slosh with coal smoke and sleet. We slowed to a halt before the gate at the west entrance. A guard stepped from the booth.

She poked her head out the window. "Good afternoon! Mrs. Gudewill and Mrs. Randolph. We're delivering the Christmas parcels from the Red Cross."

He glanced down at his metal clipboard. "Of course. Straight on through. You know the way, don't you?"

"Naturally."

We drove through the gates and stopped outside the portico, where a dull green motorcycle sat next to the curb, sidecar attached. As we rolled to a stop, a tall spindly man emerged from the door, exchanged a jaunty salute with the guard, and climbed aboard the motorcycle. The sun glinted briefly on his hair before he slid a leather helmet on his head, a pair of goggles over his eyes. I swallowed my heart. Mrs. Gudewill set the brake. "Why, isn't that Mr. Thorpe?" she said.

"Mr. Thorpe?"

"Yes, I'm sure it is. He must have been visiting the duke. *Well.* Come along. I've got a hairdresser appointment in an hour! You *are* going to the party tonight, Mrs. Randolph?"

"Wouldn't miss it for diamonds," I said.

By now, the guards and the footmen and Marshall the butler all knew me pretty well. Marshall scooped up an armful of presents and escorted us down the hall to the drawing room, where the duchess usually received me on the sofa near the fireplace, impeccably groomed, chaperoned by her private secretary, Miss Drewes, and her own enormous image above the mantel. There would be tea, and we would chitchat. I'll say no more. Today, of course, that mantel was dressed in holly, and the duchess wore a festive dress of crimson. Miss Drewes sat on the chair at her right, pencil poised.

"Why, good afternoon, ladies," said the duchess.

I perceived a trace of agitation at my side. Mrs. Gudewill, who must have been forty-five or fifty—a solid, dependable matron resembling a chintz cushion—sort of fluttered, at least so much as you *could* flutter while carrying an armload of Christmas presents.

"Good afternoon, Your Highness!" she trilled.

"Good afternoon, Duchess," I said. "Shall we just deposit these under the tree?"

"Oh, yes. Thanks *ever* so much," said the duchess, not so much as flinching from her position on the sofa.

We carried our burden in the direction of the Douglas fir—naturally, a genuine Douglas fir for Government House, and hang the expense—that stood a dozen feet tall in the corner of the room, all decked in tinsel and candles. I followed Mrs. Gudewill, and last came Marshall in his white gloves.

"Just scattered around the bottom here?" said Mrs. Gudewill.

"That will do," said the duchess.

Together we placed the presents in their thin, cheap, colorful paper atop the skirt of scarlet velvet that surrounded the base of the Christmas tree. The poor thing had already dropped a layer of needles, didn't like the climate at all. I rose and brushed my hands.

The duchess called out, "You've just missed our friend Thorpe, Mrs. Randolph. Popped by for a visit."

"We saw him on his motorcycle!" said Mrs. Gudewill. "Just leaving!"

"It's a funny thing, how you always just miss him."

"Funny, isn't it?" I said.

"But then he's constantly in and out," said the duchess.

Miss Drewes piped up. "He turned up at that tennis tournament last month, didn't he? At the British Colonial."

"I don't recall," I said. "Did he?"

The duchess laughed. "Yes, he did. I believe I caught him looking your way a hundred times, poor fellow."

There was a dainty pause. A clink of somebody's cup into somebody's saucer. Mrs. Gudewill turned back to the tree and made some admiring noises.

"Duchess," I said, fingering my pocketbook, "while I'm here. Perhaps you could spare a moment for a private matter? If it's convenient, of course."

The Duchess of Windsor met my gaze over the back of the sofa. "Of course. Miss Drewes, would you mind showing Mrs. Gudewill to her car?"

Miss Drewes rose. "Not at all."

NOW, LET ME MAKE SOMETHING clear, before I explain what happened next. You could fault the duchess for any number of defects—we all have our defects, remember—but you couldn't claim she shirked her duties as the wife of the governor of the Bahamas.

"*They* think I'm nothing but a clotheshorse," she told me, as we cruised to Cat Island aboard the *Gemini*, a few weeks after our first productive little chat in the library of Government House. "*They* think I'm some kind of lazy, frivolous socialite. Dinner parties and ocean cruises. And *nothing* could be further from the truth, Lulu."

I remember gazing at her against her tableau of pillows on the sofa— we sat inside the deckhouse, because of the draft—and recalling a certain dinner party the night before, at the home of Fred Sigrist and his wife. The Oakeses were there, and Harold Christie and his brother Frank, and yours truly, and a warm breeze off the ocean, and plenty of wine and brandy, palm trees and sea grapes and tranquility, such that you would hardly have known there was a war on at all, over on the other side of the world, where *they* existed under gloom of German bombers and English weather. Of course, there was no need to ask Wallis who *they* were. She meant David's family, her nemesis, those wicked, cold-blooded, implacable snobs, hypocrites all, determined always to cast her—Wallis—in

the worst possible light, when *nothing could be further from the truth, Lulu.*
Behind her, the ocean shimmered under the sun.

"Nothing at all," I said.

"I simply couldn't believe my eyes when we began to tour about. The
poverty! It's heartbreaking, worse than anything I saw in China. And
no one was doing a thing to help. I remember visiting a woman in her
hut on one of the Out Islands—I don't remember which one, it doesn't
matter—dirt floor, surrounded by children in rags, their bellies all swollen, another baby on the way, and she wasn't any more concerned about
the coming event than a . . . a cat might be concerned about an impending litter." Wallis shook her head. "And that's when I conceived the idea
of a maternity clinic. To *help*, you know. To help these poor creatures
take care of their young."

"And to think the newspapers report nothing but the number of
steamer trunks in your retinue."

"Oh, it's no surprise, really. That's what *they* want the rest of the world
to think of me. Those newspapers, they all have their instructions, believe me." She turned to look out one of the portholes. What a profile she
had. That strong jaw, that sharp, large nose. "It doesn't matter. As long
as I've made a difference, that's what matters. I don't care if nobody hears
about it, not a single soul. My own conscience is clear."

"I'm sure you've done a lot of good."

"You'll see. You have to roll up your sleeves, you know, you have to
weigh those babies yourself, change those napkins, feed them their bottles. You have to show these natives how to do it all properly."

I opened my mouth to ask how Wallis herself had learned to do it all
properly, not having children of her own, but at the last instant I swallowed the question and glanced down to my stenographer's notebook
and scribbled something, I don't remember what.

"It's all so primitive," she went on. "And in this modern age. They
nurse the babies themselves, like animals. No notion of proper infant

nutrition. The first thing I did, I rang up Johnson and Johnson and made them donate cans of milk. Thousands and thousands of cans we've distributed among the Out Islanders. It's done so much good. Of course, if the United States gets dragged into this damned war, they'll have to stop."

"You mean the milk? Johnson and Johnson?"

"All of it. Milk, diaper cloths, everything." Her eyes narrowed, and I remember thinking she must be concentrating deeply on something, maybe the possible new sources of supplies, some alternative means of getting milk and diapers to the native mothers of the Bahamas. I sat and watched her, pen poised.

After some time, she turned to me and pointed her finger at the leather bag containing my Kodak 35.

"Be sure you get a few good photographs," she said. "A picture says a thousand words."

Which I did, of course, and if you happen to come across that particular copy of *Metropolitan* magazine, the October 1941 issue, you'll find two photographs of Wallis illustrating the "Lady of Nassau" column on the inside back cover. The first and larger one shows her dressed to the nines in a constellation of jewels and a Mainbocher gown the color of fresh cream, dancing with HRH at some charity ball or another. In the second one, she's wearing her Red Cross uniform and an expression of deep compassion, as she hands a box of canned milk to a grateful Negro mother on Cat Island.

THERE HAD BEEN SEVERAL MORE cruises since, to say nothing of the mornings spent packing parcels and rolling bandages at the Red Cross, the afternoons at the duchess's maternity clinic in Grants Town, part of the Negro district they called Over-the-Hill. Now it was Christmas, another whirl of charity. She worked tirelessly at her causes, the Duchess of

Windsor. She was like a lioness on the hunt. Those presents beneath her tree were only the latest kill.

Together, we listened to the footsteps of Mrs. Gudewill and Miss Drewes clattering down the hallway. She still sat on the sofa, and her back was wonderfully straight, like a board, so that she only had to swivel her long neck and point her square jaw upward. She leaned her elbow on the sofa back and smiled at me. "Come sit. I have a little something for you too."

I positioned myself exactly where Miss Drewes had been. When I sat, the warmth of my predecessor seeped through the cushions into the backs of my legs. The duchess's perfume floated free. I think it was Chanel. She reached for the bell on the table and asked if I wanted fresh coffee.

"Coffee's lovely, thank you."

"Have you brought your column?"

I opened my pocketbook. "Right here. A busy month, wasn't it?"

"Oh, it was awful." She opened the drawer in the lamp table and took out her spectacles. Not everybody knew that the duchess wore readers, but I did. I had her trust, you see. She slipped them over her ears and took the typewritten page from me. When the butler arrived, he was already carrying the coffee service. He set the tray before us, piled the tea things on the existing tray, bore it all away while the duchess's eyes went back and forth, back and forth like the typewriter itself, examining each word. I poured the coffee. Considered crossing the room to the crystal decanters on their own tray, another silver tray, the place was lousy with them, but there were only so many liberties the duchess would allow, and you had to count them carefully to make sure you didn't exceed your allotment. So I added cream instead, precious cream and precious sugar, and sipped my coffee as I waited for her to finish.

"Very nice." She unhooked her spectacles and smiled at me. "Especially that bit about the bazaar. Next month you'll have an account of the Christmas gifts, won't you? Giving them away to the slum children? Poor lambs."

"Of course."

She handed me the column, which I tucked back into my pocketbook. The portico protected the room from the sunshine, and the air was cool, a relief after the unusual heat outdoors. Still, a trickle of perspiration made its way down my spine. The duchess ignored the coffee service and folded her hands on her lap. "We've worked so hard," she said. "I'm awfully proud of this Red Cross business. Between that and the clinics, my God, they can't say I haven't done my bit."

"A maternity clinic is such an ideal cause."

"Brilliant, isn't it? Of course it's desperately needed. They breed like rabbits, you know, and show about as much care for their infants."

My hands enclosed my pocketbook. I stared at her thin red lips.

"Was there anything else?" she said.

There was an expectant look on her face, around her eyebrows, which were groomed into high, thin arches that suggested perpetual interest. I thought maybe she'd heard the crackle of the envelope inside the pocketbook. I heard her voice in my head. *They breed like rabbits.*

"No," I said. "Nothing else."

"Very well, then. Let's— Oh, my darlings!"

A familiar yipping sounded from the doorway. The duchess's face lit like the Christmas tree in the corner. She held out her long, bony arms like a mother receiving a beloved child. Into those arms leapt Preezie and Pookie, panting and licking and wriggling, terrier coats as glossy as the duchess's own coiffure, festive red bows tied around their necks. Detto settled himself at her feet, looking soulful. The duke followed, although he stopped short of his wife's arms and merely stuck his hands in his pockets and grinned at the sight before him, the scene of mutual worship.

"You see," he said, "you see, Mrs. Randolph, if only the damned papers would show them this. Did you ever see such affection?"

"Hardly ever," I said. "Good morning, Your Highness. Merry Christmas."

"Yes, yes. Happy Christmas. Fine day, eh?"

"The cake, David, darling. Get me a piece of cake."

The duke bent forward and plucked a generous wedge of rum cake from the plate on the coffee tray. The duchess snatched it from his fingers and broke it in two. In her lap, the dogs went wild. "Be patient, darlings," she said, laughing, and the darlings went still, didn't they, except for the furious wagging of their identical tails, while they received their Christmas rum cake from the fingers of the Duchess of Windsor, just like your dog at home.

"Aren't they precious," said the duchess, in her throatiest voice.

"Aren't they," I said.

"It's just because it's Christmas. Ordinarily we're very strict."

"Very strict," said the duke.

"Poor darlings, they've had such a time of it. This awful, awful war."

"At least they're out of danger, aren't they? A long way from Europe."

She buried her face in the silky pillow behind Preezie's ear. "Yes, thank God. I only wish it were over, don't you? One way or another, so we can get on with our lives, so we can settle somewhere, and David can take on a more suitable job. Governor of Australia, perhaps, that's proper work for a man of his training. Don't you wish that? Just that it were *over*."

"Preferably by victory, of course."

"Oh, of course," said the duke. "Naturally one longs for victory."

The dogs, having finished their snack, now leapt back onto the rug and covered the duke's shoes. "David, since you're here," said the duchess.

"What, my darling?"

"Shall we give Lulu her present?"

"Oh! Yes, yes."

"My goodness, it's hardly—I wasn't expecting—"

"Of course you weren't. But we wanted to give you something, a little token. David, go fetch Lulu's present from under the tree. We're so awfully grateful, you know."

"Awfully grateful," said the duke. Obedient as ever, he had gone to the tree, dogs at his heels, and bent to rummage out a small wrapped box from the bounty beneath. I stared at his pinstriped back, his immaculate shoulders, his shiny gold hair, and thought, as I occasionally did, *My God, he was the king of England.*

The duchess watched him return. "It's just a token, of course."

"There's really no need at all—"

"Now, now. Not another word. David and I, there's nothing we admire so much as loyalty, Lulu, and you've been so loyal, such a good friend to us." She took the box from her husband's hand. "And I want you to know how much that means to us, in our humble little way, stuck as we are out here like this."

"You're too kind. I've done my job, that's all. Just earning a living."

She placed the gift in my hands. "We both know it's so much more than that."

The box was heavier than it looked, wrapped in green foil paper. The tag read *To Lulu, Merry Christmas from the Windsors*, the same way you might write *Merry Christmas from the Browns*, except in Wallis's elegant handwriting that no mere Mrs. Brown could possibly duplicate. I untied the bow and the paper fell apart, revealing a plain red box stamped CARTIER.

"Open it," said the duchess.

I lifted the lid, and I'll be damned if a pair of sapphire earrings didn't glitter there in a pavé diamond setting, all nestled in velvet. I remember gasping. I don't think I said an actual word. One of the dogs nipped my ankle, and I didn't even flinch.

Wallis set her hand on my knee.

"As I said. There's nothing we admire so much as loyalty."

YOU KNOW, IT'S A FUNNY word, *loyalty*. Loyalty to what? And why? And especially how, that's the kicker. It seems to me that loyalty requires a suspension of logic, of truth even. Like faith, like superstition, a thing you cling to in defiance of what lies before you in plain sight. On the other hand—like faith or superstition, like love itself—where's the comfort in a world without it? We human beings possess a marvelous capacity to fool ourselves—oh, not me, never *me*, you tell yourself, but believe me, sweetheart, *you do*—and in the course of the six months, earning a salary of my very own, hobnobbing with the haute, I had fallen into a certain fatal habit of mine, for the second time in my life, a weakness perhaps born of certain circumstances in my childhood. I mean, isn't that supposed to be the case? The circumstances of your childhood determine your character, the entire course of your future, your fate, your destiny, all of it. You are just a mere slave to your subconscious.

Anyway, the sight of those earrings. The weight of them, the twinkle. I didn't know whether to cry or vomit or run. In the end, I set the box on the cushion beside me and opened the clasp of my pocketbook.

"I nearly forgot, in all the excitement," I said. "Someone stopped by the bungalow with a special delivery."

ELFRIEDE

NOVEMBER 1900
(Germany)

A LETTER ARRIVES for Elfriede, postmarked London. She notices the edge of the envelope, the unfamiliar stamp half-hidden by a napkin, while she's pouring the coffee. Maybe her heart doesn't quite stop. But her fingers go limp, and the pot, the pot, the beautiful porcelain coffee-pot slips from her hand to land in an awful crash on the silver breakfast tray. Nothing breaks, thank goodness. Only a splash of coffee on her dress. She lifts the napkin and dabs. Reads the name now fully exposed on the envelope—hers, written in firm black handwriting, *Frau Baroness von Kleist*, and beneath it *Schloss Kleist, Westphalia, Deutschland*—and the lettering around the postmark circle. LON and the date, 2 NOV 1900, two days ago. Her fingers shake. She sets down the napkin, hiding the envelope once more.

A month has passed since Gerhard's fever broke. There have been setbacks. Relapses. But like a mountain trail, his recovery trends inexorably upward, toward some summit on which he will inhabit his old, strong self. A fortnight ago, he felt well enough to rise from his bed and manage a few steps around the bedroom, supported by his valet. Now he bathes and dresses and walks in determined laps around the upper floor. Yesterday he descended the stairs, on Elfriede's steadying arm, and spent an hour in his study. Today, the weather's improved, and Elfriede has ordered the open landau for eleven o'clock, so she and Gerhard, together with Johann and Nurse, will ride about the estate. The fresh air and wholesome sunshine will do everyone some good. And this is all as it should be. Gerhard's recovery is a sign from God, after all, a deliverance from evil. *Yea, so the penitent shall return to her husband, and he shall be saved, and she shall covet no more neighbors, she shall harbor no more sinful love, she shall do him no evil the rest of her days, amen.*

No, she doesn't think about Wilfred. Her days are busy. Her discipline is taut. The door of her mind is shut tight against ginger hair and wide smiles and gangly limbs. But she hasn't forgotten him. He's there like a ghost, like the air, invisible, unconscious, life-giving, there.

Now here. Under the napkin beneath her fingertips. She tries again to pour her coffee, and this time, though the stream wavers as it falls into her cup, she succeeds. She sips the coffee and lifts the cover from her toast. The sunshine spills through her bedroom window, warming the back of her neck. She sleeps in the bedroom suite next to Gerhard's, the bedroom that used to belong to Gerhard's mother. When Elfriede was a newlywed, she used this room only to dress and bathe, sometimes to write letters at the escritoire near one of the tall sash windows overlooking the gardens. Once Johann was born, she moved her sleeping quarters here so the baby wouldn't disturb his father during those nighttime feedings. A temporary measure, as she thought. Three years later, she's returned and thinks she ought to have the curtains replaced, the bed hangings redone in a lighter fabric. The worn tapestry rug replaced with something softer. Decent, modern plumbing installed in the bathroom.

On the other side of the wall, Gerhard's valet bathes and dresses his master. Elfriede hears their voices, though she can't make out the words—Gerhard's gruff baritone, the valet's soothing tenor. In that first year of marriage, honeymoon followed by pregnancy, Gerhard used to rise much earlier, six o'clock or even five, while Elfriede lingered abed until the maid arrived with her chocolate at eight. Now their roles are reversed. Elfriede's up at six, bathed and dressed by six forty-five, upstairs in the nursery at seven, downstairs for her breakfast tray at eight, just as Gerhard wakes and rises from his own bed. These are Herr Doktor Rosenblatt's instructions, by the way. Gerhard's an invalid who needs his rest. At nine o'clock, Elfriede will knock on his door with a breakfast tray. She likes to do this herself, to pour his coffee and butter his toast, to read to him from the newspaper because his eyes are still weak. It's the least she can do.

From the other side of the wall comes a thick laugh. Elfriede swallows her toast and looks at the clock on the mantel. Eight thirty-two. Drinks her coffee. Knocks the top from the egg in its porcelain cup. She can't taste a thing, but she goes on eating anyway. Later, she won't remember any of this. Won't remember a single bite of that breakfast, although she eats it all, every crumb, every drop, egg and toast and fruit, cold ham, coffee with milk. When there's nothing left, she looks again at the clock—eight forty-eight—and wipes her fingers on the napkin before she picks up the letter from the corner of the tray.

AND WHAT ABOUT ELFRIEDE'S PARENTS, by the way? What about her sister who stood bridesmaid, and her two brothers with their families? Why haven't they offered her any support against the united von Kleist will? Elfriede's always supposed they're ashamed of her. But maybe it's more complicated than that.

Think of the wedding feast. The Hofmeisters lined up along one side of the table, wearing their best, nails clean, hair arranged, garnets instead of rubies, small freshwater pearls instead of South Sea pebbles, tiny respectable diamonds, nervous and polite. Then the von Kleists, whose forebears built Schloss Kleist, whose forebears' forebears built the castle that had existed before it, and so on and so forth, whose clothing betrayed no particular effort, whose jewels came from vaults instead of jewelry shops. Elfriede still remembers the pain with which she gazed down that long, polished table and found her mother's white face, frozen in mortification, across from Helga's face, frozen in distaste. Probably there was some error to do with a spoon. Next to Elfriede, Gerhard was speaking to the man on his left, a grand duke who had traveled from St. Petersburg for the wedding. On Elfriede's right sat the grand duchess, who was English and spoke no German, and whose expression of cynical amusement cut more deeply than Helga's distaste. (But remember now, Elfriede didn't cry until later that evening.)

Anyway, Elfriede's mother died of pneumonia just before Christmas that year, and Elfriede was never that close to her sister, five years older, who soon married a businessman and moved to Berlin. Her father came to visit after Johann was born, but the climate of the house—Elfriede's nervous disorder, the disdain of Helga and Ulrika, the stiffness of Gerhard—seemed to bewilder him, and he's never returned. Her brothers are busy with their own families and businesses. Elfriede, by far the youngest, the baby, the afterthought, sometimes feels like a boat cut adrift to find its own shore.

STILL, SHE THINKS OF HER family often, and she thinks of them now as she holds this letter in her hand. She thinks of the last time she saw her mother, at the beginning of December, when Elfriede had been married for five months and the fatal pneumonia was just a slight cough, nothing to worry about. Naturally her mother was delighted by the news of Elfriede's pregnancy. Full of advice that Elfriede ignored and no longer remembers. (Sometimes, Elfriede wonders whether she should have taken note of her mother's strictures, and maybe then she would have avoided all the misery that followed. Oh well.) They sat in a cozy music room in the eastern wing, Elfriede's favorite part of the house, where she used to play the piano for hours and hours while Gerhard attended to business in his study. They drank coffee and ate cake, and nobody disturbed them. Elfriede's mother kept gazing in rapture at her daughter's belly, as if unable to believe that a grandchild existed therein. The conversation moved from advice to trivia, gossip and weather and so on, and Elfriede remembers thinking that her mother betrayed a certain nervous animation, unusual to her.

When the time at last wore away, Frau Hofmeister brushed away the crumbs and prepared to leave, as you might expect. Then she paused, frowned, sat back down and told Elfriede that she was not her father's child, that Elfriede had been conceived during a cure along the Baltic seaside nineteen years ago while Elfriede's father stayed home to tend the business. She met a beautiful Danish student, an artist who was staying also at the hotel, and one day he forced her—well, urged her—well, coaxed her—into his room, no, not his room, they were taking a walk together and—my God, he was so beautiful, so soulful—what could she do? It was just the one time—well, maybe more than that—maybe a dozen times, maybe most of August, it was like a dream—but it wasn't Elfriede's mother's fault, it was fate, it was God's will, and Elfriede was not ever to tell her father this thing. It would break his heart.

Elfriede doesn't remember the rest of this conversation, or how her mother made it out to the door to her carriage, or how they parted this final time before Elfriede was called to her mother's deathbed. In fact, the entire episode seems unreal to her, and she's long dismissed it from her mind as a symptom of shock. But the words return now with remarkable clarity, as she holds this letter in her hand, postmarked London. Also the brightness of her mother's eyes, which Elfriede once attributed to her incipient illness. *God sent him to me*, Mother said, and then, *That's why you're so beautiful, you know, you have his eyes and his hair and his soul*. And again: *God sent him to me, in my misery*. Until that moment,

Elfriede never knew her mother was miserable at all. Until this moment, she doesn't remember.

Eight fifty-two.

Elfriede takes her butter knife and slices open the envelope.

There was no salutation. No date.

> *Forgive me for addressing you. Not for anything in the world would I dis-turb your peace of mind. I wish only to explain how much your friendship has meant and will always mean to me, except of course that I cannot. God has not given us any words large or subtle or beautiful enough, in my language or yours. On my knees I pray for your happiness. But if happiness is impossible, if you are made to feel hurt or misery of any kind, if you have any need what-soever of a stalwart friend, you must dispatch a message to the address below. A postcard will do. W.*

AT ONE MINUTE AFTER NINE o'clock, Elfriede knocks on her husband's door, bearing his breakfast tray. The room is radiant with autumn sun-shine, and so is Gerhard's hair. She pours his coffee and butters his toast. Before she lifts the newspaper and reads him the headlines, she tells him she's ordered a carriage to convey them about the estate for an airing on this warm, beautiful morning, so exceptional for November.

NURSE AND JOHANN ACCOMPANY THEM, swathed in wool. Gerhard, gentleman as he is, tries to insist that the ladies face forward in the open landau, but he's overruled. Herr Doktor's instructions. Nurse and Jo-hann take the backward seats, except Johann won't sit, he's too thrilled by the journey. He points out the lake, the fountains, the stables, the forest, the distant hills, the driver's hat, the two smart bay horses. Once, Elfriede reaches out to touch his pale hair, and its softness entrances her.

But then he notices the intrusion and bats her away. She slips her hand underneath the carriage blanket and finds Gerhard's fingers.

Really, it's not that warm, just by comparison to the gray chill of the previous fortnight. The leaves have all dropped and the trees are like skeletons. As they pass the fringes of the wood, Elfriede can see deep inside, and the number of fallen trees amazes her. She turns to Gerhard with this observation, but he's scowling at Nurse. Some infraction of the rules. Nurse doesn't seem to notice. She's pointing out something to Johann. The breeze blows against them, bearing the true chill of November, and Johann climbs up on the seat next to Nurse and cuddles into her side.

Elfriede's used to this. Day after day, she climbs up the stairs to the nursery and plays with her son. She knows better than to send Nurse away during these hours. She knows better than to push herself on a small boy of three years, who knows nothing of mothers, only of Nurse. She's learned to bear the pain of his attachment to this woman, who has soothed all his hurts and hungers in Elfriede's absence. But she doesn't give up. Sometimes she brings sweets. Some new toy or game. Certain wars are best won by centimeters, stealing tiny parcels of ground from your opponent who looks elsewhere, until one day you're in possession of the whole.

At the moment, however, Nurse still possesses just about all of Johann. She tucks the blanket over his tired little body and puts her arm around him. Once he's secure in her embrace, she glances up and meets Gerhard's scowl with a small, private smile, before turning to admire the woodland scenery. Already Johann's long eyelashes brush his cheeks. Underneath the blanket, Gerhard's hand gives hers a little squeeze, before it withdraws entirely.

Elfriede leans forward and tells the driver to return to the house.

THEY STOP AT THE GARDENS first, however. As the lake comes into view, Gerhard orders the driver to halt the landau. They will walk the rest of the way, he says, it's only a short distance. Look, there's the house, not a quarter mile away.

The driver obeys, the horses pull up. Gerhard alights first and hands out the others, first Elfriede and then Johann—with an oversize swing that makes the boy shriek with delight—and Nurse last of all, keeping his gaze strictly on the distant hills. When the carriage moves off, he turns to Nurse and tells her—tells, rather, the top of her head, since she's only a servant—to take Johann to see the horses in the stable. Nurse looks at the two of them, Elfriede and Gerhard, arm in arm, and her face takes on a strange, hurt expression.

"Yes, of course, Herr von Kleist," she says. She clasps Johann's little hand and turns in the opposite direction, toward the stables, while Gerhard leads Elfriede along the lakeshore.

They walk quietly. Gerhard was always a man of few words, after all, even at the passionate height of their marriage, that first year that seemed so promising, emotions so new and delicate they were better unspoken. Now the words are fewer still. Limited to observations on the weather, on the headlines in the newspapers. They reach the gravel, and the crunch of their feet awakens Elfriede to their silence, to the fact that they haven't said anything at all about what matters, about their marriage, about their boy, about the past three years. Ahead, the house takes shape like a great ornament, gleaming in the sun. So entranced is Elfriede by its radiance, she takes no notice of her immediate surroundings until Gerhard lays a hand on her arm, where it links through his.

"Look," he says softly. "The summerhouse. Do you remember?"

She hesitates. "Remember what?"

"Come, Elfriede. Surely it's not so very long ago."

"It seems like another lifetime. She seems like another girl, your wife then."

"And yet she looks the same to me. This arm, it's the same arm."

"You're too gallant."

"Do you think . . ." Gerhard lifts his hand to touch the brim of his hat. "If we go inside, what do you think we might find?"

"Ghosts, maybe?"

He's rubbing his temple now, like he's trying to awaken something inside. "I don't know. Something of our old selves, maybe?"

"I don't think it's as magic as that," she says, laughing a little.

They stand in the path, at the crossing that leads to the summerhouse. The chill breeze blows on them both, erasing the faint warmth of the sun. November, it can't make up its mind. Elfriede doesn't want to go, she feels some uneasiness about the summerhouse; what's more, she feels that Gerhard doesn't want to go, either, that he shares her foreboding. Still they turn down the path together. It's beyond their control. The summerhouse has taken on its own will. It wants them there, willing or otherwise. He opens the glass door for them both. Shuts it again, because of the chilling air.

"You should sit down and rest," she says.

He sits obediently, stiffly, and takes off his hat to scratch the stubble of pale hair on his head. Invalids, she can't get free of them. Gerhard sets his palms on his large, gaunt knees. He's lost weight because of his illness, but his skeleton hasn't changed, thick and brutal as ever, only more visible. Elfriede sits down beside him. The same chaise longue. The cushions, she thinks, have faded in the sun. Maybe she should have them replaced.

"I'm sorry about that, what happened in the carriage," he says.

"What happened in the carriage?"

"He's terribly attached to her, you see."

"Do you mean Nurse and Johann? I know that. I don't mind."

"Surely it must give you pain, to see the two of them together."

"Yes, a little. But it's not her fault, is it? I'm glad he's had someone to love, someone who loves him in return. Every child needs that." Elfriede links her hands together in her lap. "I hope I can teach him to love me, as well."

"If you want me to dismiss her, I'll dismiss her."

Elfriede raises her head in surprise. "Dismiss her? Of course not. He'd be heartbroken."

He makes a noise, a kind of sigh, maybe almost a sob, and rises from the chaise to approach the glass wall that faces the lake. "I'm sorry," he says.

Elfriede turns in her seat to watch him. Lifts one of the pillows into her lap, something to hold. "Again? What is it this time?"

"These weeks . . . these past weeks . . . taking care of me . . . you've been an angel . . ."

"Oh, that. Well, I'm still your wife, aren't I? Wives are supposed to nurse their husbands when they fall sick."

"I haven't deserved it, that's all."

"But does anyone really deserve such things? Nobody's blameless. We give and receive not because of our deserts, but because we *are*. Because we are human beings, that's all, God's children. With all our faults."

He crosses his arms against his chest and bows his head.

"Come." She strokes the cushion with one hand. "You're tired. Let's go back to the house for some coffee."

"Elfriede. Are we never to say anything to each other?"

"What is there to say?"

"Everything. Everything." He shakes his shorn head slowly, back and forth. "Everything's changed. I think sometimes of our wedding day. I remember that instant you appeared down the aisle of the church, as if you were fallen from heaven itself. I thought there was nothing more beautiful on earth. I wept at the sight of you."

"Did you? I don't remember that." Elfriede pauses. "I was too nervous to look at your face, I think. It all went by in a blur. I don't even remember saying the vows."

"Ah, God," he says, anguished. "Ah, God. How is it possible we have come to this?"

"Come to what?"

"Are we never to be man and wife again? Can you love me again, do you think?"

She thinks helplessly, *But I never did.*

"Can you love *me* again?" she says. "Maybe that's the question."

"But I never stopped."

"You sent me away."

"That wasn't—my sisters thought—"

"Are you telling me that the Baron von Kleist is ruled by his sisters?" She stands and turns to face him. "You might have defended me against them. You might have remembered how much you loved me and *done* something."

His head remains bowed, unable to meet her. Oh, that short, bristling blond hair, almost white in the autumn sunlight. All she can see of him. "I didn't know what to do. I didn't understand. I don't understand. How could my beautiful angel turn into this—this—" He gropes helplessly. "It was willful, it was selfish, it was—*how* could you not love your own son?"

"I did. I did love him. But this black—thing—it shrouded me. Everything, all my feelings. I couldn't find them. It was terrifying. I had nothing inside me. I couldn't summon a single thing."

"You didn't try!"

"Didn't *try?* Oh, God. Oh, Gerhard."

He stands there like a pillar. His back is straight, his coat loose against his shoulders. What's he staring at, out these windows? The lake? The forest beyond? He says gruffly, "These—these are women's matters. I can't comprehend them. I thought my sisters would know better than I did."

"If you had fought for me—"

Gerhard turns at last, lifts his head, and his face is a picture of agony, made worse by his emaciation. He looks a thousand years old. "They told me you would kill him. The doctor—my sisters—they thought there was some danger to my son."

"To Johann? You thought I would hurt *Johann*?"

"I thought, maybe it's me. No mother would behave this way to her own child. So maybe it's me she wants to hurt. Maybe she never loved me to begin with. That's what my sisters said, when I was courting you. That you only cared about—about all *this*." He nods to the world outside the summerhouse, the estate, the schloss.

The sun has climbed overhead. The greedy glass traps its warmth. How strange to see winter lying all around you in bare, brown sticks, and yet to feel the heat of summer. Elfriede's skin prickles with perspiration. Gerhard's expression turns softer, almost plaintive. He steps forward and reaches out to take her by the elbows.

"We must begin again," he says. "For Johann's sake."

Elfriede gazes at this man, this husband, pale and gaunt and sweating, his blond hair thinning along his temples, and some panic takes hold of her chest. Some giant fear, some ache. She's nursed him devotedly, on her knees before God she has sworn fealty in exchange for her good conscience, and now he stands before her, he's only asking for something she has already promised him, and what does she feel? Panic. The heat in the summerhouse reminds her of August, reminds her of lying hazily on the chaise longue under the shadow of Gerhard's giant, straining chest. At the time, she closed her eyes—she was too shy of this daylight that illuminated their intimacy—but she remembers the sound of his grunting, the sharp, rhythmic sway of her breasts, the sweat that dripped on her skin. The roar with which he ended it all, like an African lion pronouncing victory. That's it, a lion. Except his mane, even then, wasn't long enough or tawny enough. He's so pale and crisp, and before she can banish it, she thinks of Wilfred's ginger hair, his laugh, his heat, his twenty-six freckles she dreamed of kissing.

Elfriede tries to pull back her arms, but his grip is firm.

"I must know, Elfriede. I must know if you still mean what you said three years ago."

"What did I say?"

"My God, what else? What else? Elfriede, think. I have thought of nothing else." He squints his eyes and rocks back and forth on his feet. He bows his head and whispers ferociously, "When you told me you didn't want any more children."

"Oh! That. I see."

"You *see*? Elfriede, you can't imagine—I have never felt such a blow. You sat on the bed in your dressing gown and looked at me and said this thing. In all my life, I have never taken such a blow as that."

"I never meant to hurt you. Oh, Gerhard. It wasn't that I didn't—that I didn't *want* to. I was sick. I was afraid, I was terrified of having more children, of facing all that blackness again. I wanted you to comfort me, to understand my fear. And instead you walked away from me. I still remember the sound of that door as it closed behind you."

"What else was I supposed to do?"

"To hold me! To comfort me!"

"What, you thought I could hold my wife in my arms without making love to her? After all those months like a monk? I'm only a man, Elfriede. Anyway, I thought you must loathe my touch."

Somewhere inside Elfriede's head, a voice clamors in fury: *But it wasn't about* you, *Gerhard. Why must everything be about* you? But the voice is a small one, just a last gasp of anger that dies away gently. The rest is pity. A pity she can't articulate, of course, because how for God's sake do you express pity for Gerhard von Kleist? She wears her pity on her face, in her eyes, as she gazes at her husband.

He shifts his feet and looks to the side. "Well? And now? Are you still afraid?"

Again, Wilfred's hair, Wilfred's face, which she cannot quite see. How's this possible, that his features are blurred in her memory? She can see one of them at a time, yes, his thin, plain cheeks and those eyelashes around his eyes of alpine blue. His long nose, the sharpness of his jaw, all of these dear things, one by one, each feature disappearing when she finds the next. Yet the sense of him remains in utmost clarity. The beat of him thunders in her chest. She shuts her eyes and pushes, pushes, *thrusts* him away, but it's like trying to dislodge a pillar that holds up your roof, and Elfriede is not Samson. "I don't know," she says.

"Elfriede, look at me."

She opens her eyes again.

"I must know. I must know if you're well again. I must understand what you mean by returning."

"I mean to—well, to *return*. To be Johann's mother. To be your wife."

"But what does that *mean*, Elfriede?" He pulls her elbows, pulls her even closer. "Listen to me. There, in that carriage. I thought to myself—it was all I could think—he's so lonely, a small boy among grownups. He needs brothers and sisters. He needs a family, a mother and a father who will fill his nursery."

"Gerhard, enough. Let's not talk about this yet. We'll wait until you're well again—"

"Please, Elfriede—" He cuts himself off by kissing her, with such vim she can't escape, she's imprisoned by his mouth and by his arms that lock around her. His kiss is nothing like she remembers. His lips are hard, his tongue's sloppy. What's happened to Gerhard's tender, subtle kisses? There's no fighting him. She makes herself limp instead, and he lifts his head and loosens his grip. She steps away, smoothing her hair. Gerhard sinks to the chaise longue, panting.

"I'm sorry," he says. "I am too hasty."

"You're not well enough, that's all. Look at you, you're panting."

He looks up. "Can you not even bear to kiss me, then?"

"Of course I can bear to kiss you." Elfriede sits beside him and pats his bony knee. Leans forward and places a kiss on his damp lips. "But we can't just wave a wand and make everything the way it was before. It's been three years. So much has happened. We've both been wrong."

"Ah, God." He sets his elbows on his knees, sets his head in his hands, his fingers in his hair.

"Don't, darling. Don't despair. My God, you're like a child yourself, sometimes. Just because we can't wave a wand doesn't make it impossible. Of course we can be man and wife again. We already are, remember? I don't remember a divorce. I don't remember renouncing any vows."

Instead of smiling or even laughing, he makes another noise of agony.

Elfriede touches his stiff, short hair. "Listen to me. Of course I want nothing but the best for Johann. I want him to have brothers and sisters to play with, to be his family when we're gone."

There's a little silence, occupied only by the sound of Gerhard's breath. "Elfriede? Do you mean this?"

"But we have all the time in the world for these things. There's no hurry at all. I'm not going to leave you. I won't leave my son. Never again, do you see? I've come home. So we have time for all of this. We have time to start fresh from the beginning, to wipe away the past and start again, two clean souls—"

"Yes, yes—"

"—forgive each other for these terrible sins and start again—"

He lifts his head and stares at her. "Yes, forgive me. Forgive me."

"Of course."

"Forgive me."

"Gerhard, you're weeping."

"It's nothing. It's nothing." He takes her hands and bends over them, holding her fingers against his lips, almost as if praying. When he straightens, his eyes are bright and wet, his pale lashes stuck together. He lifts her to her feet and tucks her arm back in the shelter of his elbow.

"We'll go into the house now. We'll start again, our souls clean, our hearts pure. How does that sound, Elfriede?"

Ah, what a Romantic he is, this Gerhard.

INSTEAD OF EXHAUSTING HIM, THE morning's exercise seems to have invigorated Gerhard. He escorts his wife into the house, kisses her tenderly, and practically bounds off down the hallway to his study, to be called for when luncheon's ready. Typhoid, what typhoid? He's a new man.

Elfriede, on the other hand. She glances at the clock—eleven-thirty—and considers the hour to be consumed before luncheon. She finds the housekeeper and informs her that she and Gerhard will take the meal together in the family dining room, that she and Gerhard will now be taking their afternoon and evening meals together unless notice is otherwise given. The housekeeper responds with a small smile, a tiny flicker of eyebrow that might mean relief, or satisfaction, or cynicism—who really knew the opinions of servants? Always there was this barrier. This metal shield between you and them. Elfriede returns what she hopes is a warm smile and drags herself up the stairs to her room to change for luncheon. She ought to wear something pretty, something to please her husband, something that will begin to bridge the distance between them.

Elfriede doesn't ring the maid to help her. She's used to dressing herself, and she dislikes the invasion of privacy that service requires. The poking and prodding of a stranger's hands, the foreign gaze on her skin. As she unfastens her buttons, she discovers her fingers are shaking. That her stomach is somehow sick. And why? This is only what she wants, after all. This is only the answer to her prayer. Redemption. Resurrection! In time she'll be a good mother. In time she'll be a good wife, and Wilfred—yes, say his name, don't be afraid—Wilfred, in some way she can't quite explain to herself, can't put into words, has given her the courage to do this thing, to return to her abandoned home and take up the unfinished yarns of her life and weave them together once more. She has been given this chance! She won't waste it. Just imagine Johann with a brother, a sister. Imagine the joy on Gerhard's face. Imagine a whole, happy, boisterous family. A miracle! Hers to create. Fingers, behave. Stomach, steady yourself. Button after button. White skin under sunlight. Oh God, she's dizzy. She sits on the divan and puts her head between her knees. On the floor, the tweed skirt lies crumpled. The ivory blouse on top of that. The woolen jacket, she's sitting on it. A knock on the door. She jumps to her feet and stares at the connecting door, the one attached to Gerhard's bedroom, but this knock comes from the other door, the outer door.

"One moment," she says.

One by one, she lifts the discarded garments and carries them to the wardrobe. Hangs them in place and selects a dress of rose-colored silk for luncheon, which she slides on over her corset and petticoat. The buttons go down her back, impossible to reach them all, so she fastens as many as she can and sits in the chair before the escritoire.

"Come in," she says.

Enter Nurse, in the same high-necked dress of dark green wool as this morning. Nurses don't change clothes in the middle of the day. She walks to the center of the rug, in the center of the room, and folds her hands. "I've come to tender my resignation."

"Your resignation?"

"Yes, Frau. I can no longer—can no longer—" She pulls a handkerchief from her sleeve and dabs swiftly at her eyes, which are already red.

Elfriede stares at her in amazement.

"Why, whatever's wrong? Has something happened?"

"No, Frau. I simply can't stay, that's all."

"Why not? Is it me? Can't you bear to share him with me? Because I assure you—"

"Share him? Share him?" Poor Nurse is properly crying now, mopping away at her eyes.

Elfriede forgets her buttons and springs from the chair. "You mustn't, Nurse. You mustn't. I'm not a bit jealous. We'll love him together."

"Oh . . . oh . . ."

"Sit down. Come." Elfriede leads her to the divan and makes her sit. "I'll ring for coffee. Milk? Would you rather have——"

"Stop it. Stop it. You're murdering me."

"*Murdering*——"

"I'm pregnant!"

Everything stops, the beat of the universe. The air, the sunlight crystallize in the room. Elfriede's mouth hangs half-open, in the act of saying the rest of her sentence, whatever it might have been. She never will remember.

"I'm with child," Nurse says, more calmly. For some reason, the truth stops her tears, at least for the moment. She makes a last few dabs at her eyes and cheeks and slips the handkerchief back into her sleeve.

Elfriede must say something, of course. But what?

"I suppose," she says, quite slow, "I suppose I need not ask *whose* child."

"You see why I have tendered my resignation."

"Yes, I see." Elfriede stares at her hands, clasped at her waist. Strangely, they've stopped trembling. Her stomach has righted itself. Her head's not dizzy anymore. She feels a little like she's in a tunnel, that's all, as if the sights and sounds of the room are just echoes of themselves, distant and not quite real. Gerhard and Nurse. Dear me. And then, poor Gerhard. He must have been so lonely. *Forgive me, forgive me,* he cried in the summerhouse, shedding tears of remorse on her hands. Now she understands. "How much time?" she finds herself asking.

"Since Christmas. I did try to be careful, Frau, but sometimes I couldn't——"

"I mean how much time until the baby's born."

"Oh. In May, I think. The end of May."

"Ah, then it was conceived in August. How lovely."

"*Lovely?*"

Elfriede sits on the divan and reaches out to clasp Nurse's damp hand. She says kindly, "Are you very much in love with him?"

"I—no, of course—I mean—oh, Frau von Kleist—"

"Now, don't cry. Don't weep so. Everything will be all right, I promise."

"We didn't mean it. We never meant to."

"Of course you didn't."

"I don't know what came over us."

"Hush, now. You were lonely, that's all. Both of you, and Johann between you. Of course you fell in love."

Nurse slides to the floor, sobbing.

"You must hate me," she gasps. "How I've betrayed you. Your son and then your husband. I'm a wretch, a wretch."

"Does he know?" Elfriede asks gently, stroking Nurse's hair.

"N-n-no. I only suspected—and then he was sick—"

"I see. Of course."

"It was my fault. Don't blame him, Frau. *I* went to him. I felt so sorry for him. I only meant to comfort him . . . I loved him so . . . I couldn't bear it, how sad he was, how hopeless. He thought you might never come back."

"Then you made him happy."

"No. Not even that." Nurse's sobs are ebbing now. She turns her head to the side and stares at the wall, which happens to be the one shared with Gerhard's chamber. "He felt terrible afterward. I think you should know that, how terrible he felt, the first time we did it. He wept, Frau, he wept in my arms like a child. He railed at himself. But then . . ."

"But then it got easier, didn't it? I imagine the first time must be the worst. Particularly for a man like Gerhard, so terribly loyal and full of ideals. It must have broken his heart, at first. But then once you've started, how can you stop? You've already sinned, I suppose. It's done. You might as well go on."

"A man like the baron has *needs*, Frau." Nurse sniffs. She rises from the floor and smooths her hair. "Anyway, I'll be going. The upstairs maid is watching poor young Johann. I don't want to say good-bye, it will be too hard for us both. You won't tell Ger— You won't tell Herr von Kleist, please? It's better this way."

"I don't understand."

Nurse turns to face Elfriede, and the expression on her broad, tanned, attractive face is brave and tragic, maybe a little *too* brave and tragic. "It's better he never knows. I'll go to stay with my sister. I've some money saved—"

"My dear. My dear girl. You mustn't think of it."

"I—I beg your pardon, Frau?"

Elfriede rises from the divan. Her heart is so full of—of something, some airy substance—she almost levitates. "Never knows he's fathered a child? His poor child never to know his own father? His own *brother*?"

"Frau von *Kleist*!"

She picks up Nurse's horrified hands. "We are all sinners, Nurse. We are none of us blameless in this mortal life. Why should we pile evil upon evil? You must stay here, of course. You must let us take care of you. If Gerhard has fathered a child, he must of course be a father to his child. It's immoral to do otherwise."

"But I can't! Stay under this roof! It's not—it's not decent!"

"You will please let me judge the decency of the affair. I am, after all, the wronged party." Elfriede smiles as she says this. *Wronged party*. Like a court of law, like the words on some document, impervious to the queer vagaries of the human heart, the unexpected levitations to which it's subject. *Wronged party*. She thinks of Gerhard banging away atop Nurse in the summer twilight, roaring out his ecstasy as he spent. Did they do it in the baron's bedroom? Some other chamber? By day or by night?

Surely not Nurse's bedroom, which she shares with Johann's little cot. Well, wherever it was, whenever it was. Her heart aches for Gerhard's guilt, the suffering he must have felt after the pleasures of copulation died away. *Wronged party*. If only she could laugh right now, if only she could laugh out loud and not have poor Nurse stare at her like you stared at a madwoman.

LULU

THE WAY I heard the story is this. When he first came to Nassau, at the invitation of none other than Harold Christie, who could smell money on a man the same way sharks smelled blood in the water, Harry Oakes (he had not yet been awarded his baronetcy by a grateful Empire) walked into the British Colonial Hotel in his rough clothes and his rough accent and got the rough treatment from the management. So he bought the place. End of story.

Probably the real history isn't so simple as that, but human beings love nothing so much as a tale that confirms their particular prejudices, so I'll let it stand. And the ending's the same, either way. Harry Oakes bought the British Colonial, that much is indisputable, and in December of 1941 his daughter Nancy came out into society inside the walls of its ballroom. Oh, it was a swell party, believe me. I was there.

I was there, and so were the duke and duchess, and just about everybody of note in the Bahamas, including Alfred de Marigny. Freddie came in a few minutes late, dressed to the nines, as we all were, crisp and sleek and deeply tanned. He grabbed a coupe of champagne from a nearby waiter, caught my eye, smiled, and wandered over.

"I thought I might find you here," he said.

"Wouldn't miss it. How was the hunting?"

"Terrible."

"I didn't realize you were such friends with the Oakeses."

Freddie pulled out a cigarette case and tilted it toward my neck. I shook my head. He pulled out one of his strong, brown-papered cigarettes and ejected a flame from his gold lighter, the one his ex-wife had given him for a wedding present. "I like Oakes," he said. "I like the way he is his own man, the way he stands up to these Bay Street fellows."

"Yes? Anything else you like?"

He glanced to a nearby cluster of guests. "How lovely you look this evening, Mrs. Randolph. That dress is very much becoming to you."

"Why, thanks. My housekeeper recommended it."

"Your housekeeper has an excellent eye."

"So do you, I hear."

He opened his mouth. I smiled. We had come to a certain understanding, Freddie and I, landlord and tenant. I think he had made the offer of the cottage with certain hopes, and maybe Veryl was right. Maybe I should have entertained those hopes, maybe I should have put on my red dress and perfume and invited him over for cocktails, put on a record or two, lit some candles, all those things. But I had not. I couldn't say why. Freddie was a good bet, a gentleman, someone I could like enormously and never fall in love with. Ideal, really. And now he had caught the attention of Miss Nancy Oakes, who always got what she wanted, and I wondered if the twinge I felt in my ribs had something to do with regret or something else.

"Just remember, she's only seventeen," I said. "She's got a hell of a lot to learn, even if she's the last one to admit it."

"Ah, Lulu—"

But the commotion was already starting, the entrance of Miss Nancy Oakes on her father's stocky arm. We turned to the entrance of the ballroom and shuffled back respectfully, while the orchestra made important noises. I remember Miss Oakes wore a green silk dress that perfectly suited her slender figure, and turned her auburn hair especially bright beneath the incandescent lights. I remember how her smile consumed her face and lit her skin from underneath; the way you smile when you're thrillingly conscious of everyone's gaze, when you're experiencing the admiration of every single person in a ballroom like that, when you're drinking it all in one gulp.

I remember the enchanted expression on Alfred de Marigny's face, and how I thought, with remarkable detachment, *He's a goner.*

SIR HARRY OAKES CLAIMED THE first dance with his daughter, of course, but when he returned her to the table she grabbed de Marigny's hand and said something to him, I don't know what. Whatever it was, it acted as a signal. He stubbed out his cigarette, rose and led her to the floor, or maybe she led him, I don't recall exactly. I returned to my champagne and drank it all in one marvelous gulp. Across the room, the duke drew his wife from her seat and led her to dance. I checked my watch and saw that the supper wasn't going to be served for at least another couple of hours.

I knew I should turn to my left-hand companion and strike up some kind of conversation. I knew I should engage with my fellow man, cadge a dance or two from my fellow man—why, it was part of my job, wasn't it? I was on duty. The social event of the season, don't you know, and a breathless America awaited my account of the evening. The violins sang, the trombones slid up and down, up and down. The air stank of cigarettes and perfume. Thank God it wasn't July, I thought. I opened my evening purse and pulled out my Kodak 35. The duchess wore a long, beautifully draped Mainbocher gown of sapphire blue; the duke swept her around the edge of the dancers. She was smiling, had her head

tilted back. How she loved to dance, that woman. I lifted the camera
and waited patiently until they came into profile through the split finder,
aligned, and *snap*. And again. Next to me, a stoutish, pink-faced man in a
wilted collar glanced my way and stubbed out his cigarette, as if he meant
business. I excused myself and pivoted toward the doorway, stuffing the
camera back into my purse as I went.

OUTSIDE, THE AIR REEKED OF the sea. I made for the beach, which
belonged to the hotel and in daylight hours would be spangled with cabanas and umbrellas. Now it was empty and sort of mysterious, the sand
unraked, forming cool hollows in which to lose your foot. I took off my
shoes and stepped carefully, carefully, until I found just the spot and settled there, in my dress of wine-colored silk, and lit a cigarette while the
waves lapped nearby. In the western sky, a half-moon glowed above the
horizon, gilding the length of Hog Island before me. The lighthouse put
out a faithful beam to the left. The universe beat its slow, thirsty pulse.

I heard the footsteps in the sand an instant before the voice called out,
closer than I expected.

"Abandoning hope so soon?"

I closed my eyes.

"Just the same old, wasn't it? Daddy throws a party for his poor little
rich girl, society swoons."

He dropped into the sand. Not so close as to touch me but close enough
that I felt his warmth and smelled his skin. I held out the cigarette. He
took it from my fingers and returned it a moment later. I opened my eyes.
In my other hand lay the cigarette lighter, clenched in my palm. I curled
the fingers outward, and the metal caught some light from the moon.

"Handsome object," said Thorpe.

"This?" I held up the lighter. "My father gave it to me when I was
sixteen."

"*Sixteen?*"

"He's not your ordinary kind of father."

A solemn pause. "I see."

From behind us came a crash of splintering glass. We flinched at exactly the same instant, to exactly the same degree, while a roar of laughter followed. I looked over my shoulder just as he looked over his shoulder, and our eyes met, a flash, a jolt. I turned back to the harbor.

"Aren't you going to ask?" I said.

"Ask what?"

"About my father. The lighter. It's a good story."

"I wouldn't dream of prying."

"Naturally. You're English, aren't you?"

"Half English. Well, a quarter, really. My grandmother's a resolute Scot."

"What's the other half?"

"German."

"Is that so?"

"That's so."

"Well, your secret's safe with me." I toed a little sand. "Still, it's a good story, if you want to hear it."

"I daresay it must be."

I blew out a ribbon of smoke. "The magazine, the one I write for? And that's a secret, by the way. Nobody's supposed to know the identity of the Lady of Nassau."

"Madam, I am the soul of discretion."

"I know you are. That's why I'm blabbing to you now. I mean, a girl's got to confess once in a while, and you're the nearest thing I know to a priest."

"Honored, I'm sure."

"You should be. That's the highest praise I can give a fellow. Anyway, my father's the publisher."

"Of the *Metropolitan?*"

"That's the one. My mother was his second wife, sort of sandwiched, if that's the word, between the Fifth Avenue debutante and the Austrian countess."

Thorpe took my cigarette again. "How cosmopolitan."

"Well, you've got a right, haven't you, when you're S. Barnard Lightfoot Junior, publishing scion and man-about-Manhattan. You've got the wherewithal to meet and marry whatever girl takes your fancy. Whatever girl suits you at any particular moment in your life."

There was this silence, delicate and smoke scented, while the noise of the party went on behind us. I waited for Thorpe to shift in his seat, to edge away, to make some excuse and rise and leave me alone.

Instead, he made another pull on the cigarette and said, "Well, go on."

"Are you sure you want to hear it?"

"Only if you want to tell me."

"Mind you, it's common knowledge. Dear old Daddy and his unsavory adventures. My mother was a coat check girl at the Ziegfeld. She had aspirations to the chorus line. I mean, she could dance, and boy, could she sing. I was born about a month after they married. I don't mean to shock you."

Thorpe waved his hand and returned the cigarette.

"Then my brother and sister, twins, two years later," I continued. "You can read all about us in the *New York Post*, dateline September 1925. That was about the time my father was caught in flagrante, as they say, with the wife of the Count von Enzenberg. Right there inside the count's own box at La Fenice, in fact, so you can't say they didn't have moxie."

"Ah, this happened in Venice, then?"

"Yes. Have you been there?"

"Once, a few years ago. Spent the usual disreputable year abroad, after university. Fascinating place, Venice. Rather dirty but terribly beautiful, underneath the smell."

"Interesting. I guess there's a metaphor there, somewhere." I stared out to sea, where the gleam of a sail had appeared at the western entrance of the channel, making its way down the length of Hog Island. There wasn't much wind, and the boat bore a full press of sail to catch whatever momentum she could. In her wake came a trail of laughter, as clear as next door, the kind of laughter that follows a bottle. I folded my arms and said, "Well, it was a splendid scene. As I heard the story, the count stormed in during the second act—*La Gioconda*, you know, sort of a nice little coincidence of fate, wouldn't you say?"

"Apropos, at any rate."

"It was a tremendous scandal. And that exposé in the *Post*, too brilliant. Worthy of the *Metropolitan* itself. Still listening?"

"Fascinated. I feel as if we're reaching the really good part."

He had such a nice, deep voice. I liked his voice. I thought he sounded a little wary, at the moment, but who could blame him? My cigarette was down to nothing. I tossed the stub on the sand and buried it with my toe.

"Anyway, the lighter. On my sixteenth birthday, as I said, Daddy Lightfoot took me out to dinner at the Oak Room, just the two of us. Lovely meal. I had fish, he had veal. Handed me this box at the end of it, and I don't remember what I was expecting, what I was hoping for, maybe pearls or something. A pearl necklace, that's what Daddy gives you on your sixteenth birthday, isn't it?"

"I—I'm afraid I wouldn't know."

"Well, it wasn't pearls. It was this fine cigarette lighter instead. Matches the one he gave my older brother, Barnard—Barnie's from his first marriage, you understand, the heir apparent—on *his* sixteenth birthday, except Barnie's is gold, not silver. Nice inscription, though." I'd been flicking the lighter on and off while I spoke, and now I held it up, so the fellow could make out the words engraved on the side, in the glow from the hotel and the falling moon. "Go ahead. Read it out loud," I said.

He cleared his throat. "*To Lulu on her birthday. SBL.* That's all?"

"Touching, isn't it?"

There was no movement from the man beside me, no sound at all. He seemed to have forgotten I was there. The seagulls were circling again, calling out in lazy screams, the way everything here moved and spoke at a measured pace, if it moved and spoke at all, the exact opposite of New York City.

I tucked the lighter back into my satin purse, where it clinked against the camera. Hog Island floated before us, outlined by the moon. "Tell me again about botany."

"Botany?"

"That *is* what you're studying, isn't it? Botany?"

"Yes, it is. I've spent the last year or so cataloging the native flora. Fascinating work."

I turned toward him and leaned back, propping my elbow in the sand. "You do realize there's a war on?"

He had one leg crossed over the other, and his right hand rested lightly on his knee. He stared ahead at the flickering harbor, the gilded shore of Hog Island, the sail disappearing to the east. His spectacles glinted. "My eyesight, remember? The army wouldn't have me."

"What a shame."

"Rather than sit behind some damned desk somewhere, I thought I might better serve my country by coming here."

"Oh, indeed. Where else than a tropical paradise?"

Now he turned to me, smiling. "Why, Mrs. Randolph, don't you know what treasures lie undiscovered around us, in the natural world? Think of penicillin. If our side can find a way to mass-produce the stuff, the war will be over in months."

"How so?"

"Because a vast percentage of wounded men end up dying of sepsis and other infections, Mrs. Randolph. And it seems—well, to me, at any rate—considerably more pleasant to find a way to win this war by discovering new ways to save soldiers' lives, rather than discovering new ways to kill them." He stopped, ran a hand through his hair, and grinned again. "My God, did you ever hear such a pompous ass?"

"I've heard worse."

He reached to his right and pulled a bottle free from the sand. "Nicked this from the bar," he said.

"Champagne! Why didn't you say anything?"

"Because I didn't want you to fall in love with me for all the wrong reasons."

"Did you bring glasses too?"

"Naturally."

Already he was working the cork between his thumbs. I tried to peer over his knees to see what else lay hidden in the sand, but his legs were too long, and I didn't have the strength to sit back up. The cork came free in a pop and a sigh of vapor. I watched his hands as he produced a coupe and poured the champagne at a precise right angle, so there was almost no foam at all, just pure gold. When he handed the glass to me, I discovered how cold it was, how inviting, but I waited for him to pour another for himself. When his glass was full, and my glass was full, we touched them together and drank at last.

"Oh, I needed that," I gasped.

Thorpe had not taken his gaze from my face. He lifted his index finger and touched the earring at my right ear. "Exquisite," he said.

"A gift from an admirer." When he raised his eyebrows, I laid my finger against my lips and whispered, "Not *that* kind of admirer."

"I see. Acquired this afternoon, perhaps?"

"Bought and paid for."

Thorpe settled back on his elbow, facing me. "All *that* in exchange for nothing more than a little good publicity?"

I went to drink again, but the glass was inexplicably empty. Thorpe dragged it from my fingers, refilled it, handed it back.

"No, there's more," I said.

"How much more?"

"Loyalty."

"That's a very big word."

"Covers a vast territory." I finished the champagne. Thorpe glanced at the empty coupe and made no comment, though he didn't rush to fill the void, either. Maybe he saw the dizziness in my eyes.

"How vast, exactly?" he asked softly.

I flung out my arm. "Everything! Not only am I to create this fiction but I'm to believe in it too. That's the thing about fairy tales. You hear this beautiful story told in beautiful words, you see these beautiful pictures, and you know it's not true. You know it's just a story somebody wrote to lull you to sleep. But you want to believe it so badly, you want to *sleep* so badly, perchance even to dream, yes, that's it, to dream it's *you* in the middle of that fairy tale . . ."

"My dear Mrs. Randolph."

"Call me Lulu," I sobbed, holding out the glass. He rose from his elbow and filled the bowl for me. By the time I had it back between my fingers, I'd regained control of my throat and my eyes. I apologized for the lapse.

"There's no need."

"Believe it or not, I was once a girl of ideals. Tremendous ones."

"I believe it."

"Now I'm delivering grubby envelopes for grubby people—"

"I beg your pardon?"

"Nothing." I finished the champagne and rolled on my back in the sand. The coupe fell away from my fingers. How black the sky was, how profuse the stars. That was the first thing that gave me hope, after I left New York City in the company of Mr. Randolph. Staring out the window of a Nacogdoches boardinghouse, a little the worse for wear, a little battered about, a little blue in body and spirit, and there it was: the Milky Way. I'll be damned.

Thorpe tried again. "When you said envelopes—"

"I said nothing." I zipped my lips. "You heard nothing, all right? Just a girl in her cups, talking nonsense."

"All right."

"Tell me some nonsense, Thorpe. Tell me some beautiful nonsense. Tell me a fairy tale about a girl and a boy, and the boy loved the girl so much, he brought her champagne and kept her company and listened to her nonsense—"

"Lulu—"

"—and at the end of the evening, he took her home and gave her a kiss, that's all, nothing more, just a dear little . . . a dear little kiss . . . the way they kiss in fairy tales . . ."

"But not in real life."

"No. In real life, the boy wants more than just a little kiss."

We lay together, staring at the stars. Listening to the distant party, the brittle noise of human ecstasy. The sand was still warm. My head swam. After a minute or two, our fingertips found each other, I don't know how, whether we were both searching or just me. Or him. Only the tips, you know, so that the fingers wove together up to the middle joint and no further. We said nothing about this. My dress covered the entire encounter, so that it might not be happening at all. Except it was.

"Mrs. Randolph—"

"Lulu."

"Lulu. Shall I take you home?"

"Yes, please."

HE HELPED ME INTO THE sidecar of his motorcycle, which was parked nearby, and together we headed west along the empty road. The rush of cool air sobered me, so that by the time we reached my little bungalow, ten minutes later, I was able to climb convincingly out of the contraption and stand before him and say, "That was all nonsense back there, wasn't it?"

"If you say so."

"Except you can still call me Lulu. I meant that part."

"Lulu." He touched my cheek, my hair. His hand fell back to his side. "Are you all right?"

"I'm myself, if that's what you're asking."

"Well, if you need anything," he said gravely, "just ask."

I could have said a million things to that, I guess. Much later, I asked him what he expected me to answer, what he *hoped* I would answer, and he said he didn't know. He said it was all in my hands, at that moment, which is a terrible burden for a girl to bear, though of course that was not his intention. What he meant was that the decision was mine, and mine alone. He placed himself in my hands, like a gift, only I didn't realize this at the time. I didn't recognize the gift. No one had ever given himself to me before. Always he expected it the other way around.

So I just clapped my hand over my mouth and said, "My purse!"

"Right here." He lifted his left hand, from which my evening bag dangled, a little the worse for sand, large and lumpy with camera, lipstick, compact, lighter.

I said thanks and drew it from his fingers. I leaned forward and kissed him gently on the lips.

He turned and left. Later I discovered a piece of paper folded inside the purse, on which he had written a telephone number and the single letter *T*.

FOR SOME REASON, THE SOUND of the motorcycle engine echoed inside my head long after the actual noise had faded into the night. I couldn't go to sleep after that—of course not—so I sat on my patio of crushed shells and watched the moon set, listened to the sea and the gulls, felt the salty breath of the world on my cheek. I heard nothing else, saw nothing else, felt nothing else, which was why my heart stopped the next day at the Christmas service at St. George's Church, when Mrs. Gudewill asked me if I'd heard the news. I said what news. She said it was the most awful thing. That dear Mr. Thorpe had been set upon at the docks last night by a pair of thugs, had been luckily discovered by the bartender of the Prince George and taken by ambulance to Nassau Hospital, and nobody knew whether he would live or die.

PART III

LULU

ATOP THE CHEST of drawers in Thorpe's London bedroom sits a photograph of the most beautiful woman I've ever seen. She's on a riverbank, holding a book in her lap, and she regards the camera with a touch of surprise, as if she'd been absorbed in the novel and the photographer called out her name. She wears a pale, plain dress, and her hair, gathered in a loose knot on her neck, seems to be made of sunshine. She has large, light eyes—blue, probably—and exquisite cheekbones. Her mouth forms a neat, perfect bow. Her neck is long, and so are her arms, slender and elegant, and while you can't see the shape of her nose, since she's looking at the camera, you simply assume that's as lovely as the rest of her, as well-formed, in exact proportion to everything else. I don't need to be told that this is Thorpe's mother. In the first place, it sits on his chest of drawers, in a silver frame. In the second place, while most of the rest of Thorpe seems to belong to his father, I know the eyes in that photograph like I know my own name.

Margaret confirms my suspicions in the morning, over tea and powdered eggs. "I gave him that photograph," she says. "I thought he should know what she looked like. It's the only one we had of her."

"What happened to the rest of them?"

She rises from her chair and clears her plate. Her eyes are soft and swollen, and her skin looks as if it were bleached and hung out to dry during the night. "I'm afraid I must leave for the office."

"The office!"

"If I don't turn up, it's going to look suspicious. We're lucky enough B— didn't notice me in the hotel."

"How do you know he didn't notice you?"

She's putting on her gloves. Her fingers are long and slender, just like the rest of her. "Because he'd have tracked us down already. As it is, we haven't much time before somebody remembers Thorpe's got a sister in G section and decides to ask me a question or two."

"But what are we going to do? If the—the department, whatever it's called, isn't going to help us—"

"It's called the Special Operations Executive, Lulu. SOE. In which I am a mere clerk, a secretary, transcribing documents and making German translations as required. So you see there's very little I *can* do, and what little there is depends on what I can manage to turn up today, doesn't it? In the meantime, do try not to make much noise, if you can help it. If anybody knocks on the door, don't answer. If they try to break in, you can go out the window in Benedict's bedroom. I presume you can climb down a drainpipe?"

"If absolutely necessary."

"Splendid." She settles her hat on her head. "I'll be back around six, if all goes well."

"And if it doesn't go well?"

"Then you'd better be ready to run. Get some rest, if you can. You look as if you need it."

AFTER SHE LEAVES, I RETURN to the bedroom. It was too dark last night to snoop around properly, and anyway Margaret would have heard me, no matter how softly I opened the drawers and cupboard doors and rummaged through the bookshelf.

Not that Thorpe seems to have left much behind when he departed for Nassau, two and a half years ago. Other than the photograph, nothing remains atop the chest of drawers. The top two drawers are empty, and the bottom contains only a half-dozen mothballs and a couple of knitted sweaters. I pick them up anyway and bury my nose in the wool, but the smell of him is long gone, replaced by wood and camphor.

Better luck in the wardrobe. Thorpe left his winter suits, neatly pressed, and when I stick my hand in the pockets, I retrieve a pair of theater tickets—*Apple Sauce*, the London Palladium, the fifteenth of August— and a piece of notepaper on which someone's written a brief message, followed by what seems to be a telephone number. The handwriting doesn't belong to Thorpe, and it takes me some time to decipher because of the dull light through the window and the small size of the letters. Still, my heart pumps violently in my chest, the way an archaeologist might feel at the discovery of some new artifact, some clue to a lost civilization. I consider it might be a woman, some lover of his, or else a colleague, a source, a contact. Somebody he knew before me, somebody who belonged to his life before I knew he existed. And now, at this very instant, Thorpe sits in a place I don't know, surrounded by people I don't know, and the details of his existence are beyond my knowledge, though not my imagination. So we live on faith, he and I. My faith in him, and his in me.

As it turns out, the message is only a bill from a restaurant. 2 asparagus soup, 1 turbot, 1 sirloin rare, Stilton & pear, 1 bottle Margaux, 1 brandy, 1 anise. The number at the bottom is only the total, 18/6. Dinner for two, possibly before heading to the theater for *Apple Sauce*, a pleasant night out in wartime. I tuck it back in the pocket of Thorpe's suit and sniff the collar. (Again, no hint of him.)

There's a small writing desk that offers no more than a couple of fountain pens and a pile of blank stationery, and a bookcase containing Trollope, Ovid, Goethe, and a couple of authors I don't recognize, modern stuff. In the bedside table, another pen, a laundry list, a box of matches, half-full. The very faintest whiff of tobacco.

As for the bed. The one on which I'm sitting, the one in which I slept last night like a corpse. The frame is narrow and made of iron, painted white, mattress hard, the kind of monastic bed suitable for a fellow who lives with his sister. Tuxedo curls in a ball atop the pillow. There are no ghosts in this bed, other than Thorpe, and for that small favor from the Almighty, I'm grateful.

WHEN MARGARET RETURNS HOME AT five minutes to six, I've got dinner simmering in pots and a bottle of wine uncorked on the table. She sets her hat on the stand and stares at the plates, the glasses, the folded napkins. Tuxedo gallops down the hall and tangles himself around her legs, *miiaaaaow*.

"You didn't go out, did you?"

"I would've gone nuts if I didn't. I hope you like rabbit. Game isn't rationed, apparently."

"You're an idiot and lucky to be alive. Is that a Bordeaux?"

"I couldn't resist."

She casts me a withering look and heads down the little hallway into her bedroom, followed by the cat. The flat, if you're curious, comprises a single floor of what might once have been a spacious family house. There's a small kitchen with a gas range and an oven but no icebox, the parlor in which we sat and smoked last night, and the hallway leading to the two bedrooms and tiny bathroom. The entire place is immaculate, plain and polished, devoid of the usual knickknacks you find in the homes of spinsters. I'm just spooning the potatoes into a bowl when

Margaret reappears, carrying a purring Tuxedo, wearing a housedress of navy serge and a thick cardigan, belted around her waist.

"Nice rags," I say. "Did you wear that to *Apple Sauce*?"

She drops the cat and sits in her chair. "*Apple Sauce*? Is that a restaurant?"

I set the potatoes on the table. "Never mind. Wine?"

"What a terrible idea."

"Under the circumstances, I think it's an excellent idea." I lift the bottle and fill her glass, then mine. "It's good for morale."

"There's nothing wrong with my morale."

I sit down and raise my glass. "To Thorpe."

"To Benedict." She closes her eyes as she drinks and sets down the glass with a bit of a bang. "Speaking of which. The funniest thing. You'll never guess who stopped by my desk this morning."

"Plain fellow, pockmarked, bump on the head?"

"Exactly. Told me he'd heard the awful news about my brother, assured me they would do their best to negotiate some sort of release, which of course is absolute bollocks. Nobody gets released from Colditz, especially not intelligence agents."

"No?"

"No. Political prisoners receive the worst possible treatment. The only reason they keep them alive is to get more information out of them."

"Thorpe won't reveal anything."

"You don't think so? Not even when they pull out his fingernails? Dunk him in water until he's nearly drowned? Burn him with a hot—"

Slam, goes my fist on the table.

Margaret lifts her eyebrows. "I'm sorry to have to explain a few truths to you, my dear, but there it is. That's what they do to men like Thorpe. Women too. Didn't you know that?"

"There's no proof—"

"Oh, for God's sake, Lulu. Don't be stupid. Anyway, even if they don't torture him, or shoot him after some kangaroo trial, he won't last the winter, not in Colditz. I'm sorry, I don't mean to be unkind, but it's true. It's where they send the worst prisoners, the incorrigibles. The escape artists. There's no food left, no fuel to keep them warm. The guards are all brutes. He hasn't a chance."

"Except for us."

"*Us?* What the devil are you talking about?"

"I mean you and me, working to save him."

"*Save* him? What on earth?"

"Yes. Since the War Office isn't going to help us—this Special Operations of yours—we could join efforts and—"

"Join *efforts?* Are you mad? What exactly do you plan to do, Mrs. Benedict Thorpe? Parachute into Germany and break down the gates with a siege gun?"

"Of course not. I thought you'd have a much better plan than that."

"Me? Why?"

"Because you work there, don't you?"

Margaret sets down her knife and fork. "My dear girl. I believe you've been laboring under what they call a misapprehension. I've already explained. My brother's the chap in the field, not me. I sit at my desk and shuffle papers about. Take dictation and type up reports and translate things."

"But why? You're brother and sister. You're equally capable, I'm sure."

"It's true, they recruited us both. An old childhood friend of ours was putting together this department in the War Office and called on us to join him, because we both spoke German fluently, you know, having spent our summers there at my brother's estate. But I was deemed unsuitable for fieldwork. They never told me why, of course. I suppose I can guess." She picks up the bottle and refills her glass. "But there it is. Not only am I *not* in a position to parachute into Germany—even if I were so inclined—I'm apparently unfit for the job to begin with."

"Nonsense. You're exactly the kind of person—"

"*And* there's the plain fact that it's against department policy. Don't you see? I'd have to go against my own superiors."

"You're already going against your superiors, hiding me here."

"That's different. That's for Benedict's sake."

I lean forward. "Don't you *want* to save him?"

"What a thing to say. Of course I do."

"Then why won't you do anything about it?"

"Do *what*? Don't you see? There's nothing one *can* do. You've got no idea. Sunning yourself in the tropics. You don't have the slightest clue what war's like, you little fool. We're trapped here, we're rats in a cage, waiting our turn to die. We're no better off than Benedict."

"What if I refuse to wait?"

"We already know the answer to *that*. You decided to take matters into your own hands—bold, clever girl that you are—and now look. Your little scheme of blackmail has failed, and now you're in just as much danger as he is. Whatever it is you've got against them, it's more than your own life is worth." She busies herself with knife and fork, cutting the rabbit. I have the feeling she's hiding her eyes from me. She chews for a bit, tremendous concentration. Drinks her wine like she's dying of thirst.

I push the meat around the plate. There is the music of cutlery, the damp, cramped smell of despair. A siren wails from far away. Margaret cocks her head to listen. Her eyes narrow with knowledge, with some ability to decode the keening. After a moment, she shrugs and returns her attention to her dinner.

"This is really quite good. Where did you learn how to cook?"

"My mother taught me. She's Italian, it's in her blood. And we didn't have much money, so I learned to make do."

"Neither did we. All Mummy's money went into trust, and I haven't the slightest idea what became of it. Bad investments, I suppose. Whenever I asked Granny, she wouldn't answer. She liked to pretend Mummy didn't exist. The shame, you know."

"She was so beautiful."

"Yes. She was perfectly lovely. I used to think of her as an angel. She was always calm, always patient. She never raised her voice with me, not once. I always had the feeling . . . but then, I was only nine when she died."

"What feeling?"

Margaret idles the stem of the wineglass in her fingers. It's nearly empty, and the bottle's nearly empty, and I'm tempted to open another. But oh, she's balancing right there on the edge, and the slightest breath might topple her. We are sealed tight in this chilly room, in this chilly flat, windows blacked out, curtains closed, single bulb burning.

"I don't know. That she held some kind of deep sadness inside her. Some terrible loss. She was only ever really happy when Daddy was around."

"They were very much in love?"

Margaret raises her head, and the softness of her expression shocks me. I see her mother on the riverbank in her halo of blondness, and for the first time I wonder who stood behind that camera, taking the photograph. "I was only nine," she says, "but I'll never forget the way she looked at him, and he at her. It was more than love. It was something spiritual, like a religion."

"What a comfort for you."

"A comfort?"

"Knowing that such a love even existed in the world. Knowing your parents had it."

Margaret lifts the bottle and turns it almost vertical above her glass, so that not a single precious drop remains inside. Together we watch the *drip, drip, drip*, the shimmering of the surface, until there's nothing left to give, no more wine outside Margaret's glass, and she sets the empty bottle at the edge of the table.

"Why do think I never married?" she says.

WHEN THE DISHES ARE WASHED and put away in the cupboard, Margaret turns to me and folds her arms, as if she's considering what to do with me. We're standing in the cramped little kitchen, on the floor of gray linoleum; there's a window above the sink, but it's tiny and blacked out, and the air's still rank with the odor of cooked meat and grease.

"You didn't let me finish about B——," she says.

"I didn't realize there was more."

"He was quite obviously trying to sound me out, to find out what I knew. Lucky I've got a straight face." She taps her fingers against her arm. "He said nothing about you. He said it was terrible news about Thorpe, and I said yes, jolly awful, was there anything at all we could do? And he said they would alert any active agents in G section, any informants, to stand ready to offer aid and so on. All that rubbish."

"You don't believe him?"

We speak in that low, husky tone of voice just above a whisper, and the only light comes from the bulb in the parlor, around the corner. Margaret stares not at me, but at the curtain covering the kitchen window.

"It seems to me," she says, "that if B——'s decided it's too dangerous to let *you* live with this information—whatever it is—he likely feels precisely the same way about Benedict."

"I see."

"I don't mean to frighten you."

"In other words, he's not going to do a damned thing to help Thorpe. The Germans are doing him a favor. And if Thorpe manages to escape . . ."

From some floor below us comes the sound of a telephone ringing, the thump of footsteps. A cross, muffled voice. Margaret's eyes are like discs, meeting mine. The voice drones on, a kettle whines.

"You have to understand," she says. "It's war. It's about the end, not the means. They have to be ruthless, it's their job."

"And all this ruthlessness for the sake of that—that damned pair—"

"Shh. Don't say it."

I stare at my feet, which are clad in thick woolen stockings loaned to me by Margaret. I have the feeling she's knitted them herself; they have that chunky, uneven texture with which I'm deeply familiar, from packing hundreds of boxes of same in the old Red Cross headquarters on George Street in Nassau. Ugly, serviceable socks distributed all over England by now, possibly all over Europe, possibly even Colditz.

"So what did you say to B——?" I whisper.

"What else could I say? I didn't want to raise his suspicions. I said that I would of course keep my eye on the situation, here in German section, and that I stood ready to do whatever I could to help my brother. And he said . . ."

"Yes?"

I look up to find her watching me, arms still folded. At my look of inquiry, she levers away from the cupboard and stalks out of the kitchen to the parlor, where she takes the cigarettes and the matches from the mantel. She sticks a cigarette in her mouth and lights a match, and while she's doing this, holding the cigarette in place with her lips, she says, "He said that if anyone should approach me about Benedict, anyone at all, I should come to him first. That he'd been engaged in some rather sensitive work in Nassau, and there were desperate people who might do anything to obtain that information." She tosses the spent match atop the unlit coals in the fireplace and takes a long drag on the cigarette while she stares at me. "Who might attempt to win my trust in order to discover Benedict's secrets."

"He said that?"

"He said they would say anything, tell me all kinds of lies, and I should prevent any attempt by a stranger to insinuate himself." She blows out a stream of smoke. "Or *herself.*"

"He said that? *Herself?*"

"His exact words."

"And what did you tell him?"

As I said, the light in here is feeble, because of the blackout and because we're conserving, you know, for the war effort. And it's cold and stuffy, and I feel as if I'm suffocating, and yet I can't move, and neither can she. She's folded her arms over her cardigan, and the end of the cigarette flares orange between her fingers. I think I see a twitch in the skin of her neck. Her pulse, thumping in the same rhythm as mine. I think of Thorpe, in his cold, damp cell made of stone, and whether his pulse makes this rhythm, whether this beat unites us, the three of us.

She reaches out to flick ash into the fireplace.

"I said I would be on my guard, of course. And then I took some castor oil and made myself vomit so I could take a few days off sick."

"You did what?"

"We've got to get you out of London. He'll be looking for you everywhere, and I daresay it won't take him long to visit here."

"But where are we going?"

"Somewhere safe," she says. "Somewhere we can decide what's to be done. Somewhere on a farm, so we can eat eggs and butter without having to register you for a damned ration card."

"And where's that?"

"Home." Margaret tosses the cigarette in the fireplace. "Or rather, the house where Benedict and I were born."

ELFRIEDE

JUNE 1905
(Florida)

O N THE DAY Wilfred returns to her, the weather dawns hot and auspicious, so Elfriede takes the children to the seashore while Charlotte stays home with a headache. Oh, a headache. A hangover, let's call a spade a spade. Elfriede tells herself that's how Charlotte copes with the grief.

Anyway, she doesn't mind. Let Charlotte have her elixirs of whiskey and grief, while Elfriede has the children all to herself. Johann loves the seashore. Already he knows how to swim in the surf without being swept away, though Elfriede's careful to keep him on the sand when the waves are too rough. He's big and sturdy, like his father was; in fact, he's so big and so sturdy, so whitely blond and so loyal, he might almost be Gerhard himself. During the moments she holds her son in her arms, she doesn't feel the loss of his father at all.

The girls are more content to play on the shore, except for Ursula, the indomitable elder. Well, who could blame her? Like her father, like her brother, she's built on a sturdy frame. Sometimes Elfriede looks at her and wonders where the devil they're going to find a husband for her. Yes, there's the stain of bastardy, but it's more the size of her, the strength of

Ursula. Only an unusually large, unusually strong man can cope with her. Or else a smaller man who wants to be coped with? Perhaps. Her younger sisters are more dainty. Blond and pinkish. Of course, the baby's only eleven months old, so it's hard to tell for certain. She sits on the edge of her blanket right now, under a new striped umbrella, eating sand in calm handfuls. Poor baby, Charlotte was seven months along with her when Gerhard's appendix burst. She never saw her father's face, heard his voice, felt his big hands cradling her as he had the others. These things happen. Life's uncertain. Charlotte—convinced this tragedy was the retribution of a vengeful God—took to her bed when the peritonitis set in. Didn't leave it until after Gertrud was born, one month later and four weeks early, and a little life returned to her eyes. Well, who wouldn't perk up, producing a beautiful baby like that? *The Lord giveth and taketh away*, Charlotte said, putting the baby to her breast, naming her after her dead father, and Elfriede felt her own grief lifting as she gazed at the small, sad faces in the nursery, who now loved her and needed her more than ever.

Well! But that's all in the past. Those sad faces are happy again. Children, they're more resilient than adults, and anyway their memories are fleeting. Even Ursula's too young to really remember her father clearly, a year after his death, and Johann . . . well, Johann's like Gerhard and doesn't wear his emotions like garments. An expert at pretending all's well, that certain truths don't exist.

Noon, and the sun's gone fierce, burned away the last of the haze. Elfriede, in her bathing costume of dark blue serge, feels as if she's boiling alive. Because there's no one else about on this stretch of wild beach, she removes her stockings and shoves them in the basket. The children are naturally unaffected. Elfriede climbs to her feet and lifts Gertrud into her arms. Johann has just disappeared into the guts of a cresting wave. Ursula's chasing a screaming Frederica into the water's edge. Elfriede squints and reassures herself that their hats are still in place, shielding their precious faces from the sun. She carries Gertrud toward the water. She can swim a little, but swimming's impossible when you're carrying a baby on your hip, so she just wades into the mad, bubbling wash of surf, enjoying the pull of the undertow on her bathing dress, the sting of salt against her calves, the relief. She swings Gertrud downward and the baby kicks her legs in the water and laughs, and all the while Elfriede keeps her left eye on Johann, emerging now on the other side of the wave, tossing his white hair gleefully, and her right eye on the girls as they race along the water's edge. You never stop. Always, always, some part of your brain maintains this awareness of each child. Like the hum of a bumblebee, exhausting and unceasing and necessary to life. At night, when she tumbles unconscious into bed, she'll sleep right through the bang of a Florida thunderstorm outside her window, but a single cough from the other end of the corridor jolts her wide awake. In other words, motherhood.

Elfriede glances toward the sky. The white sun sits high. Time to open the picnic basket? Johann dives again. Gertrud swings her legs so hard, the foam flies up and hits her on the cheek. The girls swerve from the water to make an arc upon the empty sand, a hundred yards away. Wait! Not empty after all.

Elfriede straightens. Returns Gertrud to her hip. Gazes at the girls as they swoop around in circles, sand flying, seaweed kicking, but really she's looking past them at the white figure sitting right at the edge of the dune grass, a quarter mile away.

It might be a dog, she thinks. It's just sitting there, a white speck.

No, it's not a dog. Of course not. Recognizing her observation, it rises to its feet, a man fully grown, dressed in a pale suit, and waves one arm. Starts forward at a long-legged stroll.

Elfriede can't move. The girls scream happily, the gulls call overhead. Gertrud pulls at her dress, wanting milk that isn't there. As she stands, immobile, the undertow buries her feet deeper into the sand. To pull herself free will require greater and greater strength, strength she doesn't have when she can scarcely hold herself upright, when she is hard put just to hold Gertrud safe against her side. A wet hand grabs hers. "Mama, what's the matter?" says Johann. "Who's that man?"

The girls, oblivious, run straight past. The man takes off his hat, a plain straw boater, and the horizon catches flame.

"His name is Mr. Thorpe," she says. "He's an Englishman."

WHEN SHE AND CHARLOTTE AND the children left for Florida six months ago, Elfriede didn't pack much. For one thing, she had few clothes suitable for the tropics. A couple of summer dresses, a hat, her under-things, her nightdresses. Her English books, to practice the language. Of sentimental objects, she packed even fewer. The Cloth of Tears—she has a superstition—and a small stack of letters from deep inside her bureau. Not many. By some unspoken agreement, they always waited months to reply to each other. When they did, the letters were not long. Maybe a page or two. They contained not the usual newsiness of letters, not even dates, not even names, not even their own. They were like poems dropped from the sky. She couldn't be sure how Wilfred perceived her missives, but to Elfriede, Wilfred's letters were strange and passionate and wonderful. Just last night, Elfriede was trying to remember the exact wording of a certain passage that she had received in the spring of 1902, so she pulled the letter from the bundle and read it through:

> There is this flower in a pot in the mean little courtyard out back, and a tiny, whirring bird called a sunbird who comes every morning to sip nectar from it. Of course, I can't be sure it's the same sunbird, but I feel that it is. He flies in purposefully and spends some time just hovering about, inspecting the flower (what sort of flower? you naturally ask yourself, reading this from the slipper chair in the corner of your bedroom while the cool rain falls on your window, and I'm afraid I'm damned if I know—it's odd and beautiful, worships sunshine, has clusters of tiny tubelike flowers that graduate in color from yellow to orange

to a vivid pink-red)—well as I said, he inspects the flower lovingly, I should say enamored, choosing where to start, until he darts in at last and plunges his long beak inside one of the buds, then the next, then the next. Eventually, having taken his fill, he flies drunkenly away. The courtyard is hot and dry and dusty, and I have taken to leaving out a dish of water to cleanse his palate, but the bird won't touch it. He must be shy of humans, I think. Anyway, I tell you all this because last night I dreamt of you lying asleep on a cushion in the courtyard, wearing nothing at all because of the heat. You were drenched in the most radiant sunshine, and a hundred tiny birds surrounded you, all hovering and not daring to touch you, though they badly wanted to. I'm not sure if I was one of the sunbirds or merely an observer, trying to glimpse you behind the blur of desperate wings. Make of this dream what you like, dearest. But this morning I sit here at the table in the courtyard with my pen and paper and the sunbird has just spurted over the wall and I'm seized by the most intense longing imaginable. Damn the rascal. He communes daily with his chosen flower. I wonder how far he flies each morning to reach her, and whether he visits any others. It seems to me that a flower so extraordinary ought to be sufficient for a single devoted sunbird. But I am not an expert on birds or flowers.

As she read these words again, just last night, the same heat spread over her skin as it always did. She wanted to know what she looked like in his dream, how she looked when Wilfred imagined her without any clothes. She wanted to know where this hot, dusty courtyard existed— surely not in England, surely not during those spring months when he would have written it—and if not England, where and why? The postmark was always the same, London. No other place name ever appeared. As if he existed nowhere at all, or maybe everywhere.

OR HERE. ON THIS FLORIDA beach. He approaches at a comfortable stroll. She notices he isn't wearing shoes, and he dangles his pale linen jacket over his shoulder by a pair of fingers. How he's filled out. He is absolutely lean, almost too lean, but he left her a skeleton and now that skeleton has flesh. Is flesh. His copper hair, all grown out. That dear, enormous head. She sees his smile first, and then his freckles, then a trim, ginger moustache above his upper lip, and last of all his bright blue eyes that tend toward green in this golden Florida light. Her feet are still stuck, and so is her face; some expression of shock, she supposes. He wades straight into the water to stand before her.

"Hello, there," he says in English.

Elfriede can't speak.

"Hello," pipes Johann, also in English. He steps forward and sticks out his hand. "My name is Johann von Kleist. I'm from Germany."

Wilfred sinks into a crouch and takes Johann's hand. "Hello, Johann. I can't tell you how delighted I am to meet you. I'm——"

"You're Mr. Thorpe. Yes, Mama?" He looks up at Elfriede, and so does Wilfred, and the pair of them in proximity, blond face and ginger face, snatches the last of her composure.

"Here," she whispers, holding out the baby. Wilfred, half-rising, scoops up Gertrud with one arm and snatches Elfriede's waist with the other, easing her slow tumble downward into the sea. He seems accustomed to such emergencies. He merely hoists Gertrud to his shoulders and sits on his knees beside Elfriede while the surf kicks around them, ruining his suit. Johann stares aghast.

"Hot day, isn't it?" Wilfred says.

"Very hot."

"Thank goodness for this lovely beach."

"Yes."

The girls have stuttered to a stop at the water's edge. Elfriede feels the charge of their amazement through the salt air. I must stand, she thinks. Gertrud screeches her delight at the color of Wilfred's hair. She grabs handfuls and kneads them in her fists. Something white bobs and floats in the water nearby. Wilfred's abandoned jacket. He braces Gertrud's leg with one hand and reaches out to take Elfriede's fingers firmly with the other one. "Up we go, then."

She rises. That hand, she can't let it go, but she must. The children. To compensate for the loss of him, she bends down and fishes his jacket from the water. "I'm afraid it's probably ruined," she says, in German this time.

"Think nothing of it."

"Gertrud, darling, stop. You can't pull Mr. Thorpe's hair. You're hurting him."

"To the contrary."

She stares at his mouth. Wide, grinning. Somewhere above, Gertrud buries her face in the thicket of ginger hair and croons. Wilfred's jacket drips from Elfriede's hand. "You're here," she says.

"Your last postcard intrigued me. How could I resist Florida? Though I had some trouble arranging for a suitable leave."

"Leave from what?"

He touches the edge of his moustache. "From the army."

"The *army*?"

"It's a long story. And we're rather wet."

"Oh, God. Yes."

"Sir." Johann tugs at Wilfred's shirt. "Sir. I beg your pardon. Which army?"

"The British Army."

Johann frowns thoughtfully. "Did you kill many Boers?"

"Ah. A few of them, possibly—"

"Africa!" Elfriede gasps. "The courtyard? With the sunbird? That was in Africa?"

Wilfred gazes down at her. "South Africa. A blockhouse in the Transvaal."

ELFRIEDE ALWAYS PACKS TOO MUCH food in the picnic basket. No excuse, therefore, not to invite Wilfred to join them under the umbrella for sandwiches and oranges, an offer he gallantly accepts. Elfriede sits at the edge of the shade, holds Gertrud in her lap and feeds her tiny pieces of bread and cheese while Wilfred converses easily in German with Johann and the girls, in between mouthfuls of ham sandwich. The children are fascinated, of course, while the two adults, Wilfred and Elfriede, hardly look at each other. Elfriede concentrates her attention on Gertrud, on keeping the sand from the little cups of lemonade she's poured from the jug, but inwardly she marvels at the gentle, effortless way Wilfred extracts everything there is to know about the children. What they like to eat and do and wear, how often they bathe, Hund the shaggy mongrel who stops by the kitchen door from time to time, accepts a scrap or two with grave courtesy, and has a particular interest in the flavor of Nurse's hand. Wilfred asks about Nurse, and Elfriede wakes from her stupor of shock and calls an end to the picnic.

"When did you join the army?" she asks him, as they walk back to the house, a mile away.

"About a month after I left the sanatorium," he answers. "As soon as I could pass the physical examination. Pulled a string or two and got commissioned a second lieutenant in the Royal Highlands Cavalry."

"I never imagined."

"It was something of an impulse. The thought of Vienna made me sick. I returned home instead and was all set to enter chambers when the news about Kitchener reached London. I thought, here's a fine way to get yourself killed."

"Don't say that!"

He laughs. "Well, maybe I didn't *want* to die out there. But I didn't really care one way or the other, at the time, and it all sounded like a great deal more adventure than studying to be a barrister over the course of a few bitter London winters."

"Why didn't you tell me?"

"I didn't want you to worry."

"Of course—"

But Johann's tugging at his shirt again. "Mr. Thorpe! Mr. Thorpe! Why aren't you wearing your uniform? Sir."

"Why, because I'm on leave, you know, and besides we're in America."

"Did you bring it with you? Can I see it?"

Elfriede falls back a pace or two and allows Johann to pelt his questions. Anyway her emotions are rising too high at the thought of Wilfred in South Africa, Wilfred riding horseback across the veldt under a blazing sun, ambushed by Boers, flies buzzing over bullet wounds. That dusty courtyard, the flower, the sunbird, all this under mortal danger! While Elfriede read his letters from a slipper chair in her bedroom, imagining him as safe as she was! She stares at his damp white shirt, his sleeves rolled to the elbow. Gertrud straddles his shoulders once more, gripping his hair; he holds her steady with one hand and carries the picnic basket with the other. Inside the basket are his jacket and his straw hat. Wilfred! Actually *Wilfred*! He exists. His shoulders, his back, his arm, his hand clasping the picnic basket, his legs encompassing the ground before hers. It's like walking in a dream. Elfriede holds Frederica's hand as a link to reality. Ursula trots ahead, blazing a trail. They reach the house and Wilfred turns, eyebrows raised, and Elfriede panics. My God, what will she do with him? What's to be done? Then she remembers she's a widow and everything is now possible. Wilfred is now possible.

TRUE, THERE'S THE PROBLEM OF a houseful of children. How is Wilfred possible when a moment of private conversation is not? She excuses herself and puts the younger children in bed for their naps, while Johann and Wilfred chatter over cake in the kitchen. Charlotte's gone, headache or no headache—in town, says the housekeeper, shrugging her shoulders. Probably buying more bottles of that Kentucky bourbon she's discovered. Elfriede waits until the children have all dropped off. She walks straight past the clamor in the kitchen and out into the garden, thundering heart, where she collapses in the grass under an orange tree. Maybe she falls asleep, God knows how when her nerves are teeming. At any rate, she startles at the sound of Wilfred's voice.

"There you are. Do you mind if I join you?"

Mind? She shakes her head.

He sinks to the grass nearby and lights a cigarette. "I'm sorry about all that. I didn't mean to shock you."

"You would have shocked me anyway. Better that than to simply knock on the door and present yourself."

"Listen to you, you're shaking." He reaches out and clasps her knee. "Don't be afraid."

"I'm not."

"If I've made you uneasy . . ."

"Not at all. Not uneasy. Just shocked." She tries to laugh. "It *is* you, isn't it? I haven't had sunstroke or something?"

"It's me, all right. In the flesh." His hand falls away from her knee, but his face remains near, his eyes contain her eyes, his long, plain cheeks contain her memory. If only she could touch them.

"Your hair is so much longer," she says.

"As ginger as ever, I'm afraid."

"And the army. My God. What if you were killed?"

"As I said, my own survival wasn't altogether important to me, at the time."

"It was important to *me*."

"Yes, I know. I suppose I knew then, as well, but I indulged myself anyway. I was suffering, you see, and it seemed only fair that, by dying, I should make you suffer a little too."

"A little? A little? How do you think I should have felt— How was I even to find out, if you were killed?"

"Oh, I left behind one of those tragic little *In the event of my death* envelopes with a trusted friend. Ridiculous and melodramatic, but I wasn't exactly myself, you know. In fact I felt I was driving myself inexorably toward madness, and I might have gotten there soon if I hadn't had to occupy myself with keeping my men alive and in some sort of fighting order." He flicks ash from the end of his cigarette. "Of course, it turns out that war's simply another avenue toward madness, but at least you feel a sense of purpose."

"Was it so terrible?"

His gaze shifts to the right, possibly to examine the trunk of the orange tree, against which Elfriede's back is resting. "That depends on what you mean by terrible."

"Did you kill people?"

"Yes."

"A great many?"

"Look," he says, "we can sit here and discuss the number of men, women, and children I've murdered for the safety and security of the British Empire, but that dear young chap of yours is going to finish his arithmetic lesson in due course, and we will have said nothing at all of what's important."

"But I want to know. I want to know everything you've endured. It was my fault, it was for my sake."

"No, it wasn't. I did it for my own sake." He leans back on one hand and sucks on his cigarette. "I'd much rather talk about you. You've made a much better work of your time. Creating life instead of destroying it."

"That's not—that's not quite true."

"I mean your children. Don't look away, dearest. There's nothing to be ashamed of. I meant it when I said I only wanted your happiness. God knows I wanted children for you, as long as you could have them without suffering the—"

"They're not mine."

Wilfred removes the cigarette from his mouth and says, "Not yours?"

Elfriede summons herself and turns her gaze to Wilfred's face. An expression of mild confusion rests there. The cigarette burns unheeded between his thumb and forefinger. "The girls, I mean. I'm their mother, of course, but they're not *mine*. From my body."

He crushes out the cigarette in the grass. "Whose, then?"

"Charlotte."

"Who the devil's Charlotte?"

"Nurse. Johann's nurse. It turned out they were sleeping together, she and Gerhard, before he got sick. By the time he recovered, she was three or four months gone with child. Instead of turning her out, I let her stay. I thought . . . at the time, I thought it was the ideal solution."

"The ideal solution to what?"

"Because he wanted more children, desperately, and I didn't want to sleep with him. How could I, after *you*? I felt no attraction to him at all. Revulsion, almost. And there she was, thoroughly infatuated, already pregnant by him."

Still, Wilfred betrays no astonishment. The same mild curiosity. He must be turning the whole affair over in his mind, examining it from all angles, making the necessary connections. Three children! One an infant! He straightens and pulls the cigarette case from his pocket. Repeats the ritual of opening the lid, selecting a cigarette, lighting it from one of the matches in the case. Smokes for some time before he says simply, "Were you mad?"

"No more mad than you were, when you sought that lieutenant's commission."

"I see. I see. And how long before you regretted arranging this neat little—little—compact?"

"I don't know. I don't remember. It's all blurred together now. It just seemed so perfectly logical, at the time. When she told me she was expecting Gerhard's child, just exactly when he'd recovered enough to—when he expected me to—when I should have slipped back into my old life. And I knew I must, I knew it was my duty to return to his bed and have children with him, that was the bargain I made with God when he was almost dead with typhoid. *Just make him well, and I'll be a good, true wife again.* But the heart, you know, the heart's not logical like that."

"No," he says softly. "It's not."

"I was in a panic. I knew I couldn't bear it, I couldn't bear him as a lover, but what else was there? And then—almost by magic—this door opened before me. And I felt such relief. I felt as if I'd been offered a reprieve from prison. Do you understand what I mean? Do you—do you think I'm dreadful?"

During the course of these few sentences, Wilfred's risen from the grass and paced a few yards away to stare at the gentle slope of the garden, which ends in a tangle of prickly, marshy wilderness. At her question—*Do you think I'm dreadful?*—he shakes his head, speechless.

Elfriede rises to her knees. It's easier to speak to the back of his head, and the words, the terrible confession tumbles forth. "So I called in Gerhard and we had this chat, the three of us. I told my husband he must take responsibility for this child, it was only right, the babe was innocent. I said I would raise the child in our nursery with Johann, just as if it were ours. Of course they were both amazed. A wife isn't supposed to be so understanding, you know. She's supposed to dismiss the other woman and pretend the whole thing doesn't exist. Instead I made my little announcement and left them together in the room."

Wilfred looks back at her, over his shoulder. "Alone, you mean?"

"Yes, alone. Except at first he couldn't accept the hint. He's very rigid, you know, or rather he's moral, he craves order and nice, clean lines of virtue and sin. Probably he was horrified at himself, at the mess he'd made, at the lust he felt for this woman. She left only a short time later, looking more upset, I think, than before. So I made myself more clear. One night I told him he should go up to Charlotte, to see how she was getting along. He said no, but I insisted. I said it was his responsibility to care for her, this woman who cared so much for him, who was bearing his child. At last he went. He came back down two hours later—I waited up, you see, to make sure—and then I knew it was done."

"Good God."

"Of course, he's very methodical, Gerhard. So he went up to her on Tuesdays and Fridays, like clockwork, whenever he was home. At first he just stayed an hour or two. You know, to satisfy a physical urge, that was all, like an itch that needed scratching. The rest of the time he spent in the ordinary way, with me and Johann or else his own pursuits, and generally ignored Charlotte because, of course, she was only a servant. Then the baby was born. We were all so happy with her, so delighted. Gerhard was enamored. He had always wanted a daughter, you know. He would hold her for hours, he would stay in the nursery and watch Charlotte feed her, he began to talk about having more children. So I suppose I wasn't surprised when he went up to visit Charlotte's room again, one night, when Ursula was a couple of months old—"

"My God," said Wilfred.

"Only it was different from before. He stayed longer this time, and he went up again the next evening. He began to go up to her four or five times a week. By then she'd moved to a separate room on the upper floor, a private room, but next door to the nursery so she could hear the children if they needed her. Eventually he had a double bed put in. He would actually sleep there with her and return at dawn. Just as soon as Ursula was weaned, Charlotte became pregnant with Frederica, like that." Elfriede snaps her fingers. "Then it was Gertrud."

"And you never put a stop to it?"

"That's the trouble. You can't. What do you say to them, it was all right yesterday but today it's not? I've changed my mind? Anyway, there were the children. I couldn't help loving them. Here were these beautiful babies, and there was no misery, no blackness, no madness. They call me Mutti, because Johann did and he was their brother. How could I give them up? So I let it go on. I told myself that she loved him and I didn't, she could please him that way and I couldn't. She might as well have his nights. I had his days, after all. He was always attentive to me, always affectionate."

Wilfred throws himself back on the ground beside her and stares at the sky. "Like brother and sister."

"Yes."

"Always?"

"Yes."

Wilfred turns his head toward her, while the cigarette hangs from the corner of his mouth. He stares at her intently, without embarrassment. "Oh, my dear love."

"There was this time, about a year after Frederica was born. I went into the study, Gerhard's study, on some household matter. I forgot to knock. I mean, why should I knock? I'm his wife. Anyway, she was there, Charlotte was there, and they were . . . they sat together on a chair, you see, her dress was open in front, her hair was down, she was on top of him. They didn't even notice I was there. I stood there in the doorway and I could only think, It's Wednesday afternoon, by God, a *Wednesday afternoon*. How dare they. Hadn't they got enough the night before?" Elfriede cackles. "I realized in that moment how much he was in love with her, not with me. I was invisible to them."

"Elfriede—"

"Oh, I know it was stupid. When there was no possibility of even seeing you again. When we are all just flesh and blood. And the months passed, the years passed, and it wasn't as if I wanted you any less, or wanted Gerhard at all. But you weren't there, you weren't real, you were an idea, a memory, a heartbeat, a stack of letters, and Gerhard was real. And I loved him, not as a lover maybe, but still I cared for him, and I'd lost him. I would hear him coming back into his room at dawn, I would wake up and hear the bed creak as he got into it, pretending to have slept there all night, while I lay there burning, my God, just to be *touched* again, maybe not by him, but to be *touched*—"

"Elfriede." Wilfred lifts himself up and crashes down next to her. One long arm takes her by the shoulders and guides her home. His shirt, her Cloth of Tears.

IN THE AFTERNOON, CHARLOTTE RETURNS. Hangs up her hat on the hook in the hallway and gapes in amazement at the fellow in the parlor, before retiring to her room for a nap.

Dinner's a failure. It's too hot and everyone's out of sorts. Wilfred makes this valiant effort to keep conversation going, and his natural charm nearly succeeds. But the awkwardness of it all. The children, scrubbed and dressed and fretful. Johann, whose natural interest in this brave British soldier turned into suspicion when he came running into the garden with his arithmetic lesson and found his mother and Mr. Thorpe lying together against the orange tree. *Mama, why are you crying?* he asked, and Elfriede, scrambling to her feet, wiping her hair and eyes, said desperately, wanting to soothe his fears, *Because I'm happy, darling.* Johann's worried, confused eyes then rose to find Wilfred, who had released Elfriede by now. But it was too late. The light of worship had already faded from Johann's eyes. Johann, who had looked upon his father as a hero among heroes, who had suffered so deeply and tearlessly as the peritonitis did its work, was not too young to realize what had transpired under the orange tree. *Because I'm happy, darling.* Stupid Elfriede. Didn't she know that a little boy doesn't want his mother to be happy in a strange man's arms? The last possible thing.

Elfriede tries to liven things up after dessert. She puts a record on the phonograph, some dance hall music, and Wilfred asks Charlotte to do a two-step around the living room. They're both excellent dancers, and the room is large. Well, the whole house is large. Large and commodious. Elfriede's a wealthy woman, after all, a baron's widow, a baron's mother. She's rented the house for an entire year from some wealthy magnate from Chicago or Cleveland or Pittsburgh, she can't remember now, one of those American cities that churn out millionaires like sausages. (Also like sausage, you didn't necessarily want to know how the millions were made.) At any rate, it's a handsome, well-proportioned house, containing a multitude of airy rooms that still manage to heat like ovens on a day like today, when there isn't much air to speak of. Charlotte and Wilfred soon break apart, panting and perspiring. Wilfred takes a handkerchief from his pocket and wipes his forehead. Charlotte pours herself a drink. Elfriede, rising from the chair, calls the children to come upstairs with her for their baths.

THESE RITUALS OF BATH AND bedtime are precious to Elfriede. By devoting herself to the children, she feels as if she's making up for the lost time with Johann, for her failures as a wife and as a mother. To-night, her mind's elsewhere. Downstairs in the living room with Wilfred and Charlotte—she keeps seeing them locked in two-step, around and around the room—and also in her study, a small room off the library, where the afternoon post contained a letter postmarked Schloss Kleist and addressed in her sister-in-law Helga's familiar, sharp handwriting.

Elfriede dislikes opening these letters. Ordinarily she just skims them, ensuring there's no emergency, it's just the same old querulous Helga, lec-turing her on her duties and her failure to execute them. How absurd, when Helga's perfectly capable of running Schloss Kleist on her own, and even (so Elfriede suspects) delighted to do so. And let's not forget the added joy of martyrdom! The moral superiority from which she can regard Elfriede, who frolics, feckless and heedless, in her American paradise.

My dear Dowager Baroness, she begins—this reminder of Elfriede's station starts off all their correspondence—*Enough is enough! Your son the Baron must be raised on his own estate, not in some American playground for the idle rich* . . . And so on. There, in paragraph two, appears the inevitable reverence to Elfriede's dead husband, the duty Elfriede owes to him forevermore. In paragraph three, up pops Helga's suspicion that Elfriede has gone to Florida specifically to engage in immoral behavior, because for what possible reason would a person otherwise travel to Florida? (Helga takes particular relish in listing the possible forms such behavior might take, all of which sound like a great deal of fun to Elfriede.)

But it's paragraph four that strikes at Elfriede's heart. *If you cannot, therefore, bring yourself to your duty, I may be forced to bring it upon you myself. Make no mistake, Elfriede. I shall not allow you to destroy the name and reputation of this family, which generations of women far worthier than you have been proud to burnish. The young Baron must return home immediately to learn his duty. He is his father's son, after all, and the only legacy that remains to my dear brother.*

Of Johann's sisters, of course, Helga makes no mention. So far as she's concerned, they don't even exist.

WHEN ELFRIEDE RETURNS TO THE living room, carrying Gertrud, the phonograph's turned to something melancholy and Charlotte sits stiff in the armchair, drinking from a tall glass of cut crystal. Wilfred stands nearby, against the wall, arms crossed over his chest. The room smells of heat and perspiration, perfume and mildew. Elfriede holds the baby out to Charlotte. "When you're ready," she says.

Charlotte sighs and finishes her drink. "Yes, of course. You'll excuse me." Rising from the chair, she nods farewell to Wilfred and extracts the sleepy Gertrud from Elfriede's arms. The scent of whiskey forms its own pungent atmosphere around her.

"Are you all right?" Elfriede asks, in a low voice.

But Charlotte ignores her. "Up we go, then, darling," she croons, carrying Gertrud to the stairs, and worriedly Elfriede watches them go, watches Charlotte's skirt whisk from sight, before she turns to face Wilfred, who has not moved an inch. His gaze asks her a question, and her nerves shatter in reply. She's exhausted by the ordeal of bedtime, confused and consumed by guilt. Johann made her read story after story. When at last she tucked him into bed and insisted he go to sleep, he sat up and put his arms around her neck instead. *You're not going anywhere, are you?* he asked, and she kissed him on both damp cheeks and assured him she wasn't going anywhere, of course not. She left the window open, screened against the mosquitoes, and thought maybe it was time to leave, to go back to Germany. Florida's getting so hot for small children. If this is June, imagine July.

"I thought you'd be gone by now," she says.

He straightens from the wall and uncrosses his arms. "I gather your Charlotte is the sort who drowns her grief?"

"Gerhard's death devastated her, I'm afraid."

"So it seems. I'm more concerned with you, however. How you're feeling. Are *you* devastated, dearest?"

"It was an awful shock, of course. I suppose we thought that if he could beat the typhoid, he was invincible. I thought we would all grow old together."

Maybe he notices that her voice grows raspy on that last sentence. He says, in a kind voice, "But you didn't really want that, did you? To grow old together?"

"I don't know. But that was what I expected. It was the future I imagined." She pauses. "He was a good man. He should have lived longer."

"Should he? I suppose none of us is given to know how long we're marked to live on this blessed earth. Well, God rest his soul." Wilfred nods to the stairs. "Everything quiet upstairs? The children are well?"

"Yes. Charlotte's nursing the baby. She'll put her to bed when she's finished."

"And then collapse in a stupor?" he inquires dryly.

"Something like that."

"Elfriede. You deserve more than this, you know."

The kindness in his face is too much. Elfriede's shot through with nerves, with shock, with an anticipation she cannot describe, like fear and desire combusting together under her skin. He's going to leave now, he's going to return to his hotel. Or is he? In the corner of the drawing room, the phonograph scratches away uselessly. Elfriede starts forward and turns it off, and for a moment stands there with her hand on the edge of the table. She starts to shake her head—but really, what's she denying?—and Wilfred, coming up behind her, puts his hand on her shoulder.

"I thought we might take a stroll in the garden, before I return to the hotel."

IT'S JUNE, AND THE DAYS are long. Twilight's just settling across the sky, a hazy indigo, and the air is hot and rich with the scent of blossom. Wilfred sticks his hands in his pockets. They stand about a hundred yards from the house, just beyond the perimeter of light from the windows, where the grass starts a long, gentle slope toward the bottom of the garden. Beyond that, Elfriede doesn't dare venture. There's a pond somewhere in the middle of all that tangled vegetation, and she's heard stories about snakes and alligators. She mentions this to Wilfred.

"Haven't you seen any?" he asks.

"Not yet. But I don't want to push my luck."

He pulls out his cigarette case and fiddles with it, as if unable to decide whether to smoke or not. "There were all sorts of predatory creatures in South Africa. I never realized how benign the English fauna really is until I went abroad."

"When do you have to go back?"

"To South Africa? Never, I hope." He turns to her and smiles. The moustache startles her anew. "My regiment was called home two years ago. But if you're asking how long until I have to report back to duty . . ."

"Well?"

Wilfred turns back to the shadows. "Next month. Four and a half weeks, less ten days on the liner." He opens the case and pulls out a cigarette. "I'm sorry about these. I was only an occasional smoker until I joined the army."

She watches him light the cigarette. She loves the way he closes his eyes as he draws in a long draft, the way he savors it. "You don't have to stay at the hotel, you know. We've got three spare bedrooms."

"That would be decidedly improper, I imagine."

"There's nobody to care."

For some time, he remains silent. Elfriede's transfixed by the orange flare at the end of the cigarette, by the choreography of fingers and lips. "I'm afraid I'm not as strong as you are," he says at last. "There have been other women since I saw you last."

"Yes."

"That's the trouble with falling in love with a married woman." He pauses. "*Falling in love*—my God, what a stupid phrase. When I think of what I *felt* upon learning that the good baron had recovered, against all probability, from an illness—I'm ashamed to admit—from an illness I expected and even hoped, yes, *hoped* would prove fatal. When I realized not only that I wasn't going to have you after all but that I didn't even deserve you to begin with. And then. *Then.* Then what I felt a year ago, when I first heard the shocking news, quite by chance, that Elfriede von Kleist was free at last."

He falls silent, implying that Elfriede should make some response, but she can't. Maybe she won't. There's just no reply possible, is there? Maybe an honest one, but not a decent one.

"Anyway," he says at last, "since the time seems ripe to confess our sins, let's return for a moment to that appalling moment in October of 1900, when Baron von Kleist vanquished the typhoid and a black future opened up before me. I began by drinking, but I couldn't seem to kill myself with it, no matter how thoroughly I bent myself to the task. So I joined the army. I thought surely the Boers would kill me, which at least might serve some sort of purpose."

"Don't say that."

"Well, it's true, isn't it? We've all got to do our bit in life. One serves one's country with a certain amount of distinction, if by distinction you mean murdering anything that dared to raise its head on that godforsaken plain, and managing to avoid getting killed oneself, despite carrying out one's duties in a spirit of desperate recklessness. Or maybe there's no contradiction. Maybe it was the recklessness that saved me. Only the careful ones get killed, after all. But I'm upsetting you."

"Yes. But don't stop. I want to know the truth. I want to know everything."

"The truth? My dear, there isn't enough time in the world." He lifts his hand to rub the corner of one eye with his thumb. "As you see, however, I didn't die. Instead I spent most of my time learning how many things there are worse than death. Or rather, how many ways there are to be dead. Then, just in time, I would receive a dear little letter from you, like a cup of water in a desert, and for a moment or two I was glad to be alive."

"Did they mean so much? They were so short. I never knew what to say. They were all just nonsense, I thought."

"They kept me alive, whether I wanted it or not."

"Then I wish I'd written a thousand."

"A waste of time. I didn't deserve them."

She starts to protest. He paces forward and turns. She can't see him in this darkness, can't see the brilliance of his hair or the saturation of his eyes. Only the shape of that round, large head against the indigo sky.

"A thousand letters wouldn't have mattered. You were lost to me, you see. You were married to another man. And I must tell you, in my despair, I often sought the particular kind of oblivion that carnal intercourse can give."

"Of course you did. I never expected you to be chaste."

"No? Well, I haven't disappointed you, then." The cigarette's finished. He tosses it in the grass and scuffs it with his shoe. "Of course, I satisfied my conscience with the knowledge that you were doing the same. Now I realize I was the faithless one."

"It doesn't matter. You owed me nothing. I had no right to ask for a fidelity I couldn't give you myself."

"And yet you gave it."

"Only by chance. Anyway, you had no way of knowing that."

"Still, I can't help feeling as if I should have known, somehow."

Elfriede sinks into the coarse, short lawn. The Florida nights are anything but silent. The bullfrogs croak, the alligators groan. The birds chatter and chatter. "Was there any particular woman?" she asks softly.

"*Particular?* They were all particular, Elfriede. Each of them human beings, God's creatures, like you and me." He lowers himself into the grass beside her. "They were all the exact opposite of you. As if I were looking for an antidote. Maybe I was. But if she existed, I didn't find her."

He smells of cigarettes and orange blossom. Or is that the air itself? But also—yes, there it is! That other, queer scent, impossible to articulate. The particular flavor of Wilfred. She hasn't smelled it since Switzerland. She lifts her hand and touches the stiff hair at the end of his moustache. "When did you grow this?"

"As soon as my commission came through. Army regulations. An officer's got to grow some kind of hair on his face, you know. Presumably lends one the necessary air of authority. Do you hate it?"

"Not at all. I love whatever's yours."

He closes his eyes. She moves her hand to his cheek, newly shaved. "You're here," she says in wonder.

"Yes."

"*It's* here. It's still here, it's the same as before. How is that possible?"

"I don't know. I never understood it to begin with. Why a woman like you should give the slightest notice to a plain, ungainly, ginger-haired chap like me. I've got nothing to offer you. A captain's pay, a trifling inheritance. A shoulder to cry on, I suppose, but—"

Then she's kissing him. The touch of his lips amazes her. The strange tickle of his moustache. She tastes tobacco and the wine they drank at dinner, this cool white Riesling because of the heat. His tongue is gentle on hers. His mouth is slow. Under her hands, he's no longer the skeleton he was. His flesh has thickened over his bones. There's simply more of him. By the time he lifts his head, she's forgotten Helga and her viper letters, she's forgotten her marriage, she's forgotten the children asleep in the house behind them, God help her. All she knows is Wilfred.

"Oh, Christ," he whispers in English.

Elfriede takes hold of his shoulders and pulls him down with her, into the grass. He goes willingly. Sheds his jacket and spreads it beneath her head. Her fingers wobble as she unbuttons his shirt.

"I do have *some*thing for you," he says. "For what it's worth. From the moment I learned of von Kleist's death, God rest him, I haven't touched another woman. Waited and hoped, that's all I did. Does that help at all?"

She finishes the buttons and pulls his shirt from his trousers, then the undershirt of white linen. Now his pale skin attracts a little light, from the new-risen moon or the house or the last echo of sunset, who knows. She places her hands on the tender hollows between breastbone and shoulders and kisses his sternum.

"Wait a moment," he says. "One more thing."

But she doesn't want to wait. She's lost all patience. Hasn't she waited enough? Years and years for him. She unbuttons his trousers. He's stiff and heavy, there's no going back. Only death can part them now.

IN THE GARDEN, THEY'RE SWIFT and efficient. Consummation, that's all. They lie stunned with relief afterward, listening to all those croaks and chirps, while their hearts thump like drums and the perspiration rolls from their skin. Not a word. What possible words? The whole world is wet and hot and stuck together. At last he eases himself out and helps her with her drawers, her skirts. She finds his shirt. They wander in a daze back to the house. In the kitchen, Elfriede chips ice from the block in the icebox and pours a pitcher of water to take upstairs. Wilfred follows her without a sound.

Elfriede's bedroom is pale and prim and hot. The windows are screened; she opens them to slight refreshment. Now there's time to un-dress each other. They have all night. She unpins her hair and Wilfred takes up handfuls to rub against his cheeks and his lips. He uncovers her breasts and her belly for the first time and falls to his knees on the braided rug. The moon's risen above the nearby sea, and Wilfred tells Elfriede how she glows in its light. He kisses every curve and hollow. He licks the salt from her skin. Like a penitent he worships her. Twice she bursts into climax—she's a bowstring, tightly wound, and each release is the flight of an arrow—and while she lies there basking a second time, he parts her damp hair from her shoulder and apologizes.

"For what?"

(They speak in whispers, because of the children.)

"I meant to ask you something, out there in the garden, and instead I forgot myself entirely."

Elfriede rolls atop his chest and presses her fingertips to his mouth.

"The answer's yes," she says, and she straddles him the way Charlotte straddled Gerhard in his chair in that far-off study, she rides him the way

Charlotte rode Gerhard, vigorous, sweating, ecstatic, shockingly deep, but when he spends a few moments later, he doesn't close his eyes and roar like a lion. He lifts his hands to cradle her face between his palms, and there, then, staring reverently inside her, he groans from his chest as if he's dying. *La petite mort*, as the French call it.

PERCHANCE TO DREAM? DROWSY, SATIATED. They lie entangled, perspiring into the night and into each other. Elfriede's stuck one hand in Wilfred's hair. With her other finger, she touches his army moustache. At last she knows the texture of his skin and the weight of his bones, which are heavier than she imagined. That lanky skeleton contains a deceptive mass. *Shanks*. She thinks of her English books, the English words she's learned over the course of the past five years. *Longshanks*. Wilfred's long, heavy leg wound around hers, his arm draped over her hip. Wilfred! A delirium of contentment settles over her. She's going to fall asleep like this, she's going to sleep all night in Wilfred's arms. And this morning she woke alone, with no notion of what was to come!

"How do you feel, my love?" he whispers in English.

How can she stop herself? The sweet, new tickle of Wilfred's moustache. She draws the tip of her tongue along his lower lip, from left to right, and tastes . . . herself.

Wery vell, she whispers back.

Against her belly, his cock stirs and stiffens. So maybe dreams will have to wait, after all.

JUST BEFORE DAWN, WILFRED RISES from the bed and dresses himself, so quietly that Elfriede almost doesn't hear him. Only a sense of parting invades her dreams, and she opens her eyes.

"Shh," he says, kissing her. "I'll be back soon."

LULU

JUNE 1942
(*The Bahamas*)

THERE'S A REASON so many revolutions occur in the summer months, and this transformation starts earlier in the Bahamas than most places. By the first of May, the furnace had begun to crank up, the heating of the air, heavy, sticky, murderous. By the middle of the afternoon on the thirty-first, as I sought refuge at the bar of the good old Prince George—window shades down, electric fans rotating furiously—you couldn't walk ten feet without your lungs turning inside out, your skin melting off your bones and into your footprints.

"Now, why ain't you lying on a beach someplace, taking in the ocean breeze, Mrs. Randolph?" asked Jack, wiping away on a glass that didn't need it. "Better yet. Why ain't you back in America with your bosom friend?"

"My bosom friend? You can't possibly mean the duchess."

"Peas in a pod, ain't you? Thick as thieves."

"That doesn't mean I'm her friend, believe me."

Jack shook his head and set the glass in its pristine row. "Coulda fooled me."

"What do you know, anyway? You never met the duchess in your life."

"I hear things."

I idled the ice cubes, around and around, *clinkety clink*. There was a slice of lime that kept getting crushed almost to death, before it popped right back to the surface, bright and green. I kind of appreciated its fortitude. "Jack, my darling," I said, "you first of all have to understand how friendship works between women. It's perfectly possible for me to see the duchess daily, to chin chin by day and chacha by evening, if you know what I mean, and not to know the least intimate thing about her."

"Aw, now, you can't fool me, Mrs. Randolph. I hear you two sit down nose to nose on the sofa *all the time*, trading all your secrets—"

"Nope."

"I stand by my sources."

"Oh, we cozy up and chatter, believe me. But you can talk for hours and hours to certain women, and never know them at all." I tilted my glass toward him to illustrate my point. "And we're both of us that kind of woman."

Jack reached behind his own back and—without even looking—picked up the next glass in the row and began to wipe, just Jack standing there wiping behind his counter, while I drank my gin and tonic and collected perspiration in the crease of my legs.

I tried another tack. "It's just business. Just business, between the duchess and me."

"Just business between her and anybody, I hear."

"*You hear.* You hear from whom?"

"From a lot of people."

"You do a lot of listening, don't you, Jack?"

He shrugged and replaced the glass. "That's my job, Mrs. Randolph. I listen to people. Pour 'em a drink or two, maybe, but mostly listen."

By now, I had sucked away most of what was useful in my glass. Only the ice remained, melting fast, and that poor, limp, defeated slice of lime. I nudged it with my finger, just an inch or two, and Jack—professional that he was—took the hint. Fresh ice, fresh lime, fresh gin, fresh tonic. The sides of the glass ran with condensation from the wet air.

"So tell me something I don't know," I said.

"See, that's exactly nothing, Mrs. Randolph. You know almost as much as I do, these days."

"I'm a gossip columnist. It's my job." I lift my finger to my lips. "Shhh."

"Well, now." He screwed up one eye and peered at the ceiling. "Say. Did you hear the one about the heiress who got herself hitched to a French count a couple weeks ago? Two days after her eighteenth birthday, yet."

"If you mean Nancy Oakes, I've heard that one. But he's not French, Jack. He's Mauritian. And he isn't really a count, not by English standards. What he *is*"—and here I removed the slim wooden stick with which I'd been stirring my ice, and pointed it toward Jack's round, pink, overheated face—"is thirty-two years old, and already divorced." I sipped my drink. "Other than that, he's a nice enough fellow."

"Her parents ain't too happy."

"Well, of course they're not *happy*. Nancy's just fresh out of school, you know, this nice French boarding school in New York City that's supposed to keep the foxes from poaching its darling baby bunnies. And now he's apparently whisked her off all the way to Florida on their honeymoon, while Lady Oakes sits and stews in Bar Harbor."

Jack whistled softly. "Florida? I didn't hear that."

"Oh, I have my own sources. All up in arms too. If there's one thing rich folks everywhere can unite against, it's a fortune hunter."

As I spoke, Jack's eyes flickered to the left, the passageway to the hotel lobby. It was just past four o'clock in the afternoon, and now that the British Colonial Hotel's former cadre of American tourists had been replaced—thanks to Pearl Harbor and President Roosevelt—by the employees of the Pleasantville Construction Company of New Jersey, building out two airfields for the use of the newly combined Allied forces, Nassau's favorite watering hole was largely empty. Just the usual old fellow at his usual old table, reading his usual old newspaper, and a couple of gents chattering confidentially in the corner, and yours truly, recuperating from her Red Cross morning. The doorway lay behind me, so I couldn't see the newcomer. Jack's gaze returned to me.

"Fortune hunter?" he said. "If you say so."

"*I* didn't say so. I'm just telling you what others are saying."

"For one thing, he ain't exactly broke, Fred de Marigny."

"He's not exactly Sir Harry Oakes, either."

"And for another thing, he ain't the type."

"You don't figure?"

"Likes the ladies too much to marry one for nothing but cold hard cash, if you ask me."

I peered at my thumbnail, pressed against the glass. "I guess I can believe that."

Jack ambled off in the direction of the newcomer, who had come to rest his elbows and his hat at the opposite end of the bar. I opened my pocketbook and drew out the Chesterfields and the lighter—*To Lulu on her birthday. SBL*—and contrived, under guise of lighting a cigarette, to catch a glimpse of the fellow. Yes, it was a fellow. Of course it was. Medium size, balding head shiny with perspiration, limp jacket slung over his arm, general air of sunstroke. Nobody I knew. I returned my attention to my drink, to the half-hearted operation of the cigarette, to the arresting spectacle of Jack's glasses and bottles in their immaculate rows, the woodsy palette, the gleam of mirrors, the blue, fragrant curls of tobacco smoke, the draft stirring my hair from the fans overhead, all of it soaked in heat, sagging with heat, heat sticking to every last molecule of everything. I slugged down the end of the drink, put out the cigarette, made to rise. The world sort of throbbed. Jack reappeared before me.

"Leaving already?"

"Column to finish. You won't miss me." I opened my pocketbook and rummaged for shillings.

"You be careful out there, Mrs. Randolph," Jack said. "You know what's been happening out at them new airfields they're building."

I laid three shillings on the bar in a neat stack and closed my pocket-book. "I know the native laborers have been demanding the same pay as the Americans, and I don't blame them. Working all day under the hot sun. Construction too. I don't blame them a bit."

Jack set his palms on the edge of the counter and leaned forward. "I hear there might be some trouble tomorrow. So you just stay in your nice bungalow, you hear me?"

"What kind of trouble?"

"The usual kind. Fellows making their point."

As he said this, Jack gave me the same stare with which a cobra might fix you. I knew he came from the South somewhere—you could hear it plain in his voice—but I hadn't once heard him say a word against the Negroes. You never could tell where Jack's true loyalties lay. He har-bored no love for the Bay Street Boys, *that* I understood, even though he served their drinks and took their tips. But as for where he stood on that complex and monumental question so delicately phrased *the color line?* Only Jack and his Maker knew.

"All right," I said. "I'll stay home."

His face relaxed. "Good. Lock your door."

"Always do."

"And that colored woman who keeps your house?"

"Veryl?"

He nodded. "She might could stay over with you, until the dust settles."

"Oh, for goodness' sake, Jack. I can't ask her to do that. There's no-where to sleep except the sofa. Anyway, it's the Bahamas, not the West Indies. They're not fire-breathers here." I tucked my pocketbook under my arm. "You just go back to tending bar, Jack, and get out of the advice business, all right? Go back to keeping your ears open and your trap shut."

There was this instant of silence, a brief and brittle standoff, eyeball to eyeball. Just long enough, you might say, for me to glimpse the alarming size of Jack's pupils before he drew back and turned his attention to the drops of condensation left behind by my gin and tonic on his nice clean counter. He took out a dishcloth and mumbled, "Suit yourself."

"I will. Have a nice afternoon."

I turned to leave, a trifle unsteady. Jack called out softly behind me.

"Another thing I heard, Mrs. Randolph?"

I paused and sighed. The room settled back into place around me. "This had better be good, Jack."

"I heard a certain fellow's out of that Miami hospital and back in Nassau. You know the fellow I mean."

Just like that, the room started up to spin again, except in a different direction this time, a different rhythm. I looked up at the ceiling to anchor myself, and what did I find but those damned electric fans, whirring and whirring without end.

"Mrs. Randolph? You heard that one yet?"

"No," I whispered. "I hadn't heard."

OF COURSE I KNEW THE fellow he meant. It was the talk of Nassau for weeks, even in the midst of all that fuss over Pearl Harbor and Nancy Oakes's ball, and while the talk had died down during the course of the spring, his name still came up from time to time.

Consider the afternoon I learned how he was attacked. I remember how the walls of the room made a kind of tunnel around me, how I went hot and then cold in the course of a few seconds, and I thought I might actually faint. Somebody asked me if I was all right—the voice sounded like it was coming from another room, from another country—and I remembering saying I was fine, just a little shocked, what a terrible thing. I remember asking questions—how had it happened, where was he hurt, who found him, were they sure it was Thorpe—but nobody seemed to know anything more. So I turned back to the hymnal in my hands, the program of service. The chords of the organ, calling the faithful to the miracle of Christmas. That steadied the shaking of my hands and brought me back to the present world, to the substance of the objects around me. Except each time I opened my mouth to sing, I had no breath. I had no voice at all.

When the service ended, I suggested to Mrs. Gudewill that we put together a few books and treats—a Red Cross parcel, if you will—and deliver them to the hospital. I thought it wouldn't be so singular if I went with a friend. By the time we reached the hospital with our basket it was past teatime, and the nurse on duty told us that Mr. Thorpe had regained consciousness a little past noon and was out of immediate danger. But we were too late to deliver him any comfort baskets. At that very moment, he was on a boat bound for Miami and the hospital there: a voyage chartered for him by the Duchess of Windsor herself.

All of which, you might think, was wonderfully good news: the kind of news that ought to make a girl feel better on the spot. Indeed it did. For that first hour or two, I felt as if I'd been loosened from a vise, from one of those devices of medieval torture that turn each limb and organ on its own separate screw, and come to understand at last the true meaning of the word *relief.* I parted ways with Mrs. Gudewill and made my way to my bungalow to pour myself a festive gin and tonic. But as I sipped at the drink, I discovered that my relief had dissolved into something else. Into emptiness, into a loss of mass, an absence of atoms and molecules I had not known I possessed. There had been something, and now there was nothing. Gone.

On a boat for Miami: the *Gemini*, the Windsors' private yacht.

THE FIRST OF JUNE DAWNED hazy and hot, promising trouble. I woke in a jolt, in the middle of some dream, seized by the conviction that someone was pounding on my front door. But as I lay in bed and stared at the ceiling, the milky air of sunrise, no noise disturbed the stillness except the palaver of birds outside the window.

There was no point in returning to sleep. I crawled from bed and crept down the hall to the parlor, where the radio rested on the sideboard, tuned to the single Nassau station. I switched it on. A plume of baroque music swept into the room, crackling with static, Bach or something. But no news. I checked the lock on the front door and went back down the hall to run a bath.

An hour later, Veryl had not yet arrived. I boiled an egg, toasted bread, started the coffee in the electric percolator. The radio now thrummed with piano. Still no news. I ate breakfast in the kitchen, standing up, because there was no room for a table. I washed and dried the dishes, poured another cup of coffee, and betook myself to my work, such as it was.

For some time, I sat at my typewriter and stared out the window, toward that small sliver of sea visible between the nearby houses, trying to think of some clever angle from which to relate the story of Nancy Oakes and her shocking elopement with Alfred de Marigny, while the radio played tinny, crackling Beethoven and the birds continued their confabulation in the trees and the sun climbed the hazy blue sky. *Stay away from politics*, advised Lightfoot, and I'd given him what he asked for, hadn't I, given it to him in spades, in monthly servings of tittle and tattle. He was going to love this scoop about Nancy Oakes and Alfred de Marigny. All I had to do was return to the typewriter and finish it, slip it into its manila envelope, carry it to the post office and collect my two hundred dollars to keep body and soul together.

In the vase next to the typewriter, right in the middle of a pool of sunshine, Veryl had set a spray of pink frangipani from the shrub outside. The scent was enough to drown me. The electric fan tossed my hair across my forehead. I rested my thumb on the rim of the coffee cup and glanced down at the newspaper under my arm, the *Nassau Observer*, headlines bristling. The labor question raged, the laborers raged, the affairs of the world hurtled along the course of history. Outside my window, the sun climbed over Nassau, hotter by the minute.

Still no sign of Veryl.

I set down the cup and went to collect my bicycle from the lean-to shed. As I pedaled hatless into town, the atmosphere was silent, eerily so, as if an invisible force had sucked away every living creature, leaving behind nothing but sunshine and heat and dread.

THEY CALLED IT BURMA ROAD, the trail newly cut through the scrub and the pine forest to connect the airfield being built at the western end of the island with Oakes Field in Nassau. The name represented some wry reference to that legendary seven-hundred-mile route across the Himalayas, down which the British had recently retreated from the Japanese forces in China. Everyone's got a sense of humor, I guess. Anyway, the airfield laborers had built Burma Road themselves, and upon Burma Road they traveled to work each day, and on Burma Road they now gathered up a few fragrant pine branches for clubs and marched back into Nassau, right past Government House—the Windsors were visiting Washington, remember—to Bay Street, down Bay Street to Rawson Square where the House of Assembly stood. I knew this because I could hear the shouting ahead, the singsong chanting, something about Conchie Joe. *Burma Road declare war on de Conchie Joe.*

And that's when I knew it was trouble, all right, because Conchie Joe was the white man, Conchie Joe was the fifteen percent of the Bahamian population allowed within the walls of high-class joints like the British Colonial and the Emerald Beach Hotel, to say nothing of the front door of Government House. Conchie Joe was the foreman on the airfield project, the merchant on Bay Street, the lawyer, the doctor, the owner of virtually all property. The legislator in Parliament, passing laws on himself and the other eighty-five percent of the population. Until now, I had always understood the word as a term of needling affection. But words, you know, they're funny things. You wake up one sultry, troublesome morning, and their meanings invert. Over and over, louder and louder, the laborers sang. *Burma Road declare war on de Conchie Joe, do nigger don't you lick nobody, don't lick nobody . . .*

A mass of humanity like that, you could hear them and smell them and feel them before you saw them. The reek of perspiration, the buzz of nervous energy. The trace of fresh pine. Nassau Street was motionless. So was George Street, stretching up to pink Government House on its hill. Not until I reached the corner of Parliament Street, not until the plaza opened up before me, the palm trees and the white-columned pink facades that constituted the seat of Bahamas government, did I discover the crowd, the hundreds of black men, a few women too, maybe a thousand or maybe even more. I braked the bicycle and touched my toe to the pavement. It was just past nine o'clock, according to the clock on the tower, and the chanting had died away into that thing called expectant silence, as if the men—having marched into the very heart of Conchie Joe's domain—now prepared themselves to listen to somebody. That was nice. Somebody who? Who the devil was in charge around here, while the Duke of Windsor was away? The colonial secretary, maybe? The crowd, rustling and grumbling, had turned toward a square pink building on the corner of Bank Lane, where some white men seemed to be standing on the steps, sweating in their suits.

From where I balanced on my bicycle, looking up Parliament Street from the harbor walk, I couldn't tell what anybody was saying. I thought one of the white men was speaking—if I strained, I could hear a high, indignant voice—but the words got lost among the perspiring bodies and the pink walls and the heavy air.

My hair stuck to my temples. The sun burned my neck, stuck the dress to my back. I dismounted the bicycle and walked it forward, up

Parliament Street, to where the stragglers milled about, trying to find a better vantage. One of them saw me and shook his head. He called out— and his voice surprised me, it was so gentle—"You gwine home, miss. Ain't you business here. Gwine home."

Of course I didn't obey him. I edged instead around the fringe of the crowd, craning for some view, some channel of clear sound to reach me. Whoever this fellow was, whatever he was saying, the crowd didn't like it. A murmuring rumbled the atmosphere, a discontent, a shifting of hot, perspiring bodies and impatient skin. Couple more shouts, somebody calling out the first notes of that chant, *Burma Road declare war on de Conchie Joe, do nigger don't you lick*—then *SMASH*. Holy God. An explosion of broken glass, too sudden and too cataclysmic even to say which direction it had come from.

I flinched and ducked, and the next instant craned my neck to see what the devil, where the devil, and the square trembled with shouts and footsteps, everybody turning at once, pelting down Bay Street, where the shops and offices of Conchie Joe lined the way, all hell broken loose and tumbling free, armed with clubs cut from the pines of Burma Road.

I DON'T KNOW IF YOU'VE ever seen a riot before, up close. It's not so much a sight or a sound as a feeling, a mayhem. A kaleidoscope, too many sensations all crammed into your brain at once, so you can't remember what happened when. I recall stumbling back from the stampede, someone grabbing my arm and dragging me away, and when I looked up I saw the man who had spoken to me before. His eyes were wide and white-rimmed, his skin blacker than I remembered it. He shoved the handlebars of the bicycle toward me and yelled, *Gwine, I said! Gwine outta here, before you gets kilt!*

"What did he say?" I demanded. "What was he saying up there?"

Gwine outta here, crazy lady! He pushed my backside. *Go, get!*

"But what—"

And he was gone, just like that, threw himself right into the pell-mell and disappeared. I stood shaking under the portico where he left me, scared to death, and yet underneath all that fear lay something more like excitement. Some charge that drew me forth, step by step, from underneath the portico to get a better vantage, to watch this extraordinary thing, this riot, this tumult of angry men, these placid Bahamians—*Oh, they'd never revolt here, they know their place, the coloreds here*—exploding into fury. Men shouting and glass smashing, the beat of two thousand feet on the sun-bleached pavement of Bay Street, drumming, hollering, howling mad, because they got paid four shillings a day to labor under the broiling sun while the white Americans got twelve, all laid out in a contract negotiated by the Bahamian government, by Conchie Joe, and they were sick and tired of that. Sick and tired.

This is big, I thought. Heart thumping.

And then: *I need my camera.*

I thought if I could maybe cross this stampede alive, I could head up Parliament Street to higher ground. I could skirt along parallel to the action—the laborers meant to smash up Bay Street, symbol of Conchie Joe's power, that was obvious—and pedal home fast to fetch my Kodak. I could take photos of this, astonishing photos, write it all up and send it to my editor, an exclusive on-the-scene account of an unprecedented race riot in Nassau, Bahamas, a spark lit to a pile of bone-dry tinder. Real news, vital news. News that was not filtered through the peculiar lens of royal privilege but was raw and genuine and needful.

I gripped the handlebars of my bicycle and pushed forward.

NOW, I SUPPOSE YOU MIGHT think this sense of adventure—this journalistic curiosity, anyway—was in my blood. Maybe that's so. I'm told I take after my father. So said my mother, anyway, whenever she caught me in some kind of mischief, like leading innocents—say, my kid brother and sister, for example—into the neighbor's orchard and climbing the trees, one by one, to drop apples into a basket held by my anxious companions. Or else that time I took the Long Island Rail Road into Manhattan all by myself, aged thirteen, and stormed into the *Metropolitan* offices to visit my father, so he could settle what you might call a domestic dispute between my mother and me. (As it turned out, my father was in a very important meeting and couldn't see me. His secretary called a taxi to drive me home.) As for the time I walked into a Columbia mixer and walked out with a certain Mr. Randolph, well, she wasn't around to scold me. But I feel sure that she would have blamed my father for that too. Certainly the shrinks would've agreed with her.

Anyway, where was I? Yes, that's right—my journalistic curiosity, my propensity for trouble, whatever you care to call it. Whatever it was that propelled me forward on my bicycle that morning, not backward; whatever it was that made me advance into the riot, not retreat. I don't know where it came from, whether it was the clamor of my Lightfoot blood or some quality particular to me, Lulu. As I recall the scene—as I watch myself from a distance, reckless girl-woman on a bicycle in wartime Nassau—I think of what my mother said, when I arrived home in the taxi Lightfoot's secretary had called for me, that day I absconded to Manhattan. She didn't take me in her arms and shower me with kisses or anything like that, because she wasn't that kind of mother. She came up to the taxi window and paid the driver and then marched me into the house, into the kitchen, where Leo and Vanessa sat in their pajamas, eyes like pies. Mama took my plate of supper from the oven and set it before me. Meat loaf and canned peas, I remember that. Also the familiar blue floral pattern along the rim of the plate, and the chip on the side near the peas. As I ate, she watched me, and when I was nearly finished she said (now this is important, so pay attention): *I don't know what you're looking for, Lulu, but whatever it is, it's going to kill you before you ever find it.* And the tone of her voice was that of someone reading her own eulogy.

I THINK OF MY MOTHER'S words often, because they hung over me from that day onward, and they sometimes return to me still, as when I recall the Burma Road riot. Certainly I had never in my life felt more vulnerable than when I pushed my bicycle into that crowd of black Bahamian men making their way down Bay Street with their pine clubs and their fury. I had also never felt more alive, more filled with purpose.

I kept my head down and drove forward. I focused my determination on the lamppost across the street, while men poured around me and into me, shouting and chanting, and the sound of smashing glass went off like a series of bombs. I don't think they even noticed me; they were intent on a larger purpose than one foolish white woman and her damn bicycle. Someone stumbled into my rear wheel and swore and moved on. A shoulder banged against mine, but I think that was an accident. As I reached the other side of the street, I looked up and traced the stream of humanity down Bay Street. About a hundred yards away, a truck bearing the Coca-Cola logo was parked against the curb. A man stood at its open rear door, handing out crates and crates of bottles, and the rioters were pitching them through windows, into walls. I clapped my hand over my mouth and turned back, but in that moment of inattention, a force took hold of my bicycle. I looked up into someone's ferocious face.

"That's mine!" I snapped.

He didn't bother to reply. Why should he? He was twice as big as I was, propelled by rage. Without any effort he tore the bicycle from my hands, lifted it above his head, and carried it down the sidewalk. I darted after him, shouting incoherent, laughable things about property and rights. A Coca-Cola bottle sailed past my ear. The man stopped, as if he'd found what he was looking for, and hurled my bicycle right into a beautiful plate glass window that had gone untouched until now.

"Oh, you bastard!" I screeched. Glass covered the sidewalk, razor sharp, and my bicycle lay just inside the broken window, in the middle of a display of fine leather goods. Already a man was picking his way inside. Blood streamed down the side of his face and stained his shirt. He bent down, kicked aside my bicycle, and gathered up an armful of pocketbooks.

Well, I wasn't going to stand for that, was I? That was *my* damn bicycle. And I had work to do, I had my camera to collect, I had news to report, a whole world waiting for this story! Without a thought, I stepped forward onto that mess of broken glass and bent over the ruined window frame to grab the bent front wheel.

And I think I succeeded. I think I did grab that wheel. I may even have lifted it a foot or two. But the victory was a Pyrrhic one, I'm afraid, because in my haste and fury and determination, I hadn't given due attention to the glass remaining in the frame. I only noticed the glitter of one transparent shard an instant before it sliced across my forearm. Split my skin clean apart, the way you butterfly a loin of lamb.

I don't remember feeling any pain. I just stood there staring at the blood as it streamed over my wrist and dripped to the pavement, and thought *You are a goddamned idiot, Leonora Randolph.* Or maybe someone said that out loud. Because I felt a little dizzy at the sight of that blood, I'm afraid, a little fuzzy at the edges, and if good old Veryl hadn't come out of nowhere and grabbed me right there, grabbed me and yelled at me and smacked some wad of material—her apron, as it turned out—into my wound, I might just have fainted.

Come to think of it, maybe that *was* Veryl's voice, shouting inside my head. Veryl's voice saying, *You are a goddamned idiot, Lenora Randolph.* And you know what? She was right.

THE GLASS MISSED THAT ARTERY in my wrist, the one that's supposed to bleed out when you slice it. *Thank goodness*, said the doctor at the hospital who stitched it up, nice-looking fellow. The nurse wound the gauze over his handiwork and thanked goodness also. *Thank goodness, you might have been killed out there.* Then they sent me in a wheelchair to a private room to stay for a night or two, just to keep an eye on me. I can't imagine why.

Now, I had slept in a hospital bed twice before in my life. Once when I was eight, to get rid of a trick appendix. The other time in Amarillo, Texas, for a reason I'd rather not disclose, if you don't mind. I didn't quite see why I should have to sleep in one tonight, although I didn't quite see how I was supposed to get home to Cable Beach through a riot, either. All things considered, I supposed I should make the best of things. To that end, I settled back in my blue gown with a magazine and a glass of iced tea. But I wasn't made for settling, apparently, because my attention kept wandering to the window and its partial view of the harbor, and how I might get my hands on my camera, and what the devil was going on out there, anyway. Whether New Providence Island stood in a state of insurrection, or whether paler heads had prevailed.

Then the knock arrived.

"Come in," I said.

A coppery head poked around the corner of the door.

"Hullo, there," said Thorpe. "I've brought cake."

THE CAKE IN QUESTION TURNED out to be Veryl's own rum cake. I shrieked and asked how he got it. He said he'd stopped by the bungalow to make sure I was all right, hadn't done anything stupid like ridden my bicycle straight into a riot, and luckily Veryl was there, packing me a few things, and explained the whole affair. Naturally—gentleman that he was—he offered to convey Veryl to her home and cake and toothbrush to yours truly in her hospital bed.

All this he told me as he took the cake and the plates from the basket, like a picnic, and put them on the table, maneuvering about expertly with his stiff leg and his cane.

"Well, kind sir, I simply don't know how to thank you," I said.

"We'll think of something. Cake?"

He raised the knife and held it above the ring of rum cake Veryl had baked the day before. A broken ring, because I'd already eaten a slice last night. Can you blame me? That rum cake was a fever dream of vanilla and sugared rum, and I mean *rum*. Just sniffing it could render you blotto. I watched Thorpe sink the knife delicately into the sponge. For some reason, his knuckles transfixed me. They were large and bony and—compared to the rest of him, anyway—rather ugly. And yet they maneuvered that knife with tremendous precision. A cake surgeon. He laid a nice, pudgy slice on a plate, added a fork, and lifted an eyebrow.

"Can you manage it?"

"Can I eat a slice of cake, you mean? I believe so."

"Because you're looking pale."

I roused myself to a sitting position and handed him the glass of iced tea. "Give me the damned cake, please."

He gave me the cake. While I ate, he cut his own cake, poured himself a glass of iced tea from the pitcher, and settled himself heavily in the armchair. I had forgotten about his leg. I stared at it now. He stretched the bones out before him, stiff as a pole and just as wasted. He had struck me as pleasingly lean in December, sturdy but not especially muscular. Now he was downright gaunt. His cheekbones sprang from his face. On his jaw, there was a long scar, still red.

I nodded at his knee. "Speaking of injuries."

"It's much better, thank you. All things considered."

"All things?"

"Look here, there's nothing on earth so tedious as listening to somebody explain the various points of his general health in full detail. I'm alive and whole. All's well that ends well."

"Did they ever catch the fellow who did it?"

"No," he said. "I don't believe they did."

"It's disgraceful."

"What, the fact that I was attacked? Or that they haven't caught the scoundrel?"

"Well, both."

"I must admit, it was rather a shock. But then I wasn't paying attention, as I should have been. My mind was elsewhere."

"Elsewhere, was it? I can't imagine where."

He shrugged his shoulders and opened his mouth to admit more cake.

"You know," I said, "I can't help thinking I'm to blame."

"You? How so?"

"Because there was another ending to that evening, don't you remember? It might have ended much more pleasantly for both of us."

He set down the plate and rested his forearms on his knees, which brought his head closer to mine. Between us, the crumbs of cake, the glasses of tea.

"Fault requires intent, Mrs. Randolph," he said. "And you surely had no inkling that a man lay in wait for me at the docks with a billy club in his hand."

"A billy club!"

"Yes."

"It's too terrible. You can't imagine how awful I feel about it. Thank God you're alive."

"Life is made up of these little crossroads, after all," he said. "A million daily forks in the road."

I studied his eyes behind the sheen of his spectacles. I thought there was something different about him—well, of course there was—some shedding of the boyish radiance that had surrounded him last December. That half-bashful exuberance. As I watched, he put his hands on the arms of the chair to lever himself upward. A wedge of sunshine passed across his face. Instead of reaching for his cane, he limped his way to the window on his own. He shoved one hand into his trouser pocket and braced the other one on the top of the window frame, while he squinted through the glass at the street outside.

"Keeping an eye on the riot?" I said.

"The riot is largely over, it seems. Good old Sir Leslie spoke to the ringleaders over at Government House and promised to look into things. Then the police sent everybody back over the hill."

"Really? That's all?"

"Not quite. I don't doubt there'll be trouble tonight. But the point is to keep the trouble where it belongs, at least so far as the police are concerned."

"Naturally. I'm sure they'll be talking about nothing else at the Red Cross tomorrow. The iniquity of the coloreds, how they should be grateful to have jobs at all, how it's just what you'd expect from a Negro to smash up the property others have worked so hard to build."

Thorpe turned his head from the window. "Do I detect a certain bitterness, Mrs. Randolph? A certain radical tenor to your thoughts?"

"I'm no radical. I just happen to think the Bay Street crowd is a pack of bigots, that's all. And the labor situation is plain unfair."

"And that's why you wandered into town today?"

"I wandered into town today because it's a story, and I'm a journalist."

"A journalist," he said. "That's all?"

"What do you mean, *that's all*? What else would I be?"

The sunshine from the window slanted across his face, half alight and half in shadow. His white shirt hung from his shoulders, which were wide and bony, and while the bones were meatless they were also thick, giving him an air of authority, of trustworthiness: the kind of shoulders that could bear a great deal, could bear the weight of his troubles and yours; could bear the weight of your resting head, if you were tall enough to reach them. Then his hair, all ablaze in the sunshine. His serious eyes, oh. You could not evade scrutiny like that. You could only bear it. You could only sit there and let him take his fill, let him examine your lines and creases, your twitches and stitches, let him judge the stuff of which you were made.

"This island," he said at last. "This damned little island. Only a few hundred square miles of barren limestone."

The electric fan whirred above us. My arm throbbed, my head ached. I said, "When did you arrive back?"

"Two days ago."

"You're still staying at Wenner-Gren's place?"

"Yes."

"But he's in Mexico, isn't he? The FBI put him on a blacklist of some kind, the second we got into the war, because of his Nazi friends. He's been stuck in Mexico since December."

"Oh, is that what you heard?"

"That's what I heard."

"Well, Wenner-Gren's not a Nazi. He's a businessman, that's all."

"Then why did the FBI blacklist him?"

Thorpe produced a crumpled handkerchief from his pocket and removed his spectacles. "I suppose you'd have to ask the FBI. I'm just a scientist, Mrs. Randolph. My concern is plants, not people."

"Some people, surely."

"Oh, I don't know. People so often disappoint one. Plants, on the other hand. They simply exist, you see. It's up to you to discover their nature." He replaced the glasses on his nose. "How's the old arm feeling?"

"The old arm will be just fine."

"All the same, I believe I'm going to sleep with you tonight."

"You're going to *what*?"

"I mean on the sofa, of course. Someone's got to keep an eye on things."

"The sofa? What sofa?"

Now the grin, like the rising of the sun. "In your bungalow, of course. I'm springing you out of here."

"What?"

"I had the feeling you're not the sort of woman who enjoys lying around in hospital beds." He tossed the basket onto the bed. "Come along, then. If you've quite finished your cake. You'll find a change of clothing in there."

"But how—the doctors—"

"The doctors in Nassau, like the rest of the population, proved remarkably susceptible to corruption." He reached for his cane and moved to the door. "And of course, I assured them I'd keep the closest possible eye on you."

SO THORPE CARRIED ME HOME to the bungalow in the sidecar of his motorcycle and fed me the dinner that Veryl had left out for us. He allowed me neither cigarettes nor the demon liquor, although after he sent me to bed with a glass of water and a couple of aspirin, I spotted him through the window on the patio chair, imbibing both without shame.

I suppose you imagine we woke restlessly at midnight, the two of us, and found our way together to make furious love by the light of a tropical moon. I'm awfully sorry to disappoint you. There was no waking, no restlessness. I suppose we were both too exhausted. Besides, we were cripples.

Instead, I slept like death. By the time I rose the next morning, the sofa was empty, the parlor neat, the blanket folded square on the armchair.

ELFRIEDE

JULY 1905
(Florida)

O NE WEEK BEFORE Wilfred's return to England, Elfriede learns she
has not conceived a baby. She informs her lover as soon as they're
alone together, taking their usual walk in the garden once the children
are in bed.

He draws a sigh. Relief or disappointment, she can't tell. "Ah. I was
wondering about that. You're sure?"

"*Quite* sure."

He stops by the orange tree and draws an arm around her shoulder.
Together they lean against the trunk. The blossoms have all fallen, the
bees have moved on. The air's grown hotter, if possible, filled with the
sultry scent of the rotting buds. "That's what I meant to ask you about,
that first night."

"And I told you the answer was yes."

"I wasn't entirely sure you understood the question. But I could have
done something about it, you know."

"Yes, I know."

Wilfred turns to face her in the twilight. "Well? *Should* I do something about it? There's a chemist in town."

"A chemist?"

"A—what do you call it. A drugstore. He ought to be able to find something for me, if I ask the right way. Of course, there are alternatives."

She smiles. "You say that as if . . ."

"As if what, my dear?"

"As if it matters."

He reaches out to touch her hair. "Of course it matters. I'd never forgive myself if I burdened you with a child you don't want to bear. I haven't forgotten why you were in Switzerland to begin with."

Here they are, dancing around the point of a needle again. Why can't they just agree to marry and make children together? Or—the other end of the needle—agree to part as friends after this halcyon interlude comes to an end? Maybe it would be simpler if Elfriede *were* pregnant, a not unlikely outcome after weeks of rapturous fucking, nightly and sometimes daily, in bed and out, filling Elfriede's womb with the stuff of life. But Nature didn't take her cue. If he likes, Wilfred can board his train to New York in eight days with warm memories and a clear conscience.

Well, will he? Why haven't they spoken of his departure at all? They've had all the opportunity in the world. True to his promise, Wilfred arrived back at Elfriede's house just before luncheon the day after his arrival. By dinnertime he'd settled into the most spacious of the spare bedrooms. By nighttime he'd settled into Elfriede's bed. During the heavenly days that followed, he and Elfriede have spent scarcely an hour apart. He's won the adoration of Gerhard's daughters, if not quite that of Gerhard's son. He's shared meals and laughter with them, he's gone on walks and swims and endless picnics, he's listened to Elfriede play the piano, listened to Elfriede teach the children to play the piano. He's almost part of the family. Except, of course, he's not. In all official respects, he's an ordinary houseguest on holiday. They don't speak of the steamship ticket tucked in the pocket of his suitcase, but it's there.

Should Elfriede speak of it now? Wilfred's face lies near hers, so familiar and beloved she can't imagine its absence. Can she keep it there? Will she keep it there? That steamship ticket. Does he mean to use it? Does she want him to? Is she still afraid?

THE REASON ELFRIEDE DEPARTED SCHLOSS Kleist in such a hurry all those months ago, packing only the essentials, was Helga.

"I've decided to take the children on holiday," she told her sister-in-law, one morning last autumn. "It will do them good, I think, after all this gloom and misery."

Helga was aghast. What could Elfriede possibly be thinking? Take Johann away from his home? From his aunts and uncle and cousins? From his education? So soon after his beloved father's death? Where on earth did she imagine taking the boy?

"Oh, someplace warm, I think, since winter's coming on," Elfriede answered. "Maybe Florida."

Florida! Florida was the worst possible idea, a hedonistic wilderness on the other side of the world. Why, Johann might forget he was German at all! In any case—Helga leaned forward confidentially—Elfriede absolutely could *not* take Those Children away with Johann. Out of the question. It was immoral. He was young and impressionable. He was a baron. He had his father's legacy to uphold. What would people think if he regarded these girls as his sisters?

"But they *are* his sisters," Elfriede pointed out, even though she knew how Helga would react to this statement of fact. (Elfriede at twenty-six was not the same creature as Elfriede at just eighteen, gazing in awe at the new relations gathered to her wedding dinner.) Then she added, "Gerhard himself acknowledged them," although in this she stood on shakier ground. Gerhard, believing himself immortal, hadn't yet troubled to compose a will in which he made explicit provision for his bastard daughters and their mother. Helga was perfectly aware of this fact.

Hardly had the mourners dispersed when she made the first of many efforts to evict the cuckoos from the nest, even while one cuckoo was yet unborn. Elfriede resisted each onslaught. But the day was coming, she knew, when Helga's arguments would prove unanswerable or her tactics invincible. So she allowed the subject of Florida to drop. She allowed Helga to believe she'd won, but when Helga left the following week to spend a few days with her sister, Elfriede packed the children and Charlotte and whisked them away.

She left behind a note, of course. During the voyage across the ocean, she took great pleasure in imagining Helga's face as she read that note.

HELGA, OF COURSE, WROTE PLENTY of her own notes during the ensuing months. But Elfriede has no intention of giving up her girls and her freedom, not yet. She knows she eventually must. Helga has some justice on her side. Johann *is* the baron, he'll return to Schloss Kleist at some point and learn to be its master. But not yet. Let him be a child first. Let him know his sisters, so he might not banish them once he gains the power to banish. Let the sun warm their hearts and blood and skin. Let them know a little of a man like Wilfred.

Elfriede thinks of all this and puts her arms around her lover's neck.

"It doesn't matter now," she says. "I'm not having a baby."

"Not *yet*—" he begins.

She cuts him off in the customary way. By kissing him.

So they keep dancing, these two.

NOW, GERHARD—A PIOUS MAN—STRICTLY OBSERVED the biblical injunctions against menstruating women, so Elfriede's amazed when Wilfred follows her into her room, in the customary way, and turns her around to unbutton her dress. She makes some stuttering protest.

"Do you *want* me to leave?" he asks, sounding as amazed as she is.

"Why . . . only if *you* want to leave."

"Why should I want to leave you?"

"Because it's unclean!"

"Look," he says, resuming the buttons, "if you don't want me to touch you, I won't touch you. But I'll be damned if I spend the night in any other bed but yours. There's a particular lump in your mattress that I simply can't do without."

She laughs. He stays. They whisper and cuddle and kiss each other, and she doesn't remember falling asleep. But she does remember waking. That's because the house starts shaking.

"What the devil?" Wilfred growls in English, bolting upright beside her.

"I think it's the door."

He looks out the window. "It's not even dawn, by God. Stay here."

"You can't——"

But he does. Throws on his dressing gown—of course he keeps one in the wardrobe—and an expression of vicious resolve, and simply marches out the door as if he owns the place.

Elfriede stares at the door in horror, bedclothes clutched to her chest. Follow him? Stay abed and trust in Wilfred's military training? She throws off the covers. The pounding stops. Voices rise up the stairway. Wilfred, of course.

And a woman. Who speaks in German.

HELGA IS A BARON'S DAUGHTER, a baron's sister, and a baron's aunt. (Through marriage, she's also the sister of a minor prince, though at some point you have to stop counting.) Is she appalled beyond her worst possible nightmare to discover her brother's widow *almost* in flagrante with an English lover, inside this house she shares with her late husband's mistress and bastard children, in Florida of all places? One can only imagine, because Helga's been bred to maintain an icy resilience in the face of such outrage to decent behavior.

"I'm so sorry to arrive at such an inconvenient hour," she says, casting a slight, proud glance at Wilfred's dressing gown, "but I'm afraid the train was delayed for some time outside of a town named Savannah, or I should have appeared yesterday evening."

"Think nothing of it, Fraulein von Kleist," Wilfred says. "Would you like tea? Coffee, perhaps? I imagine the housekeeper's awake."

"No, thank you. Elfriede, you may show me to a spare bedroom. *If* you have one." (This last with a telling, lifted eyebrow.) Then, to some patch of skin in the middle of Wilfred's forehead: "You may bring up my luggage, sir."

Elfriede leads Helga upstairs. Shows her the bathroom while Wilfred stacks her trunks at the foot of the bed of the second-best spare bedroom. (He still nominally occupies the best one.) An awkward moment passes as he makes his exit and they're forced to maneuver around each other in the corridor. For some reason, the children haven't wakened. Charlotte's probably still unconscious.

"Good night, then, Fraulein," says Wilfred, in the grave voice of somebody trying not to laugh. Elfriede refuses to catch his eye.

"Good night, Mr. Thorpe."

She and Elfriede proceed to the second-best spare bedroom. Helga stops her at the door.

"Of course, we will discuss all this in the morning," she says, and shuts the door in Elfriede's face, before Elfriede can even observe that it's already morning, according to the clock. So she returns to her bedroom, hoping to discuss all this with Wilfred first, but dawn's beginning to make itself known outside the window, and he's already left for his own room. Propriety.

ELFRIEDE IMAGINES SOME REPRIEVE, BECAUSE Helga surely won't rise until noon. But Helga's Helga, you know, and appears in the breakfast room at eight-thirty sharp. The children are shocked. Aunt Helga's face is creased, but her eyes are bright. "Good morning, my dear boy," she says to Johann. She walks around the table to plant a kiss on her nephew's astonished forehead and straighten his collar. She passes a swift eye over the remaining small fry and says briefly, "Good morning, Elfriede. Mr. Thorpe. Children. Nurse."

Elfriede rings the bell for the housekeeper. "Good morning, Aunt Helga."

"Good morning, Fraulein," Wilfred says amiably. He rises from his chair at the opposite end of the table from Elfriede. The master's chair. Charlotte sits on Elfriede's left. An empty chair to the right. Helga tries to settle herself before Wilfred can reach this chair and pull it out for her, but he's too quick, too clever. She swallows her chagrin and forces out a word of thanks.

"We will take a turn in the garden after breakfast," she says to Elfriede, as the housekeeper arrives with fresh coffee.

AT LAST, AT LAST HELGA'S spleen is set free. Elfriede, wandering among the hibiscus with her garden shears, pretends to listen. Helga gets such pleasure from her lectures, after all, such luxurious satisfaction from her exhibitions of piety. One by one, *snip snip*, Elfriede lays the hibiscus in the basket and nods along. She meditates on this human craving for moral authority, more powerful perhaps than the craving for sex. Why? What power do we gain from believing, asserting, tirelessly burnishing our virtue? To shame others, that's the point of life. When Helga pauses for breath—the heat is laying on fast this morning— Elfriede hands her a hibiscus and says, "But there's nothing improper in my friendship with Mr. Thorpe. He's a houseguest, that's all. He stays in the spare bedroom."

"Do you take me for some kind of fool?"

"I don't know why you would imagine such a thing, that's all. Maybe you possess some special insight into such matters?"

Helga's face is already pink from the heat, so there's no telling just how deeply this suggestion moves her. Her eyes widen and then narrow. "What an impertinent thing to say," she sputters.

Elfriede shrugs and turns away. "No more impertinent than what you've just said to me. It's been over a year since my husband died, Helga. I'm simply raising my children as I see fit."

"Children! You have *one* child, Elfriede, and your duty—your only duty—belongs to him."

"But Gerhard has four children, and he's left me responsible for them all. He wouldn't want his daughters to be raised under the shadow of your disapproval. I'm only honoring his wishes."

"His wishes! What do you know of his wishes?"

"My God. A great deal more than you do. I was, after all, his wife."

"His wife. If you'd been a better wife, we wouldn't find ourselves in this disgraceful situation."

That's the other thing about moral authority: there's never any use in arguing with someone who wants it so badly. Elfriede stares at the flowers in the basket, at the long, thick, sharp gardening shears in her hand. She says softly, "What a pity you never found someone to marry, Helga."

UPSTAIRS, WILFRED'S EMPTYING THE DRAWERS of his bureau.

"You're not leaving!" Elfriede exclaims.

"Not at present, no. I'm merely giving way to Fraulein von Kleist. The little room at the end of the corridor is more than sufficient for my needs."

"Oh, of course. That's kind of you."

He places a stack of shirt collars on the bed. "I can't claim all the credit. The lady herself offered the hint a short while ago, when she returned from the garden."

"Ha. That sounds like Helga."

"She's not lacking for nerve. She also asked me to confirm whether I was or was not engaging in carnal relations with my hostess."

Elfriede's palm falls away from the doorknob. "What did you tell her?"

"What did I tell her?" He turns to face Elfriede. "I denied it, of course. I lied to her face. What else is a gentleman supposed to do, to protect his lady's honor?"

"Thank you."

"Then you don't mean to tell her the truth?"

"I—I don't see any purpose in it. It will only give her one more reason to force us back to Germany. One more arrow in her quiver."

"Back to Germany? Is that the idea, then?"

"Of course it is. Not yet, of course. But eventually I must. Because of Johann's inheritance, you know."

"Yes, of course." Wilfred turns back to the bureau. "Then I suppose we'll have to observe the proprieties, from now on."

"What?"

"We can't have the floorboards creaking at dawn. The bedsprings squeaking, God forbid. She'll cotton on to us in no time."

"But—but surely we can find some way to—"

"To what?"

"Before you leave," she says. "Before you return to England."

The top drawer's empty, the contents stacked on the bed. Shirt collars and linens. Wilfred opens the second drawer. The wood's swollen with heat, and he has to jiggle the box carefully to extract it from the frame. He gives this task his full attention.

"Besides," Elfriede continues desperately, "she'll be gone before long. Once she sees it's no use."

"What's no use?"

"Forcing me back to Germany before I'm ready."

"My dear love," he says, "I don't mean to contradict you, but your sister-in-law strikes me as the sort of woman who doesn't give up until she's got what she wants. Unless you forcibly evict her, she's won't depart the premises without you and the little baron on each arm."

"I can't evict her. She's Gerhard's sister."

"Yes. Quite." Wilfred drops a pile of starched shirts on the bed. "Well, there's one silver lining in all this."

"What's that?"

"At least she didn't arrive a month earlier. She'd have spoiled our little interlude altogether."

"Don't say that. Don't say it like that. Don't call it an interlude."

"But what else is it, dearest? What future do you see for us?"

"I don't know!"

"Bring me home to Germany with you, perhaps?"

Down the corridor, Charlotte's getting the children dressed. Elfriede can hear their piping voices, their little shrieks as bathing costumes are dragged over small heads and shoes emptied of sand. Johann's old enough to dress himself, which he does in a methodical fashion in his own room. If Elfriede closes her eyes, she can picture his solemn look of concentration over buttons and laces. But she can't close her eyes. They're fixed painfully on Wilfred's face. His grave blue gaze.

"Stop," she whispers.

Wilfred steps toward her and puts his hand gently on the back of her head, near her neck, that little hollow he likes to kiss. "I wouldn't hurt you for the world, my love," he says. "The choice is yours."

"What choice? There's no choice. I've never had any choice."

"Only if you think you don't, Elfriede. That's all." His hand falls away.

He turns back to the bed and starts to gather up his shirts and collars and things. "Lend a hand, perhaps?"

Silently she picks up a few shirts, his drawers. How virtuous they look, all washed and folded, instead of shamefully crumpled on the floor of her bedroom. She follows him down the hallway to the small single room at the end, on the other side of the children's rooms, past Charlotte's stern voice and the girls' chorus of replies. Wilfred's new room is tiny, just a bed and dresser, a narrow window. Elfriede puts the shirts and drawers in the dresser and goes to open the bottom sash.

"Another silver lining," Wilfred says, arranging his clothes just so in the top drawer. "At least you're not pregnant."

THE NEXT MORNING, ELFRIEDE WAKES to a premonition. Her eyes fly open, her heart's pounding in her chest. She rolls on her side and observes the gray light of dawn, the empty pillow, which she folds into her arms. A few faint noises reach her ears from downstairs, but maybe that's her imagination. She sits up and sees the envelope on the floor, small white rectangle against the dark boards.

No! she gasps aloud. She leaps out of bed and flies downstairs, but the rooms are empty and dark. She flings open the front door, heedless of her nightgown, but the road's empty too, the air's warm and silent, the horizon pink, and she falls to her knees on the wooden porch. She simply can't stand.

THE LETTER. THE LETTER. HOW long until she can bear to read it? Not long, as it turns out. Once she drags herself inside and shuts the door again, there's nowhere she can go that doesn't contain some reminder of Wilfred. So she climbs the stairs and returns to her bedroom—no point in checking Wilfred's little chamber at the end of the hall, that will be painfully empty—and the hole in her chest is so vast, makes breathing so difficult, that she'll take anything to fill it. Even this letter.

As before, there's no salutation.

We are back to pen and paper again, my love, and this time it will be worse than before. Maybe it's better we don't write at all. I've lain awake all night, recalling every moment of the past three weeks. Do you remember that time we took the children into town for ice cream? As afternoons go I suppose it was ordinary enough. Frederica climbed on my knee and dribbled most of her ice cream on my jacket. The baby had syrup all over her face and you were trying to wipe it off. It was all very messy and loud and the proprietor, I think, wanted to throw us out of his parlor. But I don't believe I have ever loved you more. Have I made that perfectly clear? I fear I have not. In my determination to leave all decisions regarding our future in your hands—in my painful aware-ness of how little I have to offer you in material terms—our unequal stations, your duty to your children—all the obstacles that stand between us—I never told you what sort of future I selfishly dreamed of. Possibly this is the wrong moment altogether for a marriage proposal, but here it is: From the moment we met, I've longed for nothing more on this earth than to stand before God as your husband. I sail from New York in six days' time, aboard RMS Cedric. W.

AND WHAT ABOUT CHARLOTTE, AFTER all? How's she getting on with all these houseguests from across the ocean? A year's passed since the death of her lover and patron, that terrible shock she's been numb-ing in the customary fashion. In Germany it was schnapps, taken on the quiet before bedtime. Once in America, where schnapps isn't so cheap or plentiful, Charlotte turned to whiskey. Kentucky bourbon, to be exact, a type of whiskey made from corn mash, or so Elfriede understands. First Charlotte would take some wine with dinner, perfectly acceptable, and then after dinner the amber bottles came out of the liquor cabinet, one by one. Because Charlotte was generally good and soused in the evenings, Elfriede—who had started bathing the children by herself, tucking them into bed, from the time of Gerhard's death, when the heavily pregnant Charlotte couldn't summon the will to rise at all—called up Charlotte only when it was time to nurse Gertrud. Sometimes Elfriede worried whether the effects of corn mash, nicely fermented, distilled with water, and aged in oak casks, were transmitted through the human breast, but Gertrud seemed healthy enough, and anyway what else could she do?

Enter Wilfred.

If Charlotte's astonished by this turn of events, she doesn't show it. She makes no judgments. She asks no questions. Here comes this charming, odd-looking Englishman with his bright copper hair, joyously fucking Charlotte's mistress in the privacy of her bedroom, where did he come from? Charlotte doesn't care. Servants don't ask such questions, even when they're no longer servants. She just takes the Englishman's hand and dances obediently around the room with him. Maybe she doesn't stop drinking—certain habits become a biological necessity, it seems—but then Wilfred's joyousness starts to spill over into all the other rooms too, the happiness in the house becomes palpable, and how can you sit in an armchair drinking morose Kentucky bourbon when there's all this sunshine splashing over the place? She pours a glass or two and kicks off her shoes and starts to laugh a little, like she means it. Of an evening, she tells Wilfred about her humble life before she came to Schloss Kleist, her French mother raped by a Prussian soldier who eventually married her, the baby who died—it was a boy—and made it possible for her to nurse the little von Kleist infant whose mother had gone crazy. (She doesn't speak of her baby's father, and nobody ever asks.) Then Elfriede brings her Gertrud and she takes her daughter and waves the two lovebirds off into the garden. In the morning, she doesn't complain of headaches quite so much. Things are maybe not so bleak. Maybe she glimpses some future or another, who knows? Some solution to her terrible dilemma?

Enter Helga.
Exit Wilfred.

"WHERE'S MR. THORPE, FRAU?" CHARLOTTE ASKS a pale Elfriede, as they gather around the breakfast table, and the master's chair remains empty.

"I'm afraid Mr. Thorpe has been called home early."

Immediately, Frederica spills her milk, so Elfriede's rescued from having to make any further explanation. She blots and blots with her napkin, soothes the weeping Frederica. She's not quite sure whether Frederica's crying over spilled milk or over Wilfred. Maybe a little of both. By the time the spill's sopped up and the fresh milk poured, all's forgotten, because Aunt Helga has just appeared in the doorway of the breakfast room, and young minds can only occupy themselves with one dragon at a time. Well, except Johann. He keeps glancing at the chair, almost as if he can't believe his eyes, right up until the moment when Aunt Helga settles herself there, in the place formerly occupied by Mr. Thorpe.

BUT CHARLOTTE WON'T BE DENIED, not in so important a matter as this. She has her future to think of, after all. When the older children are let outside to play in the garden, she follows Elfriede to her room, carrying Gertrud.

"What's happened?" she asks. "Why has Mr. Thorpe left?"

"That's none of your business, Charlotte. What's wrong with the baby?"

"She wants to nurse."

"Haven't you nursed her already this morning?"

"No, I'm trying to wean her, she's almost a year." Charlotte pulls Gertrud's hands from the buttons of her dress, and the baby starts to cry. "Is he coming back?"

Elfriede hesitates. "No," she says, turning to the window to watch the children. "He's going home to England, I believe."

"But what about—I beg your pardon, Frau, but—"

"For God's sake, Charlotte, will you nurse the poor child? That *is* your job, isn't it?"

"*Frau!*"

Elfriede turns from the window. "My personal affairs are not your business, Charlotte. Your business is the children, that's all."

The stunned Charlotte drops into Elfriede's armchair and unbuttons her bodice. Gertrud, who's refused all breakfast in protest at being weaned, dives at Nurse's nipple and suckles frantically. The light from the window drenches them both, and Gertrud's eyes close in bliss. There's no sound in the room but the smacks of her mouth, no movement except the working of her jaw and the ecstatic clenching of her fingers. The familiar pangs start to pull in Elfriede's belly. She pivots away to her dresser and pretends to fiddle with the contents of the top drawer.

In a low voice, Charlotte says, "No, it's not."

"I beg your pardon?"

"I have a right, that's all. They're my children."

"I don't know what you mean."

"Your *personal affairs*, indeed. Your affairs are my affairs, Frau. If we're going to live here, or in England, or in Germany with that awful woman, that woman who hates me—"

"Don't worry about her. You'll be taken care of, wherever we go. You'll stay with us. You and the children."

"What about Mr. Thorpe? Does he really want—"

"Mr. Thorpe is not your concern."

"You can't just—you can't just—" Charlotte looks down at her daughter's flaxen head. "We're not baggage, you know."

"Of course you're not baggage. You're family. You know I'm as devoted to the girls as to Johann."

Charlotte shakes her head.

"It's true," Elfriede says. "I couldn't love the girls more if they were mine. I'd do anything to—"

"The girls. The girls. Yes, the girls." Charlotte looks back up. Her eyes are fierce and red. "But what about *me*, Frau? What's to become of *me*?"

"Why—why—whatever you want, of course. You're their mother."

Charlotte places her forefinger in the corner of Gertrud's mouth, breaking the seal. She tucks her breast away and buttons her bodice ruthlessly to the neck. Gertrud whimpers and claws at the fabric. Charlotte rises to her feet.

"Indeed I am, Frau," she says. "Indeed I am."

AT DINNER THAT EVENING, HELGA smiles back at her from Wilfred's chair, and the children don't say a word, let alone shriek with joy. Bath time's equally subdued, like a funeral, except the girls' nightgowns are snowy white and there's nobody to mourn, after all, nobody's actually died. Elfriede tucks Ursula and Frederica into their little beds, and Frederica starts to cry. "I want Mr. Thorpe! I want Mr. Thorpe to tuck me in!"

"Mr. Thorpe's gone back home, sweetheart. He was only here on holiday."

But Frederica's only two years old and doesn't understand. She seems to think Mr. Thorpe's home is here in Florida, with them, with her. She repeats her demand over and over until suddenly she falls asleep, with the tears still wet on her cheeks. Elfriede turns to Ursula, whose eyes are shut tight, though she's not really sleeping. Elfriede kisses her forehead and settles the thin summer blanket around her shoulders. "Good night, my love," she whispers.

Ursula opens one eye. "Where does Mr. Thorpe live?"

"In England, sweetheart."

"Where's England? Is it close to Florida?"

"Not really, I'm afraid. It's back across the ocean, like Germany. You have to take a big ship to get there, like we did to get here, and it takes days and days."

Ursula closes her eye again. "I want to make a boat and sail to England."

"That's a wonderful idea, darling. He'll be so happy to see you."

She turns out the light and lifts Gertrud, who's been playing patiently with the blocks on the floor. When she slips out the door, she finds Johann standing there in his pajamas, looking lost.

"Why, Johann! I thought you were reading in your room."

"Can't."

"Why not? What's the matter?"

Johann shrugs. "Nothing."

Elfriede takes him back into his room and settles him under the blanket with his book about Africa. "Are you unhappy that Mr. Thorpe's gone home?" she asks gently.

"No!"

"All right," she says. "But I think he's going to miss *you*. He's going to miss you very much."

Johann shrugs. "Don't care."

"Remember how he showed you how to build the kite? And you flew it on the beach together?"

Johann shrugs again and concentrates on his book. But when Elfriede straightens away and settles Gertrud back on her hip, she sees how the light from the lamp reflects some wetness in his eyes.

"I'll be back soon to turn out the light," she tells him.

As she descends the stairs carefully, holding Gertrud with both her hands, she recalls the day with the kite, and then all the other days, the other hours, the minutes, each one individually all at once, in the same way that God sees and knows a billion hearts simultaneously. Her mind grows as large and clear as the universe. *My God, what have I done?* she thinks. *Why have I not seen what was right before me?*

Because you're afraid.

Well, what if I'm not afraid anymore? What then?

In that case, the steamship leaves New York in six days.

By now she's reached the bottom of the stairs, and this thing she could not decide during the course of twenty days has now become obvious during the course of twenty seconds.

"Charlotte!" she calls out.

There's no answer. She finds the nurse in the parlor, silent and rigid in one chair, while Helga occupies another chair across the room. Of course the phonograph is still. No cheerful dance hall music for Helga. The air itself might just crack from the weight of all this quiet, the kind of quiet that's the opposite of peace.

"Charlotte," Elfriede says. "The baby's ready."

Charlotte hoists herself out of the chair and heads for the doorway, where Elfriede holds a squirming Gertrud. Instead of joining Helga in the parlor, however, Elfriede follows Charlotte and Gertrud up the stairs to the small room next to Charlotte's that serves as a nursery. Charlotte looks up in surprise as Elfriede closes the door behind her.

"Frau von Kleist? Is something the matter?"

Is something the matter! Elfriede's nerves throb, her skin's alive. She's incandescent, she's going to burst.

"We're leaving," Elfriede says. "We'll pack our things tomorrow morning. I'll check the schedule for the trains. I hope we'll be gone by lunchtime Thursday." (Today's Tuesday.)

"Leave!"

"Yes."

"But where?"

"To England," Elfriede says. "We're going to join Mr. Thorpe in New York and follow him to England."

IT'S ASTONISHING HOW THINGS ACCUMULATE when you inhabit a house for several months with several children. Every time you turn around, thinking you've retrieved it all, another object meets your eye. A toy, a book, a shoe, a pencil. They came to Florida with so little, and now there's so much—where did it come from? By evening the next day, Elfriede's exhausted, but her heart still thrills inside her chest. She keeps picturing Wilfred's face when he sees them, the lot of them, Charlotte and four children and Elfriede, a multitude of trunks and suitcases, waiting for him on that pier in New York. They will live in England, of course, hundreds of miles away from Helga in Germany, from the rigidity and formality of Schloss Kleist. The children are young; they'll be speaking English like Englishmen before long. Naturally they'll visit their native land in the summer, on holidays, because Johann after all is the Baron von Kleist. But England will be home. Wilfred will be Papa. Elfriede thinks of some rambling half-timbered house in the countryside, like Shakespeare, messy and rambunctious and filled with children. There will be more of them, of course. She's not afraid any longer. She'll have Wilfred by her side, and how could any blackness exist amid so much sunshine? She'll give Wilfred babies of his own, delightful ginger-haired babies, two or three at least, and this time she'll nurse them herself, she'll care for them herself in the bedroom she shares with Wilfred, the house she shares with Wilfred, and won't the girls be delighted at these darling new arrivals! Won't they be a large, happy family together! Why, it's all so simple! Why was she so afraid? She wants to laugh out loud.

By the time she goes to bed, it's almost two o'clock in the morning, but everything's packed and ready. She's informed Helga of her decision, and Helga for once was rendered speechless. Oh my, the look on

Helga's face! Elfriede reaches for the pillow next to her, the one on which Wilfred's head used to lie, on which she used to gaze at him rapturously while he slept like a dead man, and she tucks it into her arms. For some time, she lies awake, too dazzled to sleep, certain she's incapable of any slumber this night, until she's waking up to a bright Florida morning, sunshine irradiating the windows, Johann jumping on her bed and pulling at her shoulders.

"Wake up, Mama! Wake up!"

Elfriede sits up on her elbows and tries to make sense of the world. "Johann! Darling. What time is it?"

But Johann doesn't know the time. What child ever does? His eyes are round and blue and stricken. He tugs her arm almost out of its socket.

"My sisters!" he says. "Where are my sisters?"

IN THE YEARS THAT FOLLOW, Elfriede will recall, most of all, the emptiness of the house during that terrible day. The absence of things, the dusty absence of life, which she remembers as an absence of light itself, even though the official weather records indicate that the sun shone as brightly as ever, from dawn until dusk.

Helga's happy to explain the whole affair. The previous evening, while Elfriede bathed the children, she offered Charlotte ten thousand marks to depart the next morning with her daughters, never to return to Germany, never to make any further claim on the family, never to attempt to contact the family again. After a short period of consideration, Charlotte counteroffered at twenty thousand marks, and Helga accepted. She wrote out the cheque right there in the parlor, and Charlotte had just tucked this valuable scrap of paper into her pocket when Elfriede arrived downstairs with Gertrud. Helga relates all this while sipping her coffee, nibbling her toast. Elfriede's too stunned and enraged to speak, let alone eat. She leaves without a word, walks three miles to the train station with a bewildered Johann in tow, but the ticket master came on duty at ten o'clock, he doesn't know anything about a party of four, a woman and three small girls, who might have departed on some train at dawn or thereabouts. Elfriede, not to be denied, insists he check the receipts, the ticket log left behind by his predecessor. He tells her he's awfully sorry, but he can't do that, confidentiality or something.

But not for nothing is Elfriede so beautiful as she is. She fixes her large, angelic eyes upon this ticket master, forty-five years of age or thereabouts, thinning hair and paunchy stomach, creased uniform of navy blue, who's already stammering, poor fellow, in the presence of such a heavenly creature as Elfriede. She explains in her halting English how she's raised these girls as her own daughters, how the nurse has absconded with them, how frantic she is to find them again. Possibly a tear or two wets her long eyelashes, and who's to say they aren't real, unfeigned tears? Elfriede's desperate, after all, she's heartbroken. She's standing at the ticket office of this hot, cramped, dirty train station in the middle of Florida, atmosphere heavy with heat and the reek of coal smoke, and all she wants is her girls back, her beloved and irreplaceable girls, in the same way she wants air to breathe. And what do you expect? Within the space of a minute or two, Elfriede learns that one Charlotte Kassmeyer and her three minor children were aboard the six fifty-three to Savannah, Georgia, with tickets through to New York City.

But then the ticket master looks up regretfully, first at the clock and then at Elfriede. He's sorry to inform her that the next train north doesn't leave until noon the next day.

FIVE DAYS LATER.

Now Elfriede stands inside another ticket office, considerably more luxurious, that of the Holland America steamship line on State Street, at the very bottom of Manhattan. Here in the middle of civilization, she doesn't need beauty. Her title's enough. The Baroness von Kleist and her son are shown to a private room, waited upon by an eager sycophant. The passenger lists for the most recent sailings to Rotterdam? Just a moment, Frau von Kleist. We'll see what we can do.

They sit together bravely in a pair of armchairs, she and Johann. It's the fourth steamship office they've inhabited this morning. Yesterday it was hotels, all the famous, well-appointed hotels of New York City and then some of the lesser ones. Surely this could not be so difficult? A blond woman in her thirties, speaking limited English in a heavy German accent, accompanied by three young girls, as fair as their mother, how could you fail to notice them? But New York's a good place to hide, after all. It's a question of numbers. A thousand hotels. Railway lines going every which way. Ocean liners crisscrossing the harbor, making their way up and down the mighty Hudson River to the waiting piers. A woman and her daughters, who has time to notice them? What's that American expression? A dime a dozen. And every minute counted, at every hour the chances dimmed, the likelihood grew that Charlotte and the girls had disappeared forever.

At one o'clock yesterday afternoon, Elfriede dragged the weary Johann into a lunchroom near Madison Square and considered her remaining options. She considered what she might do, if she were Charlotte, and where she would go. This promise she'd made to live anywhere but Germany, for example. Would she keep it? Why, of course she wouldn't. Charlotte wasn't going to learn a new language. She wasn't going to settle somewhere exotic. And—Elfriede realized, in a breathtakingly clear review of the past five years—nothing in Charlotte's character suggested she regarded vows as sacred. In fact, Charlotte was most likely to do what suited Charlotte. Besides, there was that cheque for twenty thousand marks to consider. Where else could you easily cash such an enormous sum of German money, drawn on a German bank, than Germany?

Charlotte's returning to Germany. Elfriede's sure of it.

So here they sit, Elfriede and Johann, in the offices of the Holland America Line. Earlier this morning they visited the Hamburg-American Line, Cunard, the White Star. Naturally they're unable to provide passenger information on future sailings, but manifests for ships already departed, that's possible, certainly, Frau von Kleist.

The office is hot and smells of stale cigars. It's midsummer in New York, a particular urban kind of heat, dirty and immovable, the atmosphere possibly fixed in place by all those vertical walls, and the perspiration crawls down Elfriede's spine. Johann swings his legs. Elfriede aches when she sees his face, so young and so anxious, framed by wet blond curls. He should be out playing with his sisters. He should be doing battle with the Atlantic surf, not stuck in a stuffy steamship office in New York City, dressed in his jacket and short pants. Elfriede's removed her gloves because of the heat, and her fingernails dig into her palms. Her jaw hurts with the force of her teeth grinding against each other, a reflex she can't seem to conquer. Her girls, her girls. The smell of Gertrud's hair. The small, plump shape of Frederica's hand in hers. The sound of Ursula's giggle. She's going to die, she can't survive this anxiety in her stomach, this grief.

Never to see them again. No, it's impossible.

What if they're sick? Hurt? Will Charlotte care for them properly, will she notice the little signs that a fever's more than just a fever, a cough's more than just a cough, a minor scrape might be turning septic? How can anyone love the girls so passionately as Elfriede loves them?

Johann. Is he never to see his sisters again?

It's impossible.

The door opens. The officer enters, bearing some papers and an eager expression. "Here you are, Frau von Kleist. You may review these at your leisure, of course. May I bring you some refreshment?"

"Perhaps some water for my son? Lemonade, if you have it? It's terribly hot."

"Yes, Frau von Kleist. I'm very sorry. One moment."

The officer disappears once more, and Elfriede bends over the papers. So great is her anxiety, she has trouble focusing on the names, on each individual entry. She reads them without reading them. Slow down, slow down. Think. The SS *Statendam*, ten thousand gross tonnage, departed from the Hoboken pier three days ago, bound for Rotterdam. 902 passengers, 147 in first class. Another 147 in second class, the remainder in steerage. Elfriede places her finger on the paper to mark her progress down the list of names, to make sure she doesn't skip any lines. The paper's shaking a little. The names are mostly Dutch, she perceives, but also German and some English. *Mr. and Mrs. Josef Kuipers, 5 children, 1 infant. Mr. Andrew Harrison. Mr. Leopold Meisner. Mr. and Mrs. Willem Janssen. Mr. and Mrs. Rutger De Jong, 3 children.*

The door opens. A woman enters, bearing a tray with two glasses of lemonade. Iced, even. Johann reaches greedily and remembers, at the last second, to say *Danke*. Elfriede's own mouth is dry with thirst, but she can't stop to drink.

Mr. Kaspar Ryskamp. Mrs. Thomas Beecham, 3 children.

Elfriede comes to the last of the first-class passengers. She pauses to reach for the lemonade on the small, round table between the armchairs. Already Johann's finished his own lemonade. His small legs swing and swing.

"Just a few more minutes, darling," she says. "We'll find them, I promise."

"Yes, Mama," he replies.

Elfriede returns to the list. Now the second-class passengers. Because she didn't really expect Charlotte to book a first-class cabin—that's a great deal of money—unless this windfall has maybe made her reckless. But no. Charlotte's prudent. She didn't buy first-class tickets on the train to New York, and she's not going to buy them now.

Mr. Jacob Mueller. Dr. and Mrs. Henrik Schoenbrun, 1 child. Miss Roelfein Vandercamp.

AND OF COURSE, THERE'S WILFRED to consider. Beating at the back of her head, the words *I will sail from New York in six days' time, aboard RMS* Cedric. Which is today. (She's already confirmed this date at the White Star Line offices, because sometimes ships are late arriving in port, you never know for certain.) In the meantime, where does she find him? There's no time to look, is there? She can only track down one missing piece of her heart at a time, for God's sake.

At least she knows where to find him tomorrow, in the middle of the afternoon. At Pier 51 on the Hudson River, climbing out of a taxicab, carrying a suitcase and a second-class ticket for Liverpool, England.

MR. AND MRS. NICOLAAS CLOET. MR. and Mrs. John Middleton, 2 children. Mrs. Charlotte Kassmeyer, 3 children.

Elfriede sets down the lemonade and rings the bell for the officer.

"The *Statendam*," she says, when he rushes through the door. "It departed on schedule?"

"Yes, Frau von Kleist. To the hour."

"And when will it arrive in Rotterdam?"

He glances at the clock, of all things, and then at the calendar on the desk. "In eight days' time, Frau, after a stop at Boulogne. The twenty-third of July."

Elfriede looks back down at the paper on her lap. Reads the name again, just to be certain, and then lifts her head to find Johann staring at her.

"Is it them?" he asks softly.

"Yes, darling. They sailed for Holland three days ago."

Johann's jaw makes a small, desperate movement. His nose twitches. He turns away and stares out the window, and Elfriede's heart pours right out of her body and into his. Her boy, her boy. Everyone abandons him, don't they? Beginning with Elfriede, his own mother. He's sucked his lips all the way inside his mouth. He sets his jaw bravely. He's not going to cry, Gerhard's son will not cry over some girls, of all things, who sailed away from him across the ocean.

Elfriede returns her attention to the officer, who clutches his hands before her. "Your next ships," she says. "When do they depart?"

"Ah. Ah." He searches the papers on his desk and finds the one he's looking for, the sailing schedule. He runs his finger down the column. "The *Ryndam* came in two days ago, I believe, and departs tomorrow morning. The *Rotterdam* is due in next week, and departs for Rotterdam on the twenty-sixth."

"I see," she says. "You're quite sure the *Ryndam* departs in the morning?"

"Yes, Frau. She's scheduled to leave the pier at ten o'clock."

Elfriede hands him the passenger list and puts her gloves back on. Her heart beats and beats in that overheated room, and yet she's strangely cold, she has to stop herself from shivering.

"Mama?" says Johann.

"Thank you so much for your help, Mr. Patterson," says Elfriede.

"It's my pleasure, Frau von Kleist. Is there anything else I can do to assist you?"

"Yes, if you would. I should like to reserve a first-class cabin on the SS *Ryndam* for myself and my son, if there are any still available."

Mr. Patterson, of course, is happy to make this arrangement for her.

LULU

For a woman born and raised in the American South, Wallis Windsor didn't express much tolerance for the heat of a Bahamian summer. She had this fan of Chinese silk, acquired during what she called her "lotus year" in the Orient—this occurred between husbands one and two, a kind of soul searching—and she waved it vigorously as the limousine trundled up the hill toward the maternity clinic in Grants Town.

"I don't know why on earth you stand it here, Lulu," she said. "We've got no choice, of course, but you don't have to stay in this dump. You could go to Maine."

"I don't know anybody in Maine."

"The Oakeses?"

"I'd say they already have their hands full, at present."

"Oh, of course. *That* business. Do you know something funny? I'd put the whole sordid affair out of my mind." She turned her head and stared out the window. "Awful man. Did you ever meet him?"

"Yes. He seemed like a gentleman to me."

"She's a schoolgirl, Lulu."

"Nancy's eighteen and just graduated."

"He's in his thirties. Divorced. It's too horrible, really."

On my other side, Miss Drewes looked up from the duchess's appointment book, and I wondered if she was thinking the same thing I was. Ex-husbands, I mean, of which Wallis had two. If she did, she made no sign. Just tapped her pencil against her lips a couple of times and turned back to her work. Miss Drewes was an American through and through, Mamaroneck bred, a Mount Holyoke girl, but she greeted her employers each morning with *Your Royal Highness* and continued in that vein throughout the day, which was just the sort of attitude Wallis appreciated most.

"I'll tell you what he did," Wallis said. "You know he's got these properties out in Cable Beach—"

"Naturally. I happen to live in one of them myself."

"Do you really? That bungalow of yours?"

"I'm bound to confess, he's a conscientious landlord."

"Well. Apparently he built a block of luxury apartments out there, right by the golf course, and whoever rents them is entitled to play on the links and so on, rent a cabana. And do you know what he did, one season?"

"Something just awful, I'll bet."

"I don't know if I'd call it awful. Provoking, that's what it was. He took I don't know how many thousands of dollars from a pair of New York Jews and rented them apartments. The entire season! Didn't even think to ask the members if they'd mind."

"You don't say. The nerve."

"That's the sort of fellow he is, Lulu, always on the take. Never a thought for anyone else's comfort. And really, it wasn't fair to the tenants, either. I'm sure they thought everybody would take them in, you know, invite them to parties and dinners and so on, and—well. There are certain things you can't buy, you know, no matter how much filthy money you've got."

The duchess waved her fan in smart little movements, as if to drive away her own ire. By now, we'd crested the hill, and I glanced to my right, where you could see Cable Beach and the golf course as this oasis, surrounded by scrub on three sides and ocean on the other.

"You know, you've got to hand it to Hitler," I said. "Wouldn't it be convenient if we could just—oh—just *confiscate* all that filthy money for the common good? And then herd them all into camps and ghettos and shoot anybody who objects? I guess we just haven't got the guts for it."

Miss Drewes sucked her breath. The duchess snapped her fan shut. The landscape glided past the window. I remember thinking how the cabanas looked like handkerchiefs tossed on the white sand, how serene everything looked on that side of the hill. I heard the sound of metal clinking, paper rustling, the rasp of a cigarette lighter. The limousine slowed into a curve, and the sunlight shifted to enter through the rear window and scorch our necks.

The duchess muttered, "It's not the same thing, you know."

A curl of smoke made its way past my face.

"Anyway, most of those stories are made up by the newspapers, which you *know* are all controlled . . ."

I turned and lifted my eyebrows. The duchess smashed her lips together and turned her head to the side, where Miss Drewes scribbled away at her notes, red-faced.

"I forget, you're from New York," Wallis said.

The car straightened out and proceeded down the hill. The duchess dragged on her cigarette. I stared at the *snap, snap* of the Chinese fan, the whiteness of her knuckles beneath her scarlet nails.

"It's so lovely," I said. "Your fan."

Wallis stopped the waving and spread it out. "Isn't it? A gift from an admirer. I like this fellow here the best." She pointed to a chubby, smiling, naked man hiding behind a tree. "Look carefully and you'll see that's not a branch."

"Dear me."

She snapped it closed. "But we mustn't shock Miss Drewes. Eh, Miss Drewes? Not until you're married. You know, I gave one of my Chinese screens to Sir Harry, to thank him for his hospitality when poor old Government House was being redone. I believe he's put it in his bedroom."

"If it's anything like this one, I don't blame him."

She laughed. "*You* haven't been to the Orient, have you, Lulu?"

"Never. Although I'd like to go, one day."

"You should. It changes your life." She opened the fan and resumed waving. "I sometimes wish . . ."

"Wish what?"

"Nothing. Here we are at last. Look at them, poor dears."

By *poor dears*, she meant the Negro women lined up outside the entrance of the small white building to which we had just pulled up, in our giant Government House limousine with its little Union Jacks fluttering from the wheel wells. Each one bore a baby in her arms, or in a cloth sling against her body, newborns and bruisers, squallers and sleepers, in various states of dress and fretfulness.

"Frightful, isn't it?" said Wallis. "You see, they breed like rabbits."

As we prepared to climb out of the limousine, I thought that possibly some of these babies were the children of the men who had rioted three weeks ago, seeking twelve shillings a day and getting—after a soothing radio address from the Duke of Windsor to calm everybody's nerves, after newspaper pontification by the column mile, after days of fractious negotiation—five shillings a day plus lunch. Five shillings a day on which to raise a family. The duchess and I both wore our Red Cross uniforms, white and crisp, and our spectator shoes of polished brown and white leather. We hurried through the entrance, dogged by Miss Drewes and her satchel of careful records. Once the photography was out of the way, Wallis and Miss Drewes headed for the business side of things—

taking down weights, recording vaccinations, that kind of thing—while I messed about in the waiting room, played with the babies and chatted with the mothers.

It's funny, I remember how oddly cheerful they were in that moment, in that hot waiting room in the Duchess of Windsor's clinic, how confident the Duke of Windsor was going to make everything better, was going to right all of history's wrongs and begin a new chapter in the story of race relations in the Bahamas, and maybe the whole world. There had been some wonderful speech by one of the Negro leaders, made right there in the Government House annex before the duke himself, the day after the riot on Bay Street—had I heard about it? This man, he had said everything that was in the hearts of the black and colored folks in these islands, he had actually said in thunderous voice to the royal Duke of Windsor, former king of the British Empire and its dominions, *Art thou He that cometh, or look we for another?* And the duke had nodded to that. Had nodded and smiled. Oh, things was going to change, Mrs. Randolph.

On the way home, Wallis told me she was thinking of starting up a canteen for all the enlisted men due to descend on Nassau, British and American and dominion, once the airfields were completed.

"Aren't the Daughters of Empire setting one up already?" I said. "Down on Bay Street, near the British Colonial. You can't miss it."

Wallis's face turned a little stony. "And I'm sure it's a worthy endeavor. But it's teetotal, you know, and what red-blooded airman is going to hang about a canteen that doesn't serve beer? And if those boys aren't gathering in the canteen in a civilized atmosphere, they'll be causing trouble in the streets and the nightclubs."

"Fair point," I said.

"I've already spoken to Fred Sigrist. That club of his out by Cable Beach, that would be perfect. It's empty now that the American tourists have fled home. It's a bit shabby, but we can fix it up. Can't we, Miss Drewes?"

Miss Drewes glanced up. "The canteen? I think it's a swell idea. You've got such a terrific knack for decoration and entertaining, Your Royal Highness. I'd say it's right up your alley."

"We'll knock the socks off that Daughters of Empire joint," Wallis said viciously. Then she gathered herself. "Morale is so important, after all, absolutely vital. I've worked it all out. I know this fellow at the American army base in Miami, he'll help me with Lend Lease supplies. Real ham and bacon and eggs. I'm going to take such a personal role. I think it would cheer the men a great deal to have the Duchess of Windsor frying up their eggs to order, don't you?"

"I can just see it," I said.

"Just think of all the photographs you can send back to your magazine. We'll have a gala opening. It should be open by Christmas, don't you think, Miss Drewes?"

"If not sooner," said Miss Drewes.

Wallis was smiling, tapping her sharp finger on her knee, waving the Chinese fan. She gazed out the window at the passing landscape. We were climbing the hill now, back toward Government House, and the shacks of Grants Town had begun to thin out and make way for the villas and bungalows of white Nassau, soaked in sunshine. As if struck by inspiration, Wallis turned back to me.

"Of course we'll set up a canteen for the colored troops too," she said. "Where they can listen to their own music and eat their own food. Won't that be fun?"

BY THE TIME I ARRIVED home, Veryl had gone for the day, bound for the afternoon shift at the Prince George. The bungalow was shut tight as an oyster. I went around switching on the electric fans, opening the windows, but no amount of manufactured draft, no amount of fresh air— such as it was—could chase away the noontime heat of Nassau at the end of June. And the smell, the potpourri of rotting flowers and mildew. That odor, it hangs in my nostrils still.

She'd laid the morning post on the table, as was our custom since September, when the invitations began to arrive through the letter slot in their dozens, dinner parties and tennis parties and Red Cross fairs, even an occasional wedding or two. Sometimes I wonder how those couples turned out, where those lives exist now, on what continent and with how many children, or at all. On this particular night, I was due to attend both a supper dance for the RAF officers at the Emerald Beach Hotel and a dinner party at Lady Annabelle Taylor's place. The dance sounded like better fun; the dinner, like better gossip. I set my hat on the stand and straightened my hair. In the mirror, I caught the reflection of the table behind me, and the stack of cards and invitations, and beneath these small, ecru envelopes a larger one, a parcel, plain brown and wrapped in string, the parcel I dreaded.

I allowed myself the luxury of a moment's hesitation. Sometimes you have to gather yourself, you know, sometimes you need to gird your loins or whatever needs girding. In that empty instant, I recalled a dream I had the night before, just a flash of it, in which I was wandering down a hotel corridor in search of something, I didn't know what, something peculiar. The way it is in dreams.

But I wasn't made for waiting. Some people can wait around forever in the face of bad news, putting off the inevitable, insisting on living in a world that doesn't really exist, but I can't. I stepped forward and yanked the thick brown parcel from the bottom of the stack, toppling the envelopes, and sure enough it was from New York, all right, from the headquarters of *Metropolitan* magazine on Madison Avenue, sent by airmail at considerable expense. Miss Brown—Lightfoot's secretary—she always knotted that string but good. I carried the parcel into the office and found the scissors in the drawer. *Snip, snip.* The string fell away. I tore the paper to reveal the latest issue of *Metropolitan*—hot off the press, as they say, not even yet present on an actual newsstand—and flipped to the "Lady of Nassau" column on the inside back cover.

And it was no more than I expected, really. Because while my Remington and I had composed a brilliant column on the Burma Road riot last month, *clickety-clack*, had quoted from the duke's radio address, had described the scene and snapped a photograph of the smoke and ruin the next morning, called it "Now Is the Summer of Our Discontent," I had also taken the precaution of sending along an alternate column. An alternate June, in which Nancy Oakes's elopement with Alfred de Marigny occupied every imagination, and that was all that mattered.

And thank goodness for this particular precaution. Thank goodness I had lain awake all night after writing the Burma Road column, heart smacking, and counted up how many dollars might remain in Lulu's coffers if dear old Daddy decided not to run her column that month. Thank goodness I'd risen at dawn with the damned songbirds and rattled off the usual tittle-tattle, the awful scandal, the whispers, and sent it off to Madison Avenue for Lightfoot to weigh against the first. Thank goodness.

Because, according to her column in the upcoming issue of *Metropolitan*, it seemed the Lady of Nassau had never heard of Burma Road, had never wandered outside on a hot morning, the first of June, and discovered a riot. In the July 1942 issue of *Metropolitan* magazine, she had nothing to talk about but heiresses and playboys.

From between pages eighty-two and eighty-three a check fluttered to the floor, made out to Leonora Randolph in the amount of two hundred dollars. Thank goodness.

BECAUSE IT WAS SATURDAY, THE bank was closed. I tucked the check in my desk drawer and locked it—not that an enterprising thief couldn't crowbar the thing to smithereens in a jiffy—and considered the clock. Quarter past one. At least five hours remained before the evening got under way, before I would freshen up and dress, select my shoes and my pocketbook, and head to Lady Annabelle's for the dinner party before moving on to Emerald Beach, where the RAF officers would surely be dancing until midnight. After that, who knew? I was the Lady of Nassau, after all. Saturday nights were part of my job. Two hundred smackeroos to swan around paradise and flirt with the flyboys, flatter the flutterbys, you couldn't sneeze at that.

I went in the kitchen and poured myself a glass of lemonade from the pitcher in the icebox. Drank it outside, where a merciful cocoanut palm shaded the garden table. It was the time of day when you escaped your insufferable bungalow, when you made your way to your cabana at one of the beach clubs, Cable or Emerald or someplace, and took in whatever limp breeze the ocean offered you. That, too, was part of my job. People dropped the most delicious tidbits on the beach, when they were bored out of their skulls and halfway to sunstroke. Overhead, an airplane droned toward Oakes Field, louder and louder, some flyboy in training, the original cause of all our discontent, after all. At Oakes Field, at the airfield taking shape on the other side of the island, along Burma Road connecting them, the men had gone back to work under the terrible sun, five shillings a day plus lunch. Bay Street had repaired itself and returned to its ordinary rhythms. I finished my lemonade and rose to clean the empty glass in the sink. When I had returned the glass, clean and dry, to the kitchen cabinet, I went to the telephone and dialed the number on the scrap of paper Thorpe had given me last December.

"How's the arm?" he said, by way of greeting, after only three rings of the telephone.

"How did you know it was me?"

"You're the only one who knows this number."

I fiddled with the cord and caught a glimpse of myself in the mirror, flushed with heat, halfway to sunstroke. "The arm's just fine. Stitches came out all right."

"I'm glad to hear it. Any nerve damage?"

"They didn't say. What does nerve damage feel like?"

"You would know, believe me."

I turned away from the mirror and looked out the window instead, the empty street outside. "Are you busy?"

"Immensely."

"So if I packed a picnic basket and rowed myself over to Hog Island, you'd bustle me and my picnic right back?"

"That depends. Can you row?"

"Not really."

"Then I suppose I'd better jump straight in the launch and pick you up from the harbor. Half an hour?"

The rush of blood in my veins was like electricity. I dropped the curtain and spun back to the mirror, and I was surprised to see that my face was no more than normal, a little sparkly around the eyes, pink around the cheeks, despite the thunderous pulse in my ears that just about knocked me flat.

"Done," I said.

THE LAUNCH, HE SAID. WHAT he meant was Axel Wenner-Gren's motorboat, a long, beautiful blade made of polished wood, slicing the water in two. The tall man at the wheel wore a white shirt, khaki trousers, and no hat, and the wind flattened his bright hair against his skull. He pulled right up to the dock as if he owned it and tossed me a rope, which I wound around the nearest bollard. He jumped across the gap with a nimbleness that surprised me.

"How's the leg?" I asked.

"Rather better. Is that your picnic basket?"

"It's not much, I guess."

"Never mind. I've got plenty of supplies at home."

Thorpe pitched the basket in the stern, unwound the rope, and held out his hand. I grabbed the fingers. "Steady as she goes," he said, passing me over, and while I was expecting some difference between shore and ship, the uneasiness of the deck alarmed me. Thorpe followed with the rope and took the wheel.

"Off we go," he said cheerfully.

WE LANDED ON THE EASTERN end of Hog Island, the private half, where Shangri-La sat at a graceful remove from the public landing that led to Paradise Beach. I had never been there, myself. Had not encountered Wenner-Gren since that Government House party in July, because of the blacklist, remember, the U.S. blacklist that kept him from the Bahamas. Why, just last month, the duke—reluctantly, it must be said—had signed an order impounding all Wenner-Gren's commercial assets here, his bank and his dredging company and the Paradise Beach and Transportation Company, among others. So Wenner-Gren was not in residence, and the legendary entertainments at Shangri-La had come to a stop.

"Only a few caretakers left," said Thorpe, leading me down the road, "and yours truly, of course. It's rather ghostly, in fact."

"But you've got all this to yourself!" I waved my arm at the cocoanut palms, the sea grapes, the glimpses of pure, liquid turquoise between the foliage.

"Still, it does get lonely, from time to time."

In the course of our conversation, the road had begun to straighten, and the cocoanut palms to form orderly queues on either edge. I raised my hand against the sun and saw, about two hundred yards distant, a circular drive, a stone fountain—dry, I thought—and a large, shuttered building in the familiar colonial style.

"Lonely," I said. "So what do you do when you're lonely, Benedict Thorpe?"

He stopped and turned. "I work."

"Oh, of course. You work."

"It's true."

"No lady visitors?"

"No visitors at all."

We stared at each other. Some birds twittered, the ocean stirred nearby. I returned my hand to my brow and peered back at the cottage. "Do you know what I think?"

"I can't imagine."

"I think I want to see all your botany collections with my own two eyes."

THE COTTAGE WAS LARGER THAN I expected, but I suppose my expectations were to blame. Of course a man as wealthy as Axel Wenner-Gren wouldn't put up his guests in some quaint, measly, tumbledown beach shack! Thorpe led me past the main house, down a wide, tended path surrounded by tropical plants—palms, bougainvillea, sea grapes, you name it—until the fronds parted and there it stood, made of white clapboard, in that bungalow style of the British colonies: enormous, low-hanging roof, porches all around, view right down the beach to the wide Atlantic.

"Be it ever so humble," I said.

"I'm afraid it's not well-suited to visitors. Collections and equipment everywhere."

"Sounds like it could use a woman's touch."

"I'm afraid that would require a very ambitious woman," said Thorpe. We had reached the front porch. He climbed the steps, a bit stiff-legged, the knee not quite bending so well as it should. I followed without a word, through the door he opened with a flourish of his cane, directly into a single, spacious room, no entry hall of any kind.

"My goodness," I said. I stared up at the distant ceiling—there was no second story, just empty space, four electric fans hanging from the central beam, all still. The smell of wood, of trapped sunshine, of green things, of something else. Something chemical.

"As I said." He picked his way around a few stacks of wooden crates. "I don't entertain much."

"Let's be frank, Thorpe. You don't entertain at all."

"I *have* been away for half a year, remember, while my colleagues continued to ship me specimens and so on."

I trailed my index finger through the layer of dust covering the lid of a pine crate. FRAGILE—SPECIMENS—DO NOT OPEN. "And so on?"

"Mmm." Thorpe had set the picnic basket on a table and opened it. "Let's see. Apples. Sandwiches . . . what, ham?"

"Ham and cheese."

"Lemonade, excellent. And is this . . . ?" He drew out a plate, wrapped in cheesecloth.

"Veryl's rum cake."

"You're a goddess. On the beach, do you think? There's a shady spot, at the edge of the dunes."

I brushed my hands against my dress and turned in a slow circle to gaze around the room. I took my time. Such a utilitarian house, no paintings at all, no pictures, no mirrors, no decorative knickknacks. A rectangle, of which the front and back walls formed the short sides. On each of the two longer walls, a pair of doors stood snug. There was another door on the back wall, the swinging kind of door, leading presumably to the kitchen.

"Do you like it?" Thorpe said dryly.

I turned to face him. He was closer than I thought, had laid his cane on a crate and stepped right next to me. I reached up with both hands and drew the spectacles from his face. He didn't say a word. I held the glasses to the meager light and squinted through them. "Just as I thought," I said.

"I beg your pardon?"

I tossed the spectacles on the crate. "Tell me something. Do you work for the Allies or the Germans?"

If Thorpe was startled by the question, he didn't show it. He had these thick, straight eyebrows, a few shades darker than his hair, and they hardly budged. A line or two appeared between them, as if he were more puzzled than shocked.

"I'm afraid I don't quite follow you. Work for whom? I work for myself."

"My dear fellow. Are you one of those Englishmen who thinks all Americans are stupid? Or just me?" I waved my hand at the crates. "Kind of reminds me of a film set. All these nice wooden boxes with their nice labels. SPECIMENS—FRAGILE. Also untouched."

"I beg your pardon. You're suggesting I'm some kind of . . . of agent? A *traitor*?"

"I didn't say that, exactly. I asked which side you were working for. That's not the same as saying you're a stinking Nazi, is it?"

"You can't be serious."

"Can't I?"

"On what *possible* grounds?"

I held up my hand and ticked off the fingers. "One, you've taken up residence on a patch of ground that's strategically placed for Atlantic communication, to say the least, and hidden nicely from prying eyes in Nassau. Two, that patch of ground happens to be owned by a man blacklisted by the U.S. government for possible Nazi ties, among other sins—"

"Not true. Wenner-Gren's a meddling businessman, but he's not a Nazi."

"Three, you have a habit of disappearing for weeks on end, and then reappearing without warning—"

"Because I was *attacked*, Mrs. Randolph—"

"Lulu."

"I'll call you Lulu again when you cease hurling ridiculous accusations at my head—"

"Four, your eyesight is perfect."

He opened his mouth and closed it again.

"Look at you," I said. "You're all pink."

"You're damned right I'm all pink."

I stepped forward and clasped his chin, which was just beginning to stubble and had the delicious texture of a cat's tongue. I turned his head to the left, so I could make out the short, thick scar there, still red. "And *why* were you attacked, hmm? Tell Lulu the truth, now."

"I don't know. Chap wanted my cash, I suppose."

"And this thief. They never did catch him, did they?"

The muscle at the corner of his mouth made a slight twitch. He crossed his arms over his ribs. "Not so far as I understand."

"What a terrible shame. I wonder if they'll ever find him."

"The Nassau police force, alas, is not known for its competence in these matters."

"You, on the other hand. You know how to handle a fellow who needs a bit of a reprimand, don't you? Like that fellow on the airplane."

There wasn't much light inside the walls of the room. The windows were all shaded, and Thorpe hadn't switched on any of the lamps, wherever they were. The air had a dusky, dreamlike color that muted our skin, our faces, our hair. Thorpe stared at me through a million motes of dust, each one invisible by itself. To his right, a stack of crates ended just at his arm. He lifted his elbow and leaned against them. "You are the most confounded woman," he said softly. "Did it ever occur to you that if I *were* some kind of—of agent, whatever they call them, I mean if you're right, which you're not, well . . ."

"Well?"

"Mightn't I just simply kill you?" With his other hand, he waved at the room around us. "No one would ever know."

"I left a note for Veryl, to be opened in the event of my disappearance."
He lifted his face and laughed.

"Oh, believe me, you'd be a dead man if Veryl came after you," I said.

"I don't doubt it." He moved away, toward the French doors along the
back wall, through which you could just glimpse the ocean. He'd left his
cane atop one of the crates, and limped his way carefully around the various obstacles. I found myself admiring the proportions of his back and
legs, the easy way he moved, despite his injury. As he came within reach
of the glass, the handles of the doors, he stopped and made a thoughtful
grunt.

"What's the matter?" I said.

"I suppose I'm just working out how to answer you. You've clearly
reached some sort of conclusion, and nothing I say could possibly sway
you. So I find myself wondering what it is you *want* me to say. What you
expect me to do with this accusation."

"You might start by acknowledging the truth."

He turned to face me. "What if I refuse?"

"You have that right. And I have the right not to believe you."

"Fair enough." He reached for his jacket pocket, patted, frowned.
Missing his cigarettes, I guessed. "But then we're just going around in
tiresome circles, aren't we? The point is, what do you *want* from this conversation, Mrs. Randolph? What do you intend to do with your suspicions? Print them in your column?"

"My God, of course not. I'm a patriot. I'd take my suspicions to the
FBI, or something like it."

"The FBI. For God's sake." He shook his head. "Tell me something.
Hypothetically speaking, if I admitted to—well, whatever it is you're ac-
cusing me of—if I said, *Why yes, I* am *an agent for the British government*—"

"Or the German one."

"What difference does it make?"

"A great deal of difference. If you were a British agent, I'd ask to join you."

"Join me?"

"Trust me, Thorpe, nothing goes on in Nassau without my knowing it. I've got contacts all over town. I've got the perfect cover. I've got nerve, you said so yourself—"

He held up his palm. "Stop. Please. This is absurd."

"And if you're a German agent, I guess I'd just have to kill you."

"Kill me? By what means?"

"I might have something up my sleeve, so to speak."

Thorpe's gaze went to my right sleeve, my left. He said heavily, "Do you mind if we sit down? This leg."

"Be my guest."

He settled himself against a nearby crate, not so much sitting as propping himself up, and placed his hands on his knees, which was an altogether strange pose for an Englishman. They tended to hunch themselves up in this self-deprecating way, to make caves of themselves. Not Thorpe; he took a pose of readiness. "Let me tell you a little story," he said. "I happened to be in Berlin one summer in 1936, a few years after the Nazis came to power. I was visiting a friend from university, who happened to be a Jew. I rather fancied his sister, if you must know, and since I spoke fluent German—no, don't interrupt—since I spoke German, since I was familiar with Germany, having spent a number of hols there, visiting my brother—no, I said don't interrupt—I thought perhaps I might try my luck with her. Lovely girl, terribly bright, brilliant at maths and also at music."

His thumbs rubbed against his khaki trousers, over and over. My words died in my lungs. I found a crate of my own and perched on the edge, mindful of dust.

"Her name was Anke," he said. "Anke Mueller. She was sensible enough to reject my overtures out of hand, and kind enough to do it so gently, I hardly felt the wound. We continued to correspond after I returned home to England. I urged my friend Mueller to emigrate, to encourage his family to emigrate, but he refused, because to emigrate meant to give up everything, all their wealth, their friends and relatives, the damned country they loved, despite it all. Everything they knew. And then one day, I had a letter sent back to me. It had been opened and rather crudely resealed, marked addressee unknown. Anke's letters stopped altogether, and Mueller's. I made inquiries. It turned out their father's business, their beautiful apartment in Friedrichstrasse, everything had been confiscated by the state. My friends themselves had disappeared. I went to Berlin, I searched everywhere, but nobody knew where they had gone, and eventually the authorities began to make trouble for me. Arrested me, confiscated my passport, interrogations, that sort of thing, until at last I was able to make contact with the British Embassy and get them to step in."

"When—when did this happen?" I asked.

"January of 1939," he replied. "Not long after the Kristallnacht. You know what happened then, don't you?"

"Everybody knows about that."

Thorpe stared down at his hands on his legs. "Anyway, I never did hear from the Muellers again. I tried, I searched. I was frantic. After Poland, after the war started, I asked certain friends of mine to—to do what they could. Find them and get them the hell out of Germany, somehow. But I haven't heard. Anke . . ." He paused. His thumbs went still against his trousers. I couldn't see his face. I thought he was hiding from me deliberately, that he'd said more than he planned, and now he couldn't go back. But he could hide his face from me.

"Are you still in love with her?" I whispered.

Now he looked up, with an expression that seemed to regard me as if

I hadn't understood a word he'd said, hadn't understood the point of it at all. "Lulu, that was years ago. I was a boy."

"But she was that kind of girl, wasn't she?"

"She was. But she told me it was impossible, and I—well, I suppose you could say I honored her enough to believe her."

I couldn't speak. I sat there mutely and stared not at his face, which was too much, but his hair, which had caught a glint of sunlight from the window, and looked sort of rumpled, as if he'd gone for a swim earlier and not bothered to brush it afterward. *I'm sorry*, I thought, and it seemed to me that I hadn't understood the meaning of that word until now.

Thorpe rose from the crates and turned back to the French doors, to the ocean behind them. He stuck his hands in his pockets. "I can't say *what* I believe in anymore," he said. "A just God in heaven? I don't know. But if anyone deserves mercy from the Almighty, it's her."

I looked down at my hands, which were twisted together on my dress of blood orange. I had picked out this dress with great care. I thought it suited my eyes of light brown, my olive complexion, my hair now streaked with Bahamian sunshine. I had wanted to look my best for such an important encounter. How my heart had drummed away as I stood there on the dock, waiting for Thorpe to arrive in his boat.

"I killed my husband," I said.

He spun around. "*What* did you say?"

"I killed him myself. Sort of an accident, but not really. We were living in Bakersfield at that point. It was a new town every four or five months, until the bills caught up with us, and now it was Bakersfield, California. I don't guess you've ever been there. Charming spot. Hot and dry. They bring in water in ditches to irrigate the place for farming, for ranching and that kind of thing, olive groves, almonds. Otherwise you could hardly live there."

Thorpe just stared at me, waiting for the rest of the story. I thought I should hide my face from him, the way he had hidden his from me, but I couldn't look away. I said, "We met when I was nineteen. Just started my second year at Barnard. There was this party, like I said, and there he was. Somebody's older brother. Remarkably handsome, I'll give him that. I thought he was the best-looking fellow I'd ever seen, like he'd just stepped off a cinema screen. This lovely dark hair and this baritone voice. He was twenty-six and had a tremendous vocabulary. I was mesmerized. He fed me a few drinks, strong ones, and talked sweet to me. When I was good and drunk, he took my hand and said, *Let's get out of this dump*, and I said, *Sure, why not?*"

"Oh, Lulu," Thorpe said sadly.

"Well, I was just a kid. Just a dumb kid looking for something I didn't understand. I thought I'd just found it, I guess. Thomas Randolph. Tommy, to his pals. He was staying at a cheap hotel on the West Side, because—as I discovered later—he was the black sheep of a very distinguished family, and they'd had enough of him coming into town for a bender and asking for money. Anyway, I followed him to his cheap hotel like a little virgin lamb, bathroom down the hall, and we got to kissing, and the next thing I remembered, I was waking up in his bed at nine o'clock in the morning. Long story short, they kicked me out of college for that. My father was furious. Maybe I was trying to get his attention, I don't know. It turned out, I got his attention all right. He cut me off, and Tommy said, *So let's elope, two black sheep like us*, and I thought that sounded like a really nice adventure."

My voice started to splinter, so I rose from the crate and went to the picnic basket to find a cigarette. There followed some considerable effort to light the thing, given the trembling in my hands, but eventually I got the job done, sucked in a little blessed smoke, and turned to face Thorpe again, composure restored.

"Where was I?"

"You eloped with the bastard."

"Yes. Indeed, we did. Ran off to Niagara, as was customary. We fucked ourselves silly for a week or so, to be perfectly frank, had a really swell time. The scenery was spectacular, no doubt about that. And then it all started to crack up. His wicked ways and all that. I mean, the old story. Black and blue in all the wrong places. Drank whatever money came our way. Not for nothing had the Randolphs washed their hands of him, I guess, and now I was stuck with him, because I was too ashamed to crawl home, too broke, and anyway he said he would kill me if I tried."

Thorpe started to interject, but I waved him off.

"Couple of years passed. Bakersfield. By then, I'd taken to keeping a little twenty-two stashed in the bedside cabinet. Not for him, for me. I figured he was going to give me some disease, he was going to strangle me some night, and I'd decided to put a bullet in my own brain first. One night he'd gone out drinking, probably visiting the local cathouse, who knows. Commotion downstairs at three in the morning. Seemed he'd forgotten his latchkey and was breaking in through a window. Roaring about killing someone. I figured he meant me. I said to myself, *Dear me, here's an intruder, whatever shall I do*. Well, I went downstairs and shot him twice in the head, that's what I did, right in that spot behind your left ear that's supposed to kill instantly, dropped the gun, screamed for help, and that was that. Libertas."

I looked around for something in which to knock the ash from the cigarette. My legs shook. Thorpe started forward and crossed the room, right past me, through the swinging door and into the room I supposed to be a kitchen. He came out a few seconds later, holding a saucer, which he set down on the crate next to me.

"Thanks," I said. "The funny thing was, nobody ever questioned my story. I mean the imaginary intruder who broke the window and shot my husband and ran off. Not the sheriff or the townspeople. Certainly not the Randolphs, goodness no. I mean, you could almost smell the relief on them. They sent somebody to bring the body home, held a decent funeral at the family plot on Long Island. Just a terrible accident, everyone said, shook their heads. I guess they were grateful to me for solving their little problem, although they didn't say a word to me afterward, not a word, as if I hadn't existed. One of their lawyers came and offered me money, but I wouldn't take it. I didn't know what to do with myself. I wasn't sleeping, wasn't eating. These terrible nightmares. I figured I needed a fresh start, fresh career, fresh place to live. And I went and asked my daddy for a job."

"Christ in heaven," said Thorpe. He hadn't returned to his position at the doors, and instead stood right next to me, leaning against the crate by my side, so that the sleeve of his shirt brushed my elbow.

"Well? Some story, hmm?"

He pulled the cigarette from my fingers and dropped it in the saucer. Pretty saucer, Wedgwood maybe. Somehow I'd missed that part of girlhood in which you learned about china patterns. But this I knew. The blue eyes, the dark gold lashes, the skin like a cat's tongue beneath my palms.

"Christ in heaven, what a miracle," he said.

AFTER THE TEARS WERE DRY, we ate our picnic in the dunes, feeding each other morsel by morsel while the sun crossed above us. We were still dressed and decorous at that point, though the air grew hotter and hotter. I think I fell asleep on his shoulder. When I came to, he lay on his back, staring at the sky, one arm cushioning his dear head. The shape of his nose kicked the breath from my lungs. Despite the Atlantic breeze, the sweat trickled from my forehead and my armpits and between my breasts. I rose and nudged off my espadrilles and undid the buttons on my dress.

"I'm going for a swim," I said.

I'D NEVER SWUM NAKED BEFORE, certainly not in the warm, salt ocean. I can't recommend it highly enough. The water whooshed along my skin, the surf played games with me. After a moment or two, Thorpe joined me. I discovered his bare shoulders, his waist, his churning legs, his fingers wandering across my ribs to the small of my back, to the curve of my bottom. Without the spectacles, his freckles sprang from either side of his nose, and I wrapped my legs around his waist so I could gather his face in my palms and kiss each one. We met a wave or two together, holding hands, until we washed up laughing on the beach in a state of nature, Adam and Eve, paradise. I licked the brine from his cheeks and marveled at the absence of panic inside me, at the mysterious way confession draws the poison from its sac, rendering you pure again. I told Thorpe he should get out of the sun before he burned, he didn't have the right skin for it.

"But you do," he said.

"My mother's Italian." I rose and tugged on his hand. "Come on. Into the shade."

Into the shade, onto the picnic blanket. A real blanket, by the way, plucked from a closet in the cottage, scratchy but serviceable. We kissed and we kissed, until the heat and the draft swallowed up the last of the ocean from our skin, and then Thorpe sucked the salt from my breasts and stomach and between my legs while I hollered for joy. He settled himself on top of me, lifted himself on his elbows, and kissed me again. For the longest time we rocked together, a dozen lifetimes in which you fell in love over and over again, each time more deeply than the last, more comprehensive in your knowledge of the other. When we finished, we lay together unmoving. It seemed our skin wasn't meant to part.

DINNER WAS A POT OF beans and a few slices of bacon, fried expertly in an iron skillet, along with tomatoes and new carrots and some greens I didn't recognize, all grown by Thorpe in a garden he'd constructed himself. I said maybe he was a botanist after all, and he said it was perfectly true, if I came to England he would show me his degrees. Two firsts at Cambridge, he said bashfully, whatever that meant. I wore one of his old shirts and nothing else, because my dress was sweaty and caked with powdery pink-white Bahamas sand. The shirt smelled of Thorpe, of his laundry soap. After we ate, I helped him with the dishes while the sun fell and the stars popped out in the giant purple sky. We made love on the porch, in a wicker chair. Later, again, in his bedroom, atop his narrow bed under the whir of an electric fan, sweaty and indiscreet, the cry of climax like a death groan. By the time Thorpe fell asleep, it was almost midnight. We were twisted in a curiously restful contortion, Thorpe cradling me while his head rested against my belly. I remember feeling his hair in my hands, his beautiful hair, crisp with salt, and the last thing I saw was his milky skin, the bumps of his spine splitting his broad back, his scarred cheek relaxed in slumber.

I CAN'T SAY WHY I woke an hour later. I should have slept like the dead, so sapped as I was, but they do say the brain is subject to certain stimuli that the common senses can't perceive. Whatever the reason. I startled awake, as I said, and experienced a moment of utter panic. I thought it was the wrong room, the wrong man, that the past two years had been a dream from which I had just emerged, and if it hadn't been for the moonlight on Thorpe's rufous hair, blazing with an unnatural saturation of color, he might have found himself as dead as Mr. Randolph. As it was, I slumped back against the pillow and glanced out the window, and that was when I noticed the peculiar orange tinge to the horizon, which had turned Thorpe's hair such a vivid shade of ginger. I thought it couldn't be dawn already. Then I realized I was facing south, not east, and I pushed Thorpe's shoulder.

"Fire," I gasped.

Thorpe bolted awake, just as I had, and stared at me in the same confusion I had felt, then the same recognition. I pointed to the window. He swore and leapt from the bed.

"Put on some clothes," he said, running out the door at a terrible limp. "I'll ring up Government House."

BY THE TIME WE REACHED Nassau, tearing across the harbor in Wenner-Gren's motorboat, the fire had engulfed part of Bay Street and was crawling up George Street. The air flew with cinder, swirled with smoke. I tasted it on my tongue, inside my nose. I jumped from the boat and helped Thorpe secure it to a piling. He snatched up his cane and hurried with me from the docks across Bay Street, where he grabbed my hand.

"Go home!" he shouted.

I shook my head. "The Red Cross!"

He opened his mouth as if to yell back some objection, then thought better of it and kissed me instead, brief and hard. "If the fire gets close, get the hell out," he said in my ear. "I'm going to find the fire brigade."

He released me, and I pulled my shirt—Thorpe's shirt—over my mouth and nose and plunged through these terrible gray-orange billows, up George Street in the direction of the Red Cross building, where all our hard work lay in stacks and piles at the back of the building, all our supplies, our inventory, our parcels waiting to be sent overseas. I saw the duke's station wagon outside, parked at a rakish angle, the back door swung open. Out in the street, four men were running a fire hose. They were sopping wet and covered with soot. One of them raised his head, and in shock I recognized the Duke of Windsor himself. I ran up the front steps and through the doorway, smack into Mrs. Gudewill, white-faced, carrying a bundle of wool blankets.

"Mrs. Randolph! Quick, we're loading the car! She's in back."

By *she*, Mrs. Gudewill meant Wallis, of course. I raced down the hall to the back room, our warehouse, and there she was, giving out crisp orders to Miss Drewes and a couple of other ladies, stacking things in boxes, stacking boxes on each other. You might not have recognized her. She wore no cosmetics, no coiffure. Her thin lips were invisible against her skin. Her hair was in a net. Her dressing gown was belted around her waist. Only her familiar brown-and-white spectator shoes gave her away.

She gave my rumpled appearance not the slightest notice. She spoke with primeval calm. "Mrs. Randolph, thank goodness. Could you be a dear and carry these to the car? How far has it spread?"

"Halfway up George Street." I snatched one of the larger boxes and carried it back down the hall, out the door, down the steps to the station wagon outside. The crowd was growing, looking in dismay at the advance of the fire, which had begun to lick around the side of the Charlotte Hotel, next to Christ Church Cathedral, standing opposite the Red Cross. I tossed the box in the back of the station wagon and paused for an instant, staring up the rest of George Street to Government House on its hill, the end of the line. The breeze seemed to be picking up, thick with smoke, unless that was the draft of the fire itself. Someone came up to me with another box, and I recognized Miss Drewes, wearing a pair of striped pajamas.

"Where are we taking all this?" I asked.

"To the ballroom. Come along, quick."

Back we went, into the building, while the fire crept closer and the shouts of the fire brigade rang through the smoke. When we emerged, the duke and his men had set up the fire hose and begun to soak the brick walls of the Red Cross with it. I recognized Oakes among them, his rough face smudged with soot, and I remembered the building belonged to him, that he had loaned it to the Red Cross for the duration of the war. Back and forth, stacks of blankets, boxes of packages bound for London. Where was Thorpe? Back and forth, until my arms ached, and I could hardly breathe because the smoke scorched my throat and my lungs at every pulse. Across the street, the Charlotte Hotel was now fully engulfed, flames shooting from the roof, cinders flying. The station wagon was full, and another car brought down from Government House. I heard a groan, looked to the roof, and saw a curl of smoke rising from the right-hand side. I dashed back up the steps.

"Everyone out!" I shouted. "Everyone out! There's smoke on the roof!"

Out came the duchess from the back, carrying a small crate, followed by Miss Drewes with another crate.

"Anyone else back there?"

"It's all clear," said the duchess, in her calm voice. "And this is the last of the supplies. Miss Drewes, will you drive the Morris? I'll take the station wagon."

At the door, a frantic Duke of Windsor met us. He snatched the crate from his wife's arms and cried, *Thank God.*

"David. Good gracious." The duchess squinted at the scene outside. "Is that Marshall on top of the cathedral?"

We turned and followed her gaze, up and up to the peaked roof of the cathedral, where a large man stood near the spire, silhouetted in orange.

"Yes," said the duke. "God bless him. He's testing the structure. If the wind doesn't hold, we've got to dynamite the place, I'm afraid."

"Dynamite!"

"Darling, it's got to be done. It's the only chance to stop the thing from spreading all the way up the damned hill!"

At that instant, just over the duke's last few words—*the damned hill*—a low boom shook the ground. I realized I'd heard it before, the last time I went outside, except I hadn't paid attention, I'd assumed it was part of the general noise of the fire's destruction. Now I listened. There was a loud crack, and the sound of crumbling, breaking.

An expression of shock transformed the duchess's face. I don't think she had considered this, that the fire might reach all the way to Government House, to her own home, where the carloads of Red Cross supplies were right now being unloaded into the ballroom. She turned back to the cathedral roof and put her hand to her brow, as if shielding her eyes from a terrible sun. I looked too, and saw a curious thing: the large metal cross at the very front of the cathedral, atop the peak, silhouetted against the glow of flames, in such a way that the fire seemed to come from within the cross itself.

"Oh, it's going to be all right," someone said. I turned to my left and saw Miss Drewes, staring at the cross as I had. Her face glowed in the light. I would almost have said she looked beatific, except that glow was only a reflection, wasn't it? A reflection of the fire itself.

I grabbed her elbow. "Not if you don't beat it up the hill this second. Go. Get in the car."

She got in the Morris, and the duchess in the station wagon. The duke kissed his wife through the open window and waved the chauffeur away. When he turned and saw me, he started.

"Why, aren't you going too, Mrs. Randolph?"

I shook my head and opened my mouth to ask what I could do, where I could go, when a noise came from behind me, like an animal roaring. I spun around and saw flames shooting from the doorway of the Red Cross building, where I had spent so many hours, chatted with so many matrons, elicited so many morsels, banal and fascinating.

NOW THERE WERE SOME WHO said that a shower of rain intervened just as the Red Cross Center dissolved in flames, saving the cathedral, saving the rest of Nassau. I don't remember that. In the spray of water from the hoses, in the general running about, the bang and crumble of buildings under dynamite, one by one, and most of all the gnawing panic over Thorpe—*where was he, where had he gone*—I didn't notice the weather. I noticed how, in the first hint of dawn, the whole world seemed to smolder and steam, and yet the cathedral still stood, the cross reached up to heaven against a charcoal horizon. And the flames were gone.

BY THE TIME THORPE REAPPEARED in Nassau a week later, as if by magic, I already understood the obvious. That he had opened up my desk during the night of the Bay Street riot, as I slept away the effects of losing a pint or two of blood on a shard of window glass. That he had copied out the contents of the folded papers I kept in a special compartment at the back of the drawer, and replaced them without the slightest sign they'd been disturbed at all.

For the record, I didn't hold it against him.

ELFRIEDE

AUGUST 1905
(Berlin)

DAILY THEY WALK in the Tiergarten, Elfriede and Johann, because of course he must have fresh air and exercise, and so must she. Grief like this, you need something to do. Today the weather's not so good, but still they venture out, carrying umbrellas as a precaution, or else a talisman against actual rain. (Rain mostly falls when you've forgotten your umbrella, isn't that right?)

The Diet is in recess for the summer holidays, and the windows of the Reichstag wear an aspect of abandonment. Johann kicks at the gravel. Who can blame him? No friends, no family. No ponies to ride, no tennis, no woods to explore. Just a boy and his mother in the corrupt city, the hustle bustle of Berlin. Waiting for their luck to turn.

"Maybe we could visit the animals in the zoo today," Elfriede says.

"Maybe." Johann kicks some more gravel. He's a tall boy, a big boy, husky like his father. He outgrows his clothes almost as soon as they're on him. That jacket he's wearing, the one she bought him in Rotterdam because his old jacket, the one she bought him for Easter in Florida, was ruined by the salt spray on the ship? She'll be damned if the shoulders

aren't already straining when he leans forward to grip the handlebars of
a bicycle.

"We could walk," Elfriede says. "It's a long walk, but that's good exercise."

"All right."

Their feet crunch softly on the gravel. Nearby, a woman's feeding the
pigeons. They flock around her, hooting and fighting, dirty and over-
fed, and Elfriede wonders why the woman does this. The pigeons don't
need the food, clearly. Some maternal instinct, maybe? Some desire to be
needed? To be the center of somebody's universe, even if that somebody
is only a bunch of dirty, mindless Berlin pigeons? To matter, that's all.

Johann speaks suddenly, with force. "We're not going to find them,
are we?"

"What's that? Of course we'll find them. Why do you say that?"

"I mean they don't want to be found. They don't want us anymore."

"That's . . ." Elfriede pauses before she completes the half truth.
"That's not true, darling. They're your sisters."

"They're not my *real* sisters," he bursts out.

"Johann!"

"It's true. Isn't it?"

Those last two words turn plaintively upward. He's making a question,
not a statement of knowledge. Elfriede keeps walking, keeps marching
them forward, shoes grinding into the path. From the opposite direction,
a man approaches them in a pale, crumpled suit, smoking a cigarette.

"Who told you this?" Elfriede asks quietly.

"Aunt Helga said—"

"Aunt Helga. Yes, of course." Now Elfriede stops and turns, kneels
into the gravel to face her son. Above them, the clouds hold down the
stifling August air. "Listen to me. It doesn't matter what Aunt Helga said.
All four of you, you are your father's children, do you hear me, you're

all his children in God's eyes, fair and equal, and God . . . why, God does not make mistakes, Johann. Human beings make terrible mistakes sometimes, but God does not. Those girls are your sisters."

The man walks by, and the smell of his cigarette sends a jolt through Elfriede's chest.

Johann asks in a small voice, "Then Aunt Helga's a liar?"

Oh, for wisdom! For wisdom at such a moment! Elfriede grips her son's shoulders. "Don't say such a thing. Of course your aunt's not a liar. She doesn't know, that's all, she doesn't understand the truth. She thinks—she thinks I made a mistake, that's all, an awful mistake, and maybe I did, we all make mistakes, but tell me *this*! Would you rather I hadn't made this mistake? Would you rather you had no sisters at all? Would you rather they didn't exist?"

"No."

"Do you love your sisters, Johann?" She almost shouts the words.

"Yes!" He starts to cry, actually to cry, a thing he strives never to do. "Yes, Mama!"

"Then that's all there is, darling! That's all there is, to love each other! Just do that, okay? That's all your father wants. That's all God wants."

To her right, several yards away, the man spins around. "Stop yelling at your child! What kind of mother are you, making him cry like this?"

"I wasn't . . . I didn't . . ." Elfriede, gasping with her own tears, straightens and turns, and by this single act of engagement the breath flows back into her body. The strength returns to her, the tears dry against her eyes. She stares rudely into this man's face. "How dare you," she says, and she takes Johann's hand and walks away, toward the zoo.

THEY RETURN TO THE HOTEL Adlon around one o'clock, desperate for lunch. Elfriede stops at the desk, as always, to inquire after any letters, and the clerk produces two: one from Helga, who's returned to Schloss

Kleist and now, finding no other occupation apparently, fires off her little darts of poison almost daily; and the other from the private detective. Elfriede tears this one open first. (Helga can wait.)

Dear Frau von Kleist,

Further to your instructions, we have investigated fully the possible lead in Hamburg, but regret to report that the woman in question is, beyond all doubt, not the same as the subject of your inquiry. We will continue to pursue our investigation as directed.

Most respectfully yours,
L. S. Schulmann

NOW, AS YOU KNOW, THE Hotel Adlon is the premier hotel in Berlin, really the only place to exist if one must exist there at all, and naturally a widowed baroness and her son receive the most attentive treatment from the staff. When Elfriede shoves her disappointing letter from Herr Schulmann into her jacket pocket, together with the unopened poisoned dart from Helga, she turns from the desk to discover a uniformed attendant begging to escort her to the usual table in the restaurant for lunch.

Because Elfriede's so disappointed by her letters, because she's too upset to think properly, because she's used to only the best treatment from the Adlon staff, she finds nothing oddly precipitous in this request. So they cross the marble lobby, she and Johann and the attendant, and enter the restaurant. There, in a quiet corner, beyond the tangle of tables and chairs and gilding and potted palms, the scent of great expense, sits her usual table, where she and Johann take their meals when they're not taking them from room service in the suite upstairs.

But the table's not empty. A man in a handsome khaki uniform rises from his chair at the sight of them and such is his impeccable appearance, the precise ironing of his collar and creases, the knot of his tie, the shininess of his hair brushed back in immaculate order with some type of hair oil, probably, Elfriede requires a moment or two to realize that it's actually him.

Johann, being a child, takes no time at all. He utters a cry and rushes forward, all resentments forgotten, to throw his arms around Wilfred's waist.

"Have you found them? Have you found them?" he demands.

Wilfred's smile disappears. He puts his arms around Johann's back and says, "I'm afraid not, old chap, but never fear. We shan't rest until we find the girls, shall we?"

"No, sir."

Elfriede can't speak. The waiter, attempting with limited success to disguise his pleasure, draws out her chair. Wilfred catches her gaze. A little of the smile returns to his wide mouth.

"I had your letter on the ship," he says.

"I was afraid it wouldn't have reached you."

"It did. I apologize for my tardiness. I'm afraid I couldn't arrange another leave so soon."

"I didn't—of course I didn't expect—"

"But I took the liberty of making clear at the Foreign Office that if any civil service chaps heading to Germany stood in need of the services of an expert military attaché, I should be more than happy with the appointment."

"Oh." She sits down. "Oh."

The waiter stands by. Johann boldly orders lemonade. Elfriede thinks she'll need something a little stronger.

ON THE LAST DAY OF the month, Elfriede and Wilfred are married, not in Berlin or even in England, but in the small village in Scotland where his regiment is based, before Wilfred's bemused parents, a host of Scotch Presbyterian aunts, some gleeful fellow officers, and the diplomat whose timely Berlin mission provided the means for their reunion. His name, since you ask, is Mr. Cholmondeley. He's about forty, dark-haired, genial and intelligent. He thinks Wilfred's a top bloke, a pukka chap who's got all the damned luck with women, and he's tickled pink at his role in the whole affair. He gives the bride away in the small service at the regimental chapel. Johann bears the ring.

Afterward, at the wedding breakfast, Elfriede makes halting conversation with Mr. Benedict Thorpe, Wilfred's father, angular and brown-haired and shy, the sort of man who would much rather be reading a book or walking a dog. Other than his height, Wilfred seems to favor his Scotch mother, whose hair's even brighter than his, though her eyes are more green than blue. She's also the most effusive Scot in the history of the nation, not dour at all as Elfriede had imagined from Wilfred's hints. "And he never said a word, not a blessed word," she exclaims on the terrace of the officers' mess, gallantly lent for the occasion, while Elfriede strains to understand her. "Of course he had his lady friends, he's always been popular with the feminine sort, but my goodness, a *German* girl! I beg your pardon, I've nothing against Germany, splendid music, but I never imagined—well, and a widow! A baroness! Never a word until we had the telegram from Berlin a fortnight ago. And you're a beauty, how splendid. God knows the family could stand a bit more beauty. I was so cross when Wilfie turned out ginger. I'd hoped by marrying a dark-haired Englishman that the stain would quite go away, but it's like madness in the family, you know, like a bad penny. I should have loved a daughter with hair like yours. How quiet and charming you are! I can see now how he worships you. He's utterly bewitched! What a difference in him. But how naughty, to say nothing to us about it, nothing at all!" And so on.

A bit later, when Wilfred's fellow officers are giving the toasts and everybody's in stitches with laughter, Elfriede glances at her new mother-in-law and discovers she's not laughing at all. She's staring at Elfriede, or rather she seems to have been staring, because she looks swiftly away and releases an enormous bray of amusement. And yet, for an instant, Elfriede has the uncanny idea that she has been appraised in the way you might appraise a racehorse, with a pair of hard, calculating eyes.

BECAUSE WILFRED'S GOT ONLY THIRTY-SIX hours away from his duties, and because neither of them wish to leave Johann with a stranger, they spend their wedding night in the small, hastily let stone cottage that's to serve as their temporary home. "We've already had our honeymoon, anyway," Wilfred points out, as they sit before the fire and share the bottle of champagne presented to them by Mr. Cholmondeley at the end of the day. Johann's asleep in his room upstairs, and because it's Scotland, even in August, a soft rain drums on the windows.

"Yes, we had a lovely honeymoon," Elfriede replies.

Wilfred sets down his glass, crushes out his cigarette, and kneels before her. His hands, gathering hers, are large and dry, like the paws of a bear.

"I say, darling. Don't be low. We'll be happy like that again, never fret."

What possible reply? How can you, like a surgeon, untangle and extract the word *happy* from the contents of Elfriede's shredded heart, in this moment?

"I'm not fretting," she says. "I'm as happy as it's possible to be."

Wilfred, who always knows just how to touch Elfriede (and isn't that really how she fell in love with him to begin with, isn't that why she loves him so wholly) lifts her hands and kisses the backs of her fingers. "If it makes any difference, you've made *me* happy today. So happy I don't think I can altogether bear it. Like looking at the sun."

In her head, Elfriede says the English word *husband*. Two strange, intimate syllables, now attached to this plain face, these eyes, that mouth, this shock of vivid ginger, all of which now belong exclusively to her. Wilfred, hers. But not her *Mann*. Her *husband*. She'll have to learn the word all over again. She'll have to learn a new vocabulary for this strange, intimate, rain-washed marriage of hers.

Elfriede pulls her hands from his and burrows them into his rambunctious hair. "Take me upstairs," she whispers.

THEY HAVEN'T MADE LOVE SINCE Florida, and the result is a little too rushed, more relief than ecstasy. But it's enough. It's all she wants, to be held and loved. He remains inside her for some time afterward, and even when he slides out they stay clasped, unable to separate one skin from the other, unable to speak. Solid, honest bone and muscle. Damp hair and warmth, the smell of human skin, human musk, how heavenly. Against her hip, Wilfred remains stiff, plenty of life left, a young man primed for his wedding night. But leave that for later. Right now, Elfriede hears the tempo of his breath and thinks he's probably craving a cigarette desperately, and she loves that he doesn't rise to open the window and light a smoke, that he craves her more.

"Is it enough?" he whispers into her hair.

"Is what enough?"

"If we don't find the girls. To have children of our own, will that help at all?"

She doesn't answer, and Wilfred asks carefully whether she wants to have more children at all. Whether she's afraid of what this might bring, whether children are too great a risk to bear.

"No, I'm not afraid," she says. "Not anymore. For one thing, there's you. I can bear anything with you."

He reaches for her hand and kisses the new gold ring on her finger.

"Yes, you've got me, all right. Luckiest chap in the world. And what's the other thing?"

"Because I've already survived the worst," she says. "I have already lost everything."

In the years to come, Elfriede will remember those words.

PART IV

LULU

Mornings are terrible. I can just about keep the thought of Thorpe at bay during the day, what with all this business of staying alive in a foreign country, and at night, I summon memories—by force if necessary—that have mostly to do with making love to him. But when you wake, you have no discipline, nothing to distract you. You lie vulnerable. You open your eyes and there he is.

Sometimes he's lying on some cot or pile of straw, thin blanket, bowl of maggoty gruel, guards shouting. Sometimes I see him injured, his wounds untended, blood and pus, his skin hot with fever. Sometimes I see him parched with thirst while the guards taunt him through the bars of his cell. Now, it's true, I don't know this place, Colditz. It's a castle, that's all, so what I see—and it changes, from morning to morning, it's never quite the same cell or the same jailers—what I see is like a medieval dungeon, like something the brothers Grimm might conjure up. Maybe the reality's different. Maybe they're playing checkers with the guards before a nice toasty fire. But that's not what I see. I see him suffering. The anguish fills my chest and leaks from my eyes until I throw off the covers and rise, shaking, to meet the day. And the next.

ONLY TWO WEEKS REMAIN UNTIL Christmas, but nobody on the train displays much holiday cheer. Margaret and I share a compartment with a woman and two young boys, aged perhaps three or four, and it says something for our state of gloom that even the tots are subdued. We're traveling north, you see, and if London was dark and bleak, the landscape now clattering past the window seems to have been cast in iron.

Margaret catches my expression and checks her watch. "Only another hour or so," she says, hushed voice, because the boys have piled up asleep on the seat, like puppies. The single lamp casts an anemic glow, and the air smells of stale cigarettes and an intractable damp. At our feet, Tuxedo lets out an anxious *miaaaow* from his wooden box.

I return to my newspaper. By now, I've read every story twice, and I've started on the personals. *Widow, aged 26 with one child, experienced nurse, seeks elderly gentleman for purpose of companionship and matrimony.*

AT EDINBURGH, WE CHANGE TRAINS for the line to Inverness. The sun set long ago, and we might be rolling through Timbuktu for all I can tell. The compartment is empty except for the two of us. Margaret lights a cigarette and stares out the window at the passing shadows, black on black, while I settle myself against the corner and listen to the rhythmic clatter, metal on metal. Her eyes grow heavy, and so do mine. I summon up Thorpe's face in my memory, as I do whenever the tedium of the journey sinks its teeth into me, his face drenched in the sunshine of Shangri-La, just before he kisses me.

To my despair, I can't quite make out his features. Only the color of that golden light as the sun prepares to set.

I WAKE IN A LARGE, shabby room papered in blue toile and filled with sunshine. For a moment, I can't remember where I am. I imagine I'm in

Nassau, in California, in Texas, and the confusion's so acute, I almost feel myself floating between the two worlds, the two sides of my life, before Thorpe and after him.

Then I become aware that the tip of my nose is frozen, and I recall I'm in Scotland, and the sunshine is not an ordinary feature but a miracle. I recall the night before—the arrival at the terminal in Inverness, the silent, gray-haired woman who met us there in an asthmatic Morris, the bouncing, skidding journey across what seemed to be the entire goddamned frozen Highlands before we arrived at what Margaret called the Pile, as if that were its name. I learned from the retainer, who showed me to my room, that it was really named Dunnock Lodge, and that this was where Thorpe was born, twenty-seven years ago. I can't remember the retainer's name, however. It's escaped me in the night.

Already the image of Thorpe has started to crowd into my head, obliterating everything else, the certain knowledge of Thorpe's milky, beautiful back crisscrossed by welts. Something leaps on my stomach and starts to purr. I reach out to clasp Tuxedo, but he has other ideas, probably to do with getting fed, and leaps back off. I throw aside the covers and hurry down the hall to the remembered bathroom, which seems to have been installed in the house before Thorpe himself. The water's icy, and the smell of rust reminds me of blood. Through the walls comes the distant noise of voices, the clatter of plates. I wash swiftly, dress swiftly, throw on my coat for good measure, and head downstairs in the direction of these signs of humanity.

THE FUNNY THING ABOUT MARGARET, she's not all that interested in Nassau, in the Windsors, the glamour. Last night, on the train, I explained how we met, Thorpe and I, and how I worked for *Metropolitan* and went to parties for a living, and her face took on this distant expression, and her mouth curved with something that, if it wasn't quite disapproval, was certainly disdain. Fine, then. Margaret Thorpe doesn't give a damn about parties and duchesses. I might have guessed.

The only thing that moves her is Thorpe. When I told her how he was attacked on the docks one night, her eyes turned glossy and she reached for her cigarettes, just as she's doing now, sitting at the kitchen table at Dunnock Lodge with a plate of eggs—real ones—and a cup of tea before her. At the giant, ancient range, a woman fusses about, skinny and silvery. It's a moment before I realize she's the same woman who drove the Morris last night. For one thing, she's speaking. Scolding Margaret about not giving more warning.

"Annie, there's a war on," she says. "I can't just— Oh, there you are, Lulu. I was beginning to think you'd sleep all morning."

Annie whirls from the stovetop to face me, wiping her hands on her apron. Her round eyes convey awe, in much the same way the Red Cross ladies regard the Duchess of Windsor, I guess.

"Mrs. Thorpe. Would you—may I offer you breakfast?"

"I don't suppose you've got any coffee?"

A panicked expression overtakes Annie's face. I step forward and pull back a chair from the table, where a place is already set for me, plate and cup and saucer (somewhat the worse for chips) and cutlery. "Never mind. Tea's just fine, thank you."

"We've got eggs," she says proudly. "Toast."

I'm about to say *Just toast*, but then I recall I ought to be eating better, ought to be filling myself with good, wholesome food. I lay my napkin on my lap and smile at her. "Thank you, Annie. Sunny-side up, if you don't mind."

Across the table, Margaret lifts the cigarettes and her eyebrows. I shake my head. She shrugs and continues to smoke, continues to nudge her eggs around the plate. "We used to have our breakfast right here, Benedict and I, when we were little," she says. "Didn't we, Annie? You made us boiled eggs and toast soldiers. There was so much butter, then.

He used to sit right there, where you're sitting. I remember the sun coming through the window to shine on that hair of his."

"Lit up the whole kitchen, it did. When it was sunny, of course."

"Which wasn't often." Margaret stubs out her cigarette and lights another. Her mouth is pale, she isn't wearing lipstick. There's a stirring in the region of her lap, and she lowers her hand to stroke some object I presume is Tuxedo. Settles back an inch or two and stares at Annie. "He was the sweetest boy, you know. After Mummy died, Granny and her sister moved in to take care of us. Of course, the war was still on, and they're the sort of thrifty Scots who light the fires only when the temperature gets below freezing. If we complained about the cold, they would tell us to put on a jumper and run around the halls. I don't think I even knew what it was to be warm until Johann started inviting us down to Germany during the summers." She pauses to drag on her cigarette. "But Benedict, you know, he never would complain, not the least noise."

"I'm not surprised."

Margaret flicks the ash from her cigarette into a nearby ashtray. "I remember he was such an awfully big baby, but then he got so skinny after Mummy died. Whenever he got sick, I thought he was finished. But they're stronger than they look, you know. Babies."

"Are they? Or just him?"

"Well, I wouldn't know, would I? He's the only baby I've ever properly encountered. Annie? More tea, if you don't mind."

Annie carries over a fresh pot, which she pours first for me and then for Margaret. As she lifts the spout and turns away, she mutters, "More tea and less cigarettes, if you ask me."

"But nobody *did* ask you, Annie," says Margaret, so crisp.

I look for the sugar and can't find any. Instead, there's a pot of honey. I pour in the milk, stir in the honey. "Maybe he had to be strong. Maybe it's just bred into him, from the beginning. Maybe it's a good thing the house was so cold."

"We'd like to think so, wouldn't we? We'd like to think he can endure it. The alternative's too awful to contemplate."

Annie brings me a pair of eggs, cooked together so that the yolks are like a pair of yellow eyes regarding me from a white face. Also brown toast with butter.

"Why does Mrs. Thorpe get *two* eggs, Annie?" Margaret asks. "And all that butter on her toast, it's obscene."

For an instant, Annie meets my gaze. "No reason," she says softly, and returns to the range. Margaret glances at the clock on the opposite wall and drums her fingers against the saucer. A pair of black ears pops up from her lap. An inquisitive feline face, interested in the egg that remains on Margaret's plate.

"Do hurry," she says. "I'd like to take a walk before it starts to rain. Oh, damn. Never mind. It's already started. How I hate the weather here."

"I don't see how you can live in London and complain about the weather anywhere else."

"Because it can't make up its mind, that's why. First one thing and then another."

Annie, washing dishes at the sink, turns her head over her shoulder. "Mackintoshes are in the boot room, Miss Margaret."

Margaret heaves a sigh, stubs out her cigarette, gathers the cat, and rises from the table. I stare out the window and listen to the sound of her footsteps on the floorboards. A drizzle's begun to patter, sure enough. When the footsteps disappear, I turn to Annie.

"Don't say a word to her, do you hear me?"

She shuts off the faucet and faces me. "You can't hide it much longer, mind."

"Oh? And what do you know about it?"

"Because Mrs. Thorpe used to look the same way when she was breeding, that's why." She clasps her hands together. "It's true, then? A wee babe? Dear little Benedict's sweet child?"

"Why, didn't you know for certain?"

"Oh, aye, you can never be *sure*, Mrs. Thorpe, not until the lady says so herself."

I smacked my forehead. "It's a secret. Remember that."

"What's a secret?"

Margaret stands in the doorway, arms full of raincoats, face all stricken. Her hair's coming loose from the knot at her neck. She looks from me to Annie and back again, and her gaze slides downward, to my breasts, lower still. The raincoats slide to the floor. Tuxedo, galloping past her legs, makes a heroic last-second leap.

"Bloody hell. When did *that* happen?"

"July," I say. "The night Oakes was murdered."

LULU

JULY 1943
(The Bahamas)

EVERY MORNING, THE Liberators took off from Oakes Field and flew in formation over the ocean, like a flock of ungainly birds. It was all part of their training, and it made a terrible noise. I used to sit at my desk and grit my teeth against the immense, subterranean racket as each airplane lumbered down the runway and out to sea, four Rolls Royce engines churning in unison to drown out the ancient *clackety-clack* of my Remington typewriter.

Sometimes I counted them as they roared above the rooftop. More often I leaned forward and concentrated ferociously on the words before me, because mistakes were made when you weren't paying attention, and you couldn't afford mistakes in a gossip column, believe me. One misplaced letter or, God forbid, number might cause the guilty to go free or the innocent tossed in the slammer, metaphorically speaking. Or worse, might bring the wrath of Wallis upon your head. So I concentrated on the typing and blocked out not just the noise of the Liberators but the thought of them. Their existence altogether. It was better that way, right?

Every so often, I rose and went to check on the man sleeping in my bed. A racket like that, surely it would wake him. But poor Thorpe was so exhausted, he didn't even flinch. So I went back to work while the sun climbed carefully above the palmettos of Hog Island. I was due for the morning shift at the duchess's canteen at eight o'clock sharp, and the "Lady of Nassau" column was due in the post at high noon, and something had to give. My hours of rest, apparently.

I finished the column with just enough time to spare. In the bedroom, Thorpe still lay in his torpor. I shrugged off my dressing gown, sank back down on the damp sheets and curled myself around him once more. He was here, that was all. Had come to life in my bedroom in the middle of the night, still wet from a bath—I smelled the soap on him—and from the squall that had drenched him on the way across the harbor. He'd stopped on Hog Island only long enough to drop off his kit and clean up, he said, and then he had come to me, to Lulu, his Lulu, *at last, my God*, had spent himself in less than a minute and dropped senseless on my pillow. Just like that. Where he'd slept the night before, I had no idea. Where he'd slept the previous twelve nights, I had even less idea. He was here, that was all. His heart still thudded away, thank God. A snore rasped in his nose. He was alive. I gathered him in my arms and listened to the sounds of his sleep, which—unlike the noise of the airplanes outside—belonged to me, and only to me.

That was all.

I WAS JUST DRIFTING OFF again when he woke. For an instant, his body went rigid, and then he recognized the room, the bed, the whore at his back. I felt his relief like a downpour. He turned in my arms and apologized.

"For what?"

"For last night."

"Last night? That was nothing. Makes a change from the everyday." I ran my hand over his hair, which was short and bristling, God knew why. The smell of his soap, how I'd missed it. This humid little intimacy of tangling in bed together at dawn.

"Everyday, eh?" he said.

"Everyday. It's how most people live, you know, one day the same as the other. Sleeping in the same bed with the same woman, night after night. Some find it a little dull, I guess."

How that wide, red mouth grinned at me. I still remember that smile, the shape and size of it. He rolled me on my back, kissed me on the lips and throat and breasts. "I believe we can do better than that, my love," he said. And you know how it is. The sunshine, the smell of the sea through your window, your lover returned to you after an absence. A lover's body you know as your own, each bone, each sinew, each twitch of muscle, each hair, each flavor, each word before he says it, each thought. When the end approached, I threw back my head and came like the Southern Pacific, and he arched his back and collided head on, an awful crash. Together we shuddered and steamed. The quiet, pale room. The damp sheets, the fan that whirred above us.

Eventually the shuddering slowed to a tremble, a stillness. We lay stomach to stomach while the light gathered above our heads. Still I trusted him. He lifted himself on his elbows and pulled out slowly. Shimmied off the rubber and said he'd be right back, don't go anywhere. When he returned, I stood at the French door to the patio, staring out to sea, smoking a cigarette. He put his arms around me and rested his chin on the top of my head.

"Why, what's the matter?" I said.

He took some time, while the surf tumbled in under the sunrise.

"I've been recalled back to London," he said.

NOW, I DON'T KNOW WHY everything caught up with me at that particular moment. I hadn't shed a single tear, not one, throughout the length of Thorpe's most recent absence. I was used to them, after all. Sometimes he went away for a week, sometimes a couple of weeks. Sometimes he would return for a day or two, sometimes for a week or two, and once— dear, blissful February—he stuck around for almost an entire month. And I never knew which it was. He never gave me the slightest clue. He turned up and disappeared without prior notice. Well, he couldn't ex- actly emblazon his intentions in the sky, could he? So I'd learned to take him as I found him, each episode of his company a surprise, each kiss, each clandestine bender at Shangri-La, each stolen night at my bun- galow, careful always to make sure we never gave ourselves away at a party, greeted each other coolly, flirted with others, left separately, raced to Cable Beach where Thorpe waited for me under one of the enormous, mature sea grape trees that brushed the patio. He had resumed his ciga- rettes, maybe because of the additional strain of hiding a mistress from the world, and I always saw the curl of smoke first, then his hair and his skin in the moonlight. Sometimes, when the party had proved es- pecially unbearable, the tension between us too excruciating, we got no farther than the trunk of that tree for quite some time, and I still remember the scratch of sea grape bark on my spine with a certain sadis- tic pleasure.

Then he would vanish, and I tried not to think of him at all. I plunged myself into the socio-charitable whirl of Nassau. When Freddie and Nancy de Marigny returned from their honeymoon, such as it was— she'd had a terrible case of typhoid when they got to Mexico, followed by trench mouth, innumerable dental surgeries, just awful—I gave them a dinner party at my bungalow that went off quite well, I thought, un- der the circumstances. On Christmas Eve, we opened the duchess's can- teen at Fred Sigrist's old Bahamian Club with a grand party chock-full of handsome young servicemen, and I'd been working shifts there most mornings since. So you see how terribly busy I was, how unable to spare even a moment to indulge in self-pity. The appearance of these tears shocked me. What was it about Thorpe? I never cried anywhere except with him.

I SPUN TO FACE HIM. "*What* did you say?"

His face was heavy with remorse. "I've been called back to London."

"And you *agreed*?"

"Don't, Lulu," he said. "You know I haven't got any say in this."

"I know!" I shoved away the tears with the back of my hand. "Don't you think I know? But you don't know what it's like, to be left behind. Not a word. Just helpless. You might be in Timbuktu or dead, and I'd never know. Nobody knows about us, except Veryl. Your family's never heard of me, have they? *Have* they?"

He answered with a frown. I threw up my hands.

"You see? Where do I go if you never come back? Whom do I turn to? I'm nobody to you, as far as anyone else is concerned."

Thorpe released me and sat on the edge of the bed. He stared at me from what I called his thinking face, which was really no expression at all, just this blankness, topped by a furrowed brow. He'd worn it often during the past year, usually right after making love. I suppose there's something about fornication that gets you thinking. His eyes, catching the yellow sunlight, were nearly green.

I stepped to the chest of drawers and stubbed out my cigarette.

"When the war's over," he began.

"When the war's over you'll be dead, Thorpe, and I'll be alone, or worse, I'll be pregnant with some baby who has no father to speak of, no family to speak of." I sat down and gathered the pillow in my lap. "And with my luck, he'll have your goddamned hair!"

Thorpe rose from the bed and pulled his trousers from the floor. "Now, hang on a moment, darling. I thought you liked my hair."

I threw the pillow. He dodged it and reached for his shirt.

"Where the devil do you think you're going?" I yelled.

"Out, of course. Veryl should be swinging through the door any second."

"Veryl already knows about us, you bastard."

"Keep your voice down. The neighbors will hear."

"I don't give a tinker's damn what the neighbors hear!"

He leaned over the bed and kissed my forehead. "I'll come back, my beauty."

"You always say that."

"And I always do. Eventually."

An instant later, I was staring at the door. Which was not at all how I'd imagined this scene would end.

YEARS LATER, IN HER AUTOBIOGRAPHY, the former Mrs. Wallis Simpson calculated—among other things—some thirty thousand eggs personally fried by her bony, capable hands in the kitchen of the United Services Canteen of Nassau, but I dispute those numbers. For one thing, she wasn't exactly there every day. For another, the woman can't count up much else except pieces of eight.

Still, she did her share. Duty called. She took Sigrist's shabby old club and refurbished those rooms into a canteen de luxe. And I can attest she cooked up eggs and bacon for hundreds of these starstruck young men, dazzled them all with her famous charm, organized supper dances and concerts and what have you, anything you could imagine to keep up morale and keep servicemen writing home in rapture about how the Duchess of Windsor herself served them eggs by the plateful, any which way you wanted them.

And when we opened the place last Christmas! Oh, that was a party, all right. I'd had some last-minute appointment with the duchess, I don't remember what, and wound up driving to the joint in the Windsors' own limousine with the Union Jack flags. If only the folks in Bakersfield could've seen me. The canteen was already jumping, buzzing with Red Cross ladies in a spirit of tremendous female cooperation, laced with Christmas cheer. Standing in a disorderly queue outside, held back by a tolerant police officer of the white-glove variety, milled our first customers in their best dress uniforms. The duke and duchess stopped to wave—slow, decorous waving like they were screwing in a pair of light bulbs. *Pop, flash* went the cameras. *Your Highness, Your Highness* went the newspapermen, while Miss Drewes and I slipped right up the front steps and into the duchess's canteen de luxe. Someone tossed me an apron and a gin fizz. We took about a million orders, and afterward Miss Drewes and I handed out presents from beneath the tree, since the duke and duchess had left shortly after their official performance.

Best of all, when I arrived home, someone was waiting for me beneath the sea grape tree, bearing a bottle of champagne and a small white box, the best kind. Not a ring, of course. But I'd worn that diamond pendant like a talisman ever since, as if it could ward off evil, as if by the act of wearing it I could lure my lover back to me, however far he roamed.

It dangled now between my breasts as I bicycled through the soupy air to the canteen, apron neatly tied for the eight o'clock shift. As I climbed the steps in my natty uniform and headed into the kitchen.

HALF AN HOUR LATER, THE orders poured in. Bacon and eggs, bacon and eggs, yet more bacon and eggs, because these chaps were accustomed to everything powdered and canned back home in darkest England, apparently, and here in Nassau we still had the genuine article, sent over from the Lend Lease office in Miami in vast American quantities from vast American farms. The smoke of frying bacon filled the kitchen. My arms flew. Spatula in each hand, the right turning eggs and the left turning bacon. I still remember that rhythm, still remember how the air inside that kitchen turned always as dense and hot as July, whatever the actual season—but especially in July—and how the perspiration collected on my scalp and ran down my temples and my spine. I remember the noise of the men enjoying their breakfast, the clatter of china and cutlery, as if that canteen still exists inside my head somewhere. Maybe it does.

On this particular day, however, the duchess was absent. To her credit, she showed up most mornings, picked up her spatula and flipped her share of eggs over easy, but she never did enjoy the best of health, and today was one of those days that word came down the telephone wire from Government House. Her Royal Highness—no giggles at the back, please—was unwell, and sent her regrets to the canteen staff.

At the time, I didn't imagine there might be another reason for her absence. Like I said, the lady was subject to spasms of sickness from time to time. Mrs. Gudewill took the call—Mrs. Gudewill had a fondness for ringing telephones that I never could understand, I mean a ringing telephone was a harbinger of disaster so far as I was concerned—and announced the news. I don't remember thinking anything at all about it. I just shrugged and wiped away the perspiration from my temples and turned back to that canteen grill, flipping and turning. There was a knack to sliding a finished egg whole onto its plate without folding over the white on itself or, God forbid, breaking the yolk. You had to concentrate a little, especially in that heat. You had no time to think about absent duchesses and murdered husbands and lovers sailing back to jolly England in a time of war. You had no time to think about your silly old conscience. And maybe that was why I dedicated myself so thoroughly to that canteen. Not for the morale of the troops, not to do my bit or to

share in the excitement of war, the bumper crop of virile young men that
wanted sowing in the dining room behind me. Because it was something
to do. It occupied the long, lean hours. It occupied the space between my
ears that might otherwise be filled with anguish.

AT HALF PAST ONE O'CLOCK, I hung up my apron, washed my face and
hands in the lavatory, and climbed back on my bicycle. The air outside
was dark and hot, threatening the kind of rain that did nothing to refresh
you. Sometimes a gust of wind came off the water to batter me on my
bicycle. I trundled on past my cottage, past the golf course, the stretch of
barren road along the shore. There was a rumble of thunder. Then the
good old British Colonial, brooding in the heat. Hardly a soul reclined on
the sand outside. The harbor, now. That was bustling. A steamship was
in the process of attaching itself to the dock. I cycled carefully around the
excitement and came to a stop outside the Prince George. It was now past
two o'clock, plenty late for a drink. I propped the bicycle against the wall
outside and made straight for the bar.

   To my surprise, Jack himself stood behind the counter. Surprise because Jack didn't usually saunter to his duty until later in the afternoon,
on account of staying up all night to hear everybody's secrets. Some
younger fellow watered the lunch crowd, I never could remember his
name. Today that fellow had his back to the room, however, was polish-
ing the glassware one by one with a clean white cloth, and Jack faced the
tables and stools, braced his eight fingers and two bony thumbs on the
wood, shirt crisp and waistcoat black. The ceiling fan whirred directly
above his head. I slid into place and told him his countenance was looking wilted today, was something up?

   He stepped away and reached for a glass. I laid my arms on the counter,
one folded over the other, and watched him pour me a gin and tonic.
Because of shortages, there was no lime. Just bottled, concentrated lime

juice, an unsatisfactory substitute that tasted of metal. Jack set it before me on the counter and assumed his original stance.

"You ever think of moving back home?" he said.

"Home? This *is* home."

"I mean back where you came from, Mrs. Randolph. Where you was brought up. Family and friends."

I set down the glass. "I come from nowhere, sonny. I've got nobody."

"You have a mother and a father. Brother and a sister."

"What makes you say that?"

"Family's family, Mrs. Randolph. They might could help you find what you're looking for."

"Oh? I didn't notice I was looking for anything."

"Everybody's looking for something. If you ain't looking for something, you're trying to get away from something. Ain't that so?"

He had lowered his face a little, so that when I raised my face a little, we met right in the middle, eye locked with eye, tonic fizzing our chins, fan stirring our hair.

"Where *do* you get your ideas, Jack?"

"I'm just saying you might want to get out of town, Mrs. Randolph. That's all I'm saying. Get the devil out of Nassau, and maybe take with you whatever you care about."

"What's happening?" I said. "What have you heard?"

Jack straightened up and glanced at the doorway. "Just that someone's at the end of his rope, that's all. And there's a lot of fools swinging on that rope, you know what I mean? A lot of fools."

"Fools like me?"

There was a commotion taking shape on the opposite side of the room, near the doorway where Jack had just glanced. He gave me a last look and stepped away, straightening his waistcoat, to nudge his colleague at the glassware. I tipped back my glass—it was a thirsty afternoon, all right—and reached for my pocketbook to rummage out a cigarette. As

I did so, I contrived a sweep of the room beyond my shoulder. But it was only Freddie de Marigny and his cousin Georges de Visledou, laughing over some joke. I turned away and lit my cigarette.

"Why, Mrs. Randolph!"

"Freddie. How nice."

The stool beside me scraped back a few inches. De Marigny's long body took possession. He laid a palm on the counter and made some gesture to Jack with the other hand. His cousin Georges made me a salute and reached for an ashtray.

"How's married life?" I asked.

"A bit lonely, at the moment. Nancy is in Vermont for the summer, learning to dance."

"To dance? Doesn't she already know how?"

"I mean real dancing. This famous dancer is teaching her, this Miss Graham. You've heard of her? It's a retreat of some kind." He paused to light a cigarette. "Nancy doesn't like the heat so much."

"Why don't you join her?"

"Because I have business interests, Mrs. Randolph. I'm a working man. Anyway, I don't want to spend the summer dancing. Georges, now." He nudged the other man with his elbow, and Georges, who had been staring around the room, idling his cigarette, made a start. "Georges, you good-for-nothing. Why haven't you made some escape from this inferno, like Nancy?"

Georges looked at me and then the floor. Turned around to scrabble for the ashtray. His cheeks were pink. He was a handsome devil, all right: strong Gallic looks, dark shiny hair.

Freddie just laughed and leaned toward me. "My dear cousin has an *amour*, you see. That's why he stays here. But what's your excuse, Mrs. Randolph? This column of yours? Or something more interesting, like Georges here?"

"Habit, I guess. I don't mind the heat so much."

Jack set a pair of glasses in front of the two men. I met his gaze for a second or two, but there was no telling what he was thinking, no expression at all on that flat, white face. Still, I had the idea he was communicating something, some idea. *Someone's at the end of his rope*, he'd said.

I circled my finger around the rim of my glass. "Say. Your father-in-law's in the same boat, isn't that right? Wife scampered off to cooler climes."

"Yes, Mrs. Oakes is in Maine, as usual."

"Poor Sir Harry. The way he stomps around without her. You ought to keep each other company."

Freddie winced. "I'm afraid I haven't seen Sir Harry in some time."

"On the outs, are you?"

"For the moment. He's something of an autocrat, you see—"

"You don't say."

"And I—well." Freddie put his hand to his heart. "I am not so easily brought to heel, I'm afraid. He knows I don't want his money, and it irks him."

"Irks him? Isn't he pleased you're not after Nancy's fortune?"

"Not at all. A man like that, money is the only power he knows. Without it, he's just an ordinary fellow. And a son-in-law who can't be bought—*well*. But we will mend fences. He's got a temper, that fellow, but he's like me. The storm passes, and everything is like it was before." Freddie sipped his whiskey. "Anyway, he leaves for Maine in a day or two. That should cool him off."

"Meanwhile, he sits at Westbourne with Harold Christie."

"Christie's with him?"

"That's what I hear. In a plush guest suite, whispering into the old man's ear. What's the matter?"

Freddie was shaking his head. "Christie. You know he double-crossed Sir Harry last year, on the deal for the land for that airport? He had better watch himself. Sir Harry plays a long game. And Christie owes him a great deal of money."

"Does he, now?"

"A great deal." He glanced at Georges de Visledou, who had taken his drink and his cigarette and gone over to speak to a pair of women at one of the little round tables. "I will tell you something else. A few months ago, just before we had this last little disagreement, Sir Harry told me he was going to leave Nassau."

"Oh, that's been going around for ages."

"No, but he means it. He doesn't like the way the women here treat his wife, for one thing. He doesn't like all the scrutiny, you know, this British oversight in his affairs. He's been sending his money away for some time, to this bank in Mexico, and you may take my word for this, Mrs. Randolph. By this time next year, Oakes will be out of the Bahamas for good."

As he said all this, de Marigny had lowered his voice, had positioned his head in close proximity to mine. I glanced to Jack, who was quietly rearranging his bottles behind the counter, and Jack, who had been watching us, looked away. I thought of the papers locked in my desk drawer on Cable Beach.

"Which bank?" I asked. "The one in Mexico?"

"Banco Continental, of course. Wenner-Gren's outfit."

I stubbed out my cigarette. "Fascinating. And also illegal, isn't it? Moving your assets overseas in a time of war?"

"What does that matter to such men? But come. You're not leaving?"

"I only stopped by for a little refreshment."

He touched my hand. "We're having a little dinner party tonight, Georges and me. You must join us."

I opened my mouth to offer my regrets, to say I was otherwise engaged, but then I wasn't, was I? Otherwise engaged. For all I knew, Thorpe was on his way back to London right now. For all I knew, I had seen my last of him. This idea—the loss of Thorpe—inserted itself at the top of my head, penetrating deeply, and then drew a slow gash right down the middle from skull to viscera, splitting me apart the way you might filet a trout.

I laid a few shillings on the counter and rose to my feet. "Why, how lovely of you to think of me, dear Freddie. Eight o'clock all right for you?"

He took my hand and kissed it. As he bent over my fingers, the light glinted on his hair.

"Eight o'clock is perfect."

WHEN I STEPPED BACK OUT into the simmering air, the first thing I saw was the Government House limousine sitting by the curb, Union Jack flags hanging limp from their tiny flagpoles above the headlights. The chauffeur stood against the wheel well, checking his watch. He saw me and straightened.

"Mrs. Randolph?"

"Indeed."

"Her Royal Highness requests a moment of your time, if it's convenient."

I glanced at the rear window and back at the chauffeur, who stared back steadily, in the same way that Jack regarded me from behind his counter. The heat laid its oppressive hands against my cheeks, my chest. Already I felt my dress warming against my legs.

"You can put my bicycle in the back, I guess," I said.

IT'S A STRANGE AND RATHER empty sensation, riding in a limousine by yourself, a giant official limousine like the one that ferried the governor and his wife about the island. I thought of that *Life* magazine cover, the two of them in the drawing room I now knew so well, resting against those cushions I now knew so well.

We drew up the hill, toward the west gate, and glided past the guard booth. Came to a stop before the portico, where I had once made the acquaintance—if you could call it that—of Sir Harry Oakes. Sir Harry Oakes, who was also on his way out of Nassau, if de Marigny's information was straight. I tried to imagine this, the Bahamas without Sir Harry, and could not. He was part of the landscape. From time to time, as I rode my bicycle about the island, taking exercise to keep my mind off my lover's absence, I might see him clearing land somewhere. He drove the bulldozer himself, back and forth, digging up scrub and palmettos and what have you, taking a kind of boylike glee in the destruction. Always he raised his hand and greeted me. Why, just the other day, I'd stopped my bicycle to chat with him, because I knew that Nancy and her mother had decamped for New England once the heat descended on Nassau, and a fellow like Oakes was sure to be bored and restless. It was late afternoon, and we were both perspiring freely, but he didn't seem to notice the discomfort. I asked about his wife, and he said she was doing well in Bar Harbor, and I asked (rather more carefully) about Nancy. "Doing much better, thanks," he said. "Away from that sex maniac husband of hers."

"Oh, be fair, Sir Harry," I said. "They're newlyweds."

Hmph, Oakes said.

"Now, don't be grumpy. He *is* a handsome devil, after all. Maybe she couldn't resist his charm."

He stuck out his lips a little, but he wasn't really angry at me. We understood each other, Oakes and I, the way two outsiders will always feel a kinship in a place like this, a place like Nassau.

"He's not such a terrible character, you know," I went on. "He does love her. He's enchanted with her. It's not the money."

"Of course it's not the money. The fool sent me a damned notarized

letter, right after they eloped, giving up any rights to it. He's just a—
damn it all—"

"He's a son-in-law with a will as stubborn as yours."

Hmph, he said.

"Sir Harry. She's nineteen, isn't she? She's not a child. And she might
have done worse, believe me. *Much* worse."

Possibly he knew what I meant. I always maintain that man had more
human perception than most people gave him credit for. At any rate, we
parted on good terms, almost affectionate, though I don't know why I
should have thought of him as I climbed from the rear seat of the limousine and walked under the portico to the front hall of Government House,
where Miss Drewes stood waiting for me, mouth twitching. Maybe it
was because of Freddie's revelations that afternoon. Maybe it was some
fleeting visitation of the cataclysm to come.

MISS DREWES AND I HAD NEVER quite become friends. I don't know
why. I liked her—efficient, intelligent, sly sense of humor lurking beneath that Mount Holyoke polish—and I believe she liked me. But like a
pair of neighboring cog wheels that couldn't seem to match their respec-
tive teeth, we never really clicked together, if you know what I mean. I'd
always presumed this was because she was so terribly protective of the
duchess, and I had been trusted with altogether too much power, in her
estimation.

And yet, as she greeted me in the hall, as she led me upstairs to the
duchess's suite, I had the feeling that Miss Drewes was suppressing the
desire to laugh. Her mouth twitched, as I said. She had almost nothing
to say to me, in contrast to her usual experienced patter. I asked what
this was concerning, and she said it was a private matter, and the duchess
would explain herself. Upstairs, the air was warm and musty, smelling of
the usual Bahamas mildew, of dampish wood and rich flowers. When we

arrived at the duchess's door, Miss Drewes seemed to hesitate before she raised her hand to rap on the wooden panel. She cast me a small, nervous smile and knocked twice. The duchess's deep voice floated back: *Come in.*

Miss Drewes turned the knob and stood aside for me.

Unwell the duchess might have been, but she paced the blue-and-white carpet of her blue-and-white dressing room with true American spirit. The suite was decorated in the French Provençal style, awfully elegant, mirrors all over the place that surrounded you with a thousand off-kilter versions of yourself. On the settee, Wallis had draped a number of splendid gowns. She didn't bother to greet me, only waved her hand at the dresses and said, "There you are, dear Lulu. I've been cleaning out my wardrobe. So many dresses. I was wondering if any of these might fit you."

I suppose I gave her a shocked look, because she laughed.

"Oh, don't be shy. We're about the same height, aren't we?"

"And that's *about* where the resemblance ends, as anyone with eyes can see."

"Let's give them a try anyway, shall we?"

I crossed my arms. "I'm terribly grateful, but I'm sure it wouldn't be any use."

But the duchess had already lifted one of the garments in question, a sunset-yellow number, made of silk and long, elegant sunbeams. She carried it across her forearms and presented it to me along with an expression I recognized, that of the indomitable inner Wallis who wouldn't be told no.

"I don't like yellow," I told her.

She held the sleeves to my shoulders and cocked her head to the side. "Oh, do give it a try. Please, Lulu."

I took the dress and went behind the Chinese screen in the corner, though not before checking the angles of the mirrors around me. As for the frock, I hadn't much hope. Along with the olive skin and brown eyes, my Italian mother had bestowed on me a set of curves that required posted warnings in certain states, a predicament Wallis had never faced in her life. I stepped into the dress, reached around back, sucked in all the breath to the bottom of my lungs, and pulled on the zipper tab.

And here's the funny part: I met no resistance at all. That dress, castoff of Wallis Simpson, whose figure resembled a clothes hanger more than a living woman, slipped right over every hill and plain. "I'll be damned," I muttered, and stepped from the screen. Wallis clapped her hands.

"Oh, I knew it," she said. "A perfect fit. Yellow's your *color*, darling, with that skin. You look like a dream. Come along, let's show the duke."

"The duke!"

"He adores a woman in a fine dress."

"I can't possibly—"

"Don't be shy. He's not busy at the moment."

She took my hand—Miss Drewes had disappeared—and led me out of the suite and down the hall to the stairs, toward the duke's private study. The dress reached all the way to the floor, thank goodness, disguising the rather serviceable saddle shoes I'd worn from the canteen. The duchess was in a strange mood, ebullient, mischievous. Whatever she was, she was not unwell, and I wasn't such a dunce that I didn't smell a rat around the place, by now. Why, the whole affair stank to high heaven. But it was not until the duchess opened the door to the duke's study— she didn't knock, of course not—and, linking arms, drew me into the room, that I discovered the source of this aroma.

He stood next to the duke, at his massive desk, wearing a neatly pressed tropical suit of pale linen and a hibiscus flower in his buttonhole. Also a wide, shy smile, which he offered to me now, along with a small white box, the best kind.

This time it did contain a ring.

ELFRIEDE

JUNE 1916
(Scotland)

ACCORDING TO THE doctor, the baby will be born in ten more weeks. On the other hand, the doctor's nearly eighty years old and possibly deaf, and Elfriede—counting back for the hundredth time to Wilfred's last leave at the end of November—now considers whether it might be sooner.

"Does it matter, really?" asks Wilfred. "One week or the next. Anyway, in the end it's up to the baby."

"Of course it matters. You've got to be here when it's born, and in order to arrange leave—"

"My dear love. You can't be serious."

Elfriede rises on her elbow and stares down at Wilfred's face. In June, the Scottish day never seems to end, and the light streaming through the window gathers cruelly on the lines that spread across his forehead and out from the corners of his eyes, the lines that form a pair of parentheses around that wide mouth. She cups her hand around the side of his face and touches his moustache with her thumb.

"But you must. You must be here with me."

Wilfred sighs deeply and heaves himself out of bed. Except for his face and hands, his skin is so pale as to be almost white. He finds his jacket, crumpled on the floor, and bends to pick it up, to shake it out and hang it on the back of a chair, to extract the cigarette case from the breast pocket. Elfriede, still propped on her elbow, examines his body like a doctor searching for symptoms. Of course he's as lean as ever. His long, spidery limbs flash as he moves about the room, cigarette stuck in the corner of his mouth, picking up his discarded clothes in a military way. "Darling, you must understand there's a war on," he says. "I can't simply lark off back to Blighty whenever the mood strikes."

"Whenever the mood *strikes*? Your wife is having a baby!"

"As do the wives of my subordinates, on a remarkably regular basis, without any promise or even chance of their getting leave."

"You're a major, aren't you? Doesn't that mean anything?"

"Yes, it does." He removes the cigarette from his mouth and leans his palms against the sill of the open window. "It means I'm obliged to set an example. It means I'm obliged not to ask my men to do anything I wouldn't ask of myself. It means I'm the last chap who gets leave."

"That's not fair. Look at you, you've lost weight. Your face, it's aged a decade since I saw you last—"

"Unkind."

"Don't joke. Your daughter needs you. Your wife—your wife needs you terribly—"

"Yes, and so do the wives and children of all my men, as I said, and several of those men, those husbands and fathers, they're dead, Elfriede, dead, gone, buried under white crosses in France, or hadn't you heard? Tucked away in a nice, warm, dry house, plenty to eat, not a gun in sight. Hadn't you heard there's a fucking war on, darling?"

By the end of this speech, Wilfred's voice roars out through the open window and shakes the trees outside. His elbows are locked, the cigarette burns from his right hand.

"You'll wake the house," Elfriede says.

He straightens and takes a deep drag from his cigarette. "I'm sorry."

"Of course I understand there's a war on. My God. How many damned socks have I darned, how many bandages, how many hours do I spend with all your widows, Wilfred? How many hours in the hospital dressing wounds?"

"I know. I know."

"My son. My son is fighting in some regiment in Poland, and I don't know where, and he might be dead this minute. Johann might be dead, and God knows when I'm going to discover that fact. In some letter from the Red Cross, I suppose, or from Helga, even worse. My own husband is the sworn enemy of my own son. If you meet him in battle, Wilfred, what will you do? Will you kill him?"

"Not if he kills me first, obviously."

Elfriede swings her legs out of bed, hoists herself up, and snatches her dressing gown from the floor nearby.

"Elfriede?"

She shoves her arms in the holes and belts the robe over her swollen breasts, her swollen belly. The door's shut tight; she swings it open and lumbers down the hallway and down the stairs, outside, outside, even though the air's cooling fast and turning damp, because she can't stand another minute of her husband. Not *this* husband, anyway. The word's taken on a strange new meaning over the past two years.

THEY BOUGHT DUNNOCK LODGE TEN years ago, just before Margaret was born, from a wealthy Englishman who'd gone bankrupt on railroad shares. It went unsaid that most of the money for this purchase came from Elfriede, for whom generous provision was made in Gerhard's will. The house was far too big. In a spirit of great hope, they intended its spacious rooms to shelter not just the four of them, Wilfred and Elfriede and Johann and the new baby, but Johann's three sisters and, of course, all further babies God might send them in the bright, new days to come. What optimism! When you're big with child, when your marriage throbs and hums with mutual adoration, anything seems possible. But that was before the horror of Margaret's birth, the protracted labor, the breech presentation, the botched delivery that nearly killed them both. The blackness that descended afterward, just as the dark, dank Scottish winter set in, how futile. What's the old saying? Man plans, God laughs. The years went. Charlotte's whereabouts remained a mystery. Johann grew from boy into man, and Germany inevitably claimed its baron back. And no more babies came along.

Until this one.

THE BABY'S LARGE, SHE KNOWS that much. After seven months of pregnancy, Elfriede feels so big and so ungainly. Already she's caught herself waddling. At the hospital, the wounded men cast her looks of alarm, as if they're expecting her to lie down and give birth at any moment. Now, when she tries to run down the lawn to the river, she discovers she can't quite breathe, because the baby's stuffed in there all the way to her lungs. She slows to a walk. A rapid walk. Upon reaching the riverbank, she crosses the bridge to the small, tree-covered island where the Englishman had built a folly, as Englishmen do, inside which she and Wilfred have made love more times than she could possibly count. In fact, as she steps from the bridge onto the turf, bathed in the slow, blue twilight of a Scottish June, she recalls tramping over these grounds with Wilfred and the estate agent ten years ago, in a similar state of pregnancy, and how she and Wilfred had spotted the folly at the exact same instant, and looked at each other with the exact same thought. On the night they moved in, as soon as Johann was tucked in bed, they hurried here through the rain, hand in hand, and consecrated first the cushioned bench along the eastern side, and then—an hour or so later—the steps that led back down to the riverbank. Both of them soaked and laughing and consumed with each other. Eight days later Elfriede was bleeding to death. The Lord giveth and the Lord taketh away. Nearly a year passed before she and Wilfred made love again. Then he was off to India with the regiment. Two long years. Seven and a half months after his departure, Elfriede gave birth to a stillborn boy. She steps inside the folly and sits down on the cushioned bench along the eastern side, not for old times' sake but because her feet can't stand another bloody second.

Finally the sun's going down. What a relief, the departure of light.

Elfriede closes her eyes and leans her head against the pillar. Some nearby robin whistles a brisk tattoo at the dying sun. How they sing, the robins of Dunnock Lodge. They woke her this morning at the first instant of sunrise. She was too thrilled to fall back asleep, because Wilfred was coming, a few days' leave at last, he'd sent a telegram from Boulogne the night before. The shock of it, after all those months on the front! And the robins woke her at dawn. She tried on five dresses and none of them made her belly look any less disgraceful. Poor Wilfred, to come home at last and discover a hippopotamus instead of a wife.

OF COURSE THEY WERE USED to these absences. That was the trouble with the army, wasn't it? When Wilfred returned from India for three months of home leave, they discussed whether Elfriede and the children should accompany him back. It was too unbearable to live apart like this. Certainly Margaret was old enough. But what about Johann? He'd settled happily into boarding school at Winchester, and he was expected in Germany over the Christmas and summer holidays. And the climate was so unsuitable for young children, disease so rife. In the end Elfriede and Margaret stayed in India only six months, during which time Elfriede miscarried twice, the second time off the coast of Ceylon during the voyage home. She never told Wilfred about that one. What use? The news would only grieve him. Another year passed, another home leave. Another excruciating separation. Then the war. The regiment hurried homeward, but only to embark for France. A few hundred miles of separation instead of several thousand. But what was the difference, really? Letters arrived sooner. Theoretically, Wilfred could be home in several hours instead of several weeks. But in exchange for these blessings, Elfriede now had this monstrous crushing fear, the terror that sometimes paralyzed her; a compound terror because Johann, visiting Germany as usual during the summer of 1914, accepted a lieutenant's commission in the Germany army upon the outbreak of war. He's on the Eastern Front somewhere. They don't know exactly where. Some bloody steppe. His letters, when they arrive at all, are months late and contain no more than assurances of health and of his continued devotion to his mother, his sister, and his stepfather. Love thine enemy, that's what the Bible says.

So you will understand the tremendous power of this small word *leave* in Elfriede's life. For the past decade, her world's swung around it. She's orbited this sun called leave, she's anticipated its rise and fall in her sky, she's taken all life and light and nourishment from her husband's faithful return. In November, of course, the sun's scarce in Scotland, and Wilfred's leave—also on short notice—was maybe more like an explosion in the middle of the night, like fireworks. The telegram came from London just after lunch, delayed because all the telegraph boys were run off their feet with news from the front, and she had just enough time to jump inside the Wolseley with Margaret and drive into Inverness to meet her husband off the train. Margaret spotted him first. (Elfriede's nearsightedness gets a little worse each year.) She screamed and dashed off down the platform, and somewhere in the tangle of khaki arms and khaki legs a man lifted her up high, yes, this spindly blond girl of nine years, and spun her around in a crushing embrace. Elfriede stood absolutely still, a paralysis of joy. In her head, she heard some woman say, *It's a special kind of love, you know, between a father and daughter.* Wilfred, still holding this daughter in his arms, whispered some question in Margaret's ear, and Margaret pointed back up the platform toward Elfriede, and Elfriede, looking upon her husband's face for the first time since the end of spring, felt the sun rise at last in her sky. That's what leave is like.

And yet. And yet. Even in November, something wasn't quite right. That marvelous candlepower of Wilfred's charisma had somehow dimmed, she thought, as she drove the Wolseley and Margaret kept up a thrilled chatter from the back seat, to which Wilfred replied with occasional and mechanical *Yes darlings* and *Oh jolly goods*. Later, when Margaret was asleep, he made love to Elfriede without a single word, rolled away and fell unconscious, woke sometime in the night to smoke beside the window, returned to bed, repeat. Elfriede counted thirteen stubs in the ashtray the next morning. And for the next five days, he did nothing but eat and sleep and copulate. Well, not entirely. In Margaret's company, he tried his best to summon up the old sunshine and sometimes succeeded, but these efforts depleted him, and Elfriede had only his silence. His long, quiet walks around the grounds. His distant gaze at breakfast and dinner that reached across the room and through the walls to someplace far from Elfriede's imagination. His wordless, relentless, tobacco-scented fucking in the middle of the night, sometimes the middle of the day, filling Elfriede's womb with the stuff of life while she clung to his neck, his shoulders, his buttocks, straining for the same elusive object. She waited until the end of February to tell him she was pregnant. She wasn't sure if the news would delight or upset him. He replied by telegram.

DEAR BELOVED ANGEL STOP RECEIVED YOUR LETTER AN HOUR AGO STOP HAVE NOT STOPPED WEEPING STOP FORGIVE THIS BEAST YOU CALL HUSBAND STOP TAKE EVERY POSSIBLE CARE FOR YOUR DEAR SELF STOP CAN BEAR ANYTHING EXCEPT LOSS OF YOU

STOP NAME HIM FOR MY FATHER STOP ALL LOVE
FROM ONE WHO HAS ALWAYS ADORED AND NEVER
DESERVED YOU=
=*WILFRED*

In short, more affection than she had received from him in . . . well,
since the previous leave, probably.

BUT NOW SHE WONDERS, AS she leans against the pillar in the folly and
listens to the robin. Affection, really? Or remorse?

Across the damp air, a man's voice calls out. Elfriede's eyelids fly
open. Her heart leaps: *Johann!* (Thus the maternal mind, swinging back
and forth between child and mate.) Then she remembers that Johann's
in Poland, probably, and this voice must belong to her husband. To this
Wilfred so unlike the old Wilfred, this husband who only eats and sleeps
and copulates. Yes, there it goes again, a bit louder, thick with longing
and exasperation.

Elfriede!

He's coming closer. Naturally, if he's taken the trouble to find her at
all, he'll check the folly first. And maybe Elfriede already knew that.
Maybe she came to this place for a reason: to be found. To be found *here*,
in the scene of their old lovemaking, where every square inch of bench
and floor and wall and step has been consecrated by one act or another,
in one position or another. It's like an album of their marriage, the carnal
aspect of it anyway, in which the photographs are memories. Elfriede's
come here to be found by her husband. There must be a reason.

MAYBE IT'S LUCY MACLEOD? MRS. MACLEOD, you know, whose
husband—a lieutenant under Wilfred's command—was killed last winter,

blown apart by a shell in the middle of a muddy February day, somewhere near Albert. As you might expect, there wasn't much left of Lieutenant MacLeod's body to bury. Just the identification tags and some
disarticulated bones and burned flesh. (Lucy doesn't know these details,
of course; Wilfred confided them to Elfriede in one of his more candid
letters.) Elfriede's visited Mrs. MacLeod frequently over the past several
months, providing comfort as duty requires the commanding officer's
wife. Duty, and maybe a little fear too, because doesn't Elfriede know
all too well how catastrophe strikes? And by easing the suffering of others, can't you earn some reprieve from suffering yourself? Of course,
Elfriede doesn't actually make this cold calculus in her own head as she
brings books and toys for the little MacLeods, as she sits by Mrs. Mac-
Leod on the sofa and holds her hand. It's more like an instinct, a moral
instinct, a game played deep inside the region of the subconscious mind.

Anyway, there they sat together on the sofa, Elfriede and Lucy Mac-
Leod, just last week. Mrs. MacLeod was having one of her bad days,
which seem to come more frequently now than when the terrible news
was still fresh. Grief is like that sometimes. She'd lost patience with having her hand held. She got up and checked the window—Margaret was
playing outside with the MacLeod fry—and lit a cigarette. She stared at
the photograph of her husband on the table, stiff and constipated in his
dress uniform, and told Elfriede how she found some love notes among
the personal effects sent home with Lieutenant MacLeod's kit.

"This must have been some comfort," Elfriede said, in her careful English.

Mrs. MacLeod laughed. "I guess it would have been, if they were
mine."

Elfriede set her teacup in her saucer. "Yours?" she asked stupidly.

"Of course I know how it is," said Mrs. MacLeod. "We all know how
it is, when they're away. But it's still a shock, all the same, to see another
woman's handwriting. Some woman in Paris, of course. They all do it."

Elfriede, too shocked to reply, watched the movements of Mrs. Mac-Leod's arm as she smoked her cigarette, staring at her dead husband's photograph. Over a decade now, and Elfriede still doesn't understand these Englishwomen. True, the chariness is mutual. The regimental wives never did regard her as one of their own, did they? She's too foreign, for one thing, too *German*, a fault now almost unforgiveable. For another thing, she's shy, and shyness in a beautiful woman will always be seen as arrogance. So most of them dislike her and gossip about her endlessly at all the parties and luncheons to which she's not invited. She knows this, naturally. Women have an instinct for knowing these things. But she tries her best to ignore the antipathy, to soldier on in the grand tradition of army wives, to drink their damnable tea and pretend an earnest interest in the weather and the cultivation of roses. And maybe these efforts are finally having some effect on her. As Mrs. MacLeod studied Lieutenant MacLeod's faithless face in the photograph, Elfriede found herself glancing at the window in a fruitless search for some weather to discuss.

"They all do it," Mrs. MacLeod said again, almost to herself.

"Not—not all, surely," whispered Elfriede.

Mrs. MacLeod turned. "Oh, you poor thing. Do you think your husband's the exception?"

"He—he would not—"

"Wouldn't he?" Another laugh. "Two years at a time in India, and you think he didn't find some native women to suit his fancy, like all the others? Don't you *know*?"

"I really don't think we should—"

"My God, look at you, so happy. So untouched. Husband still alive, baby on the way. How nice. Major Thorpe's pretty wife, who stayed at home when the regiment went to India, never mind her husband's needs. Imagined he could last two years without it, apparently."

"It?" Elfriede said faintly.

"*It.* You know, dearie. What goes on between husbands and wives.

Between husbands and other women, when they haven't got it at home, and very often when they have."

Well! So much for the weather and the roses. As Mrs. MacLeod spoke, the gray light from the window illuminated the smoke of her cigarette, and it rose from her hand like a ghost. How pink and swollen her face was, how slurry her words. She gripped the table behind her with strange ferocity. When Elfriede first arrived, she thought she'd interrupted Mrs. MacLeod in some paroxysm of grief, but later—remembering also the strong odor of eau de cologne filling the room—she wondered if she'd interrupted Mrs. MacLeod in some paroxysm of Scotch whiskey. It was only eleven o'clock in the morning, but still. That would explain everything. Her appearance, the sound of her voice, the spite of her words.

"Now, Mrs. MacLeod," Elfriede said, in her most conciliatory voice, "it's so natural to make suspicion, from time to time, while our husbands are away—"

"Suspicion! Oh, Lord. Suspicion, indeed. My dear, they all do it, whenever and wherever they can. My husband, your husband. It's war, after all. Battle puts up their animal instincts, you know, and they're all just animals at heart, aren't they? Men."

Elfriede rose from the sofa. "Perhaps I should leave, Mrs. MacLeod. I will return when you feel better."

"Oh, God. Oh, God. You think you're ever so much better than the rest of us. Is it because you're so beautiful? Our precious little German princess, you think he won't stray? Poor Mrs. Thorpe. They all do it."

"Mrs. MacLeod—"

"I'll tell you another thing. You ought to ask your husband about that woman *he* sees in Paris. Those twenty-four-hour passes of his, those important meetings. Everybody knew about it. My husband wrote me, before he died. It was the joke of the regiment. Major Thorpe's woman in Paris. Everybody knew."

With that, she crushed out her cigarette, directly onto the wooden table, not far from her dead husband's photograph, and turned away.

So Lucy MacLeod has her own opinions on the state of Elfriede's marriage, and the significance of leave.

NOW, ELFRIEDE—A PRINCIPAL IN THIS marriage, while Mrs. MacLeod is not—probably should have discarded these opinions as unworthy and ill-informed, as maybe even spiteful and conceived in a perfectly understandable state of bitterness. Grief will do that.

But certain opinions, once presented, are so difficult to ignore. Do you think that when Elfriede went to pick up her husband from the train this afternoon, she didn't search his face for some expression that would belie Mrs. MacLeod's extraordinary claims? Do you think that when they retired to the privacy of their bedroom this evening, Elfriede wasn't conscious of the hippopotamus grossness of her belly as her husband pulled her free from her dress and her petticoats?

Do you think, as he arranged her carefully at the edge of the bed and plunged headlong into her body, Elfriede didn't torture herself with the image of Wilfred plunging into some woman in Paris?

Do you think she didn't hold his sobbing shoulders afterward and wonder: *Affection? Or remorse?*

WILFRED'S VOICE GROWS LOUDER STILL. How big this voice has grown over the course of their marriage, how commanding, how gravelly. That's what happens with age and cigarettes, Elfriede supposes. We all grow older, we grow from idealistic youth into an adulthood of compromise and necessity. In between these desperate utterances—*Elfriede! Elfriede!*—the robin makes his joyful call. Then, in a flutter of wings, he's gone. Wilfred steps into the folly and sees her in the twilight. He slumps against a pillar and whispers, *Thank God.*

"Go away," she tells him.

He just stares at her, not with any particular expression, unless his absence of emotion is an expression of its own. The old light flattens away the lines of his skin. He's wearing a linen undershirt over his trousers. Braces over his shoulders. Barefoot, a thing Elfriede notices at the very edge of her vision.

"I apologize," he says. "I shouldn't have said that. I forget you're not accustomed to gallows humor."

Elfriede has to think for a moment before she remembers. *Not if he kills me first.* Oh, that. She casts about for some reply, and ends up shaking her head.

"Do you think it doesn't grieve me?" he says. "I've loved him like a son. I've raised him like a son. To imagine him inside enemy trenches—"

"Raised him? You? *I've* raised him. I've raised them both, Wilfred. You were on the other side of the world."

"And he was in school, but we had our months and years, and we made what we could of them. The army's my *job*, Elfriede, we both agreed I shouldn't resign. Remember when the regiment got orders for India? I was the one who couldn't bear the thought of leaving. You were the one who convinced me to go."

"Because I thought you'd regret it one day, if you resigned. I knew how you loved adventure. I knew you wouldn't be happy in a bank or in chambers. I loved you too much to make you stay at home. And I trusted your love."

"You might have joined me out there at any time. At any moment, I'd have—I'd have died of joy, to have you with me."

"Would you? Really? With so much variety at hand?"

He gapes at her. His crossed arms fall apart. The robin, returning, begins to sing again, and Wilfred spins on his heel and walks back into the darkness.

Elfriede releases her breath and hangs her head, slumping, gripping the bench beneath her with much the same ferocity as Mrs. MacLeod gripped the table on which her husband's photograph stood. Oh, the photograph. Why hadn't Mrs. MacLeod put it away, in the face of the evidence? Why hadn't she smashed it, destroyed it, scissored out those faithless eyes from existence? Only because he was dead? Did his death, did his suffering somehow expiate his sacrilegious disregard of a promise, made before God, to love no other woman before Mrs. MacLeod?

But Gerhard, she thinks. Didn't Gerhard break this same vow, while Elfriede was away in Switzerland? And didn't she forgive *his* faithlessness? Isn't this a weakness common to men, who are made to range far and spread their seed, while women, cursed creatures, must remain at home to reap it?

And Gerhard loved her so. Surely no man could have loved a woman more passionately than Gerhard once loved Elfriede. Still, when faced with a nurse, sympathetic to his struggles and his sexual needs, he cast aside these vows.

"Elfriede."

She lifts her head. Wilfred's returned to the entrance of the folly. The river lies behind him, an impression of movement, almost impossible to distinguish from the purple sky.

"Your woman in Paris," she says. "What's her name?"

"My *what*?"

"Your woman in Paris. The one you visit on your twenty-four-hour pass, which isn't enough time to travel all the way to Scotland, of course, so you have to make do——"

"Christ. Christ."

"I understand. I've been very stupid, very naive. You told me yourself, all those years ago, when a man's at war he needs—what was it? Oblivion, you called it, the oblivion of carnal intercourse. He needs the comfort of women—"

"Christ."

"I just want to know her name, that's all. Her Christian name. What is it? Marie? Josephine?"

"And here I thought this was all about our son, about Johann and me on opposite sides, about your goddamn existential grief—"

Elfriede jumps to her feet. "Of course it's about that! For you I've given up everything, I've given up my country and my language, I've given up my own son! To give you a daughter, I nearly gave up my own life! Every day I sit among these English women who hate me, I drink their tea and listen to them talk about those barbarian Germans, this terrible country, these men who spear babies and rape women, barbarians like my own son! I do this for you, Wilfred. For you I'm forced to pray against my own homeland. To pray against the child of my own body. Now I'm going to die to give you another child. And this is how you repay my loyalty. I thought my loyalty might somehow guarantee yours, like a treaty between countries, but I guess we've seen what comes of that—"

"Elfriede, stop—"

"At least, when this baby kills me, you'll be free. You can have all the women you like, you won't have to hold yourself back—"

He crosses the floor and grabs her shoulders. "Just be quiet. For God's sake. I can't stand it."

"Let go. Let go."

"You're not going to die, do you hear me? Is that what this is about? You're strong and healthy. You're not going to die. Elfriede, you can't die."

Inexplicably, her arms have circled his neck. She can't seem to pull them away. "It doesn't matter," she whispers. "Never mind. It doesn't matter. It's God's will."

"You're not going to die."

"I'm thirty-eight. I'm not the girl I was. You're not the man you were, you've changed, you're not Wilfred anymore—"

"Yes, I am."

"You're not. It's changed you."

His chest moves slightly, as if he's about to reply. Nothing comes, however, no denial. Instead the truth settles upon them like a single shroud. A Cloth of Tears.

ELFRIEDE TOLD HER HUSBAND ABOUT this cloth about a week after Margaret's birth. The doctors had stopped the bleeding, but she was so pale and depleted she couldn't lift her head from the pillow, and now a fever had set in. Every two hours, she demanded the nurses bring her the baby so she could feed, even though she couldn't hold Margaret on her own, she simply could not move her arms. A nurse kept the little body in place at her breast while Wilfred paced and paced along the corridor outside. Elfriede remembers lying feverishly in bed, feeling the pull of Margaret's mouth as the only thing attaching her to the living world. Soon even that sensation had begun to dim, she began to feel instead the separation of her soul from her body, and she called for Wilfred.

He came, white-faced and skeletal, full of remorse. He had done this thing to her, after all, he had fathered this child that had drawn away Elfriede's lifeblood. His bright hair stuck out from his head. From his jaw, too, from his chin, because he hadn't shaved all week. When he saw Elfriede's face, he dropped to his knees beside the bed and tried to speak. He didn't know she couldn't really hear anything, that her ears had retreated from the world. With tremendous effort, she shook her head. She told him, in broken, whispered words, about this handkerchief in her drawer which was to cover her face when they buried her.

On Wilfred's face, remorse turned to anguish. He didn't understand.

This relic from her first marriage? From her wedding to the baron? She wished to be buried with *this*?

So Elfriede tried to explain that this tradition was all she had left of her old life, of her family, of Germany itself. She had kept it in her drawer to ward off sorrow, and sorrow had come anyway, so the Cloth of Tears must be buried with her. It was the only way. You couldn't break a custom like that.

No, he said. *No*. He laid his hand atop her face, as if to check for breath. *You won't die, my love, you cannot die. Elfriede, you cannot die.*

Somehow, though she couldn't really hear, she heard these words. Maybe it was the vibration, or the movement of his lips, or something deeper than words that moved between them, because after all his heart still beat in her chest, and her heart beat in his. Anyway, she remembers thinking as she lay there, listening to Wilfred by whatever means, held down to earth by his fingers along the bridge of her nose, by his palm hovering above her mouth, *But I am already dead.*

This is my Cloth of Tears.

CLEARLY, THE IDEA WAS PREMATURE. From that day, that hour perhaps, Elfriede began an almost imperceptible climb back to health. The blood returned to her veins, drop by drop. In a month, she could sit up in bed as her daughter nursed at her breast. How she stared at that downy blond head, how she stroked that round, hungry cheek with her finger, as if by doing so she could summon some emotion, some tiny spark, anything at all to lighten the despair that enshrouded her. As if, by touching this creature who had innocently broken her, Elfriede could repair her defective self. Of course, she couldn't.

Take her, she sometimes said to Wilfred, who hardly left her side even to wash. Take her away. Go somewhere, all of you. You don't deserve this, you deserve more than me.

But he wouldn't go. Persistent, perverse, pumpkin-headed soldier. He did exactly the opposite. Week after week, month after month, he would, in these blackest moments, climb into the bed beside her and hold her in much the way you might hold a child, in a way that asked nothing at all of her except her mere existence in that bed, being held. Sometimes he would call in Johann too, and the four of them would lie there together, and Wilfred would say something silly to make Johann giggle, and the day eventually came when Elfriede, despite herself, giggled too. The next morning she rose from the bed and saw that it was springtime.

So the Cloth of Tears remained where it was, inside her drawer, untouched and nearly forgotten.

AND NOW, A DECADE LATER, those words have returned. *Elfriede, you cannot die.* Husband and wife stand before each other in the darkened folly, enshrouded by truth. The robin's fallen silent with the arrival of night. Elfriede's head makes a slow, heavy descent to Wilfred's chest.

"This barbarous war," she says.

"Yes."

"We can't survive it."

"Nobody can."

For some reason, although she's rested against Wilfred a million times, she thinks of that morning in Switzerland, when she sat on the fallen log and her head touched Wilfred's chest for the first time. How she listened to the beat of his heart and the movement of air in his damaged lungs. How they seemed like a miracle to her, these vital signs, these proofs of Wilfred's existence. She listens to them now as if they're new to her, as if they belong to a different man, and as those thuds and whooshes fill her head, Elfriede realizes that she and Wilfred have been speaking in German, for the first time in two years. Of course, from the beginning of their marriage, they always spoke English in public, in front of the servants and Wilfred's family, but German remained their private language, the dialect of their intimacy. Until that catastrophic summer of 1914, when a major in the British Army had—like Caesar's wife—to set himself above suspicion, and Elfriede's native tongue disappeared from their lives as if it had never been spoken. Now it returns, just as the last instant of sunlight vanishes over the curve of the earth, and they have nothing left to say to each other.

Or do they? Elfriede senses a stirring in Wilfred's chest, like something wants out of there. She thinks, *No, don't say it, don't say some stupid, comforting thing, some wretched apology*. But it's not enough. Something *must* be said.

"I should have given it up, shouldn't I? I should have resigned my commission when we married. Taken some position at a bank."

Elfriede rouses herself. "No. You'd have been miserable at a bank. You're too good at this."

"Anyway, it's done."

"Yes."

Elfriede's feet ache. They always ache, carrying this enormous baby around. More and more of her weight comes to bear on Wilfred, she can't help it, but he stands firm. Hasn't he always stood firm?

"Where did you hear this thing?" he asks softly, somewhere near her hair.

What thing, she might ask. But isn't it obvious?

"From Mrs. MacLeod. You remember her husband died last winter. Apparently he had a woman in Paris too. But I expect you know more about that than I do."

"Oh, God. MacLeod. Poor devil."

"Some might say he had it coming."

Wilfred makes some Scotch kind of noise. "So the punishment for adultery is to have oneself blown apart beyond recognition?"

"That's a merciful death. He didn't suffer. He didn't know any pain."

"But his widow does, you mean."

"I wasn't thinking of her. I was thinking of me."

"Elfriede—"

"Not *that*. The baby. I was thinking of my own battle. I know it's selfish. But you see, I don't have a platoon or a company. It's just me, fighting an enemy that takes pleasure in inflicting the greatest possible suffering—"

Now he moves, now he grips her, except there's no room to embrace like this, they can't fit, the giant belly comes between them. "I know it, I know it," he says.

"I only survived Margaret because of you."

"That's not true."

"You, keeping hold of me all those months. You wouldn't let me die."

"You're wrong. It's the other way around. I survived it because of *you*."

"What a stupid thing to say."

"No, it's true. I'm the weak one. It's me, it's always been me, holding on to you for dear life."

"Holding on to whatever you could, anyway."

Wilfred doesn't answer. Elfriede has this idea that he's chewing her words, digesting them. She feels the small, careful convulsions of his chest. How strange that she still can bear to touch him like this, that she can bear to lay her head on his chest in this intimate way, when some other woman's head has lain there too. And maybe she's just weary. Someone's got to hold her up. Why not Wilfred, then, why not the man who toppled her to begin with.

"Elfriede," he says at last, "there is no woman in Paris. There's no woman anywhere, except you."

It's Elfriede's turn to remain silent.

Wilfred removes her arms from his neck and steps away. "Well?"

"Well, what? What am I supposed to say? Am I supposed to believe you?"

"Don't you?"

"You said yourself once—a gentleman will lie about this—he'll lie through his teeth to protect a woman's honor—"

"Do you mean to say—my God, do you really mean to say that you don't trust me? You think I'd *lie* to you?"

"Apparently, I've been naive," she says. "To believe that a man could go two years in India without—without copulation. I've been naive to think my husband could face the horrors of war without the chance to relieve his physical needs inside the body of some woman."

"Mrs. MacLeod told you this?"

"Yes."

"With what possible knowledge?"

"Everybody knew. It's the joke of the regiment."

"Everybody knew. I see. Everybody knew. And does everybody also know—does Mrs. MacLeod also know—what exists between *us*, between you and me? Does she know how we met, how we fell in love? Does she understand the particular quality of this bond that ties us together? This passion, does she know about that? Does she think—do *you* think—this is how a man behaves when he's been satisfied elsewhere?"

"She says you went down to Paris regularly, like her husband, on twenty-four-hour passes to see some woman, or women—"

Wilfred turns away, lifts his fist, and slams it against the wall. "I can't, Elfriede. I can't listen to damned Mrs. MacLeod any longer. I can't listen to this."

"You can't tell me she's lying. You can't tell me that any man will go months and years without wanting to fuck somebody."

"A *man*? What about a woman? Don't you burn as I do? Do you think I don't suffer, wondering whether some damned local squire's been sniffing around—and for God's sake, you're the most beautiful woman alive—"

"Me! How can you say such a thing?"

"*Wanting* to fuck somebody. Christ, yes. Didn't you? Yes, God knows, I wanted to fuck somebody during the course of many long months spent away from my wife. I wanted it badly. Yes, during the course of those months, I met women I might have liked to go to bed with, in another life. I daresay you've met a few gentlemen you fancied well enough. But in *this* life—*my* life—I met you instead, I loved you, I worshiped you, I married you, I swore to God I'd take no other women, you swore to God you'd take no other men, and so—amazing, isn't it—I didn't fuck somebody else, I didn't go to bed with this or that woman I met, I went home alone and I dreamed, Elfriede, *dreamed* of what we'd do together when I saw you again. Christ. *Christ*. Some woman in Paris. And there I was an hour ago, actually sobbing, Elfriede, weeping with gratitude in your arms, because I hadn't felt the inside of a woman in seven months, I'd spent in two minutes like a schoolboy, and I thought—I thought—don't laugh—here's what I thought, I was actually thanking God for this wife who understood and forgave me, who could take my passion and fling it right back at me—"

He breaks off just in time to catch Elfriede as she sinks to her knees. Her feet just can't take the strain another instant. Her thick ankles. Wilfred supports her to the bench, a few steps behind, and crashes next to her, panting.

"I went to Paris," he says, "but not to see a woman."

"Then why?"

"Another reason. A bit of a secret, for the moment."

"Oh, a *secret*."

"I've been a beast, I know, a boor, selfish, tyrannical. Whatever you want to call me. I deserve it all. Except that. Don't accuse me of that."

The baby stirs. Kicks out an arm or a leg, like he's testing the water, and Elfriede folds her hands across her stomach and stares at the glimmering shadows where the river lies.

"The problem with leave," Wilfred says softly, "is you have to face what you're missing. All you've lost. In France, on the front, you can just about bear it. Home is just a dream, it's another life, it's like heaven. You can't touch it. Then suddenly you're back. You think, I don't deserve this. I should be with my men, getting killed, instead of making love to my wife. I should be back in hell. I'm no longer fit for heaven."

Elfriede absorbs the green smell of the river, the faint perfume of the night jasmine. A pair of tears rolls away from her left eye, quick quick, drip drip. Then a single one from the right. She wipes them away.

"Then you know," she says. "You know what it's like."

"It?"

"The blackness."

"Elfriede. Darling love. I've always known. I've felt your blackness in my own heart, believe me. When you were sick, I took it inside me. But now it's mine, isn't it? It's my own blackness."

Wilfred's legs stretch out past hers. His long, awkward legs, the same as ever. The body, yes, the body's all Wilfred. How she's adored this flesh! Oh God, how many times, over the years, how many countless times she's strained to unite herself so perfectly with this man's body that—for an instant, anyway, for that moment of union—she might share his soul. And yes, at certain times she *has* felt this communion, she *knows* that sublime fragile existence as a part of Wilfred, Wilfred as a part of Elfriede, each inhabiting the other at the same time. And isn't this the supreme bliss of which humans are capable? Not the physical gratifi-cation, however pleasurable, but the spiritual one. You wake up the next morning and it's still there, you feel as if you're waking from a shared dream, and then the light intrudes and separates you. If you're lucky, when the night returns, you'll find it again. When the night returns, and you can't see his legs properly—they're just shadows—but in the knob of his knee, you recognize yourself. Yes, you! Your own self, in the knob of his knee, and it's so beautiful you can't look away from this thing you don't really even see.

"Elfriede," he says, "I swear before God—"

"Never mind. It doesn't matter."

"Doesn't *matter*? A moment ago it was the *only* thing that mattered!"

"It's just—oh, never mind—I was thinking—"

"Well, it matters to *me*, by God! It matters to *me* that I've kept myself for you, when—"

"Do you remember Florida?"

The knee slips. The air stops. The universe rotates around a single word. The salt sea invades them, sand against skin, the noise of water, the color of twilight. The hot, drowsy air. The trunk of an orange tree.

Wilfred says, "Yes, I remember Florida."

"Those three beautiful weeks. The only real joy we had, before we lost the girls. I remember how we fell asleep each night. I don't think I've ever slept so deeply in my life."

Outside the folly, along the riverbank, the frogs have started up. Or maybe they were croaking all along, and Elfriede's only just noticed them. A lumpy frog chorus, like the chorus of night creatures in Florida, outside her window made sacred by love.

"I remember the morning I saw the blood in my drawers, and how *shocked* I was. I'd thought I must surely be with child, after all we'd done. And it grieved me. I wanted it so. I wanted to be pregnant by you, Wilfred, to grow your child inside me. I still remember that shock and grief, and how I knew, in that moment, just how much I loved you. I loved you so much, I wanted a baby from you. I loved you so much, I forgot all the sorrow. And that was the moment our sorrows began."

"But life is never without sorrow. You can't—Elfriede, you can't mean to say you were unhappy all these years? You can't mean to say that we didn't have our joys, just because there was grief too?"

Elfriede reaches for her husband's hand, which turns out to be folded against his chest, under his arm. She draws it across the arc of her belly to rest near her navel. The baby rumbles around beneath.

"I don't know what I mean. I want it back, that's all."

"Want what back? Florida?"

"You'd been with other women then, when we were apart, and I didn't care, because you were mine. And maybe . . . don't you see? Maybe it doesn't ever matter, as long as—as long as—"

Wilfred's hand pulls free from hers. He takes hold of her sash and unties the knot. He parts the dressing gown and lowers himself on his knees, between her knees, holding her womb between his palms.

"Here's what I remember," he says. "I remember lying in the grass with you. I remember it was hot, I remember licking the salt from your skin. I remember how you took me in your hands. I remember the sound you made when we joined, the exact noise, and how I thought it was a miracle, how could this incandescent woman possibly allow me inside her, how could she possibly love me like this. I remember feeling as if you were consecrating me. When I spent, it was a holy thing. I had never felt so close to God. And we lay there in the grass, and I thought, well, it's done. I'm all hers. I have left myself in her. She's taken my soul into her soul. So I only *live*—I'm only *alive*, how do I explain, I'm only united with my own soul—in her." He presses his mouth against her skin. Her head falls back against the wall. "You might not give a damn about my fidelity, Elfriede, but I do. I can't live without it."

"But I've only brought you misery."

"You've brought me life. I only have life in you."

Now the tears roll from both eyes and down into her ears. She holds his head against her, his lips against her skin.

"You can't die, Elfriede. You cannot die. I'm inside you, I'm existing in you alone. Just allow me to stay, for God's sake."

What can she say? Nothing. She holds his head, that's all, and only makes a low, soft cry when she spends in deep spasms against his mouth. The rest is silence.

WAR OFFICE, LONDON.
TO: MRS. ELFRIEDE THORPE, DUNNOCK LODGE,
INVERNESS

4 JULY 1916

DEEPLY REGRET TO INFORM YOU THAT MAJ W. B.
THORPE KILLED IN ACTION 1 JULY STOP LETTER
FOLLOWS SHORTLY

LULU

JULY 1943
(The Bahamas)

IN THE COURSE of my journalistic research—no snickering, please—I once came across the wedding photographs of the former king of England and his American bride. The service was held in the south of France, I understand, at some magnificent villa owned by a friend of theirs. (Oh, the Windsors and their useful friends.) And if you'd listened to the king's heartfelt address over the radio—*the woman I love*—and you assembled all these facts, the longed-for union, the wealthy friends, the villa, the south of goddamned France, you'd think what a happy couple they must be, married at last in the middle of paradise, troubles consigned to the past and all that. So the photographs might startle you.

I'm told the duchess's dress was made by Mainbocher out of Wallis blue satin, to match her eyes, but of course you can't tell about color in a black-and-white photograph. Suffice to say the dress fits the occasion, long and rather demure, flattering all the same. No surprise there. It's their faces, my God. Her face, and his face. I mean, they're not smiling, either of them. In fact, they remind me of a pair of aristos about to board the tumbrel. She wears an expression of taut stoicism, and he looks scared out of his wits. I believe Cecil Beaton himself took those photographs. I sometimes wonder what he was thinking as he snapped the shutter.

THERE WERE NO CAMERAS AROUND as I took for my second husband, for better or worse, Benedict Wilfred Thorpe—good Lord, what a moniker—in a private service officiated by the former king of England, if you will, witnessed by the notorious Wallis Simpson, his wife, and Miss Jean Drewes of Mamaroneck, who laughed out loud and handed me a bouquet of hibiscus plucked straight from the gardens of Government House. It was a long way from the clerk's office in Niagara, I'll say that, and certainly the groom was a decided improvement. But I'll never know what we looked like, side by side, facing the world as husband and wife for the first time. I do know that my dress was yellow, not blue. The color of old sunshine and telegrams.

The duchess, that miraculous woman, had ordered a proper wedding tea laid out in the formal dining room. We drank two bottles of iced champagne and ate a great deal of cake. Afterward, she took me aside and wished me happiness. There were tears in her eyes, I'm not kidding. We sat on a pair of armchairs in the drawing room while the Duke of Windsor and my brand-new husband laughed and smoked cigars at the mantel. Those Union Jack pillows adorned the sofa nearby. She leaned forward and said, in her throaty voice, "How do you feel? Were you surprised?"

"Awfully."

She laughed. "For a moment, I thought you were going to be sick. That's all right. I felt the same way."

"You? The romance of the century?"

We still held our glasses, the last of the champagne from the two vintage bottles, both of which had been smuggled out of France ahead of the Nazi advance. Wallis looked away from me and toward her own portrait, above the mantel, right between our two chummy husbands. I thought how strange it must be, to sit beneath this monumental version of yourself, day after day. She idled the glass between her fingers and said, "Have you ever been skiing, Lulu?"

"No."

"It's exciting, really. You stare down that slope and you think what a thrilling ride it's going to be. In your head, you map out exactly where you're going to turn, how fast, how damned magnificent you're going to look as you swish your way downward. Then a glorious finish to start all over again. Rapturous applause from the poor slobs waiting at the bottom."

"Sounds like a scream," I said.

"That's the general idea, isn't it? Or nobody would try. So you push off, all dressed up in your fine new skiing clothes, and at first it goes exactly how you expect, just exhilarating fun, everybody admiring how you've mastered the hill. Until you find a patch of ice, maybe, or the slope turns steep, or you take a wrong turn, and all at once you've lost control. You're flying and flying and there's no one to stop you, no one to catch you, no one to save you. The slope becomes your master instead of the other way around. You see the end approaching, and there's nothing you can do to avoid it anymore. You've started the whole thing in motion, and you've got to see it through, no matter how bad the crash at the bottom. How many people you strike down along the way." She lifted the glass to her lips and drained the last of the champagne, all the while staring at her own elegant, painted face, or maybe the two men who stood on either side of it. It was hard to tell from this angle. Thorpe propped his elbow on the mantel, listening to the duke. How I loved that profile of his. That thatch of strawberry-gold on top. The cigar dangled from his hand. As I searched for words, the duchess wiped away a smudge of crimson lipstick from the rim of her glass and added, "Of course, it's different for you, lucky thing."

"Different how?"

"You're so beautifully in love with him." The duchess turned to face me. Her eyes glittered. "Dearest Lulu. May I offer you a word of advice?"

"Yes, of course."

She laid her left hand on my left hand, ring to ring. "Never marry a man thinking you'll change him."

AFTERWARD, THEY OFFERED US THE Government House limousine to take us home, but I said I'd rather start married life in the sidecar of Thorpe's motorcycle. The duchess said I'd ruin the dress. I said I'd take my chances.

"Thanks for everything. The dress, the surprise. The lovely party."

She waved her hand. "Oh, it was my pleasure, Lulu. You know I'm nothing but an old romantic at heart."

I glanced at Thorpe, who was shaking hands with the duke, chortling amicably. The sunlight turned both heads the same shade of golden-white. "I never realized you were a skier."

"I'm not," she said.

I turned back in amazement, but before I could ask a thing, she was hustling me toward the motorcycle.

"Go on, now. I'll have your things sent back by car. Your bicycle and dress."

Thorpe helped me into the sidecar, made sure my dress was tucked inside. I still carried my bouquet of pink hibiscus. The smell reminded me of my bungalow, of Cable Beach, of the bark of the sea grape trees on the edge of the patio. I looked at Thorpe's face, which had lost its smile, and now looked tense with shock. I touched my cheek and realized I felt the same. As I said, thank God there was no Cecil Beaton in Nassau to pop from the bushes and immortalize that.

"Which home, though?" I said. "Mine or yours?"

"Yours. Mine smells like something's got in and died there."

Thorpe went around the side of the motorcycle, climbed aboard, started the engine. From the portico, the duke and duchess, Miss Drewes, Marshall the butler all stood and waved.

"Off we go," said Thorpe, and I tossed my bouquet just as the motorcycle jumped from the curb. I thought I sent it in a nice, clean arc toward Miss Drewes, but when I glanced back, I saw the pink flowers inside the bemused palms of George Marshall.

At the end of Cumberland Street, Thorpe stopped the motorcycle. The British Colonial Hotel loomed before us. To the left, West Bay Street ran along the shore toward Cable Beach. To the right lay the business district, the docks, the ships alongside, the smaller boats bobbing at their moorings. I realized that the trembling came not from the rumble of the idling motorcycle engine, but from within. I glanced up at Thorpe's profile and thought, *My husband.*

FOR NO PARTICULAR REASON, AS the motorcycle turned left down West Bay Street, I thought of Tommy Randolph's funeral. Did I mention it was May when I killed him? Well, it was. It was early May and the air was turning hot in Bakersfield, California, hot and dry, so the medical examiner had packed his body in enough ice to freeze an elephant before they shipped it by train across the country to some mortician chosen by his parents.

The day they buried him, however, the weather had cooled considerably. It was one of those May days in which you can still glimpse the retreating spring, and the air tasted of damp and melancholy. Not grief, mind you. As I said, nobody really mourned Tommy. You saw the relief in everybody's eyes, the guilt at the relief, the narrow, shameful stares at the coffin as the pallbearers inched it into the ground and the breeze picked up as if to hurry them along, get that bastard inside the earth where he belonged, that much closer to hell. The new leaves shivered in the trees. I remember the good reverend father spoke his lines hastily, so that the words slurred together, *Wecommendtoalmightygodourbrotherthomas*, and that a little glint of sunshine caught the lid before it disappeared from view. Then it was all mercifully over and we turned away from Tommy and from each other. I shook hands with the Randolphs without meeting a single eye. My mother was there too, although the twins were both in college, Leo at Harvard (the Lightfoots were Harvard men) and Vanessa at Skidmore, and couldn't come. Or perhaps it was thought best that they didn't come, tender lambs as they were. Meanwhile, my father had avoided the affair on principle—he hadn't attended the wedding, and he damned well wasn't going to attend the funeral—so it was just the two of us on my side, mother and daughter, against the various Randolphs, and I'd like to say that we forged a bond in that moment, that this harrowing encounter brought us close together at last.

But you see, I was still so shocked, so numb with horror at myself. I couldn't speak to my mother at all. I caught her glance only once as they nestled Tommy's coffin in its eternal hole. During the service, they had left the casket open, because a well-placed shot behind the ear leaves your face remarkably unscathed and Tommy's face was the only noble part of him, and as I'd stared at his waxy skin and his eyes for the last time, his lashes that remained as long and lush as in life, I'd felt terrifyingly little emotion. Maybe a speck of pity, that was all. So I was reflecting on this apathy as the breeze nudged my widow's veil, wondering whether it meant I was a monster, a sociopath or whatever they called them, and I happened to glance at my mother just as she was glancing at me, and I saw at once that she knew exactly how Tommy had died. Mothers know, don't they? They gave birth to you and suckled you and tended every inch of you. They can peer straight through your eyes and part the drapes of your soul.

I remember looking away and thinking, *Well, that's that.* I can't return home, not ever. She'll have it out of me, one way or another, and once the deed was committed to words, once it floated free of my mouth and into the atmosphere, it became truth. I had killed my husband with my own hand and a .22 caliber revolver I'd procured myself and hidden in the bedside table. I had killed Thomas Randolph. So my mother and I walked away from that cemetery without saying a word to each other, not a blessed word. She'd returned to my childhood nest in Great Neck, and I'd found a room in a cheap hotel in Murray Hill, and I hadn't seen her since.

Come to think of it, maybe *that* was why I felt this shiver of memory as we sped along West Bay Street. Why the smell of leaves returned to me, the rotting earth, the fear, the breeze that was nothing like the tropical draft that swept against us from the road. Not fear or premonition, or anything like an echo from one husband to the other. It was the opposite. I recalled Tommy's funeral because at that moment, standing before his grave, I'd decided I never would confess. I never would tell a living soul what had happened in Bakersfield.

Surely no person existed whom I could trust like that.

WHEN WE CAME TO MY bungalow, Thorpe stopped the engine and dismounted to help me from the sidecar. The heat billowed from the asphalt, the wind sang. The surf was picking up; you could hear the noise all the way from the road.

To my surprise, the doorknob turned before I had the chance to insert the latchkey. "Hello?" I called.

"Miss Lulu?"

"Veryl!" I went down the hall, just as she emerged from the study, duster in hand. "You're still here? Aren't you supposed to be finishing up at the Prince George?"

"They give me the day off," she said. "Why, what that on you finger?"

I looked at my left hand and saw, rather to my shock, a slim gold band adorned with a row of tiny diamonds. "I got married."

Veryl put her hand to her heart and took a step backward.

"You see, Thorpe came home last night, as I'm sure you noticed, and he asked me to marry him—well, didn't exactly ask—"

"Oh, Lord, Miss Lulu."

"I'm still rather shocked, myself."

"Oh, Lord. Where he at?"

"Putting the motorcycle out back."

I went into the kitchen and pulled a bottle of champagne from the icebox.

"Miss Lulu?" said Veryl, from the doorway. "That fellow be back here today."

"Which fellow?"

"The one be giving you they letters."

I turned from the icebox. "What did you say to him?"

"I say you at the canteen, be home after lunch."

"Well, I won't be back. I'm through with all that. I won't be carrying letters for anybody, from now on."

"That so?"

"That's so. I'm Mrs. Thorpe now, Veryl. I've hitched my wagon to another star."

Veryl still held the duster, dangling from her hand. The ceiling fan was on, rotating the stuffy air above us. I set the bottle on the washboard. "What's the matter, Veryl? Do you have something to say to me?"

She hung the duster from its hook on the wall and straightened her dress. "I does, Miss Lulu. I be giving you notice."

"Notice? Notice of what?"

"Leaving," she said. "Leaving my position. At the end of the month."

"Oh. I see."

"My cousin Iphigenia and me, we be saving up wages. We gwine open a little tea shop, down Victoria Street."

You might have thought she'd have some trouble looking me in the eye with this news, but she didn't. Not Veryl. She tilted her chin and caught me square with those dark, serious peepers of hers and told me her mind in a formal voice. She had finished straightening her dress and her arms hung rigid down her sides like a pair of sticks. She looked awfully brave.

"Well," I said. "This is all rather sudden. I had no idea."

"You been generous, Miss Lulu, and I appreciate that. You paying thirty shillings when the other ladies be paying fifteen—"

"Have they, now?"

"—and I been saving that money, week after week. So we be opening our own tea shop, Effie and me, the fifteenth of August."

The champagne bottle was already dripping sweat. I pushed the hair from my damp forehead. "Well," I said again. "Well, that's grand. I'll be the first one in line. You'll be serving that rum cake of yours, won't you?"

"Now, what does you think, Miss Lulu?"

"Good, good. And if you don't mind asking around the Prince George for another housekeeper, I'd be much obliged."

"I be asking already." She untied the apron from her waist. "One thing more, Miss Lulu."

"What's that?"

Veryl was folding her apron carefully, applying all her concentration to the creases. As always, her hair was parted down the middle and pulled back into a snug knot at the nape of her neck, and though she scraped it all into pitiless order, still the curls made tiny, stubborn ripples all the way down. When she first came to work for me, I used to wonder what it looked like when it was loose, how long it was, whether the curls all sprang back to life as soon as they were set free. Of course, I never did find out. That was the thing about what they called the *color line* around here: neither one of us had the nerve to cross it.

"Well?" I said.

"You be careful, is all."

"Careful? Careful of what? Of Thorpe?"

She looked up. "All them. Them Government House, they friends. Something bad gwine happen, Miss Lulu. Be brewing in the air, like some storm."

"Well, that's why I'm washing my hands of that business, like I told you," I said. "Now where the devil are the champagne glasses, hmm? I thought I put them away."

Veryl stepped to the cupboard and pulled out a pair of coupes, which she set on the counter. "You ain't finished until they-all finished, Miss Lulu. You remember that."

Over the last of her words, Thorpe ducked through the doorway into the kitchen. "Remember what, Miss Veryl?" he said cheerfully. "To make her husband breakfast every morning? Oh, champagne. I knew I married the right sort of woman. I hope you're going to stay and toast us, eh, Veryl? Failing that, you might offer Lulu your condolences."

"Now, stop," she said, as he kissed her cheek. "You gwine down the beach, you two. Never mind Veryl."

"I'll give you a lift home, shall I?"

"No, sir. Bus be rolling by any second. You take good care of my Miss Lulu, now, or you be hearing from the end of my good broom."

When she left, the bungalow turned quiet. The champagne dripped on the counter with the glasses, which Veryl had smuggled in—along with most of the glassware, chinaware, and cutlery, not to mention the towels—piece by piece from the Prince George. The ceiling fan swirled about a centimeter from the top of Thorpe's head, and as I stared at the blur of blades, I felt a premonition come over me. Thorpe stepped closer and kissed my lips. "Everything all right?"

"Everything's just fine," I told him.

THORPE CHIPPED SOME ICE FROM the block in the icebox and filled the champagne bucket, which also bore the Prince George crest. I wandered to the patio and stood there in my yellow silk dress, gazing down the beach to the mounting surf. The sea grape trees bent in the wind. I kicked off my shoes and stepped on the sand, outside the shelter of the patio. Behind me came the sound of Thorpe, setting the bucket and the glasses on the table. I thought we were the only two people alive under this sinking sun, this restless sky. The only two people alive in the world.

"Good evening, Mrs. Thorpe," he said. "It's a fine day to be married, isn't it?"

He stood only a few yards away. I remember thinking that he bore not the slightest resemblance to the man I'd met on a Pan American airliner, two years before. He was his old self, the man I liked to think was the true Thorpe. I thought that this was what he must have been like, before the war came. Charming and spindly, subject to romantic impulse, bristling with new, crisp enthusiasms that seemed odd to other people, and wonderful to the woman who loved him. I thought how ridiculous I must look, my hair all askew, my dress stained with sweat, my lipstick long gone. I thought what a leap of faith he had taken, what a leap I had taken, how we were falling together through an unknown space to land in a foreign country.

He'd removed his jacket, and his shirt was wilted, unbuttoned at the collar. The skin beneath was flushed. He had his hands on his hips, his feet square beneath him, his head bare, his jaw glittering with new stubble. His freckles stood out from his apricot face. His hair spiked from the top of his head like the fur of a puppy. His lips were red and round and damp. I could not comprehend that he belonged to me. I could not imagine us in a neat, rectangular house somewhere, cooing over a baby while the pot roast grew tender in the oven. I couldn't imagine a future for us at all, any kind of future. I thought, this will never work, we're doomed, we haven't got a chance in this crazy world.

Thorpe was grinning, though. He seemed to have forgotten any doubts. He pulled off his shoes and socks and joined me on the sand. I smelled his soap and his sweat. I went on my toes and kissed his nose, his eyes, his chin, his mouth. He snatched my hand and dragged me down to the water, where we plunged into the roiling surf and kissed some more, kissed with hysterical abandon, because we were married now and it was our right to kiss each other in full view of the world. Eventually the surf became too rough, the kissing too important, and we staggered back onto the beach. The dress came off, the trousers, the shirt, all ruined. We moved into the shadow of the patio. I saw the bruises on his ribs, the scar on his jaw, the profuse nicks and flaws on the surface of his skin. I pressed my fingertips on his collarbone, then my lips. I said clearly, "Don't go back to London."

He didn't answer. I don't know if he heard me. His pupils were giant in his blue eyes, his skin was flushed. This husband of mine wasn't looking at my face, no, he was looking at my breasts and the dent of my waist. He was lifting me into the hammock that hung between the sea grape trees. I mouthed the words, *Don't go back, don't go back, don't go back*, and I must say they formed a nice syncopation to the beat of his pale, bony hips. *Don't go back, don't go back*. We swayed dangerously in the hammock. The hot air pooled in the hollows of our bones. We were married, we were made into a single, sacred flesh, consecrated by the holy water of our mutual perspiration. I gathered his wet buttocks in my hands and arched my back. He came an instant later. *Don't go back*, I gasped, but he was already gone. The hammock swung with our dead weight. The sea grapes groaned with it.

WE REMAINED OUTSIDE ALL EVENING, in the ocean, in the shade of
the sea grapes, drinking champagne. Thorpe was right, nobody else
was outside on a day like this, at least not at this end of the beach. The
surf was picking up mightily, in big, urgent waves. Thorpe had once explained the science of them, how a single ripple traveled across miles of
ocean, and I was entranced by the idea of this packet of energy passing
between molecules of water, the way sound travels through air, the way
light travels through space. I stuck my toes in the water and thought,
*This wave began with a gust of wind, and that gust of wind began as a beam
of sunlight warming the air, and that beam of sunlight began as a fusion of
atoms inside the sun, and that fusion of atoms* . . . well, here I got a little
murky, but you see what I mean. This wave now breaking on the beach
had a whole history of its own, which I could never learn, just as we're all
upon this earth ignorant of the vast, complicated histories of those living alongside us. Why, on the other side of this very ocean, men were
blowing each other to pieces; at this very moment, some fellow lay on
the sands of North Africa in the act of dying, bleeding, suffering, while
I stood here on the sands of Nassau and knew nothing about him or the
hearts due to shatter at his passing. You look out into the teeming air,
and you have no idea what's going on outside your own square yard of it.

I mention all this because I remember how the gathering storm sent
us scurrying back indoors at half past ten o'clock, and while we did this,
a few miles away, Harold Christie was finishing up a game of checkers
with Sir Harry Oakes and a couple of dinner guests at Westbourne. But
of course I didn't know that fact, at the time. Of all that happened at
Westbourne that night, I was blissfully unaware until later.

THORPE AND I SCURRIED INDOORS, as I said, and closed the shutters against the spitting rain and the gusts of tropical wind. A flash of
lightning illuminated the sky, and the crack of thunder followed swiftly.

Thorpe asked me if I was afraid of storms, and I said I hated the damn things, you never knew what might happen in a storm.

We crawled between the sheets. Having made love twice already, marriage safely consummated, we felt no urgency. I stretched back and wiggled my toes, and Thorpe lay on his side against me and examined every inch of my figure while the rain beat noisily against the shutters and the tin roof. He spread his hand over my stomach, a gesture I loved for some reason. The sensation of that palm on my navel.

"Tell me something," I said. "Why were you recalled to London?"

The room was dark and motionless, only the sway of the electric fan, while all hell slammed against the walls of our cottage. I kicked off the sheets from my legs.

"Well?" I urged.

"Can't say."

"Can't you? Your own wife?"

"It isn't a question of trust."

"Isn't it?" I said, and when there was no answer I went on in a loud whisper near his ear, so he could hear me over the storm. "You've put them in a bind, haven't you. Those chaps of yours, back in London. You did your job too well. And now they know you know about the whole thing. You know the duke's a traitor."

Thorpe reached out and put his finger on my lips. I pushed his hand away and linked my fingers at the back of his neck.

"Let's fly away. You can't go back. They'll never let you live with this knowledge in your head. Fly away with me."

"No."

"One of the Out Islands, maybe, or somewhere else. The other side of the world. Indochina, maybe. Have the Japs invaded there yet? Or Tasmania."

"We can't go to Tasmania, Lulu."

"Just think. The two of us. I'll make you happy, I swear it, we'll have our own little world together, a little home, sunshine and babies and—"

"No," he said.

"But—"

"No." He rolled on his back. Side by side, we stared at the ceiling, and the shadow of the electric fan as it swept the air. Outside the window, the rain poured down on the roof, drowning out the noise of the thunder. His pale skin stretched across his ribs. I thought of the rubbers in the nearby drawer, untouched.

"When do you leave?" I said.

"Tomorrow. They've got a place for me on a Liberator leaving at dawn."

"At *dawn*?"

"Yes."

"Dawn *tomorrow*?"

"Yes."

"Exactly when were you going to tell me this?"

"I'm telling you now."

For an instant, a streak of lightning turned the room as bright as noon. A boom shook the house. We lay there on the bed, holding hands, and waited for it to pass. Another streak, another boom. Underneath it all, the rain roared on the metal roof, and the tears ran from the corners of my eyes and down my temples to the pillow, because I understood. Now I understood.

"Do you remember what we said to each other on the airplane?" I said.

"Every word."

"Is that so?"

"Try me."

"Well, you remember how I called the Windsors a pair of romantics, and you said they weren't romantics at all?"

"I remember."

"You said that it was a modern thing to do, choosing love over duty."

"Ah, yes. Rather facile of me, wasn't it?"

"You mean you don't believe that now?"

"I mean, at that point, I'd never really loved a woman before. I didn't know what sacrifice meant."

"Maybe the duke didn't know about sacrifice, either. I don't believe he ever really wanted to be king. Do you?"

Thorpe released my hand and reached over to the bedside table to find a pack of cigarettes. He offered it first to me. I shook my head. He tapped one out for himself and produced a match. "Well, I imagine he wanted the privilege of kingship, right enough. It was the responsibility that went with the privilege, that's what he didn't want." He lit the cigarette and smoked it thoughtfully, one arm tucked behind his head.

"Yes. He discovered that being king didn't mean you *could* have anything you wanted, but that you *couldn't*. And he wanted *her*."

"Yes. And he got her. *And* his freedom."

I rolled on my side to face him. The lightning came again, the wind howled against the walls.

"My God," I said. "*You're* the romantic, aren't you?"

"Rubbish."

"Yes, it's true. I see it now."

"You see what you want to see. The truth is, I've betrayed every ideal I ever held. I've killed men who never saw me coming. I've lied and stolen. Then you. I saw you and wanted you and seduced you—"

"You fell in love with me."

He shrugged and reached for the ashtray. "I was also searching your papers, allowing you to continue serving as a courier for information that was more than your life was worth, at least to the men on either side of it."

"But I knew. I let you."

"I betrayed you."

"And you hated yourself for it. And I loved you for hating yourself. I love both sides of you, the sweet, idealistic boy you were before, and the man you've had to become."

Thorpe reached over to the ashtray and crushed out the cigarette. I glimpsed the side of his face as he returned his head to the pillow and folded his two hands beneath. "My parents are both dead," he said, and though the thunder covered his words, I still understood him. "I was raised by my grandmother, who still lives in our old place in Scotland, outside of Inverness, with one of the maids who takes care of her. She's going a bit soft in the head these days, I'm afraid, but she's the sort of woman who will probably outlive us all."

"Why are you telling me this?"

He turned his head on the pillow and stared at me, though he couldn't have seen much, just the reflection of light in my eyes and the bridge of my nose, my cheekbones, the way I saw his. "My half brother lives in Florida, up the coast. My mother's son with her first husband, a German. His name is Johann."

"Johann," I repeated.

"My sister's name is Margaret. Margaret Thorpe. She never married. She lives in London, Draycott Avenue, works for the War Office. If anything should happen to me, go to one of them."

"If anything happens to you, I'll track you down to the ends of the earth, by God. I promise you that."

He was staring at me the way you stare at a painting, at an altar. He seemed to be straining for something. I thought, *Just take it, for God's sake.* He looked nothing like the boy on the beach when we arrived a few hours ago. He cupped his hand around my jaw. When the lightning came, I saw a silver track along the side of his cheek, falling into the scar.

"I believe you," he said. He dragged me over his hips. When we had fit ourselves together, from base to stem, he wrapped his arms around my waist, and I wrapped my arms around his neck, and so we remained, stock-still in the rumpled sheets, while the storm raged and crashed out-side the window.

OVER AT WESTBOURNE, HAROLD CHRISTIE had picked up a copy of *Life* magazine and headed to his guest room, adjacent to the bedroom of Sir Harry Oakes. Oakes retired soon after. He drew the mosquito netting around his bed, took a revolver from the drawer of his bedside table and laid it under the lamp, as was his usual habit, and settled himself to sleep.

IT WAS SOME TIME BEFORE Thorpe and I went to sleep. I don't know exactly how long we made love, just that it went on without end, that we were afraid to stop. Maybe we felt some kind of premonition, I don't know. Maybe we were simply wise enough to take what we could from each other, to stockpile what we needed, like squirrels who understand there's a long winter ahead. I couldn't get enough of his skin, or the little hairs that grew in a trail below his navel, or the tips of his fingers. His hip bones, his eyelashes, the smell of his hair. I was delirious, I was woozy with him.

At one point, we wandered into the kitchen for the pitcher of water in the icebox. When we had finished drinking, he drew me back against him, one palm on my breast, one palm on my womb, his teeth at my shoulder, and we stood there, perfectly balanced, listening to the fury outside.

I said, "When did your parents die?"

My head swam from pleasure and fatigue and dread. I was leaning against him, I knew, suffering him to bear my weight, because my legs had already given him all they could. I listened to his silence, and at last I put my hand on top of his.

"My father was killed at the Somme," he said at last, "about two months before I was born."

"Oh. Oh, no. No."

"Margaret was nine years old, nearly ten. He was a career officer, a major in the army. Went down gloriously, of course, for king and country."

"But your mother."

"Well, they were deeply in love, from what I was told."

There was a long pause, in which the shutter over the kitchen window came loose from its mooring and started to bang. *Bam, bam, bam,* like someone pitching rocks at the wall. Neither of us moved. His mouth was in my hair; I felt his breath near my ear, shuddering a little. We smelled of each other, of perspiration and human love, of salt and ozone. I turned in his arms and looked in his bleak eyes, his pale, freckled face that glittered with stubble.

"They were deeply in love," I said.

"Yes, they were. So deeply, in fact, that she drowned herself in the river shortly after giving birth to me."

WE WENT BACK TO BED. Thorpe turned me on my side, eased back inside me, and came at last in a series of quick, sure spasms. In the next instant, he was asleep, and so was I.

And at some point, either before or after this final culmination of ours—nobody can say exactly when—a person or persons entered the bedroom of Sir Harry Oakes, struck him three times behind the left ear with an object also unknown, covered him with feathers and gasoline, and set fire to his body.

I CAME AWAKE TO AN empty bed, some hours later, and called Thorpe's name. He arrived instantly, dressed and smelling of soap.

"What's the matter?" I murmured, reaching for him.

"Time for me to go." He kissed my lips and set my arms back in the bed. "I'll come back to you as soon as I can."

ELFRIEDE

AUGUST 1916
(Scotland)

ON THEIR ELEVENTH wedding anniversary, the day Elfriede goes into labor with their second child, Wilfred's kit arrives home at last. There was some delay, explained in official letters and telegrams that Elfriede didn't read. Anyway, there it sits on the library rug, delivered by special courier along with a note from Wilfred's batman that describes how carefully, how reverently the contents were packed up. How beloved Major Thorpe was, how cruel his loss for the men. Those who remained alive, anyway, after that disastrous July day on the Somme.

These are words Elfriede will read later, however. For now, the letters remain stacked on her desk, unopened. Dozens of them, from Wilfred's men, from his fellow officers, from the War Office, from this batman of his. Private Collins, who's been with Wilfred since India and is now shattered.

She notices the smell first. Like a charnel house, like the mud of a thousand dead men. And then the sound of screaming, Margaret screaming. Elfriede runs, or rather lumbers, toward the source of both sensations, smell and screaming, and that's when she sees what remains of her husband. Some canvas thing, and Margaret collapsed on top, wailing in primal agony.

As for Elfriede, she hasn't wept yet. Not a single tear. They simply won't come. Margaret cries for them both. Wilfred's daughter hasn't stopped shedding tears for her father, it's like a fall of continuous grief, never ending, and Elfriede must be her sponge. Her Cloth of Tears.

SO PROVE IT. THERE'S NOTHING real about Wilfred's death, is there? If Wilfred were really dead, Elfriede—his lover, his wife, his blood companion, the mother of his children, she who harbors Wilfred's heart inside her own chest, his soul inside her own skin—if he were dead, she'd feel his death in her bones, in the corridors of her body, and she feels nothing at all except the kick of Wilfred's baby in her womb, and the wetness of Margaret's tears on her chest, her arm, her lap. (What there remains of her lap, anyway.) Well, really. How can those blue eyes be closed? How can those limbs, which were made to tangle around hers, made for this single purpose and none other, to hold and soothe and make love to Elfriede—how can those limbs have gone still? How can that mind, which was made to give laughter and life to others, be lifeless? It's impossible, obviously. No physical evidence whatsoever exists to prove that Wilfred Thorpe is dead.

Except, perhaps, this lump of canvas, on which their daughter weeps.

Elfriede staggers carefully to her knees and pulls Margaret into her arms. She sits on the floor with Wilfred's children, born and unborn, and holds them close. Margaret's sobs take the form of words—*I can't, I can't live without him, he can't be dead*—and Elfriede answers her in kind. *He's not, darling, he'll always be with us, Daddy would never leave us.* The baby, who knows nothing of the outside world, just throws out an elbow or a foot or something. Elfriede thinks of that last night of Wilfred's leave, and the way the baby shifted and turned between them, making his father laugh for possibly the first time in the entire five days he'd been home. *He's a busy chap, right enough,* Wilfred said, and Elfriede, lying on her side, facing her husband, drinking the gentle sound of his laughter, put her hand on his cheek and said, *Like his father.* More laughter, and *Are you quite certain of that, my love? A chap at the front has to take his wife's word on these matters,* so naturally she pondered for a minute and replied, *Well, it's either you or Jock Cholmondeley, every other man's gone off to France,* and Wilfred smacked his forehead and said, *Cholmondeley, that rascal! I always knew he was in love with you,* and pretty soon they were giggling like old times, like before the war, like Florida, and one thing led to another until Wilfred and Elfriede, baby or no baby, were once more exchanging proofs of their enthusiastic devotion to each other, like before the war, like Florida. How could you be more alive than that?

When Margaret's wailing subsides at last into hiccups, Elfriede calls for the downstairs maid, who appears almost at once. Pale, stricken face. Even the household staff adores Wilfred.

"Annie, I need your help with Mr. Thorpe's kit," she says, matter-of-fact.

"Shall I—" The maid gulps fearfully. "Shall I unpack it for you, ma'am?"

"Unpack it? No. You must bury it. Bury it in the garden, I don't care where. Just bury it." She strokes her daughter's hair and bends awkwardly to kiss the small, trembling ear. "It upsets the children."

"B—bury it?"

"Yes. Straight away. What are you waiting for? Bury it!"

And Annie scrambles to obey.

SOON AFTERWARD, THE SPORADIC TIGHTENING of the muscles around her womb strengthens into regular, progressively deep contractions. She takes Margaret to her grandmother, who's been living in the guest bedroom at Dunnock Lodge since July, managing the household in a spirit of tremendous Scotch efficiency, and rings up the doctor herself. "It seems to be advancing quickly," she tells him calmly, and he promises to be on his way at once.

On her way back upstairs, she pauses outside the music room while a contraction grips her. They're boiling the water in the kitchen, preparing the linens. There's a baby on the way, after all, poor Major Thorpe's wee babe, we must all do our bit for the major's sake. Elfriede rides out the pain the way you ride a wave in the Atlantic surf, don't fight it, let the wave do the work, let the wave carry you into shore. She holds herself upright on the doorframe and stares at the piano, remembering how Margaret played for them both on that last evening, before Wilfred returned to the front, and Wilfred himself took his daughter upstairs to tuck her into bed a final time while Elfriede, wanting them to have this moment of private farewell, stayed downstairs and played Chopin. Wilfred, returning, came to a stop in the doorway, exactly where Elfriede stands now in the iron-hot fist of a contraction. *What's the matter?* she asked then, looking up to find his strange expression. *You played that in Switzerland,* he told her. *That one always reminds me of Switzerland.* She finished the piece and Wilfred came to sit by her on the piano bench, saying nothing at all, just sitting and staring at Elfriede's hands on the keyboard.

When the contraction subsides, Elfriede lets go of the doorframe and continues to the stairs, up to the bedroom, where her maid, Mary, summoned from the mending, waits anxiously to change her into a white nightgown.

"You'll be just fine, ma'am," Mary says, for the third time. "Only think, a beautiful new baby to remember him by, a precious wee gift from the Lord. You'll be safe in His hands, ma'am."

Elfriede knows better, of course. When the nightgown is on and the dressing gown draped over her hardened belly, she checks the dresser to make sure the Cloth of Tears sits in place, folded neatly in its box in the far corner. In her head, she hears Wilfred's voice, over and over.

You cannot die.

I'm existing in you alone.

She settles herself in the armchair to wait for the doctor.

A MERE HOUR AND A half later, Elfriede gives birth to an enormous boy, nine pounds four ounces, as the British measure these things, burly and red-faced, squalling handsomely. The tuft of hair on his head is paler than his father's but unmistakably ginger. Elfriede touches it with her finger as he nurses. "Well, there's no doubt who's his dear father," Mrs. Thorpe says weepily, holding the entranced and dry-eyed Margaret close to her side.

"No doubt at all," says Elfriede, and she waits for the blackness to descend.

LULU

DECEMBER 1943
(Scotland)

THE DRIZZLE COMES in angry bursts against our backs, blowing in from the northeast. Margaret settles her chin inside the collar of her raincoat and her hands inside her pockets. We both wear rubber boots that squish against the grass as we walk. Mine are too big. Margaret tells me they belonged to Thorpe when he was thirteen or so. Just before he started sprouting up, she says.

Behind us, Dunnock Lodge is grim and wet and rambling, like Wuthering Heights or something. The slate roof gleams with rain. We tramp across a meadow that looks as if it used to be a lawn, and sure enough, a fountain emerges from the thickets. When I peer into the bowl, I see about three inches of brown water covering a layer of dead leaves.

"It's where Mummy used to have garden parties for the officers' wives," Margaret says. "She tried so hard, and they never did like her, except for a few. She was so beautiful. Jolly foreign too, which set their backs up. And of course she wasn't cheerful or chirpy, either, at least with them. She kept herself hidden from them."

"Didn't she have any friends at all?"

"One or two. I think they knew she had this dark place inside her, and they were afraid of it. They were afraid of getting sucked in. Even Granny. Only Daddy wasn't afraid."

The drizzle's paused, and she's smoking again, staring into the bowl of the fountain. Outdoors, her eyes are very blue, almost as blue as her brother's. Her pale hair lashes against her cheek.

"You noticed a lot for a ten-year-old."

"I sometimes think I was soaking up the details on purpose. I remember so clearly the last time I saw Daddy. He had to leave early for the station, to go back to the front, and I was supposed to be asleep. But the sun rises so early in June, you know. I looked out the window and saw them in the drive, Mummy and Daddy. It was only half past four, and he helped Mummy climb into our old Wolseley—she was expecting Benedict, she was just enormous with him—and then he got into the driver's seat. He was wearing his uniform, no overcoat. I remember wishing he would take off his hat so I could see his hair. He had the most wonderful hair. It was much redder than Benedict's, like flame." She tosses the cigarette in the water. "And that was it. They drove away. The telegram arrived a week later."

"It was the Somme, wasn't it?"

"Yes. The very first day. One of his captains went down in the first surge, and most of the lieutenants, so he picked up his rifle and led the company himself. He was a major, a career officer. So he knew, you see. He knew what war was about." A wave of drizzle comes across the meadow. She squints angrily at the sky. "Come along. There's a place we can shelter."

I'd like to tell her that I don't want to shelter, that I welcome the hardship of a cold rain, but she's already tramping onward. The ground's begun to slope, the bare trees to gather. I smell the river before I see it, a giant, teeming perfume of freshness and rot. The branches part, and there it is, about a quarter mile across, brown and rambunctious with rainfall. Inside the shelter of the trees, the larks sing earnestly. It's December, after all, and no time for fun and games.

"That's where my mother drowned herself," Margaret says. She lifts her arm and points to a ruined building, choked with vines, on a small island connected to the riverbank by a footbridge. "It was November, a few months after Benedict was born. She would feed him and put him to bed and then come here, in the middle of the night. And one night she just went down those steps and didn't come back. I woke up to this terrible fuss. Benedict was screaming for milk, and the maids were crying, and all these men were tramping over our lawn. Granny had taken charge, she was giving people orders left and right. I saw them carrying Mummy into the ambulance. She died in hospital a few hours later. They wouldn't let me see her, the disgrace was too awful. And she couldn't be buried in consecrated ground, so they had to bury her on the estate."

"Where?"

Margaret swivels and points back toward the house. "Somewhere over there. Granny took charge of that too. It was all such an awful disgrace, she didn't invite anybody. I wasn't allowed to go, it was just Granny and her sisters and the minister, so I never got to properly say good-bye. It's not even marked. Mummy wanted to be buried next to my father's kit, apparently."

"His kit?"

"His kit bag. It came home after he died, and Mummy couldn't bear it, so she made Annie bury the thing."

"Oh, poor Annie."

"It was jolly awful for her, I imagine. Everybody adored Daddy. He was the most—the best—the most wonderful—"

I don't say a word. What can I possibly say? I kneel in the clean-smelling mud next to Margaret while she goes to pieces. The larks keep on yammering, as if nothing's happened.

WHEN WE RETURN, MARGARET CLIMBS the stairs for a nap, and I return outside. I'm too restless to lie down, my head too crammed with new ideas, new images, this damp, heartbroken childhood of Thorpe's.

The drizzle's eased, leaving behind a bleak landscape, December gray. I walk past the carriage house and its air of abandonment, its missing roof tiles, broken door. I think how it must have looked thirty years ago, and how long it's been left like this. Whether Thorpe might have learned to ride a pony here, or whether the decline had already begun. The ground's soft beneath my boots, the grass limp and dying. I realize I'm headed toward the place Margaret pointed out, the place where Thorpe's mother is buried, next to the effects of her husband, but when I reach that place, the general area indicated by that long finger, there's nothing to see. No marker of any kind. The same grass, the edge of a thicket. And yet they're there, the two of them. The grief, it's inside the soil.

I hear the sound of squishing footsteps an instant before the brisk Scotch voice. "You ought not to be out like this, Mrs. Thorpe."

"Annie! You startled me."

"You ought to be inside, where it's warm."

"I don't mind the cold. It makes me feel closer to him."

"Won't do him a bit of good, though. Nor his babe."

I nod toward the thicket. "Is that where they're buried?"

She hesitates. "Who, ma'am?"

"Margaret said they're buried here. Her mother and—well, not her father, but his kit bag. You buried it."

"Yes, ma'am," she says, but there's a note to her voice that sets something stirring in me. You know how it is when you've been reporting on people's tittle-tattle for the past two years. You recognize the sound of someone wanting to unburden herself. I turn my head. She's wearing a worn raincoat, worn rubber boots that must be several sizes too big for her, a strange floppy oilskin hat like something a fisherman would wear in a gale. Her hands fret about inside her pockets.

"Something the matter, Annie?" I ask.

"Poor Master Benedict. Poor lad. Just like his father. And you! Expecting a wee babe, just like his mother."

"I'm not anything like his mother."

"Oh, but you are. There's only a few who love like that. Only a few that can bear it."

"But she didn't bear it, did she? When he died, she couldn't bear it." I gesture to the thicket. "She made you bury his things."

"That was just the darkness in her, ma'am. I knew she didn't mean it. She had a darkness in her, like my mum had. Came on when she had her babes. Poor wee thing. I knew she didn't mean it."

She's looking off into the thicket now, as if she sees something inside it. I turn to face her, and still she doesn't regard me, so I reach out to take her elbow. I left my gloves behind, and my hands are wet and raw, and her raincoat is about the same.

"What does that mean, Annie? What are you trying to say?"

"I did keep it safe, ma'am. All these years. The poor dear major. It wasn't right to bury his things in the dirt."

LULU

I WOKE TO the sound of a ringing telephone, sometime past eight o'clock in the morning. At first I thought it must be Thorpe, but then I remembered how, a few hours earlier, I had settled in the dark sand and watched the sun crawl over the edge of the world, until the drone of the Liberators merged into the noise of the ocean and Thorpe was gone, my husband was gone, and I had staggered back to bed.

The telephone persisted shrilly. There was no closing your ears to a sound like that, repeated over and over by a person who evidently meant to get his point across, one way or another. I raised my head from the pillow. My brain ached with champagne and sorrow. I lifted my hand to the sun that splintered through the shutters and saw the ring on my finger like an exotic object, a thing never before seen in human history, a band of gold clamped above my knuckle. I rolled over and fell from the bed, aching in every joint and sinew, each tendon screaming with its own particular anguish. Like the telephone, over and over. I stumbled naked out of the room and found the receiver in the parlor. The shutters were still closed, the room streaked with bands of light.

"Hello?" I said.

A man's voice. "Mrs. Randolph."

"Who's this?"

A rush of static came over the line, like the fellow at the other end was simply breathing into the mouthpiece, considering his words. "Mrs. Randolph, it's Jack," he said at last.

"Jack! Jack from the Prince George?"

"That's right."

"You're up awfully early. Say, I've got a little news for you—"

"Listen, Mrs. Randolph. It's important. You got a minute?"

"Sure I do. But it's not Mrs. Randolph anymore, you know. It's—"

"I know, I know." He made a sound of impatience, a grunt. "Listen up. You heard the news about Oakes?"

"Sir Harry? What about him? Has he left town already?"

"He's left town, all right," said Jack. "He's dead. Murdered last night in his own bed."

JACK WANTED TO MEET ME all the way out at Lyford Cay, an odd and awfully inconvenient location, because he had something important to tell me, and you couldn't trust a telephone line not to have an operator listening at the other end. I was shaking a little, from shock and lack of sleep. I asked what about, and he said he couldn't say, just that it was important, Mrs. Rand— Mrs. Thorpe. I said I had my shift at the canteen, the ladies were counting on me, which was true. I said how about after lunch, and he hesitated and said all right, in such a way that I felt it wasn't all right at all. Then he hung up so suddenly, the telephone swallowed the last of his words to me.

Sometimes I wonder how things might have turned out if I changed my mind and called in sick, as I had any right to do, having just been married the day before and seen my new husband off to jolly England a few hours later. But you can't second-guess yourself, I've found. You don't know what lies in that parallel dimension, you don't know what fate is contained inside those infinite hypothetical worlds in which you made other choices. Anyway, what can you do about them? They're like the past itself, they're gone. You can't just get on your bicycle and travel there.

In this world, the world in which I hung up the telephone and stared at the wall and said to myself, *Harry Oakes is dead, he's been murdered*; the world in which I ran a bath and scrubbed away the sweat and salt, the remnants of Thorpe from the hollows of my body, and the water felt like ice on my skin; in which I dressed and brushed my hair and bicycled to the canteen, repeating *Harry Oakes is dead* to the rhythm of the bicycle wheels, and served a hundred and seventeen men their bacon and eggs and coffee; in which I pieced together gossip about what was happening down at Westbourne—most of which turned out to be false—and then borrowed Mrs. Gudewill's Buick for the ride out to Lyford Cay: in this world, in this history I now recount, I never did discover what Jack meant to say to me, and whether it would have made a difference.

IN DISREGARD OF THE HEAVY sky, I drove Mrs. Gudewill's Buick with the top down, all the way along New Providence Island while the draft warped around me and the ocean spread out to the horizon. I passed the drive to Westbourne, now crawling with men, without stopping. *Harry Oakes is dead*, I thought, but still the words made no sense, so I kept driving. The white beaches went by, mile after mile, and I thought how lovely it would be to stop and bathe in that sea, to lie on that beach with your lover, your husband, the sand on your skin, his hair in your hands. The road streaked west along the extreme edge of the coast, while the palmettos and the scrub crawled past on my left. Above the pitch of the Buick's engine, I heard a different noise, deeper and larger, and I looked up and saw a massive airplane dropping gracefully from the hazy sky, wheels down, aiming for Windsor Field. The din was enormous, like the end of the world. Foolishly I ducked my head as it passed. The screech of tires followed a moment later. Ahead, I saw a commotion to the right, away from the road, on the beach. I brought the automobile to a stop.

For a moment or so, I rested my toes on the brake pedal and stared at the knot of fishermen who were hauling a bundle of wet clothing with great proficiency over the side of their boat. My fingers turned cold on the steering wheel, though the day was as hot as ever, the air turgid in the wake of last night's storms. I got out of the car and walked closer. A couple of men stood by, arms folded, and I asked them what was happening.

"There's a body." He pointed to the water. "They found a body in the harbor."

"*Who?*"

The fellow shrugged. "Never seen him before."

I worked my way closer, until I saw them lay out the body on the damp, hard sand. I wondered why nobody had called the police, and then I remembered the police were dealing with matters at Westbourne. As they arranged the fellow just so, his wet clothes sopped around his body, his head lolled to one side, for an instant—and just for that instant—I caught a glimpse of his blanched face. In my shock, I thought it was Tommy. That was the only dead man I had ever seen until now, so irrationally I saw that pasty skin and those blank open eyes and screamed to myself, *Tommy!* and my body reacted accordingly, the jolt of energy, the splintering of nerves against the skin.

Then I saw his ears that stuck out like wings from his head, and I knew it wasn't Tommy, of course not. Tommy lay beneath the earth of Queens in the Randolph family plot, under a headstone that nobody visited or cared for, because Tommy had been the kind of fellow to raise love in someone's heart only to slay it afterward, until nothing was left of that love. But Tommy was a handsome devil with neat, flat ears. This face belonged to the man I knew as Mr. Smith, the man who'd delivered to me the envelopes addressed to the Duke and Duchess of Windsor.

OF LYFORD CAY, HAROLD CHRISTIE'S great dream, for which he had mortgaged himself to Sir Harry Oakes, there wasn't yet much. He had spent a fortune laying out pipes from the other end of New Providence Island for water and electricity and so on, but all the houses and golf courses and tennis courts had yet to be built. Lyford Cay was just an investment, was a piece of land cleared of scrub and pine and swamp and waiting for a future.

I waited some time at the entrance to Lyford Cay, but Jack never turned up. Only some workmen, back and forth, who took no notice of me. I found a rock to sit on and tried to seize some kind of control of my rattled nerves. I felt as I had in the days after I killed Tommy Randolph, like I had been flattened out by God's rolling pin, and though my body strained for sleep and my head felt like it was made of dough, my brain kept spinning round and round inside. I mean, could you blame me? A day earlier I had stood inside the drawing room at Government House and been married to Benedict Thorpe by the Duke of Windsor. Now my husband was gone across the ocean, Sir Harry Oakes was dead, Mr. Smith was dead, and it seemed to me that evil seeped from the stones around me and hung in the air like a cloud of poison gas. I started breathing in shallow sips, so as not to draw it into my lungs. My watch ticked away. An hour passed. Across the empty, landscaped ground of Lyford Cay there was a marina, and I remember thinking what a remote, convenient location it was, that dock, if you wanted to land on New Providence Island incognito, or depart it the same way, with no more noise or notice than a cloud of poison gas, say.

Or maybe I'm remembering wrong. Maybe I had this thought later, in the weeks before the trial, when stories of the night of Oakes's murder began to sift into my ears.

Eventually I got into the car and drove back to the canteen, exhausted. The fishermen on the beach with the dead body had left by now, but the crowd remained milling outside of Westbourne as I passed. I didn't stop, I made straight for the canteen and returned the keys to Mrs. Gudewill. I had the feeling that I didn't want to know, I had no desire at all to learn how poor Sir Harry had died. Instead I got on my bicycle and pedaled into town through the same taut, warm silence. I walked straight into the Prince George hotel in my canteen uniform, wet with perspiration, but Jack wasn't there, he wasn't anywhere. Like a lot of fellows over the course of those strange months following the murder of Sir Harry Oakes, he had simply disappeared.

THE NEXT DAY, WHEN I bicycled to the canteen, the ladies were all abuzz with the news. Had I heard? The chief prosecutor of the Bahamas had arrested a man and charged him with the murder of Sir Harry Oakes.

Not, as you might expect, the fellow who had slept in the adjoining bedroom the night of the murder, who had discovered the body the next day, who had been in debt to the dead man to the tune of untold thousands of pounds.

No, they arrested Alfred de Marigny, the son-in-law of Sir Harry Oakes. After all, the two of them were known to be on the outs, and de Marigny was a scoundrel of a man, a fortune hunter, a mountebank.

LULU

DECEMBER 1943
(Scotland)

I DON'T UNDERSTAND," Margaret says to Annie. "Why didn't you tell me?"

"Why, you were too young, Miss Margaret. And then I was too old and forgot."

"How could you forget a thing like this?" She sinks into the straw and lifts her hand to touch this thing, this brown canvas bag, the leather straps, one by one, the way you might touch a holy relic.

We're speaking inside the hayloft of the carriage house. They hay is largely gone, as you might expect, and the bag's sitting snug underneath the eaves. When she first deposited it here, Annie covered it with a striped horse blanket, which she now holds in her hands, folding and unfolding and folding again. The rain drums softly against the roof and drips in places to the floor.

I kneel next to her on the old wooden floor, the bits of hay and dust. The air is musty, but if you taste it carefully inside the chambers of your nose, there's a horse there somewhere, long absent from the stalls below. There's also the smell of gasoline, because the Morris occupies the center hall, next to a stately old brougham, coated in dust. Margaret's in some kind of trance, just staring and staring at something nobody else can see, some memory. I say gently, "Should I open it? Or do you want to do it?"

"No, you do it."

I unbuckle the straps, which is no easy chore, believe me. The leather's stiff, the metal rusted. At last they pull apart, and I lift the flap at the top and reach inside. One by one, I pull out the objects, the socks, the field dressings, the gun oil, the gas mask, the shirts, the soap, the mess kit, the shaving kit—

Margaret snatches up the shaving kit and unties the knot with her fingernails, *pick pick pick*, until at last it comes loose and the belt unrolls, the scissors and razor and brush all stuck in their little slots, gleaming as if they were new. She pulls out the scissors and touches the tip with her fingers, and I think of my bathroom on Cable Beach, and how I kept shaving soap and razor and toothbrush in the cabinet, and how I liked to lean against the windowsill and watch my lover shave, fascinated at his concentration, the series of contortions, the new pink skin revealed in the stroke of the razor, the smell of the soap, his naked shoulders. How, when he was gone, I would sometimes rise in the middle of the night and take the razor from its jar and inspect the blade to see if some tiny hair still clung to the edge, some relic of Thorpe.

An hour passes. Margaret inspects each item, strokes it, sniffs it. She doesn't cry, she doesn't say a word. I think it's too much for tears, too much for her to comprehend all at once like this. Annie sits with her knees to her chest, her arms wrapped around her legs, watching us. At one point she checks her watch and says old Mrs. Thorpe will want her lunch.

"All right," Margaret says. "I suppose we can come back this afternoon."

She staggers to her feet, and so do I. The cold and damp have had the same effect on our living flesh as on the leather. For a moment or two, she stands there staring at the bag, the artifacts placed around it. She sets her hands on her hips.

"Coming?" I ask.

She bends down and picks up a bundle of letters and a notebook.

"Coming."

OLD MRS. THORPE KEEPS TO HER bed, thoroughly senile, next to an array of pill bottles and powder packets. She married young, Margaret explained on the train, but Thorpe's father arrived only after several years of fruitlessness, like one of those flowers that blooms every century or so. Margaret's not sure precisely how old she is, but probably ninety-five, God bless her. Now she's propped against the pillows on what will probably become her deathbed, while Annie spoons soup into her mouth and replies patiently to all her crazy talk. I think of my mother back on Long Island, at the table in the kitchen, drinking her coffee while her chicks fly free.

"Let me do it," I say.

Annie looks up in surprise. Over by the window, Margaret puts down her cigarette and laughs. "Decent of you, Lulu, but it's not going to bring him back."

"It's not for Thorpe." I settle on the chair, take the soup from Annie, and peer into Mrs. Thorpe's hopeful face. Her hair is uniformly white, but something tells me this is the redhead in the family tree. I should mention that she's chattering away as all this takes place. You can't really understand the words—aside from the Scotch brogue, she's got no teeth—but whatever she's saying, the woman's got a lot of it to communicate. I wait until she pauses for breath and stick the spoon in the hole. She swallows it down and smiles gummily, like when the twins were babies, and I think it's maybe just as well I'm getting the practice, isn't it? How, if we're lucky to survive the measles and the tree climbing, the wars and the childbirth, disease and famine and Hitler and Tito and the crosstown bus barreling down Fifty-Ninth Street, we come right back to the beginning before heading west into the unknown, to meet our Maker just as we left him, helpless.

THE FEEDING OF MRS. THORPE TAKES some time, and Annie and Margaret retire to the kitchen, where at least there's a range to keep the air warm. I occupy this hour by telling her a little about me, about how I met her grandson, what a dear fellow he is, how the king of England married us, how I've got a bun in the oven already, her great-grandchild. I leave out the part about Colditz, not because I don't want to upset her—she doesn't understand a word I'm saying—but because I don't want to upset myself. It seems to me that this is a moment for fairy tales, for a story that ends well, for a fiction you know is a fiction that comforts you anyway.

When the spoon scrapes a final time against the bowl, and the lady deigns to accept this offering, I wipe her mouth carefully with the napkin, settle her comfortably on her pillows, and ask if there will be anything else, Mrs. Thorpe.

"Johann," she says clearly.

I beg her pardon.

"Dear boy. Hair like his mama."

(Understand, if you please, that she speaks in a toothless, whistling lisp, so I may not be translating precisely.)

"Ah. Yes. They were both blond, weren't they?"

"But she was mad, poor thing. What could I do?" She looks at me earnestly, like a moment of clarity has come upon her and she wants to know this thing, she really wants to know what she could have done, other than what she did.

"Buried her properly, perhaps."

"I couldn't let the children see her, not the state she was in."

"I'm sure she forgives you," I said, not that I had any such confidence. On the other hand, from the look of things, Mrs. Thorpe would be discovering the limits of her daughter-in-law's forgiveness firsthand, before long.

Mrs. Thorpe claws a little at the edge of the sheets. "I had no choice. But he understood. He's a good boy. A good son."

"Do you mean Wilfred?"

Her eyes make little spasms of effort, remembering. She nods and says, "Wilfie," and then the words fall into babbling again. I give the blankets a final pat and rise from my chair, bid her good afternoon, tell her Annie will be back soon with her tea. And indeed, when I descend the stairs and find the kitchen, the kettle's whistling on the top of the range, and Annie's spooning leaves into a blue-and-white teapot. Margaret sits at the table before a dozen or so letters, arranged in orderly rows. A cigarette smokes away in the ashtray at her elbow. She makes no sign of noticing my arrival. I carry the bowl and spoon to the sink and wash them, dry them, set them in the cupboard. Through the window, I spy a patch of blue sky, a gleam of sunshine on the wet grass. I sit down at the table and Annie sets a cup of tea before me. When I reach for one of the letters, the nearest, Margaret snaps—not looking up—*Don't touch!*

"Sorry." I stir in the milk and the honey.

Margaret lifts her cigarette, drags lengthily, places it back in the ashtray. She's holding a letter in her left hand, and though I don't mean to snoop, I can't help noticing that it's typewritten.

"Find anything interesting?" I ask.

"They're all interesting."

"I mean anything in particular."

"Annie," she says. "Tea."

Annie rolls her eyes and sets the teacup in the patch of bare table next to the ashtray. Brings the milk and the honey. Margaret adds both and stirs with the teaspoon, *clinkety clink*, without taking her eyes from the paper before her.

"What's that?" I say. "The Magna Carta or something?"

"It's in French, that's all."

"Let me have it, then. I'm practically fluent."

She shoots me a murderous glance over the top of the paper. "So am I. It's just that I can't make heads or tails of what's in it. Annie?"

"Yes, Miss Margaret?"

"You don't remember any legal dealings in Paris, do you? Oh, Lord. Of course not. You were the housemaid."

"It's from a lawyer?" I ask.

"Yes," she says, snapping again.

"Do you mind if I—"

"It's none of your business."

I set my hands around the teacup. "I disagree. I think it is my business. He's my father-in-law, isn't he?"

"He's my *father*."

"I'm carrying his only grandchild."

She tosses the paper to the table. "Are you *certain* of that, darling?"

"What the devil does that mean?"

Margaret picks up the cigarette, smokes it; picks up the tea and drinks that. The cup rattles in the saucer when she returns it. Her eyes are a little glassy, I think.

"Maybe that's not his only grandchild, I mean." She makes a thin, bitter smile. "It seems my father was paying a lawyer in Paris to track down a certain woman and her daughters."

"Oh, dear."

"And what's more, it seems he succeeded."

"How—how—"

"How the mighty are fallen, perhaps?" She points her cigarette to the letter. "See for yourself, then. I don't give a damn."

I reach across the table and pluck the letter from atop the layer of envelopes, all of which are addressed, I perceive, in the same elegant handwriting, to *Maj. W. B. Thorpe.* Except this one, typewritten, dated the thirtieth of June. The day before he went into battle. Margaret lights herself another cigarette and rises from her chair to stare out the window above the sink. She's wearing another of her shapeless housedresses, which hangs from her slender frame, reminding me a little of the duchess. The same shape, except it's not cultivated, it's not fashioned the way you fashion a mannequin, it's not displayed to its best advantage. It's just what it is, a woman who's naturally slender, who isn't eating as well as she should, smoking too many cigarettes, fretting.

From time to time, the duchess liked to speak to me in French, in order to polish her fluency. So while it's been some time since I picked up a work of French literature, or wrote out a sentence or a paragraph in that language, I find I can read the words pretty well, without stopping to translate in my head. When I come to the woman's name, I look up.

"Charlotte Kassmeyer? But that's not a French name."

"No. They're German. Look at the children's names."

I turn back to the letter. "Ursula, Frederica, Gertrud. How odd."

"There's nothing odd about it. Probably some woman he met when he was stationed somewhere, before the war. He arranges for her to live in a nice little flat in Paris, so as to be conveniently nearby. Men, they're jolly clever, aren't they?"

"Then why was he paying a lawyer to find her?"

"I don't know. I don't especially care. It all adds up to the same sum, doesn't it?" She blows out a cloud of smoke. "Poor Mama. No wonder."

"No wonder?"

"No wonder she was so unhappy. All that time, you know, I thought they were in love. I thought—I thought they were like a fairy tale, like the prince and princess in a story for children—"

"You don't know that. He might have been making arrangements for another officer, someone who was killed. That would explain—"

"*Stop*."

"But—"

She whirls to face me. "Stop, damn it. Read me those names again."

I pick up the paper and skim the paragraphs. "Ursula, Frederica, Gertrud."

Margaret marches back to the table and snatches up the letter. "Ursula. Ursula Kassmeyer."

"What's the matter?"

"It must be a coincidence."

"Miss Margaret! The cigarette!" cries Annie.

The corner of the page has begun to smoke. Margaret swears and drops the cigarette in the ashtray, pinches out the flame with her fingers. The smell of scorched paper fills the air.

"What's the matter?" I say. "Who the devil's Ursula Kassmeyer?"

"It's got to be a coincidence." Margaret looks up and meets my gaze, and the gloss is gone from her eyes. They're a bright, pale blue, animated, sizzling with life. "It's just that we've got an operative by that name in the German section. One of our best. She runs an escape line into Switzerland for downed pilots and Jews."

PART V

LULU

NOVEMBER 1943
(The Bahamas)

I HAVE SAID before that there was more than a little of the American spirit in the Bahamas, the American way of doing things, owing to the fact that Miami lay a trifling distance to the west, whereas London rose from an island on the other side of a notoriously tempestuous ocean. Still. Bahamians clung to certain inscrutable British traditions, and a Nassau courtroom is just about indistinguishable from Old Bailey itself, down to the frizzled gray wigs and the so-called dock in which the prisoner is kept during the proceedings, like an animal in a cage.

IT'S A GRAVE THING, AFTER all, to put a man on trial for his life. A grave thing, to accuse a man of murdering another man, and—like marriage—not to be undertaken lightly, or for base purposes. On the last day of Alfred de Marigny's trial for the murder of Sir Harry Oakes, I sat in the press gallery for some time after the concluding arguments were made, after the judge gave his summation and instructions to the jury, after the members of the jury filed out of the courtroom to deliberate de Marigny's guilt or innocence.

I stared at that prisoner's dock, now empty, and considered all I had witnessed in the past several weeks, the testimonies, the facts I had already known and the startling facts I had learned. The faces. There was Freddie himself, of course, all calm demeanor and earnest eloquence. Lady Oakes, crushed by grief. Nancy de Marigny, resolute, pretty, courageously pale. Harold Christie, white knuckles gripping the rail, perspiring ferociously, though it was autumn and the courtroom was not especially hot. The two detectives from Miami, old associates of the duke, whom he had flown in specially to lead the investigation on the morning of the body's discovery, because the Bahamas police (he claimed) were not up to the task. Slick, handsome, bumbling, all at once. In my head, though not my daily dispatches to the Associated Press, I called them the Keystone Kops.

Then you had the faces we *didn't* see, because their owners had disappeared, or died, or—as in the case of Colonel Erskine-Lindop, the former Bahamas police superintendent, a man of known integrity—been transferred abruptly to Trinidad. Those absences were perhaps more interesting, as I pointed out to my readers. More telling, you might say. Among them, the Duke and Duchess of Windsor. It seemed the royal couple was called away to visit friends in the States just as proceedings got underway, so they could neither appear in court nor testify, although I understood that the duke arranged for detailed reports on the trial's progress to be cabled to him daily from his good friend, Harold Christie, at no small trouble or expense. Which was good of him, don't you think?

By now, I sat alone in the gallery. The other journalists had rushed to queue up at the telephones and send their dispatches to eager editors around the globe. Even in time of war, it seems, people still give a damn about a single dead man on a small island off the coast of Florida, because he was rich and because he was a friend of the Duke of Windsor. Before me, a clerk gathered papers on the prosecutor's table. The courtroom had turned hot and stuffy with the heat of so many people and so many electric lights. A rising wind rattled the windows. I rose from the bench and made my way downstairs and across the street to the Central Police Station, where Nancy de Marigny awaited the verdict on the second floor.

I FOUND HER ON A sofa, flushed and fluttery, smoking an anxious cigarette. Her mother was elsewhere, having taken exception to Nancy's support for the accused, and I thought there was something rather moving about Nancy's solitude.

"Oh, there you are," she said to me. "What do you think?"

I settled myself rather heavily on the cushion beside her. "What do *I* think? I think twelve sensible men couldn't convict Bonnie and Clyde from the evidence presented. But then again"——I shook my head at the cigarette case she presented to me——"I'm not a man, am I?"

She made this hysterical little laugh. I figured she must be on her last nerve by now, but what did I know? I had begun to harbor a tremendous admiration for Mrs. de Marigny. Most women, already shocked by the brutal murder of a beloved father, would succumb to nervous collapse at the mere suggestion that a beloved husband had committed this atrocity himself. But Nancy, you understand, was not most women. She seemed almost to thrive under the scrutiny of the press, the attention of every spectator. No actress could have played her part more heroically in that witness chair. She waved away a little cigarette smoke and said, "Well, I hope you're right."

"Oh, you heard the judge. My goodness. What did he say in that summation of his? Never in all his years seen a case handled like that, evidence mishandled, testimony fabricated, et cetera. I wonder if he really meant that bit about recommending an investigation into the whole mess."

"I hope so. I'll hope it's got them scared, all right, I mean everyone who had a hand in this. Everyone who wanted to take Freddie down."

"Thank goodness they were so incompetent."

She laughed shrilly. "Those Miami policemen! I never saw such a pair of dunces. That idiot Barker was on the stand, sweating and stuttering and backtracking. Everybody could see those fingerprints were planted. *Everybody.*"

She laid such an emphasis on that last word, I flinched. "Well, it won't be long now. He'll be vindicated, I'm sure of it."

Even to me, the words sounded hollow. Nancy looked at the clock. Six fifty-six in the evening, not even two hours since the jury had retired. Across the room, a pair of policemen lounged about their desks, pretending not to notice us.

"What will you do when it's over?" I asked.

"Over? My God. I don't know. Just to settle down with my husband, I guess."

"You deserve it. Everyone admires how you've handled yourself."

She flicked a little ash from her cigarette. "Except my mother, it seems. Speaking of which, where on earth has *your* husband gotten to? He's missed all the excitement around here."

"You know how it is in wartime," I said. "When you're called away to serve king and country and all that. He sends his warmest regards."

"Does he? That's kind." She rose from the sofa and stepped to the window, a few feet away, overlooking the street outside the courthouse. "Just look at all those folks standing there. They all support Freddie, you know. They love him."

I made myself rise, too, and came to stand with her by the window. By "those folks" she of course meant "the Negroes." The Windsors and the Bay Street Boys might not abide Freddie, but the greater part of the population, the colored part, the part that didn't sit in parliament or on juries, stood firm behind him.

"Anyway," Nancy said, "however things turn out. I appreciate your support. I mean that. Seeing you up there in the gallery, every day, it just gave us strength. Both of us."

"I wouldn't have been anywhere else. Anyone could see he'd been framed. Just as anyone could see who the real culprit was."

A twitch involved the corner of Nancy's mouth. She stubbed out her cigarette on the windowsill and turned to me.

"Anyone could *see*, sure," she said, "but do you think anyone's got the guts to say it out loud?"

Across the room, a telephone rang. We both jumped. One of the policemen answered it, speaking in low tones, glancing in our direction. Nancy grabbed my hand and dug her fingernails into my palm with such ferocity, my eyes stung.

The policeman hung up the phone and rose. "Mrs. de Marigny. It seems the jury has reached its verdict."

BY THE TIME I ELBOWED my way back to my seat in the press gallery, the courtroom was packed, the air electric. Freddie was back in his cage. From the opposite wall, in its place of honor, a portrait of the King of England stared nobly into the distance, as it had done throughout the trial. The resemblance to the duke unsettled me. At certain moments, it had seemed as if the brothers had switched places, as if the duke himself were somehow staring through the bland eyes of his successor, as if he presided over us—participants and spectators alike—from a point higher than that of the judge himself.

When the jurors had filed back inside the courtroom, Sir Oscar entered and resumed his seat on the dais in his robes and his curling wig. The court registrar asked the foreman of the jury, a grocer named James Sands, if they had reached a verdict.

Yes, we have, said Mr. Sands.

How silent that room was, how taut, how stifling. There was not the slightest sound, not a movement. I remember I stared not at Mr. Sands, or the judge, or the portrait of King George there on the wall, but at

Freddie in his cage. I remember how I looked at his face and realized he might actually die, that his life hung on this decision, on these words, and who on earth could willfully put an innocent man through such an ordeal? Who could frame a man for a capital crime he did not commit? It was murder, absent the courage of murder, the moral conviction of looking your man in the face and pulling the trigger. It was cowardice, the act of a runner. Freddie stared at Mr. Sands, waited for his fate, and for a terrible instant I forgot all about Sir Harry Oakes. I forgot about the Bahamas and the Windsors. For a terrible instant, I thought we were in Bakersfield, and it was Tommy's murder being tried, it was my guilt for which Freddie would hang.

I heard the registrar speak.

How say you, is the prisoner guilty or not guilty of the offense with which he is charged?

He is a goner, I thought. God forgive me.

Mr. Sands called out, *Not guilty.*

IN THE PANDEMONIUM THAT FOLLOWED, I was possibly the only person who kept my seat. While my colleagues stampeded for the telephones, I stared at Mr. Sands, whose lips still made words, though you couldn't hear them in all that noise. In the corner of my vision, Freddie was leaping from his cage to embrace his wife, a free man.

Well, so are you, I thought. You're free, aren't you? Freddie's acquittal is your acquittal. But I was not free. The world spun in frantic loops around the small, fragile core inside my womb, the piece of himself that Thorpe had left behind. I rose from my seat and shouldered out of the press gallery. I found a telephone and communicated my dispatch to the Associated Press, and to this day I've got no idea what that dispatch actually said. By now, everybody had tumbled out of the courthouse and into Rawson Square, where Freddie was hoisted onto the shoulders of the crowd—white and Negro—and carried through the evening air to his car. I stood there on the steps and watched it all. A sense of dread overcame me, of imminent disaster, and I fought to master it. The Lady of Nassau had a column to write and transmit by two o'clock in the morning, after all, just in time to set the press for the December issue, and since Lightfoot had agreed—with many a grumble—to pay me a thousand clams for said column, I needed my conscience at its clearest and my pencil at its sharpest. No morbid thoughts, no impending doom. *Not guilty*, remember?

A man stood next to me, checking his watch. Godfrey Higgs, Freddie's barrister.

"Why, Mr. Higgs! There you are. The man of the hour."

He looked up. "Mrs. Thorpe. You give me too much credit. The prosecution laid a contemptible case. Any competent barrister should have won acquittal."

"Any barrister *should*, maybe. But they weren't exactly scrambling to take on the defense, were they? Just you."

"I did my duty, that's all, Mrs. Thorpe."

"Well, at least you were wise enough to leave certain questions unasked. I wonder if we'll ever see justice?"

He shook his head, and I saw how weary he was, not that I blamed him. The poor fellow probably hadn't experienced a good night's sleep since July.

"Mr. Higgs," I said. "I thought I saw the foreman speaking, after the verdict. Only I couldn't hear him in all the racket. Was it something important?"

Mr. Higgs turned his head to watch Freddie's car as it drove slowly through Rawson Square, parting the crowd, honking its joyous horn. "It was," he said. "I'm afraid there was an addendum to the verdict."

"An addendum? What do you mean?"

"Mr. Sands went on to say that the jury recommended—in spite of the verdict—that Mr. de Marigny and his cousin, Georges de Visledou, be deported from the Bahamas immediately as undesirables."

"*Deported?* Undesirables? Why?"

"A very good question, Mrs. Thorpe. I shall seek answers as soon as possible, although I don't imagine it will make any difference."

Across the square, Freddie's car had disappeared around a corner, and the jubilant glow of the headlamps arced across a building to dissolve into blackness. "Why not?" I whispered.

"Because I suspect that certain elements of the government will move heaven and earth to see that the deportation is carried out forthwith."

I turned to gaze at him. He had removed the wig, of course, and while I privately thought these wigs an absurdity, Mr. Higgs did seem to have shed a certain air of importance along with his gray curls.

He went on. "I haven't told him yet. I thought he should have a few hours to celebrate."

"Mr. Higgs," I said softly, "could you perhaps offer me a lift home?"

WHEN MR. HIGGS DROPPED ME off at the door of my bungalow, he wished me a sober good evening and conveyed his warmest regards to my husband.

"Yes, of course," I replied. "And he returns his to you. Naturally, he's followed news of the trial with the utmost interest."

This was a lie, of course. Benedict Wilfred Thorpe hadn't sent any regards at all to Alfred de Marigny or Nancy de Marigny; had not sent a single word, in fact, to his own wife, or to anybody—at least so far as I'd heard—since disappearing on the morning of Harry Oakes's murder. Of course, a lot of people disappeared around that time, and nobody showed the slightest curiosity about that singularity. Everybody just carried on, and since the fact of our marriage was indisputable—why, the Windsors themselves confirmed the story, terribly romantic, and what cachet to have been married by the governor himself, everybody was so envious—the fiction of Thorpe's urgent, unfortunate business elsewhere stood pretty firm, thank you. There was a war on, after all. Everybody understood that.

And so I walked up the path to my bungalow alone that night, the fourteenth of November. I unlocked the door and went into my empty house and checked the rug, the hall table, as I always did.

I found no note, no letter, no message of any kind. But a fellow stood in my living room, a blond giant of a man, wearing a creased suit and a sober, anxious expression.

"Who the devil are you?" I cried, hand on heart.

He opened his mouth and spoke in impeccable English, though a pronounced German accent. "I beg your pardon, Mrs. Thorpe. Your housekeeper was kind enough to admit me. My name is Johann. Johann von Kleist."

"Johann?" I whispered.

"I'm afraid I have taken the trouble to come to you with some grave news."

I covered my mouth with my hand.

"It's to do you with your husband," he said. "My brother. Benedict Thorpe."

ELEVEN DAYS LATER, ON THE twenty-sixth of November, I followed Marshall into the drawing room of Government House, where the Duchess of Windsor was supervising the erection of a tall blue spruce in full needle. The air smelled deeply of pine. For a moment, I stared at the back of her head, her trim waist in its blue jacket, belted in yellow, and I couldn't quite comprehend what was going on. Then I remembered. Christmas.

"Madam," said Marshall, "Mrs. Thorpe is here."

The duchess made no sign of having heard him, except that she raised one finger in the air. "A little to the left," she said, and the footman moved the spruce to the left.

"Will there be coffee, madam? Tea?"

"No, thank you. That will be all, Marshall."

Marshall bowed and turned. I believe, in passing, he offered me a look of sympathy. But I might have been mistaken. When it came to poker faces, Marshall could have cleared the card table in Amarillo, Texas.

The duchess rested one hand on her hip and tilted her head. So far as I could tell, that Christmas tree could have modeled for the *Saturday Evening Post*, but then it wasn't my job to present the world with a picture-perfect picture of life inside Government House, was it? It wasn't my job to create that kind of fiction for a living. Not anymore, at least.

I knew better than to say anything. Let her enjoy the exercise of petty power, after all. It cost you nothing and meant the world to her. She told the footman to move it an inch thataway, then thisaway. Preezie nibbled at her ankles. She held up her finger at last and said, "There. Thank you, Brown. That will be all. You may send in the maid to clean up the mess."

"Yes, ma'am," said the footman. He dusted off the needles and hurried out, and the duchess began a slow, deliberate turn to face me. To my surprise, she was smiling.

"Mrs. Thorpe. How good of you to stop by. I was going to send for you. We were only back from the States last night."

"Yes, I heard."

She leaned her head to one side, regarding me as she had regarded the spruce tree. "I read your column, Mrs. Thorpe."

"Did you, now? I'm flattered you found the time, what with all the Christmas shopping."

"Of course I found the time. We've been very important to each other, haven't we? Of course I found the time to read this column of yours." She lifted her finger and waved it back and forth, the way you might scold a naughty child. "Not your best work, Mrs. Thorpe. Not at all."

"No?"

"I don't know how that scoundrel de Marigny wormed his way into your affections—I can only *guess*—but really, I was embarrassed for you. To say nothing of all those *dreadful* insinuations."

"I'm sorry about those. I would've been delighted to accuse outright, but I don't want to get killed, like everybody else."

"I beg your pardon?"

The face she presented me was thoroughly shocked, and I had no doubt of its sincerity. Women like Wallis never, for a single moment, imagine themselves really guilty of anything. Each action is perfectly defensible, each enemy perfectly vile and deserving of whatever fate casts his way.

"Never mind," I said. "That's not why I came."

"I don't understand you."

"I came to discuss my husband. To be frank, I've been concerned, since I hadn't heard a thing from him since the morning we learned poor Sir Harry was murdered."

"The day you were married," she said.

"Yes. And eleven days ago I learned that instead of flying back to London under the care of the Royal Air Force, he was captured by German agents that very morning, on his way to Windsor Field."

"No!"

"Someone had betrayed him as a British agent, you see, and he's presently imprisoned in the fortress at Colditz."

"In Colditz!"

"Yes."

"My goodness! Poor Thorpe. How very awful for you. My deepest sympathies."

"Yes," I said. "Quite."

"Why, you can't possibly think—"

"No, of course not. Perish the thought."

We regarded each other for a moment or two, eyes of Wallis blue to eyes of plain brown, American to American, both of us all tangled up in the affairs of a country not our own.

I went on softly. "It would have been awful, wouldn't it, if anyone had ever laid the finger of suspicion on Harold Christie. If Scotland Yard, say, had taken over the investigation, instead of those two incompetent specimens of the Miami Police Department the duke put in charge the very first morning. My God, heaven knows what they might have found. They might have found what my husband found. What my husband had already reported to his superiors back in London."

"I don't know what you mean."

I reached up to my earlobes and unscrewed the first earring. "What would you say, Duchess, if I told you that I had made copies of all those documents I passed along to you? All those interesting financial statements."

She stared, transfixed, at my fingers. The earring came free, and I went to the other ear.

"What, for example, would those documents be worth to you and your husband? I'm just speaking hypothetically, of course. It's not as if I mean to blackmail you."

"Mrs. Thorpe. Lulu. Really." She forced her gaze away from my left earlobe and made a brittle laugh. "This has gone far enough. What documents do you mean? I'm afraid my memory fails me."

I held out the earrings in my palm. She looked down, but she didn't touch them. At her temples, a few beads of perspiration had begun to form. I thought I smelled something peculiar in the air, something tangy.

"How we trusted you," she whispered.

"I trusted *you*, and now my husband's imprisoned in Colditz."

"I—we had *nothing* to do with that. Nothing at all. How could we? We are loyal servants of the Crown, Mrs. Thorpe. Loyal servants."

"No doubt. In which case, I'm sure you'll be more than happy to give me what I need to save him."

"What do you need?"

I took her hand, stuck the earrings in the middle of her palm, and closed her cold fingers around them. Her eyes met mine, round and vulnerable. I thought of my dear, empty bungalow, my belongings packed in a few wooden boxes, on the slow boat back to the United States. I spoke softly, so as not to frighten her further.

"What I need, at your earliest convenience, is a place on one of those Liberators taking off from Windsor Field."

PART VI

URSULA

JANUARY 1944
(Germany)

MAYBE THERE'S SOME truth to what they say about second sight, or intuition, or whatever you want to call it, because on the morning Ursula Kassmeyer receives the message from Scotland, she wakes up thinking vividly of Mutti.

Her sisters don't remember this woman they once called *Mutti*, but Ursula does. There's a little irony in this, because Frederica and Gertrud were the ones who wept so bitterly as that long-ago train rattled northward from Florida to New York, who cried and cried for Mutti's fragrant, loving arms, while Ursula remained dry-eyed and comforted them. But eventually the younger ones dried their tears, they called for Mutti less and less, and by the time they were settled in a little villa outside Paris, near a village on the Marne river where Maman's uncle still lived—Nurse said she was not their nurse anymore, but Maman—only Ursula stayed awake in her bed at night and remembered all the little details of Mutti, her smile and her kisses, her patient instruction at the piano, her pale hair that felt like silk against your cheek. Only Ursula gazed upon the painting of the Madonna in the village church and thought of Mutti.

Only Ursula recalled the beach and the picnics, the magical man with the ginger hair and the gigantic laugh who swung you up screaming in the air and caught you just before you dunked in the water. *Mr. Thorpe*. She even remembered his name.

Maybe if Maman had been less drunk, if she had spent less time sick in her bed or else out all night, sometimes all the next day or even several days together, Ursula might have forgotten Mutti, instead of holding the little shards of memory close to her heart and turning them over and over, examining each tiny facet, each glint, each inclusion. But what other comfort did she have? Only God and her great-uncle, who was old and not well himself. When he died—this was maybe a year or so before the Great War started, when Ursula was twelve years old—Maman moved them all into Paris itself, a few grubby rooms on the top floor of a building in the Montparnasse, where there was little food, less heat, and almost no money at all.

But isn't this how Ursula became what she is today? Those lean days in wartime Paris, scrounging for food and knowledge. This morning, as Ursula forces her body out of bed, the dark, frozen air brings back the memory of those nights in Paris, huddled under a moth-eaten blanket with her sisters. The days in Paris, helping out Madame Pistou at the boulangerie around the corner, shaping the dough into endless loaves, in order to earn some bread for them to eat. The stinking gutters, the wounded soldiers hobbling down the street with their stricken faces.

Now it's a different war, different soldiers, but the cold and the hunger and the despair are as familiar to her as her own raw fingers, as her own reflection in the scrap of mirror above the washstand. Outside the window, rimmed in frost, Berlin staggers to its feet and begins another day. At nine o'clock, an elderly woman wearing a plain blue headscarf will be waiting on a certain bench in the Tiergarten, feeding pigeons from a bag of crumbs. Ursula must be there to meet her.

STILL, AS URSULA SLIPS PAST the doorway of the boardinghouse and into the frigid morning, she can't shake the image of Mutti from her head. She realizes that she was actually dreaming of Mutti—bits and pieces of that dream return to her now, or rather impressions of the dream—and that was why she had woken this way, whispering *Mutti, Mutti*. Now, to be fair, Ursula thought of Mutti often anyway. Mutti made a shrine in Ursula's imagination. *Maman* was dead and unlamented—she had died just before the end of the war, simply collapsed on the stairs one midnight—but Ursula had always nursed the idea that Mutti remained alive, golden and glowing, in some distant and happy home somewhere.

Indeed, that was why Ursula had left France and taken the girls to Germany after the war. They had gone in search of Mutti, had tracked down some woman whose name appeared occasionally in the letters Maman had left behind. Helga von Kleist turned out to be a very grand lady who lived in an enormous, baroque schloss in Westphalia. She told Ursula she had no idea who this Mutti could possibly be, but that their Maman had been a prostitute in the village many years ago, and she had given Maman money to take her immoral ways elsewhere and start a new life. She had actually offered Ursula money to do the same but Ursula had proudly refused. She had gone to Berlin instead and become a waitress to support her sisters, in a café frequented by artists and philosophers, some of whom she slept with, some of whom painted her or put her in their stories, an interesting bohemian existence. She learned how to draw and sold her illustrations to magazines and newspapers. Her sisters grew up and went to school (Ursula paid the fees) and married, and all the while Ursula never stopped looking for Mutti in the face of every woman she served at the café, every woman on a bus or at a shop or on the street itself.

She does it now, in fact, as she navigates the piles of frozen slush to the Tiergarten in her patched coat of brown wool, her creased, ancient shoes.

Some habits you can't break. Though you wouldn't know it from looking at her—in fact, you wouldn't look at her to begin with, because Ursula's an expert at passing beneath your notice, hunching her wide shoulders and sturdy frame, practically melting into the pavement and the shop windows and the lampposts—Ursula's examining every forehead, every chin, every pair of eyes that passes by. From beneath her eyelashes she rakes in each detail of her surroundings and records it to memory.

Oh, her memory. There it goes again, taking a snapshot of this woman on the corner, aged about sixty-five, skeletal, threadbare gray coat, pale, narrow eyes, who might be a bank teller or a manager at a munitions factory or a Gestapo agent. Always Ursula has had this tremendous power of recollection, this capacity for storing and retrieving information, human faces especially—it's what's kept her alive these past four years, while committing endless acts of treason right here in Berlin beneath the very noses of the Gestapo. Longer than that, even. Since before the war. When the Nazis came to power and passed their laws, many of her Jewish friends began to disappear, so that it was natural to try to help them out of Germany, using her drawing skills to forge documents and so on, a hobby that became a vocation when the war came and one of her old lovers, an Englishman who had been studying in Berlin before the war and now worked for the British intelligence agency, the so-called Special Operations Executive, recruited her as an agent for the German section. It turned out that, in addition to her prodigious memory, she had a knack for subterfuge, an amoral willingness to sleep with any man or woman who might further her cause (or else kill him, as necessary), a feral bravery when it came to crossing forests and hayfields and alleyways in the dead of night. In short, she was a natural.

And just where has it got her?

Here. Skidding on a patch of ice, grasping at a lamppost, clutching her bag of crumbs to her chest. Bitten with cold. The man on the corner looks her way and squints, like he's seen her before and can't remember where. Ursula composes herself and strikes off across the street, between weary bicycles and streetcars, hungry, exhausted, feminine Berlin. We are so sick of this war. We want our men back, our food back, our good times back. Our dignity, our trust in each other. What's that? What about our Jews? Maybe not them. But everything else. A new coat for winter, one that actually keeps out the chill. Hot coffee made from genuine beans, not ersatz. Meat. Schnitzel, sauerbraten, schmaltz to spread on your bread in the morning. Remember that?

Ursula reaches the safety of the street corner and trudges on, without expression. She learned early in life that you kept your thoughts to yourself, your emotions to yourself, cradled carefully in your chest so that no one else could see them or touch them or hear them, and this, too, has served her well in her chosen field. An offhand glance over her shoulder reveals that the narrow-eyed woman has turned her attention elsewhere.

HOW DIFFERENT THE TIERGARTEN LOOKS. In the old days, even when times were bad, it was full of men and women walking their dogs and their children, lovers walking each other, picnics, roller skates, green grass, each flower and shrub in immaculate order, not a speck of gravel outside its allotted bed. Jews playing their violins for the spare change tossed in the open cases at their feet. Now it's barren and unkempt. The lovers have parted, the men are at war, the women have no energy left for walking, the Jews are in the camps, the dogs have been discreetly boiled for soup, the January sky dyes the world gray. On a bench near the Brandenburg Gate, an old woman sits with her bag of crumbs, feeding a flock of skinny, ravenous pigeons. Ursula joins her.

It feels good to sit. Together they toss their crumbs and watch the bobbing and jerking of the pigeons, the frantic, nasty pecking. Like the sky, the birds are colored in shades of gray. Neither woman says a word. A policewoman passes by, eyes them carefully, moves on. After a few minutes, Ursula picks up the bag of crumbs and moves on too.

Except it's not the bag she arrived with.

BY THE TIME URSULA ARRIVES home—stopping along the way at the grocer, the newsstand, just an ordinary Berlin woman making her morning rounds—and decodes the messages inside the bag, she's forgotten about Mutti and the vivid, half-remembered dreams of the night before. Which makes her shock all the greater when she reads the third message, received from a radio operator near Bremen on a relay from Denmark, originating in Scotland, from somebody code-named Dunnock who works in G section. She reads it three times, and even then she has some trouble understanding what it means. Boiling down this meaning to a single devastating essence.

Mutti and Mr. Thorpe have a son who is imprisoned in Colditz.

For four years now, Ursula has maintained a network of friends whose loyalty to humanity exceeds their loyalty to Germany, who are willing to commit treason in order to provide a bed or a meal to a downed airman, or a Jew, or another agent whose identity has been discovered. This is dangerous work in the occupied countries of Europe, where most of the population hates the Nazis, but in Germany it's suicidal. Ursula expects to die. She's surprised she's still alive, in fact. She continues to exist, day after day, only because of luck, or possibly the grace of God. (She debates this point with herself all the time.) But as long as she continues to live, she'll dedicate that overdue life to rescuing others, to sending men and women from safe house to safe house, south toward Switzerland, where a few organizations exist inside that cocoon of neutrality to receive the fugitives. She can't tell you why, exactly. Just that she must, that she cannot imagine herself otherwise.

To spirit a man out of Colditz, however, that was another story.

How did you extract someone from between the stones of Germany's most notorious fortress? And then, once the alarm was sounded, smuggle him across the border to Switzerland? It was madness. It was impossible. Were this prisoner any other man, Ursula would refuse the request outright.

But he's not any other man. He's Mutti's son, the son of Mutti and Mr. Thorpe, and Mutti is the only mother Ursula's known. Mr. Thorpe is all she can remember of a father. So this prisoner, Benedict Thorpe, is her brother.

Still, the message is worded strangely. Instructions for reply are detailed and specific, routing through Scotland instead of London. The idea itself is crazy. It's unprecedented. Ursula understands at once that Dunnock—whoever he is—possesses intimate knowledge of her past, considerable expertise in SOE operations, and no formal authority whatsoever. By any objective assessment, it's probably a trap of some kind.

On the other hand, Ursula dreamed of Mutti last night. She woke with Mutti's name on her lips. Who else but Mutti would know of her connection to Benedict Thorpe? Isn't that a sign of some kind? A stamp of faith? Maybe all these years that came before, all Ursula's long apprenticeship in subterfuge, her continued survival in the face of impossible odds, has led to this single operation. After all, nobody else in Germany stands a better chance of freeing a prisoner from Colditz. If the thing can be done at all, only Ursula can do it.

In fact, as she stares at the paper in her hand, lit by a single flickering bulb that causes the letters to squirm on the page, she's sure of it.

Ursula takes a scrap from the pile in the drawer, sharpens her pencil with a knife, composes a reply, and translates it carefully into code.

LULU

MARCH 1944
(Switzerland)

IF YOU LOOK at a map of Germany—and God knows, I've done little else for the past nine weeks—you'll notice that the town of Colditz, tucked into the forests and farmlands of Saxony, lies at a considerable distance from the border with Switzerland. About four hundred miles, to be exact, across farm and forest and mountain, and then you get to the shores of Lake Constance, the Bodensee. You raise your hand and peer across the water, and on a nice clear day you can see Switzerland.

Or, if you're standing on the opposite rim of the lake—as I am, as I've done for ten days now, bundled in a thick wool coat that bulges over my middle—you see Germany.

Because of the pregnancy, and because I don't speak German, and because I don't have any training in this kind of thing, Ursula Kassmeyer made it absolutely clear that I was not to set foot, or attempt to set foot, on the wrong side of this border that stretches invisibly along the length of the lake: the border that separates Germany from Switzerland, enemy territory from neutral territory. Bad enough that I exist here on false papers, on a stack of clever, delicate lies. Bad enough to have made my way by train through occupied France, across strictly defended borders, on a passport that identifies me as Lenore Schmidt, a Swiss national born in Geneva, married to a Zurich banker, returning from medical treatment abroad in the company of my sister, Marguerite, whose hair, eyelashes, and eyebrows are as dark as mine, thanks to a brunette rinse obtained in an Edinburgh drugstore. Bad enough that at any moment, we might be captured and tortured and expose brave men and women to capture and torture. *Nein.* I was not to enter Germany. I was not going to make a shambles of a finely wrought plan, I was not going to make some clumsy American mistake and shatter this line she had developed and nurtured herself, for which she would give her own life. No, no. She would get Benedict Thorpe out of Colditz, all right, for the sake of his dead father and dead mother, who had apparently once been like a real father and mother to her, but she wasn't going to babysit the pair of us fine ladies, by God. Once we crossed into Switzerland—*if* we crossed into Switzerland—we were to proceed to Lake Constance for our health (mine is a difficult pregnancy, you understand, most fragile) and wait there for a man called Stefan, who runs a safe house across the lake on the German side. By cover of night, Stefan crosses the lake with Jews and pilots and messages. He'll find us. He'll deliver Benedict Thorpe to safety.

So. Here I sit, on an elegant bench along the esplanade, as I've done for the past ten mornings, the past ten afternoons. The wind is brisk today, the pigeons hungry and cross. The lake ripples before me, reflecting the sun, and behind all this (rather distant) you see the Alps and their sharp, snowy peaks against a sky of winter blue. Margaret—I beg your pardon, Marguerite—has gone off for a walk and a smoke and, possibly, a continued flirtation with the woman who runs the bookstall near the pier, the one that sells racy French novels. There was a giant fall of snow the other day, and while the sun's made an earnest effort to melt it all into puddles that soak the turf and flood the gutters, the piles of slush remain.

And the lake itself? Well, there are the fishermen, plying the waters. There are the patrol boats, mostly German. In times of peace, there were countless pleasure craft, but nobody sails Lake Constance for pleasure at the moment. Margaret explained to me that there is a peculiarity of borders on this lake, which is really just a wide spot on the Rhine; that no official treaty governs exactly what belongs to Germany and to Switzerland and to Austria. The Swiss believe the border runs right down the middle of the lake. The Austrians believe everybody holds it in common. And the Germans, well, they've got no official position at all, so that everybody sort of dances about on this water, patrols circling each other edgily, a choreography of suspicion. About a quarter mile out, a fishing boat hauls in its net; I can just see the little ant-men and their miniature spiderweb.

"Excuse me, madame. Is there room on this bench?"

For an instant, I think it's another one of the Swiss guards, patrolling up and down the esplanade with his rifle. But it's only a civilian, a man in a gray overcoat and felt hat, medium build, handsome as the devil. He's addressed me in French, too, whereas most of the Swiss in this part of the country speak German.

I slide a foot or two to the right. "Naturally, monsieur."

He sits with a flourish. "A beautiful afternoon, isn't it? But I think the weather may turn."

"Do you think so?"

"Yes. The lake is notorious for storms. The winds, you see, come down from the mountains in astonishing gusts. Sometimes the waves reach two or three meters in height."

"Dear me. How dangerous."

"Yes. The fishermen stay in port, even the patrol boats stay in port. Only the foolhardy venture out."

He's got a beautiful, rich voice, this fellow, and he doesn't seem to notice that my accent—while excellent, I do admit, having a certain ear for music that helps in such matters—isn't exactly authentic to a native speaker. (Neither is his, if we're keeping score.) Like me, he seems to be staring ahead, watching this fishing boat haul in its catch. A small, jagged line of white forms and disappears on the surface of the water, as if to confirm his words.

"The foolhardy," I say, "and also the brave."

"Brave? I wouldn't say that. Desperate, perhaps. Like a bear in winter."

I repeat the words slowly. "A bear in winter."

"Yes, madame. A bear. *Ursus*, if you prefer the Latin name."

"Ursus. Yes."

"A bear and her cub. I've heard—on the radio, just this afternoon— they wait for just such a night as this one, when the weather is too terrible for anyone else to risk their lives."

"It sounds dangerous."

"Ah, but not when the boat is accustomed to such waters. Courage, my dear madame. The bear will arrive safely." He rises, turns to me, and lifts his hat. "Good afternoon, madame."

"Good afternoon, Monsieur Stefan."

He winks. "Until the dawn."

Then he's gone, ambling down the esplanade, whistling some song, while my breath chokes in my lungs and my heart slams into my ribs. Eventually I rise and walk to the railing, just to calm my nerves. The wind is picking up, the whitecaps are spreading, the fishermen are heading into port. I curl my hands on the railing and fill my chest with the clean air that tumbles down from the Alps.

After a half hour or so, Margaret returns, cheeks all pink, hair straggling from beneath her hat. The brunette suits her, I think.

"My goodness, look at that water," she says. "I think it's going to storm."

AFTER DINNER THAT EVENING, I remove some papers out of the lining of my suitcase and fold them into an envelope. Just by themselves, no note. Though I have carried them with me since leaving Nassau, sometimes right next to my skin, I experience no sentiment at all, no pang of loss. *Good riddance*, I think, that's all. I seal the envelope and address it to *Mr. B——, War Office, London*. Outside, the wind's picking up, the clouds scudding across the darkening sky. I stop at the front desk to purchase the necessary stamps, and the desk clerk offers to hold my letter for the next morning's post. I refuse politely and walk out the door, down a few streets to the post office, where I push the letter irretrievably through the metal slot marked INTERNATIONALE.

THE OLD DREAM RETURNS TO me that night, during the half hour or so of sleep God grants me. The dusty town, the train, the man passed out drunk on the bed. This time I'm bleeding from within, and I can't seem to stop the flow. I can't seem to clean it up, and of course I've got to clean it up, every drop, or else he'll wake and find it. But there's no keeping up. Turn and wipe, turn and wipe, more blood on the floor now the carpet now the bed

Eyes open. Heart smacking. I turn my head and stare out the window of the hotel to the blackness beyond. The wind rattles the frame in its casing. The baby punches a tattoo in my side. I touch the diamond pendant underneath the nightgown, between my breasts. In the other bed, Margaret stirs. I ask softly if she's awake.

"Christ, what do you think?"

"Was I making noise?"

"Yes," she says. "Who's Tommy?"

I fix my arm behind my head. "Just an old beau."

"All that for an old beau?"

Another gust strikes the window. The room is as black as outer space, not a hint of light. I widen my eyes into this nothingness and consider telling Margaret about the time I found Tommy paying the rent on the landlady's parlor sofa at two o'clock in the morning, and how he got so mad at being discovered he delivered me a knockout punch to the gut, saving himself the money for the abortion we'd been arguing about, though we did have to skip town directly from the hospital bed. I actually catch my breath on the first words of the story, *There was this winter we spent in Amarillo, Texas.* But she doesn't need to hear about this, and I don't require her pity. I don't even know why Thomas Randolph visits me now, in this hotel room in Switzerland, when I've been free of him for years. It's just my dream, that's all. The one that comes to me in the dark of night.

"This woman," I say instead. "Ursula Kassmeyer."

"What about her?"

"Well, what do you think of her? Can we trust her?"

"Haven't the foggiest. I've never met her. I do know she's regarded as something of a saint by the chieftains at SOE."

"And you never knew you were related to her?"

"No." She pauses. "I knew about *them*, of course. Mummy didn't talk about them often, but I knew I had sisters, German half sisters, Johann's sisters, and they were taken away by their nurse before I was born. And that Mummy missed them. She missed them terribly."

"But I don't understand. How could the nurse have taken away the children like that?"

There is a long silence from the other bed, until I begin to think she's fallen asleep. Then, in a sharp voice, higher than her usual pitch: "I don't think they were hers, exactly. I think the baron had them with someone else."

"What? What makes you think that?"

"I don't know. Just a feeling. I was a child, you know, just a little girl when she told me these things. I don't know *how* I know. Until a few weeks ago, I'd forgotten all about it. The missing girls. It was like a story one's told at bedtime."

"But your mother loved them."

"Yes. I know she loved them. Even though they weren't hers."

From one of the windows comes a loud noise, like an object crashing against the glass, a stick or something. My nerves startle, but my head, as if detached from all this commotion, revolves around this idea of Margaret's mother, Thorpe's mother, taking in her husband's strays as if they were her own. I consider my own mother, who went about the mechanical duties of motherhood so thoroughly, the cooking of dinners and the enforcing of bedtime, all the while creating the impression of wanting to be elsewhere, wanting something else, someone else.

"Sounds as if your mother had a big heart," I say.

"She did. She loved us passionately. That was her trouble, I think. She loved too much. She staked everything on people she loved. When they were gone, it destroyed her."

"And she never knew your father had found the girls again."

"Apparently not." From the darkness beside me, Margaret made a noise of mirth. "Just imagine if that lawyer in Paris had sent his letter to Papa a week earlier. Or if the generals hadn't sent them into battle on the first of July."

"Then Ursula Kassmeyer wouldn't exist. I mean she wouldn't exist where she is now, helping Benedict escape."

"Yes. That's irony, I suppose. Or is it coincidence? Sometimes I can't properly tell the difference."

"Maybe it's the hand of God," I say. "Maybe it's hope."

"Oh, for Christ's sake, Lulu. You can't possibly think there's a God anymore. That he gives a damn about the world, even if he exists."

The last few words are buried beneath the noise of another gust striking the windows, the rattle and shriek, and in its wake there doesn't seem to be any point in talking. Why talk when the weather just eats up everything you say? But after this gust comes silence, a full minute or two in which the wind goes flat and the windows lie still, and you can hear yourself think, and you forget the possibility of annihilation.

"Tell me a story," I say. "A fairy tale."

"I don't know any of those."

"Yes, you do. Somebody read them to you when you were little."

"Oh, Mummy read stories, all right, and they were all frightful, gory tales, in High German. They didn't end well."

I listen to the thud of my heart inside my chest. "My mama used to read from the Arabian Nights. I used to imagine I had a djinn of my own, hiding in a lamp somewhere, and all I had to do was to find him. I used to rub every lamp I saw, hoping he would turn up and grant me my wishes."

"Well, there's the difference between you and me, I suppose. You've got hope left in you."

I roll heavily onto my side to face her, although of course she's no more than a suggestion of a shadow in that black room. "So do you. You wouldn't be here if you didn't."

"You're wrong, Lulu. I'm only here because of you. If Benedict turns up tomorrow with our German friend, I'll die of shock."

I close my eyes, and for some reason, some optical trick, the world seems lighter when I do. A few feet away, Margaret's bed creaks. The sound is swallowed by the window, rattling again in the grip of another gust of Alpine wind.

The soft hiss of a match, as Margaret lights a cigarette.

"But you keep hoping, Lulu," she says. "You can hope for both of us."

THERE'S NO MORE SLEEP. THE clock ticks toward six. The sun rises in an hour. I swing my legs to the floor and start to dress.

OUR INSTRUCTIONS ARE TO TAKE a stroll at sunrise along the esplanade, and somewhere between the two piers we will encounter Ursula and Benedict, another couple out for a stroll with the papers to prove it.

The trouble is, who takes a stroll on a morning like this? The wind tunnels between the buildings, shrieks around the corners. I can smell the lake, the ozone, the churning water, from three streets away. The sky's lightening by the minute. A violet stain appears behind the peaks to the east. Margaret's cigarette goes out. She swears softly and drops it in a pile of slush.

By the time we reach the esplanade, the violet's turned to pink, and the sky is taking on texture, taking on movement, as an array of clouds hurtles over us. An enormous wave crashes against the wall and sends up a spray like a waterspout.

"My God," whispers Margaret. "How can they survive it?"

"They will. Stefan assured me. He's used to these storms, he waits for them because the patrols don't go out."

"He's an idiot."

"Well, you can ride out the waves, can't you? But you can't ride out a German patrol boat."

"Christ. I need a fag."

"Listen to me. If a patrol comes along, we're just here to see the storm. We *adore* storms, do you hear me? We find them thrilling."

"Oh, jolly thrilling."

I put my arm through the crook of her elbow. "Come along. Let's go south first, away from town."

We tuck our heads into our collars and hold down our hats with our hands. Every so often I make a screech of delight and point to some wave or another, toppling over its mates, just exactly like one of those idiots who gets his kicks from Nature's wrath, the ones who line up on the beaches to witness a hurricane. We've only gone about a quarter mile when a pair of figures resolves from the shadows. My heart stops. Then I see the gleam of rifles, the curve of caps.

"Patrol," I mutter.

"What's that?" she says, because the wind is so noisy, and then she

sees them too. She turns to the railing and squeals. I join her and pretend
to laugh. The Swiss guards approach us.

"*Damen!* You shouldn't be out, it's too dangerous."

"Oh, but we love storms. Don't we, Lenore?"

"*Ja*," I say, which is about all the German I can safely utter without
raising suspicion.

"But she's expecting! You must go home."

"Now, my dear fellows. This is nonsense. We'll be careful, of course."

"Frau, you're very foolish."

"Please."

The two guards look at each other and shrug. "It's on your own head,
then," says the one on the right, or something like that, and they continue past us, shaking their heads. I release my breath. When I glance
down, I see my hand is laid over my belly like a bandage, and I wonder
what the devil good that's going to do, should a Swiss guard decide I'm
a suspicious character, should some rifle discharge some bullet on this
wind-whipped esplanade, where only the foolhardy and the desperate
tread.

We linger another moment, gazing at the water as if in rapture. The
sky behind the mountains is now bright and angry, a bundle of nerves,
shedding light on the lake which is now more akin to an ocean. The
waves hurtle along the surface and fling themselves on the shore. Our
coats are wet with spray, our hats dripping. "It's impossible," Margaret
gasps.

I can't stand here like this, doing nothing. I take her elbow and drag
her down the esplanade. A half mile away, the second pier juts out into
the lake, surrounded by churning water. I march toward it, searching
the path, searching the rocks beneath the esplanade for any sign of human movement. Another figure becomes visible, walking toward us, but
it's only a man with a large, shaggy dog of some mountain breed, I
don't know what. The dog takes a lunge at us as we pass each other, and

the man hauls on the leash and doesn't say a word. There's the pier, just beyond, empty except for the spray kicking up on all sides. The pretty gazebo at the end, painted in green and white stripes, looks like it might blow away like an umbrella. I am swallowing back panic, clenching my teeth with the effort of keeping myself from shaking to pieces. Over and over, I think, *It can't end like this, he can't have gone this far and then drowned almost within sight of us.*

"Maybe we missed them," Margaret says.

"Not if they were here, we didn't."

"Let's double back and make another pass."

I stare another second or two at the pier and start to turn. Margaret tugs on my arm. "Wait a moment," she whispers.

She squints at the pier, or rather beneath the pier, near the place where the stairs disappear into the rocky base of the esplanade. I follow her gaze. Hold myself still, or so near to still as you can hold yourself when you're trembling as I'm trembling, when you're as godawful frightened as I am in that moment.

And then. Something moves.

I make a little cry and dart forward. Margaret's behind me. We trip down the steps to find a hollow cut into the stone, beneath the wooden pier, in which a man and a woman huddle together, and the man is inspecting the woman's leg, her ankle. He hears us and looks up, and my heart slams in my throat when I see it's the wrong man, his hair is dark and wet, his features all wrong.

"*Stefan?*"

"She came down hard when we landed," he says, in French. "The ankle's twisted. She can't get up the stairs."

I look down into the face of a woman I've never seen, blond, irritated, built like a draft horse. "Ursula?"

"Shh! Get me up."

Margaret calls down. "Patrol!"

"What about Benedict? What about Benedict?" I cry.

Stefan says, "There was nobody else. Just her."

I put my arm around Ursula's ribs and haul her upright, not without effort. Thick bones, thick muscle. She grunts in pain.

"All right?" says Stefan.

"Stay there!" I hiss. "I'll lead them away!"

And I don't know how the devil I do it. I guess that kind of necessary strength just arrives in your sinews when you need it. I lift Ursula up those steps somehow, lift her to the esplanade where the guards now run toward us.

"*Hilfe!*" I scream, in German.

Margaret swoops in to take the weight of Ursula's limp body. "Help!" she screams. "She's fallen into the lake!"

IN THE HOTEL, WE TAKE Ursula upstairs in the elevator. The attendant looks at us strangely, wet and seething as we are, almost bursting. "Fifth floor," he says dully. He stops the elevator, opens the grille and then the door. We step out, supporting Ursula on each side. At the door, I fumble with the key, drop it, attempt to bend. My mind has gone numb, my fingers and my heart have gone numb.

"I'll get it," snaps Margaret. She leans down and snatches up the key, opens the door. We stagger through and ease Ursula on the bed. She's shivering, nearly blue. I pull the blanket from my bed and wrap it around her.

"He's dead, isn't he?" I say, in French.

"Yes. I'm sorry."

"When?"

"At Colditz, a month ago."

I sink to the rug.

Margaret takes Ursula by the shoulders and screams—first in English, then in French. "Then why are you here? You might have just sent a message. Look at her, my God. How could you get her hopes up?"

"Quiet!" Ursula says. "Listen to me!"

"How did he die?" Margaret yells.

"A fever, that's what they told me. Listen to me! And then a woman— a woman—"

"My God, what's the matter?" says Margaret.

I stare at the iron bedpost, the indentation in the rug. Ursula's brown, wet shoe before my face. She's sobbing a little in her chest, this woman who's a hardened operative, for God's sake, running an escape line through Germany, and I think, *I'm the one who's supposed to be crying. He's my goddamned husband.*

Somewhere above me, Ursula's speaking. "A woman—a woman came to take possession of the body."

"What? *Who?* Who took him?"

Ursula chokes back another sob and says, *Sa mère.*

"His mother? *My* mother? That's impossible! She's dead, don't you know that? She's been dead for years! Dead!"

"She's not dead," whispers Ursula. "She's in Switzerland."

ELFRIEDE

MARCH 1944
(Switzerland)

IN THE AFTERNOONS, Elfriede still plays the piano. She likes to think it keeps her fingers from getting stiff, but the truth is more sentimental than that. She follows the same chronology as always, all the way up through Chopin and no further, because really what comes after Chopin? Nothing anybody cares about. There was a young woman ten years ago who asked her if she knew any Gershwin. Elfriede said she'd never heard of him. The woman said she would find the music, she would order it from this shop in Paris she knew, but she never did. Just packed her suitcase and left one day. Oh, well. Never mind Gershwin, then.

Outside the window, the sun's come out. They've had a warm spell over the past few days, and much of the snow has melted. Some of the infirmary patients were outside this afternoon, soaking up the sunshine, and one still remains, bundled in a woolen coat, reading a book. Elfriede smiles and turns back to her music. From the refectory comes the clink and clatter of tables being set. The children do this, it's their job. Elfriede believes firmly in the importance of children having jobs, and so the children set the tables while the adults make dinner, and everybody's mind is relieved of its troubles for a short time. Because she's an early riser, Elfriede takes her turn at breakfast. Never ask your troops to do anything you wouldn't do yourself, that's what Wilfred used to say.

WHEN SHE COMES TO THE last note, she pauses for a moment, eyes closed, fingers resting on the keys. In that space of time, while the music still exists in her head but not in the air, she feels Wilfred's spirit in an especially pungent way, as if she's absorbed him inside her body, as if she's become Wilfred. Then the notes fade, and so does Wilfred, but not entirely. He's still there, only less immediate, which allows her to rise from the piano bench and take her cardigan sweater from the top of the piano, where she's left it. She shrugs her arms into the sleeves, belts the waist together, and heads down the hallway to the garden door.

NOW THAT ELFRIEDE OWNS THE clinic, now that the clinic runs not as a mountain retreat for wealthy invalids but as a refuge for the up-rooted, the unwanted—Jews, mostly, but also some Resistance, some downed pilots—that daily hour of music is sometimes her only interlude. Still, she tries to spend some time outdoors each day, even in the middle of winter, clearing snow from the pathways and so on. Exercise is abso-lutely vital for one's psychological health, she feels. During the spring and summer, there's the garden to plant and tend, the livestock to care for. In autumn, it's the harvest. She requires all the able-bodied guests to pitch in. Thus there's always food to eat, even when they're snowed in for weeks, and everybody feels as if they've contributed, even those who arrived here with only their clothes. Friendships are made, some-times love affairs. One couple married last October. Shortly after, the American embassy in Zurich approved their visas. (In special cases like that, Elfriede sometimes asks Johann—who seems to have some trusted friends inside the American government—to pull a string or two.)

In fact, she's holding a telegram from Johann in her hand right now. It was delayed a bit because the melting snow caused some flooding in the valley, blocking the roads, so perhaps the news inside is old. Still, she wants to share it with the man in the garden, soaking up the sunshine on the bench next to the wall. He's reading a book, and he looks up when he notices her approach. His hat hides his hair, but she knows the color, she knows every note of him. She asks if she can sit with him. He nods yes.

"There's a telegram from your brother," she says.

"What does it say?"

"I don't know. I thought we might read it together."

She hands him the yellow envelope, and he opens it with his bone-thin fingers. She remembers Gerhard, recovering from typhoid, and she reminds herself that this frailty will pass, that he's over the sickness, his strength will build rapidly in this good, clean mountain springtime, her abundant homegrown food.

She bends over his arm and reads aloud, because Benedict's eyesight is still a little blurred at close range.

RECEIVED CABLE AT LAST FROM MRS. THORPE STOP
PRESENTLY WITH MARGARET IN SWITZERLAND . . .

"*What?*" shouts Benedict. "What did you say?"

Elfriede puts her hand on her son's sleeve. "Shh. Listen."

. . . WITH MARGARET IN SWITZERLAND UNDER
BELIEF BENEDICT DEAD STOP MY REPLY RETURNED
UNDELIVERED STOP NO FORWARDING ADDRESS
STOP WILL ALERT U.S. EMBASSY ZURICH STOP YOURS
ALWAYS=
=*JOHANN*

The yellow slip starts to crumple. She slides it gently from Benedict's trembling fingers. He makes an anguished noise from his chest and tears his hat from his head.

"Don't worry," she says. "Johann will find her. Just think, she's in Switzerland. Wherever she is, it's not far."

"She can't be here. She's in Nassau."

"Well, it seems she's not. She came after you."

"It's impossible," he says.

"She's an intrepid woman, I suppose."

"She was supposed to stay in Nassau!"

Elfriede folds the telegram and slips it in her cardigan pocket with the envelope, all the while cursing herself for not reading the thing first. When would she learn? Telegrams always contained something shocking. Benedict's bracing himself on the arm of the bench, trying to rise, and the image of Wilfred, sitting on this very bench, and her young self poised on the wall behind him, almost staggers her. But not quite. She keeps enough wit to reach out and take his arm.

"Benedict, no. Where are you going?"

"To find her."

"Don't be silly. You can hardly walk yet."

"I thought she was safe," he says. "I thought she was in Nassau."

"Well, it seems she came after you, like a good wife should. Now sit down."

"Why didn't someone tell her I was alive?"

"Because by the time your brother was able to get word to his old army friend and arrange that little ruse in Colditz for us, she was already gone. Sit, please. You're alive, she's alive. Johann will find her somehow. *Sit*, Benedict."

But Benedict will not sit. Just like his father, she thinks, as she follows him down the paved path, piles of slush to the left and the right of him, the mild smell of springtime leaking from the stones, and back inside the walls of the monastery. You can't just keep a man like that away from this woman he loves. They will have to dig up one of the old straitjackets from the cellar or something.

BUT ISN'T THIS NO MORE than she deserves? Maybe she had no choice in the beginning, when Mrs. Thorpe had her moved from the hospital in Inverness to a— Well, let's call it what it was, a loony bin. Naturally, Mrs. Thorpe, being the sort of woman who never spent a sunless day in her life, who saw the bright side even of her own son's death—*He died a hero, just as his father would have wanted, remember that, Elfriede, don't dishonor his memory with these stupid moods of yours*—thought it best for the children to remove this sodden, dangerous influence from their lives. A woman who tried to drown herself, what next? Drown the children?

And maybe she was right, who knows. Elfriede remembers little of the next couple of years in this loony bin that—true to its name—actually made you loonier each day you lived there, smack in the rainiest possible corner of the rainiest possible country, who the hell thought of that? Some crazy person. It was not until Johann arrived after the war and dragged the secret out of poor Mrs. Thorpe, who made him promise not to tell the little ones in exchange for allowing him to take charge of Elfriede, take charge of his beloved mother, bring her to Switzerland and care for her devotedly until, bit by bit, she discovered enough of herself to survive. By that time, years later, what could you possibly do? Announce yourself back in your children's lives? They would hate her, she was sure. She and Johann argued fiercely over this point, right up until Johann abandoned his post in the German high command and fled to the United States in 1938. She couldn't do it. She was brave enough to live, brave enough even to take over the clinic, run it herself to give refuge for those who were uprooted and unwanted, but she was not brave enough to introduce herself to these children she had failed. She was not brave enough to summon up that fierce, passionate love once again, because why should these children want this love of hers thrust upon them? It poisoned whatever it touched. No, she kept her love locked tight in her heart, where it could do no one any harm.

Until Johann cabled her four months ago with the news about Benedict. Then she understood what she was meant to do. What she had been waiting the past twenty years to do. What Wilfred *needed* her to do. So she had done it. This impossible thing, to rescue a man from Colditz prison, she had done, employing Johann's old ties and her own ingenuity. She had bartered him out of prison—oh, the first sight of her youngest son, her baby, fevered and weak and limping, unfocused blue eyes and matted hair of indeterminate color, how it wrecked her—and then carefully maneuvered him south by train and horse cart, an injured German soldier on his way to a Swiss cure, according to the perfectly faked papers Elfriede had obtained in Zurich from a man who had found refuge in her clinic a year earlier. She had nursed him and fed him and healed him. She had saved her son, Wilfred's son, *their* son, with the strength and singlemindedness of her love. So there.

And now here he goes, this lost-found son of hers, her personal redemption, her gift to Wilfred, staggering down the path, cane plunging, hair glittering in the late sunshine, and she thinks, *Damn it all, Wilfred, could you have made him just a little less like yourself, please?*

BUT THEN. THIRTY OR SO yards from the old wooden door, something funny happens. The script changes without any warning at all. The door swings open, and a woman comes tumbling out, pale blond, blue eyes so well remembered that Elfriede stops dead. The woman's gaze slides right past Benedict, who has also turned to stone, and finds her, Elfriede. They recognize each other at the same time. As if this courtyard is a bedroom in Florida, a picnic blanket, an ice cream parlor, and the decades have compressed into nothing. As if the air smells of salt instead of spring.

Mutti! Ursula gasps.

SO ELFRIEDE MISSES THE MOMENT when her son reunites with the woman who lumbers along behind Ursula. She's on her knees, holding Ursula to her chest, and doesn't see the brunette with the enormous belly, crying and crying, sinking on the stones beside her, wrapped around Benedict who is wrapped around her. That meeting will have to wait until she wakes from this dream she's having.

Somewhere in the middle of the dream, though, Elfriede happens to squint upward—maybe by chance, maybe by human instinct, maybe by the nudge of some unseen hand—to discover a third woman, who stands near the door, arms folded. The sun beats down on her brown hair. A cigarette dangles from one hand, and she's smiling a little.

Her other hand wipes at her eyes with a small, square linen cloth.

EPILOGUE

LULU

JUNE 1951
(RMS Queen Mary, *At Sea)*

I HAVEN'T GIVEN much thought to the Duke and Duchess of Windsor over the course of the past seven years. Like you, I've seen their names in the newspapers from time to time, some dateline from Biarritz or Paris or New York—never Nassau, of course, and certainly not London—but the stories are of so little interest to me, so little relevance to my own life, this party or that party, this magnificent necklace or that extraordinary bracelet, I generally don't linger. I simply don't give a damn.

And I'm chasing the twins down the promenade deck when the luggage comes aboard, twenty-eight steamer trunks in all, and the demi-royal couple emerges from the back of a chauffeured limousine to the crump of a hundred flashbulbs and the cheering of a gullible crowd of admirers. All that fuss occurs at a distance, scarcely noticed, because Maggie's about to throw her left shoe down a ventilation shaft, so I learn the news hours later, as we're dressing for dinner. The ship's already well past the tip of Long Island, steaming out to the open ocean. My husband straightens his tie, eyes me in the mirror, and speaks in a voice of forced cheer. "I say. Jolly coincidence. Have you heard the Windsors are aboard?"

LOOK, I'VE BEEN BUSY. AT seven, Wilfred's finally acquired a midge of sense, but Maggie and Jack turned three only last month, so you can imagine. I'll be *clackety-clacking* away on my typewriter one minute, elbows-deep in a story about the Rosenberg trial, say, when a crash comes echoing down the hallway, followed by the telling pause, followed by the howl, followed by the nanny's hushing. I'm supposed to let her sort everything out—as Thorpe reminds me time and again—but biology's an autocrat, wouldn't you agree, and inevitably I've got to rise and witness the unfolding disaster for myself. And once you're up, you're up. It's an hour or more before you can disentangle yourself from the ties of motherhood and find your typewriter again. Sometimes Thorpe wanders in, bemused, while I'm still on the kitchen floor playing horsie with Jack and Maggie, and I'll look up and say accusingly, *One more, you said. Let's have one more baby.* And Thorpe will scoop Maggie or Jack (or both) into the air and say, *Twins run in your family, beloved, not mine. Anyway, which one of them would you send back?*

So we muddle on, me writing freelance for whatever magazine will have me, and Thorpe teaching botany to dewy undergraduates at this small college at the western edge of New Hampshire where we've chosen to settle, God knows why. Each June, we board one ocean liner or another and cross the Atlantic to spend the summer in Switzerland with the aunties and Gammy. (Wilfred dubbed her that when he was a year and a half old, and it stuck.) This June, it happens to be the same ocean liner selected by the Duke and Duchess of Windsor for whatever whim presently moves them to Europe. What are the odds?

AS IT HAPPENS, OUR PATHS don't cross until the fifth evening of the voyage. This is mostly because the Thorpes—a botany professor and his journalist wife, together with their three small children—are traveling cabin class, wedged together in a berth on D deck near the engine room, whereas Wallis and Edward occupy a massive suite of staterooms on the main deck, near the center of the ship where the noise and motion are at a minimum, don't you know. Also—and if you haven't traveled by ocean liner across the Atlantic with three small children, you might not fully comprehend what I mean by this—our hands might have been a little full.

Still. On the fifth night, which is fair and warm, my husband pays one of the stewardesses to mind the children for the evening, while he whisks me away to the glamour of the second-class dining room for drinks and dinner *à deux*, all dressed up, just like old times. He's looking especially handsome. The burnish on his strawberry-blond hair might be fading a trifle, and he still walks with a hint of a limp, but the sight of Thorpe in his dinner jacket never fails to set my heart thumping and my back itching with the memory of a certain sea grape tree on an island, far away. After dinner there's dancing, and after dancing we spill onto the deserted promenade deck for what my husband likes to call a spot of kissing. Mind you, we've both drunk a great deal of champagne, and as soon as I inhale Thorpe's good, clean smell, the kissing turns serious, and there we are, necking desperately against the railing like a pair of teenagers, Thorpe's wicked hand down the front of my dress, when some damned kids start yelling for their mama and papa and spoil the fun. Especially when they turn out to be *our* kids, followed by the exhausted stewardess we hired to prevent just such an interruption. Oh well.

But Thorpe responds in good humor. He swings Maggie into one arm and takes Jack's little palm in his other hand, and Wilfred trots along after them, explaining how he *tried* to get the twins to stay in bed, *really* he did. I look around for the stewardess, but the ship has swallowed her up. Not that I blame her.

Now, it's June, remember, and we're fairly far north, and even though it's past ten o'clock, the sun hasn't quite set. The air is filled with this incandescence, this golden light, and for an instant or two I allow myself the pleasure of watching my husband bear our children down the deck, gilded in sunshine. The beauty of it drenches me. I think my heart stops. And that's when I spot them.

God only knows how long they've been standing there like skeletons, not twenty yards away. She's wearing a long, sleeveless dinner dress in her favorite shade of blue, and her chest and neck and arms are crusted in jewels. He's wearing a dinner jacket identical to that of my husband. The years have not been kind. Her features have hardened into something more resembling a mask than a human face. The eyebrows are a painted caricature of their former selves. As for him. He's haggard and goggle-eyed, and his thick gold hair is turning thin and gray. But it's them, all right. You can't mistake them. Their expressions are frozen in shock. We meet eyes, and I can tell they recognize me. I can tell they've witnessed the entire scene, the necking and the children, the late, golden sunlight drenching us.

For a moment, as we stand there arrested in silent, mutual recognition, I'm reminded of the duchess once telling me—I can't remember where or when—how she hoped that their faithful years of service in *this dump*, as she called it, would lead to bigger things. I think she expected a governorship in Australia or Canada. Something suited to their station and his imagined abilities. And in these two stricken faces, which seem to have aged twice those seven and a half calendar years since I've seen them last, I believe I read the story of all those disappointed hopes, the glister,

the vapid pointlessness of their lives. Standing before them, on a patch
of wooden deck in the middle of the ocean, I imagine those painted faces
are like shells around a hollow core.

Possibly I should say something. Certainly I should feel something.
But I do neither of those things. I simply can't summon them up. The
strap of my dress hangs down my arm—I can feel it tickle my skin—so
I secure it back atop my shoulder and proceed in the same direction as
Thorpe and the children, toward the hatchway that leads to the staircase
that leads to our humble cabin, where perhaps Wilfred and Maggie and
Jack will eventually fall asleep and I can sneak into my husband's bunk
for the kind of silent, giggling, undercover lovemaking that is our present lot in life.

As I pass them, I nod my head and say good evening.

Good evening, Mrs. Thorpe, says the duke.

His wife remains silent. But salt breeze nudges her hair, and the setting sun flickers on her jewels.

HISTORICAL NOTE

My book ideas come from all kinds of sources, from newspapers or cocktail parties or when I'm researching something else, and this one started with my editor, Rachel Kahan. I was heading off to the Bahamas with my husband for a long-anticipated Weekend Away from the Kids, and she reminded me the Duke of Windsor had been governor of the then-British colony during the Second World War, and wouldn't that be a terrific setting for a book?

So I did a little research, and I spoke with our hosts—Sean and Kara Nottage, who are lucky enough to make their home in Lyford Cay—and discovered all kinds of fascinating lore about the Windsors and the island they called home for nearly five years. It took some time, however, for the right story to take shape in my head. Generally speaking, while my novels take place in historical settings, I prefer to write from the perspective of a fictional protagonist, and in order to navigate all the significant episodes in wartime Nassau without taking a historical figure as narrator, I had to make a giant, complex imaginative leap. Lulu was the product of that leap.

Most of the major events in this novel actually took place, and many of the characters Lulu encounters actually existed. The murder of Sir Harry Oakes remains one of the most intriguing unsolved mysteries of the twentieth century, and I'm not the first novelist to take on the subject. Each detail of his life and his untimely end are as accurate as I could make them, and I refer anyone interested in further research to the excellent *Blood and Fire*, written by the journalist and Bahamas native John Marquis, and to Alfred de Marigny's memoir *A Conspiracy of Crowns*, both of which were indispensable to my understanding of the crime and the personalities involved. Keep in mind, however, that this novel is a work of fiction, and both Lulu's involvement in the affairs of the Windsors and her speculation as to the true identity of the murderer derive solely from my imagination as inspired by the known evidence.

As for the Windsors themselves, endless ink has already been spilled trying to get to the bottom of them. I recommend Anne Sebba's *That Woman* and Philip Ziegler's *King Edward VIII* for a wealth of biographical information and psychological insight into one of the most notorious couples of the century, as well as Andrew Morton's *17 Carnations* for an examination of the case against the Windsors' activities—and possibly their loyalties—during the Second World War. I have tried to be fair, however, and the short memoir *The Windsors I Knew*, written by Jean Hardcastle-Taylor (formerly Miss Drewes, the Windsors' private secretary during their Bahamas years, who makes a few appearances in *The Golden Hour*) provides a fascinating counterpoint to the largely negative portrait of the couple that emerges from history. Many of the details of everyday life inside Government House—including the red bows tied around the necks of the Windsors' beloved Cairn terriers during the Christmas season—come from this invaluable source.

As for the larger historical context of the Bahamas, I consulted a variety of sources, both popular and academic, in trying to understand the racial and social history of the colony. I count Gail Saunders's *Race and Class in the Colonial Bahamas, 1880–1960* as the most comprehensive study, but Owen Platt's *The Royal Governor . . . and the Duchess* and Sir Orville Turnquest's *What Manner of Man Is This? The Duke of Windsor's Years in The Bahamas* lent crucial details and insight. I also spent hours scouring old maps and sources to imagine Nassau and New Providence Island as they existed decades ago, before the enormous development that took place in the postwar years. While *The Golden Hour* is not, and was not intended to be, a scholarly history of the Bahamas and the Windsors, I've striven to re-create this setting and its real-life inhabitants as accurately as possible.

As for the scenes in wartime Europe, I'm indebted to Lynne Olson's excellent and absorbing books—*Last Hope Island* and *Citizens of London,* for starters—for providing context and spurring my imagination, and to Max Hastings's *The Secret War* for further background on the intelligence services during the Second World War. To understand the operation of the escape lines that channeled Allied pilots and other refugees out of German-occupied territories, I read Peter Eisner's exhilarating *The Freedom Line*, which I highly recommend as a first-class example of narrative nonfiction.

From the beginning, I wanted to weave Lulu's story with that of another character, Elfriede von Kleist Thorpe, who first appeared offstage as the (supposedly) deceased mother of Johann von Kleist in my earlier novel, *Along the Infinite Sea*. Having given her such a tragic backstory, I wanted to write more about my German woman who wove her fate into Great Britain at such an interesting moment in history, and then bore a son of possibly murky national loyalty. To understand her and prewar Germany further, I had the great pleasure of reading the brilliant and utterly mesmerizing *1913: The Year Before the Storm* by Florian Illies, which catapulted me straight into my setting, wholly inspired. Elfriede forms the moral backbone of *The Golden Hour*, and her journey is that of women everywhere.

ACKNOWLEDGMENTS

As with all my books, so many wonderful people played a role in the creation of *The Golden Hour*, starting with my editor, Rachel Kahan, who planted the first idea in my head a few years ago and kept at it with her watering can until the buds began to form. Huge thanks to her and to the rest of the William Morrow team—publisher Liate Stehlik, marketing maven Tavia Kowalchuk, publicity panjandrum Lauren Truskowski, branding brigadier Kathryn Gordon, and many others—for making it their mission to put my novels in the hands of readers. Special thanks to my copyeditor, Candace Levy, who had the dread task of catching all the little timeline errors and inconsistencies that occur in a book of complicated historical narratives, and to Mumtaz Mustafa for her gorgeous jacket design.

My literary agent, Alexandra Machinist of ICM, has been on my team from the beginning, as coach, general manager, and cheerleader all rolled into one. Huge thanks to her and to her capable assistant, Ruth Landry, for all the efforts I know about and especially for those I don't.

This book is all about strong women and sisterhood, which I'm blessed to have in abundance in my life. Gratefulness always to the other two thirds of the Unibrain, Lauren Willig and Karen White, who have talked me down countless trees, untangled various plot threads, and poured all the necessary coffee and wine down my throat. To the extraordinarily generous and talented Elin Hilderbrand, no amount of thanks is sufficient—this woman is simply a superstar human being. It's impossible to name all the other brilliant people who champion women writers and women's writing, and who have lit so many candles in my life this past year. Thanks to you all, and with special gratitude to Andrea Katz of Great Thoughts, who always has our backs.

Thank you to my readers, new and old, who send the most lovely encouragement my way just when I need it most. I appreciate your kindness, your energy, and your loyalty, and I strive to be worthy of it with every book I write.

I'm also grateful to Sean and Kara Nottage for their friendship and their kind hospitality during our visit to the Bahamas, which set this book idea into motion.

Finally, my family puts up with all my travel, my periodic hibernations, my random outbursts, and the mood swings that come with life in an audience-facing creative field, and gives me (well, mostly!) nothing but love in return. Thanks and love, always.

ABOUT THE AUTHOR

Beatriz Williams is the bestselling author of nine novels, including *The Summer Wives*, *A Hundred Summers*, *The Secret Life of Violet Grant*, and *A Certain Age*. A native of Seattle, she graduated from Stanford University and earned an MBA in finance from Columbia University, then spent several years in New York and London as a corporate strategy consultant before pursuing her passion for historical fiction. She lives with her husband and four children near the Connecticut shore, where she divides her time between writing and laundry.